HOLLY GREEN

Workhouse Girl

EBURY
PRESS

First published by Ebury Press in 2020

1 3 5 7 9 10 8 6 4 2

Ebury Press, an imprint of Ebury Publishing
20 Vauxhall Bridge Road,
London SW1V 2SA

Ebury Press is part of the Penguin Random House group of companies
whose addresses can be found at global.penguinrandomhouse.com

Penguin
Random House
UK

Copyright © Holly Green, 2020

Holly Green has asserted her right to be identified as the author of this
work in accordance with the Copyright, Designs and Patents Act 1988

This novel is a work of fiction. Names and characters are the product
of the author's imagination and any resemblance to actual persons,
living or dead, is entirely coincidental

www.penguin.co.uk

A CIP catalogue record for this book is available from the British Library

ISBN 9781785035654

Typeset in 12.25 pt/15.5 pt Times LT Std
by Integra Software Services Pvt. Ltd, Pondicherry

Printed and bound in Great Britain by Clays Ltd, Elcograf S.p.A.

Penguin Random House is committed to a sustainable future for
our business, our readers and our planet. This book is made
from Forest Stewardship Council® certified paper.

MIX
Paper from
responsible sources
FSC® C018179

Workhouse Girl

Chapter 1

Liverpool, October 1867

Patty Jenkins stood on the quayside and watched the *SS Royal Standard* steam out into Liverpool Bay. The ship's rails were lined with passengers waving their last farewells, and the quayside was crowded with people waving back, many of them in tears. The ship's ultimate destination was Australia, and they all knew that the chances of meeting their loved ones again, when they were going so far away, were very slight.

By straining her eyes Patty could just make out one figure among all the rest: a slight, almost girlish form wearing a surprisingly stylish bonnet. She was waving, like the rest, but it was not to Patty. A little distance away, a young man was waving back, his expression distraught. He had shouted something as the ship drew away from the quay, but Patty had not been able to hear what he said. Patty recognised him. His name was James Breckenridge and he was a solicitor's clerk, a respectable young man with good prospects, but for the last few months he had been keeping company with May Lavender, the girl on the ship. How someone in his position came to be walking out with a milliner's apprentice, an orphan brought up in the Brownlow Hill workhouse, was a mystery to Patty. May had not made any secret of the relationship but she had kept her friends at arm's length when it came to any discussion of it. And now, without any warning, without even saying goodbye, she had booked a passage on this new steamer and was off to Australia. The only reason Patty was there to watch her sail away was because one of the sales girls at Freeman's Department store, where Patty worked in the kitchen, had told her that on the previous day May had been going round the shop with a note from Mr Freeman himself, instructing the staff to allow her to choose anything she needed for a long voyage to a warm country. Then, she had managed to worm out of one of the porters the information that he had been instructed to carry May's new suitcase down to the docks and see it put on board the *Royal Standard*.

Patty turned away with a heavy heart. She and May had been friends ever since they were children in the workhouse. They had been separated when they were both sent into service, she to work in the kitchens of Speke Hall, the great mansion a few miles from the city, and May as a maid of all work for the Freeman family.

Patty had thought she was the lucky one to start with, but she had soon learned that being the lowest of the low in a house with a large staff was a miserable position, whereas May had found the opportunity to demonstrate her skill with colour and design and caught the eye of Mr Freeman, who was then just building up his haberdashery business into the first department store to open in the city. He had placed May as an apprentice to his milliner, Nan Driscoll, where she had soon acquired a regular clientele of her own for the hats and bonnets she created. Patty knew she had been less than happy when Nan had retired and was replaced by Miss Jones, who had very firm ideas about the place of an apprentice. But surely that was not reason enough to suddenly throw everything away and rush off to the other side of the world? Patty was mystified and hurt. She was going to miss May very badly.

When she entered the big kitchen, which catered for the employees of Freeman's store, she was berated by Mr Carton, the head cook, for being late for work. Since, like many of the staff, she slept in a dormitory on the premises, she had no reason not to be prompt. Patty ducked her head and muttered an excuse about waking up with a headache and having gone out for some air. None of the other kitchen staff had known May well and she did not feel like discussing what had happened with them.

She washed her hands and set to work on the pastry for some apple pies. She enjoyed making pastry and cakes, and she was good at it. The one bright spot from her time at Speke Hall had been the chance to work with M. Blanchard, the pastry cook. He had taken pity on her, and in the rare intervals when she was not being hounded. from scrubbing dishes to fetching water to building up the fire in the great open range, he had taught her how to make crisp pastry for tarts and light-as-air sponges. There was little opportunity to try to copy some of his fancier creations where she worked now. It was more a case of good plain fare to feed a large number of people, but at least her work seemed to be appreciated. None of her pies or tarts were ever left over at the end of a meal.

Usually, Patty was never happier than when she was up to her elbows in flour, but today she found it hard to keep her mind on her work. The question kept nagging at her. Why had May gone away in such a rush, and why hadn't she even said goodbye?

There was only one person who might be able to answer her questions. May must have explained her decision to Mr Freeman when she gave in her notice, and he must have approved, otherwise why would he have given her the freedom to choose whatever she wanted from the stock? He had a reputation as a philanthropist who cared for the needs of all those who worked for him, and she knew he had a particularly soft spot for May, who had been badly treated by his wife and his housekeeper when she'd worked for him, until he'd found out and put a stop to it. Nevertheless, Patty's memory of her first encounter with him was not a happy one.

She had lost her job at Speke, dismissed for helping herself to some game pie left over from the dining table of the gentry. As the most junior member of staff, she had been expected to serve all the others when they sat down to eat at the long table in the kitchen and was not allowed to eat herself until they had finished. Often, there had been very little left for her. Perpetually hungry, she had watched dish after dish being sent up to the dining room, so that the ladies and gentlemen had plenty to choose from, and much of it was sent back, untouched. Some of it was then stored away to be served up at the next meal for the staff, but a good deal was scraped straight into the bucket of scraps that went to feed the pigs. One evening, finding herself for a brief moment unsupervised, she had slipped into the larder and cut herself a slice of the game pie. Some of it had been eaten already, so she thought that a small piece would not be missed, but when she came out of the larder, still chewing, she came face to face with one of the footmen, a man who had always treated her as if she was something the cat dragged in. He had reported her to Cook, who had spoken to the lady of the house, and Patty had been summarily dismissed without a 'character', and with nothing more than the clothes she stood up in.

Starving and friendless, she had seen no alternative but to resort to prostitution, but even that scarcely gave her enough to keep body and soul together. Skinny and poorly dressed, she had little attraction for any but the most desperate men. The 'professional' ladies who occupied the most favourable positions drove her away whenever she showed her face and she was left roaming

5

the back streets on the fringes of the city. She had been standing on a corner, shivering and faint with hunger, when May had passed on her way from the store to Nan Driscoll's house, where she'd lodged at the time.

For three days May had hidden her in her own room, until Nan had found out. An hour later, she'd found herself in Mr Freeman's office. It was due to him that she had been sent to a home where she could learn a trade and later been given a job in the kitchens at Freeman's Store. She knew she had a great deal to thank him for, but still the memory of that first interview made her go hot and cold with shame, and the thought of walking into his office to ask for an explanation of May's sudden departure was intimidating.

'Patty? Mr Freeman wants you in his office.' It was one of the messenger boys.

Patty gasped. It seemed as if her thoughts had somehow transmitted themselves to her boss. How could he possibly have known that she was plucking up courage to knock on his door?

'When?' she asked, when she had got her breath back.

'Now, of course.'

Patty looked at the pies she had been making. They were ready to go into the oven. She turned to the woman working alongside her. 'Maisie, can you put these in the oven for me and watch them? Mr F has sent for me.'

'Sent for you? What have you been up to?'

'Nothing! I don't know what he wants but I'll have to go.'

''Course you will. Don't worry, I'll see to the pies.'

Patty took off her apron and washed the flour off her hands and headed up the back stairs that led to the main part of the store, the part the customers saw. Mr Freeman had an office on the first floor, and Patty knocked on the imposing oak door with a pounding heart.

'You sent for me, sir?'

'Ah, Patty.' He looked up from a ledger. 'Yes. I want you to do me a small service.'

'Service, sir?'

'A week or two ago I asked the kitchen to produce a cake for the birthday of one of my longest-serving staff. I understand that you were given the job.'

'Yes, sir,' Patty responded doubtfully. Had someone complained? There had been nothing wrong with the cake; she was sure of that.

'Don't look so worried. It was an excellent cake. I tried a slice myself. Do you often make cakes?'

'Sometimes, sir. If one of the girls in the dormitory has a birthday I sometimes make a few cakes for their tea. But,' she added hastily, 'I always ask Mr Carton if he can spare the butter and the sugar first.'

'Of course. I'm not suggesting that you have been misusing company property.' Patty was relieved to see that Mr Freeman looked slightly amused. 'Where did you learn the skill? Did Mr Keogh teach you?'

Patrick Keogh was the chief pastry cook in the Freeman's kitchen.

'No, sir. When I was in service at Speke Hall I some-times worked for M. Blanchard, the pastry cook there. He taught me a bit.'

'I see. Well, now what I want you to do is this. The day after tomorrow I have invited some ladies and gen-tlemen to tea, here in the store. That may seem a little strange to you, but I have my reasons. There will be six of us, and I should like you to produce the food. You know the sort of thing – some sandwiches, perhaps something toasted, and some nice cakes. Do you think you can manage that?'

Patty struggled for a response. 'I'm sure I could, sir. But I don't think Mr Carton will let me have the time off to do it.'

'I will speak to Mr Carton and tell him I want you to be relieved of any other duties for two days and given what-ever ingredients you need. Does that allay your worries?'

'Well, yes, sir.' Patty's brain was churning as she strove to grasp this extraordinary turn of events. 'Yes, if he agrees, I'm sure I can do what you want.'

'Good, that's settled then. I have arranged to have the tea table set up in the ladies' fashion department, so my guests can see all the latest creations while they eat. Tea at four o'clock. I am relying on you to do me and the store proud.'

'Oh, I will, sir. I'll do my very best.'

'I know you will. Now, you had better get back to the kitchen and start planning your menu. Ask Mr Carton to come and see me.'

'Yes, sir. Thank you, sir.' Patty made a small curtsy and started towards the door. Then she hesitated. There would never be a better opportunity to ask the question that was plaguing her.

'Please, sir, can ask you something?'

'What is it?'

'I was down at the quayside this morning, watching the *Royal Standard* sail away – and May Lavender was on board. I was wondering why. It's so sudden.'

Freeman frowned. 'My goodness, did she not tell you she was going?'

'No, sir.' Patty's lip trembled. 'She didn't even say goodbye.'

Freeman took a long breath and let it out on a sigh. 'Oh dear. That must be distressing for you. I know you were close friends.' He thought for a moment and went on. 'I can't go into details. She spoke to me in confidence, but I can tell you this much: she received a letter from her brother, Gus. You knew he had gone out to Australia?'

'Yes, I knew that.'

'May has gone to join him. The ship was sailing today, so she had to make a very quick decision. But that's really no excuse for not finding the time to say goodbye to you.'

'No, it's not, is it?' Patty agreed. She thought for a moment. 'Did you know she was walking out with James Breckenridge?'

'Mrs Breckenridge's son? No, I did not. I'm not sure his mother would approve of that.'

'I bet she doesn't,' Patty agreed. 'I only mentioned it because I saw him this morning, standing on the dockside, waving. He looked pretty upset.'

Mr Freeman considered. 'That's understandable, if he was fond of her. But it's probably for the best. It would never have been a suitable match. But now you mention it, I did wonder if there was more to May's sudden decision to leave than just the prospect of a new life in Australia.'

'You think she realised it was never going to work, so she decided to put an end to it?'

'That seems quite likely, don't you think?'

'Maybe that's why she didn't want to talk about it to me. She knew I always thought she was making a mistake.'

'That's possible, I suppose.' Freeman pulled a ledger toward him. 'Now, I haven't got time to sit here gossiping, and nor have you. You'd better get on.'

'Yes, yes, I must, mustn't I? Thank you explaining things to me.' She curtsied again and left the room.

Back in the kitchen she went up to Mr Carton, who was standing over a large pot of stew with a spoon in his hand, about to taste it.

'Excuse me, Chef. Mr Freeman wants you in his office.'

He glowered at her. 'What, now?'

'Yes, please, Chef.'

A look of sardonic enlightenment dawned on his face. 'Oh ho! You really have been up to no good, haven't you? Am I going to have to look for a new assistant pastry cook?'

'I don't think so, Chef.' Patty kept her eyes demurely lowered so he did not see the triumphant gleam in them.

Carton turned to one of his assistants. 'This needs more salt. See to it, will you?' He pulled off his apron and dusted himself down. 'Right, young lady. Let's see what you've done to cause all this disruption.'

As soon as he had left, Patty tore a strip of paper from a sheet that had been wrapping some cabbages, took a pencil from a collection in a jar on one of the shelves, and slipped into one of the big larders leading off the kitchen. She found a stool and pushed aside some jars of pickle to make a space. Biting the end of the pencil in concentration, she set about making a list of cakes for Mr Freeman's tea party.

Sandwiches – that was no problem. The kitchen baked bread every day and there were always cucumbers. 'Something toasted', Mr Freeman had suggested. She searched her memory of afternoon teas at Speke House. Yes! Balmoral cake, baked in a loaf tin and flavoured with caraway seeds. That could be sliced and toasted. Gingerbread, that was easy and always popular. What else? In her free time, when she strolled through the streets window shopping, she often stopped outside bakers' shops or tea shops to look at the cakes on display. It was not just that they made her mouth water, it was curiosity about what the experts were creating and a longing to try her own hand at something similar.

Remembering what she had seen brought new inspiration. Recently many windows had exhibited a sponge sandwich layered with jam and cream. These were often labelled 'the favourite cake of our dear Queen'. So that would certainly be popular with Mr Freeman's guests. But she wanted something else, something spectacular that would really impress them.

At a loss, she began to search along the larder shelves looking for inspiration. At one end there was a stack of different shaped baking tins. Most of them were too big, intended for large numbers of people. She sorted out some that would be more suitable. Then, at the back of the shelf, she came upon a dusty mould in the shape of a fluted dome and the sight sparked a memory. Savoy cake! She remembered that M. Blanchard made them for special occasions. With suitable decoration one of those would make a perfect centre piece. But try as she might, she could not recall the recipe.

Giving up, she went back into the kitchen to ask advice. Mr Carton was chopping onions. His expression when she approached him was irritable but he was no longer as threatening as before. She sensed that he was seeing her in a different light. Nevertheless, he was not pleased with this new development.

'What's all this new-fangled nonsense about afternoon tea?' he demanded. 'Aren't three meals a day enough?'

Patrick Keogh pricked up his ears and came over. 'What's all this?'

'Mr Freeman has taken it into his head to entertain some ladies and gentlemen to afternoon tea, in the ladies' fashion department, would you believe?'

'Has he really? Well, I can see what he's thinking. From what I hear, afternoon tea has become very fashionable among the gentry. I believe Her Majesty herself is partial to a cup of tea and some cake at about four o'clock. So, Mr Freeman invites ladies to take this fashionable meal and at the same time they are surrounded by the latest fashions in gowns. It makes sense to me. So what are we giving them?'

'Don't ask me,' Carton responded grumpily. 'He's given the responsibility for the arrangements to Patty.'

Patty looked at Patrick, expecting his face also to express irritation, perhaps even outrage. This was a responsibility that, surely, should have been his. But instead he smiled.

'Has he, by Jove? Well, it's a great opportunity for you. Make sure you use it to the best of your ability.'

'I will!' Patty said. 'But really it should be you.'

Patrick shook his head. 'No, no. That's not my kind of thing at all. Good plain cooking is my style. If the boss had given the job to me, the ladies and gents would be lucky to get anything more exciting than a rock bun for their tea. I've watched you at work and I can see you've got a lot more imagination than I have. Make the most of the chance!'

'Thank you,' Patty said, and her gratitude was heartfelt. Then she added, 'Do you happen to know the recipe for Savoy cake?'

'Savoy cake? Now that's really out of my league. I've seen one or two, but I wouldn't know where to start making one.'

'M. Blanchard at Speke used to make them for special occasions,' she said, 'but I can't remember the quantities.'

'Let's see,' he said. 'I've heard that one or two ladies have published books of recipes lately. You might find what you need there. Why don't you pop across to the library and see if they can help? It's only just over the road.'

'The library?' Patty hesitated. 'I've never been inside. Would I be allowed?'

'It's intended for everyone. That was Mr Brown's idea when he paid to have it built. Of course you're allowed. Go and try.'

Patty looked at Mr Carton. 'May I, Chef?'

He waved her away with a dismissive gesture. 'Go, go! Mr Freeman says you're to be relieved of all other duties for the next two days. It's up to you how you use the time.'

'Very well.' Patty braced her shoulders. 'I'll try.'

William Brown's imposing library was only a short walk from Freeman's store but it had never occurred to Patty to go inside. She had been taught to read at the workhouse, though she had found it a chore and resented the time spent in the schoolroom. Miss Bale, the schoolmistress, had been a hard taskmaster and Patty had hated her. But, since leaving, she had realised that there were others of her own age who had never acquired the skill, or had only a shaky grasp of it, and she had come to understand that she was privileged to have had any sort of education. She remembered, as she made her way there, that May had got into the habit of going to the library when she'd started walking out with James, determined to prove herself a worthy wife for him. She had asked Patty to go with her, but Patty had always refused. She was regretting that now.

As she passed through the columned portico, Patty's knees were shaking, and at the sight of the smartly dressed lady and gentleman behind the reception desk she nearly turned and ran. But she told herself that she could be as brave as May and went forward.

'Can I help you?' the man said politely.

'Please, I ... I'm looking for ... do you have any books of recipes?'

'Cookery books? Your department, I think, Miss Smith.'

Miss Smith stepped forward with a friendly smile. 'Yes, we do. They seem to have become quite popular lately. Would you like me to show you?'

'Oh, yes, please. If it's not too much trouble.'

'Not at all. This way.'

She led Patty up a flight of stairs and into a huge circular room with a domed ceiling. All round the walls, on more than one level, there were shelves laden with books. Patty stared, open-mouthed. She never seen so many books, and she found it hard to imagine who

could have written them all. How on earth could anyone find a particular book amongst all these? But Miss
Smith led her confidently to a shelf.

'Is there anything in particular you were looking for?'

'If you please, miss, a recipe for Savoy cake.'

'Cake? Well, I think you should find all you want in
this book. It's by a lady called Eliza Acton. I've tried
some of her recipes myself and they do seem to work.'
She took down a large volume, bound in leather with
a tooled design on the front. 'Now, I can't let you take
this away, I'm afraid. It's for reference only. But if you
find what you want you could copy it out. There's a
desk over there and I can give you some paper and a
pencil. Will that suit you?'

'Oh, yes, very well,' Patty said breathlessly. 'Thank
you.'

As Patty sat down she became aware for the first time
that there were others, mainly men but some women,
seated at similar desks all round the great room. All
seemed absorbed in what they were studying, and no
one paid any attention to her. She began to relax and
turned the pages of the great book lying in front of her.
It took some time to find the chapter dealing with cake,
and at first reading she was disconcerted to find that
Miss Acton did not approve of cakes. She called them
'sweet poisons' and wished she need not give them so
much space in her book. She gave way, however, in the
face of general taste and proceeded to discuss methods
and recipes, and there, at last, was the one Patty was

looking for – Savoy cake. Slowly and painstakingly she copied the instructions and then made her way back to Miss Smith at her desk.

'I've left the book there, miss. I didn't want to put it back in the wrong place.'

'That is quite right. I'll see it goes back on the shelf. Did you find what you wanted?'

'Yes, I did, miss. Thank you very much.'

'Good. Remember, you can come here and look up whatever you want to find. That was Mr Brown's purpose in creating this library.' Miss Smith smiled. 'And good luck with your cake.'

Over the next two days, Patty worked harder than she had ever done in her life. She made her way up to the first floor and braved the formidable Miss Clarke, who presided over Ladies' Fashions. Once again, she expected resistance; surely she could not approve of this disruption to normal routine. But she found Mr Freeman had smoothed her path and Miss Clarke was delighted with the prospect of introducing her latest fashions to discerning customers. Arrangements had been made for a table to be set up in the centre of the room, napery and cutlery had been organised and Mr Freeman was providing the tea service from his own home. Patty remembered May's stories of the horrible Mrs Wilkins, the Freeman's housekeeper who had made her life a misery when she was in service there, and wondered how she had reacted to that.

This all satisfactorily settled, she set to work to assemble the necessary ingredients for her list of delicacies. Most of them were easily available, since flour and butter and sugar were staples for any sort of baking. But some of the more exotic items were lacking. She took her problem to Mr Carton, who seemed to have decided that this new venture could only enhance his own standing with his employer, and had given a note to the grocer who normally supplied the kitchen, instructing him to allow her to choose what she needed and add them to his monthly account.

Patty had never had to shop for food. She had passed her life in various institutions where the meals, however meagre, had been provided for her. She lived in at Freeman's, in common with quite a few of the staff, and ate in the communal canteen. Walking into the grocer's shop was like walking into some magical eastern bazaar. Her nose was assailed by a symphony of different odours. There was the heady scent of spices, cinnamon and nutmeg and cloves, and the more down to earth scent of herbs, sage and thyme and mint; there was the sharpness of cheeses and the tang of hams hanging from the ceiling and the sweet smell of sugar and chocolate from open barrels of biscuits.

When her turn came to be served she presented her list. The caraway seeds for the Balmoral loaf were readily available, as was the ginger for the gingerbread, but she wanted something special with which to decorate her Savoy cake. On a high shelf she spotted exactly what she needed; candied rose petals and crystallised orange slices. Delighted with her purchases, she headed back to the kitchen.

The Balmoral cake was to be toasted, so could be made in advance, and the gingerbread would benefit from maturing for a day, but the sponge sandwich and the Savoy cake must be made fresh. She rose next morning with a quiver in her stomach that was partly fear and partly excited anticipation. The sponge turned out well and could be filled at the last moment and she turned her attention to the Savoy cake. The basic recipe was for a simple fatless sponge. It was the use of the mould and the decoration that made it special. She remembered from watching M. Blanchard that the preparation of the mould was crucial. She melted some kidney fat, better as a grease than butter, and swirled it round the mould to coat it. Then she added some caster sugar and finally some potato flour. Then it was time to make the batter, and soon her arms were aching from beating the mixture, but that was only the start. She added a fine grating of orange zest. Then she had to beat up the egg whites. She soon understood the meaning of the term 'elbow grease'. She folded the whites into the batter and poured the mixture into the mould. Then all she could do was put it into the oven and hope.

An hour later she took the mould out of the oven, but it had to be left to cool completely before it was turned out. When the moment came she held her breath. She set a decorative plate on top of the mould and turned it over. For a terrible moment nothing happened, then she felt the cake slide onto the plate. It had turned out perfectly and the outside had a crisp, shining sugar coating, exactly as she had intended. The mould had a central funnel, which left a hollow down the middle of the cake. Patty filled it with sweetened whipped cream flavoured with orange zest. The shape of the mould produced a domed structure with a small ledge halfway down. On this, Patty arranged rosettes of candied rose petals interspersed with slices of crystallised orange. She put more of both around the base and crowned the top with a small pyramid of orange slices. Then she stood back, eased her aching back, and gazed at her creation. It was exactly what she had hoped for.

She had been given a small corner of the kitchen for herself and the other staff had been too occupied with their own jobs to pay her an attention, for which she was grateful. But now she called Patrick Keogh over.

'Look! What do you think?'

He gazed at the cake. 'My word, that's a right bobby-dazzler of a cake, and no mistake! You'll knock them sideways with that.'

Patty felt a glow of pride, but there was no time to stand around admiring her handiwork. There was still the sponge sandwich to be filled and the cucumber sand-wiches to make, and she had less than an hour until four o'clock. She managed it just in time and enlisted the aid of one of the kitchen porters to carry most of the food up to the first floor. She carried the Savoy cake herself, trusting it to no one else. A curtain had been erected to screen off a small area near to the door leading to the back stairs and a trolley had been provided from which to serve. Patty arranged her sandwiches and cakes on it and peeked round the curtain to check that all was in readiness there. The department had been closed to general customers and a table set up, covered with a pristine white cloth on which Mr Freeman's bone china was laid out. The silver teapot waited on the trolley to be filled. With a gasp, Patty realised she had forgotten all about the boiling water for the tea. She raced back down to the kitchen and as luck would have it found that one of the big kettles that stood always on the hob was full and boiling. She lugged it back upstairs, just in time to hear Mr Freeman's voice as he conducted his guests to the table.

Patty waited a few moments until they were settled, then she pushed her laden trolley out from behind the curtain. There was a small murmur of pleasure as the guests reviewed the spread on offer – but Patty had kept back her *pièce de résistance* for later. Peering through a small gap in the curtain she watched the proceedings. The models, who had been organised by Miss Clarke, had begun to parade around the table. Attention was focused on them and she heard several ladies commenting favourably on the new designs. She knew that it was considered impolite in good society to discuss the food, but then to her delight she heard one lady say to another, 'Isabella, do have another piece of this delicious gingerbread.' 'Thank you,' that lady replied, 'I have already had two, but why don't you try a slice of this sponge. It's so light I could eat it all!'

There was a brief interlude in the clothes show while the models changed and Patty judged this was her moment. Proudly, she carried in her Savoy cake.

'Oh! Oh! My goodness. Look at that! Isn't it beautiful?' It was the lady called Isabella.

'How lovely!' said her friend. 'It looks almost too good to eat.'

Patty set the cake down in front of Mr Freeman and caught his eye for a fleeting moment. He smiled and gave her a quick nod and she knew she had done all he'd expected.

When the guests had gone, and Patty went to clear away the dishes, there was very little left on the table. She was glad that they had enjoyed what she had worked so hard to create, but a little disappointed too. She had been looking forward to tasting some of it herself, and perhaps sharing it with Patrick. But there was still a sliver of Savoy cake left, and feeling rather guilty she ate it herself before she took the dirty dishes down to the kitchen.

Next morning Mr Freeman sent for her again, and this time she went without misgivings.

'Patty, you did Freeman's proud yesterday,' he said. 'Well done!'

Patty curtsied. 'Thank you, sir. I'm glad you were pleased.'

'That Savoy cake was a tour de force. I did not know you were quite such an accomplished pastry cook.'

'I went to the library to find the recipe,' Patty explained.

'Did you?' He studied her for a moment. 'That shows initiative. Now, let me get to the point. Yesterday's tea party was not just a passing fancy of mine. It was in some ways a trial run for a much bigger idea. I am thinking of opening a tea shop within the store, for all our customers. One of the chief attractions of a department store like Freeman's is that it is place to which ladies can come without requiring to be chaperoned or accompanied by their husbands. It is a place where they can not only buy all they need under one roof, but meet friends and socialise. Now, it's generally recognised that the longer someone spends in a shop the more she is likely to buy, and what better way of detaining them than to provide an opportunity to chat to friends over a cup of tea and some really nice cakes? Does that make sense to you?'

Patty was wondering why she was being treated to her employer's thoughts at such length and was surprised to be asked her opinion. 'Oh yes, sir,' she said. 'I think it's a very good idea.'

'Good! So how would you feel about taking charge of the venture?'

'Me, sir?'

'Yes. You've proved what a good pastry cook you are. I wouldn't expect you to concern yourself with the general running of the tea shop. I shall have to advertise for a manager or manageress to see to all that. But you would be in charge of providing the food. I don't think we should expect something as spectacular as your

23

Savoy cake, except on special occasions perhaps, but I'm sure there are plenty of other little delicacies you could produce to vary the menu. What do you think? Will you give it a try?'

Patty swallowed and drew a long breath. This seemed almost too good to be true. 'Oh, yes, sir. If you really think I'm up to it. I should like that very much.'

'Excellent. You will need an assistant in the kitchen. Is there anyone you can suggest? Someone you could take on as a sort of apprentice?'

Patty thought hard. 'There is a girl, Maisie. She's only been with us for a few weeks, but she helped me out a bit yesterday. She seemed to be interested in what I was doing.'

'Well, try her for a week or two and see if she's the right person for the job. Now, there's no need for you to concern yourself about the practical arrangements. I already have an area in mind on the ground floor and I will see that all the necessary furniture and equipment is procured, and, as I said, I shall look for someone to take care of the day-to-day running of the place, and deal with the financial side. Once it is organised I will let you know how many customers we may expect. All you have to do is produce enough cakes and other such things to satisfy them. Is all that clear?'

Patty felt breathless. 'Yes, sir ... I think so. Does Mr Carton know what I shall be doing?'

'He will, soon. I shall make it clear to him that you have important responsibilities and he needs to facilitate your efforts in any way you require. Oh, and there is one more thing: with added responsibilities comes added remuneration. You can expect a pay rise at the end of the month. Any further questions?'

'No, sir. Not that I can think of.'

'Good. I expect to be able to open the tea shop at the beginning of November, so you had better get back to the kitchen and start making plans.'

Chapter 2

Liverpool, April 1868

Patty straightened up and reached for a towel to dry her hands. 'Right you are, girls. That's the last of the washing-up. You can help yourselves to a gingerbread lady if you want one.'

'Gingerbread ladies' had become Patty's signature bake. Her gingerbread had always been one of the most popular items in the tea shop, and gingerbread 'men' were a staple offering in most bakers' shops. One day it had occurred to her that, as one of the objectives of the tea shop was to introduce customers to the dresses for sale in the fashion department, it would be an amusing conceit to produce her gingerbread in the form of an elegant lady with the most fashionable silhouette. After asking around she had found a blacksmith who had crafted a mould in the desired shape, and gingerbread ladies now made a regular appearance on the tea tables.

'You've got some leftover?' said Maisie. 'That doesn't often happen.'

Patty caught her eye and winked. 'Don't tell any-one, but I'm cooking slightly larger quantities than I think will get eaten. Well, I don't see why the customers should have all the enjoyment and us workers never get a taste, do you?' She held out a plate. 'Here, have one. Have two, if you like.'

She looked around her corner of the kitchen. It was quiet at this time of day. The rest of the staff would arrive shortly to begin preparing the evening meal, but that no longer concerned her. Outside, the spring sun-shine was brightening the grey city streets. It was April, and the tea shop had been open for four months; four months in which it had become increasingly popular, justifying Mr Freeman's trust in Patty's skill. She now had her own staff, not just Maisie but a young girl called Lucy, whom she had chosen herself from among the orphans brought up, as she had been, in the workhouse. Lucy followed her with adoring eyes and called her 'miss'. Patty had told her that was not necessary, but she could not suppress a small glow of pride. She had never expected to be given that sort of respect.

'We're finished here,' she said. 'I'm going upstairs to take the weight off my feet. Are you off home, Maisie?

Maisie's home was a few streets away, so she was able to live there rather than in the accommodation pro-vided for Freeman's staff.

'No, I've got some shopping to do,' Maisie said. 'You coming with me, Luce?'

'Yes, please,' the girl replied.

'See you in the morning, Maisie,' Patty said. 'And you make sure you're not late for supper, Lucy.'

'I will. Never been known to miss a meal, you know me.'

The two younger women put on their bonnets and shawls and went out, and Patty made her way up the back stairs to the top floor where there were two dormitories, one for the women, one for the men, and a common room where they could meet and relax. There was a table in the middle of the room, where letters addressed to the occupants were placed, but Patty never bothered to look there. After all, who would ever be likely to write to her? She had no relatives, that she knew of, and her friends were all on the staff of Freeman's.

That day, however, as soon as she came in one of the other girls who worked in the kitchen said, 'Hey, Patty! You've got a letter – from Australia!'

Patty picked up the envelope with a quickening of her pulse. There was only one person who might write to her from Australia, and that was May. She had given up hope of ever hearing from her friend again, but now here it was! She found a chair, put up her feet on a low stool, and slit open the envelope.

> *Freshfields*
> *Rutherglen,*
> *Victoria,*
> *Australia*
> *January 2nd 1868*

Dear Patty,

Merry Christmas and Happy New Year! I realise that by the time you receive this letter that will seem a very odd thing to read, but you will see from the date that those festivities are only just over as I write. Before I go any further, I need to apologise to you for going off without even saying goodbye. It was thoughtless and unkind. Can you ever forgive me? I can only say in excuse that I was in such a state that I hardly knew what I was doing.

How are you? I hope you are well and have not missed me too much. I think about you often and remember the times we had together – the good times and the bad ones. Did you have a good Christmas? It really doesn't feel like Christmas here. The weather is so much the opposite of what it is like at home. (I must stop saying 'at home' meaning Liverpool. This is my home now.) It is really hot here, hotter than I can ever remember it being in England. The sun beats down all day, every day. It's wonderful to wake up in the morning and see the sky, clear blue with not a cloud, and never have to worry about wrapping up in gloves and shawls. I'll never forget how cold we always were in the workhouse, and how much our chilblains used to hurt when our shoes pinched. Sometimes I catch myself wishing it was a bit cooler here, but then I remind myself of that and I don't mind the heat – though the flies do make me irritable at times.

I need to explain why I was in such a hurry to leave. You remember that I was walking out with James Breckenridge? I never let you know how serious it was, though I think you must have guessed. I was in love with him – I still am, and he with me, I believe. But I always knew it could never come to anything. His mother was determined that he should marry a 'suitable' girl from a 'good' family. Someone who would make a good wife for a rising young solicitor. And her idea of suitable did not include a milliner's apprentice, let alone a girl brought up in the workhouse. But she did not know that last bit, nor did James until shortly before I left.

If you remember, I concocted a story about having been brought up by relatives after my parents died, because I was ashamed to admit the truth. Then one day James asked me to marry him, and I knew I had to tell him the truth. He was shocked, not surprisingly. He told me it didn't make any difference to the way he felt but he suggested that we keep it secret and stick to the story I had made up. But I knew that could never work. One day we would meet someone who recognised me from when I was a maid-of-all-work for the Freemans, or ask questions about where I grew up and went to school that I couldn't answer. The more I thought about it, the more

I realised I couldn't marry James and live a lie, and he shouldn't ask me to.

I was in a desperate state, trying to see a way forward, when I got a letter from Gus. You remember he decided he wanted to settle in Australia? You know I always thought my father had drowned at sea. That was what my mother told us when she was still alive. Well, it wasn't true. He had been sentenced to transportation to Australia for smuggling, and she was so ashamed that she made up the story about him being lost at sea. Now I know that when he had served his sentence he decided not to come home, because he had not heard anything from my mother and thought she had probably married again. He met people who had come out to dig for gold and decided to join them, and he struck lucky! He is now a very wealthy man.

Gus had a job in a hotel in Melbourne and one day our father just happened to walk in and took a room in the name of Lavender. Well, it's not a common name and so he and Gus soon discovered that they were father and son. Father – it still seems very strange to write that word – has invested his money in a piece of land and gone into partnership with a Spaniard called Pedro to grow vines and produce wine from them. Gus's letter invited me to go and join them, and enclosed a warrant for a berth on the Royal Standard. *Well, it seemed like the perfect solution to my dilemma. I wrote to James and told him that I couldn't marry him and booked my passage. The only snag was that by the time I got the letter I only had two days before the ship sailed. I had a frantic rush to get ready. Mr Freeman, who has always been so kind to me, let me go without giving proper notice and even let me choose new clothes and other things for the journey. I was so caught up in all the preparations that I am afraid I never even thought of saying goodbye. And I was still feeling hurt and upset about breaking up with James, so much so that I did not want anyone to see me leave or wave me goodbye. Can you understand that?*

I thought by the time James got the letter the ship would have sailed, but it must have been delivered very early. I was standing at the rail, taking a last look at Liverpool, when suddenly I saw him on the dockside. It was quite a shock, as you can imagine! He shouted to me that he would marry me, and he wouldn't ask me to lie, and he begged me to come back. Well, by that time the ship was moving, so it was impossible. I shouted back to him that if he really loved me he would get the next boat, and he promised he would. But of course I realised as soon as the words were out of my mouth that it was impossible. His mother is very sick and he is the only son. He couldn't leave her. And then there are his final exams, to qualify as a solicitor. It would be stupid to waste all those years of study. I wrote him a letter, explaining that I understood that, and posted from our first port of call. Then, just a few days ago, I got a letter from him, saying almost the same things and apologising for not keeping his promise.

He says that as soon as his mother no longer needs him, and once he has passed his exams, he will come to join me. It's terrible to think that we are both waiting for his mother to die. The doctors say it is only a matter of months. James takes his final exams just before next Christmas, so by then he may be free – but even then it will be over a year before he could get here. He doesn't ask me to wait, but of course I shall. The question is, will he? That's an awful thing to say, but a year is a long time and his mother is determined to see him married to some- one suitable. I'm afraid he may find himself being pushed into a marriage, even if he still really wants to be with me.

I must try to trust in him. I'm sure he loves me – but it would be so much easier (and probably better) for him to marry someone else. I can only wait and hope.

That's quite enough about me! I really only intended to explain why I went off in such a hurry. There is so much to tell you about my new life here – but my hand is aching already. I'll write again soon, but you will have to wait until another ship can bring you my letter. It's very hard, waiting for news, when it takes three months for a letter to reach England and another three before you can get a reply.

Do write to me as soon as you can. I'd love to have all the news from Freeman's! I hope everyone is well and that Chef isn't giving you too much of a hard time. I'll tell you one thing I really miss out here – your deli- cious cakes!

Your affectionate friend,
May

C/O Freeman's Department Store,
Lime Street,
Liverpool,
England
April 3rd 1868

Dear May,

I'm not much good at writing letters. You were always the clever one in our class at the workhouse, and I always hated the lessons. That horrible Miss Bale was always hitting me over the knuckles with her ruler for blotting my work. But I'll do my best to give you all the news.

I've had a real stroke of luck. You remember I always liked making cakes? Well, Mr Freeman has decided to open a tea shop inside the store and he has asked me to be responsible for making the cakes and all the other things to eat. I've been given a pay rise and I have my own corner of the kitchen, with one of the new gas stoves to cook on. It frightened me to death to begin with. When you light it it gives a great pop, as if it's going to explode. But I'm used to it now and it certainly beats the old coal range they are still using in the main kitchen. I also have two girls working for me. Imagine! Me, a boss!

The tea shop opened in November and it's going really well. Lots of people say my cakes are delicious and they come back for more. It's wonderful to have a job I really enjoy.

There isn't much other news. Freeman's is doing good business, they say. And there are always plenty of people shopping in the store. Mr Freeman gave all the staff a bonus at Christmas to say thank you.

The weather here is chilly for the time of year, but I don't mind that. It's always warm in my kitchen.

I can't think of any more to say, except of course I forgive you for not saying goodbye. I can see you were in a bit of a state, what with one thing and another. I'm sure James will keep his promise and come to join you next year. But even if he doesn't, I bet there are plenty of nice-looking young men out there who would jump at the chance of marrying you. Just don't wait too long.

Write as soon as you can. I'm dying to hear all about life in Australia. Have you seen a kangaroo yet?

Love,
Patty

Chapter 3

Rutherglen, Australia, April 1868

May Lavender rubbed the back of her hand across her forehead. Although it was April, it was still hot and the sweat was threatening to run down into her eyes. She looked at the long table set out under the veranda. A white cloth had been spread over it, and on it were silver knives and forks, china plates decorated with a pattern of ivy leaves and cut-glass goblets, which sparkled in the evening sunlight. She looked at Maria, the wife of Pedro, her father's chief vigneron.

'I think everything is ready.'

'Ready and waiting,' Maria responded with a smile. 'We've enough food and drink to satisfy half of Rutherglen.'

'Sometime it feels as though we've invited half of Rutherglen,' May said. 'My papa certainly knows how to throw a party!'

'It's been a good season. The grapes are all in and it's time to celebrate,' Maria said. 'Now, why don't you go and change and get ready to receive your guests?'

'I suppose I had better,' May agreed. 'You're sure you don't need me to do anything else?'

'I've told you. It's all ready. Now go! And stop worrying.'

'Thank you, Maria,' May said. 'I don't know what I'd have done without you. I wouldn't have known where to begin.'

Until May's arrival, four months earlier, Maria had been in charge of the domestic arrangements at Freshfields. Three years ago, when George 'Ginger' Lavender, newly rich from the gold fields, decided to buy a 'run' of land just outside Rutherglen and go into the winery business, he had taken her husband on as his partner and chief adviser. Since he had no wife – as far as anyone knew – it was natural for Maria to act as housekeeper. Then, one day last autumn, he had returned from a trip to Melbourne in the company of a young man with the same flaming red hair and introduced him as his son, Augustus. He had learned that his wife was dead, but he had a daughter of seventeen and he had immediately sent for her to join him. Naturally, May was now the 'lady of the house', and Maria was quite prepared to cede her authority to the new arrival, but it had been clear from the start that May had no intention of supplanting her. She had made it abundantly clear that she knew nothing about running a household and was willing to defer to her in all practical matters. In Maria's experience the mistress of the house was not expected to sully her hands with domestic chores but

May had no intention of 'sitting on a cushion and sewing a fine seam', whatever her favourite song said. She had shown herself willing to work alongside Maria and had quickly picked up many of the skills required, but Maria understood that, because of her background, she had very little confidence in herself as a hostess.

'That's what I'm here for,' she said now. 'All you need to do now is smile and look pretty, which will be very easy for you. Off you go.'

May cast a last glance over the table. Her father had invited neighbours from around the area to celebrate the completion of the vendange. A little further away, under the shade of a tree, a second table had been set up for the workers, mostly Chinese, who had been employed to pick the grapes. She had queried this separation when the arrangements were discussed but her father had pointed out that the Chinese preferred their own food and had, in fact, brought their own cook with them. They would be much more at ease, he said, celebrating with their own kind than sitting with the Europeans. Away to the other side of the garden a whole hog was turning on a spit over a bed of charcoal, the appetising smell wafting across the space and bringing the saliva to her mouth. Satisfied that all was in order, she turned away and went up to her bedroom to change.

Waiting there was a girl of fourteen, a slender creature whose arms and legs seemed too long for her body.

May caught her breath on an apologetic gasp. 'Betsy! I'm so sorry, I didn't realise you were waiting for me. Have you been here long?'

Betsy shrugged. 'Not long. 'Bout ten minutes. Thought you'd want to take your time getting ready.'

'I suppose I should – but I wanted to make sure everything was ready downstairs'

'No need to worry,' the girl said. 'I 'spect Maria's got it all in hand.'

'Yes, she has,' May agreed. 'It's just … well, you know I'm not used to this sort of thing.'

'You'll be fine,' Betsy said. 'Least ways, as long as you're dressed before the guests arrive.'

'You're right. I had better get on. I'll just wash my face and hands.'

May had greeted the suggestion from her father that she should have a lady's maid to look after her with laughter.

'I've managed for myself all my life,' she'd said. 'I don't need someone to dress me. There was a time when becoming a lady's maid myself was the height of my ambition. I wouldn't know what to do with a maid of my own.'

'Well, you're the lady of the house now,' her father had responded, 'and you need to dress suitably, at least when you're in company.'

May had had to recognise the force of that argument, and it was true that dressing herself was not always easy. There were corsets to be tightened, and dresses that buttoned down the back, and doing up her own hair in a fashionable style was something she struggled with. So a compromise was agreed on. Betsy was the daughter of the local draper. Most of the time she worked in the shop, but she was fascinated by fashion and delighted to be given the opportunity to assist in transforming May into the image of the ladies she saw in the fashion plates in her father's magazines. So on special occasions, like this, she came to help out.

The relationship had been uneasy at first. Betsy made it clear that she was not to be treated as a servant, but when she discovered that May had been in service herself and was not about to put on airs and graces, she relaxed. May shared the same love of colour and design and very quickly a bond was formed between them. Sometimes it seemed to May that they were both engaged in a delightful game of dressing up. There were moments, though, when she felt a pang of guilt. What right had she, a girl brought up in the workhouse, to enjoy such luxury, when others she had grown up with were still living in poverty and servitude?

Her dress for that evening had been laid out ready on the bed. It was a creation of pale-green silk, with a flounced skirt trimmed with rosettes of darker green and drawn back over a bustle to create a short train. It had been made by a dressmaker in Chiltern, a woman who had learned her trade in London and Paris but who had given it all up to follow her husband to the new world. She had been overjoyed when asked to create a new wardrobe for May, who had arrived with only the most basic requirements. May thought this dress was probably the most beautiful she had ever worn.

'Do you know,' she said, as Betsy helped her into it, 'this reminds me a bit of the first proper evening dress I ever had. That was green, too, a bit darker than this, and I made it myself.'

'You made it? I'd never have dared try that.'

'It was that or nothing. I couldn't afford to go to a dressmaker, and even ready-made dresses like that were too expensive. And I have always been good with my needle. That's how I got my job as a milliner. I altered a dress of Mrs Freeman's, when I worked for her, to bring it up to date. So I borrowed a sewing machine from the shop and set to work.'

'Was it for a special occasion?'

'Yes, it was.' May paused, caught by a moment of nostalgia. 'Or it was for me. I'd been invited to a concert by ... by a gentleman.'

'A special gentleman?' Betsy probed.

'Very special – at the time.' May moved away to the dressing table and added, with a sudden change of tone, 'Come and help me arrange my hair.'

She found it hard to explain to herself, but she had never told anyone in her new home about James, or the reason why she had been so eager to accept her father's invitation. His letter had promised that he would come to join her as soon as he was free, but she kept the hope to herself. If in the end he did not arrive, there would be no need to explain her disappointment. She could keep her broken heart to herself.

Betsy brushed her hair and parted it in the centre, then coiled the rest into a chignon at the base of May's neck and fastened it with a circlet of green ribbon, the same as that used for the rosettes on the dress, and small white flowers. May shared the colouring of her father and brother, but in her case it was more subdued, giving her hair the sheen of polished mahogany. When Betsy had finished she stood up and looked at herself in the long mirror on the wall. It was hard to get used to this new, elegant May. Sometimes she hardly recognised herself, but tonight she had to admit that she was pleased with the effect.

'Will I do?'

Betsy looked at her with her head on one side. She was not given to flattery. 'It's a pity you haven't got a bit more up here—' she indicated her own bosom '—but apart from that … yes. You look pretty good.'

The sound of wheels and horse hooves outside drew May to the window.

'Goodness, people are here already!'

She looked down. A pony and trap had just drawn up outside the front door, escorted by two young men on horseback. One of them was her brother Gus, and as she watched he swung himself down from the saddle, threw the reins to his companion and went to hand down the occupants of the trap. Watching him, May was suddenly suffused with tender pride. This was the scrawny, pugnacious waif she remembered from their workhouse days, determinedly refusing to accept that 'lost at sea' meant drowned and convinced that their father still lived somewhere; the surprisingly tough boy who had come back to her after a year aboard the Confederate ship *Shenandoah*; the restless youth who had finally decided to seek a new future in Australia. And now look at him! At sixteen he was on the verge of manhood, with the potential for their father's broad shoulders and capable hands but the lithe grace that must have been their mother's legacy.

You were the one who had faith, Gus, she thought. You were the one who brought us here. Without you I should still be a milliner's apprentice – and probably without a job, and without any prospect of marriage.

The passengers in the trap had now all descended. The first was Kitty O'Dowd, the pretty Irish girl whose attractions had played a large part in Gus's decision to emigrate. After her came her mother, Deidre, her sister Maeve and her father, Patrick. There were two younger ones, but clearly they had been left with a neighbour. Gus and Kitty's brother, Liam, were now leading their horses round to the stables behind the house. May shook herself out of her reverie and hurried downstairs to greet her guests.

Very quickly the rest of the guests began to arrive. Many of them were fellow vignerons who had come from various parts of Europe to try their hand at establishing vineyards. Predominant among them were families of

German origin. There were the Ruches, the very first to set up in Rutherglen, and the Voherrs and the Schluters. There were English families too, the Lindsey Browns and the Chambers. Not everyone was involved in the wine trade. There was the Scot, John Wallace, owner of the Star Hotel, one of the best in Rutherglen, and the American Hiram Crawford, who had set up a coaching firm in the nearby town of Chiltern. It was, May's father had declared with pride, the cream of local society.

In the flurry of greetings May had no time to think about correct protocol. She had presided over one or two small dinner parties since her arrival, but this was the first large gathering and an important occasion. She had worried that she might not know how to conduct the formalities in the way other people would expect. But she need not have concerned herself. The rigid rules governing behaviour that applied in the society of Victorian Liverpool no longer held sway here. The atmosphere was relaxed and people mingled easily.

Very soon they were all seated and tucking into slices of roast pork with potatoes baked in the ashes, washed down with copious amounts of the previous year's vintage. Maria had drawn on her Spanish heritage to create a dish of sweet red peppers baked with tomatoes and stuffed aubergines. The vegetables were bought from a Chinese man who had given up on the hunt for gold and planted a market garden. May had never seen many of the things he grew before she left England, but the new flavours and colours made food very appealing to someone brought up on workhouse gruel and lobscouse. Afterwards there were jellies in jewel-like colours and sweet pastries and bowls of ripe peaches and bunches of purple grapes. All her life May had found that colour and scent combined to produce something almost like music to her senses, and tonight she was treated to a veritable orchestra of sensations.

During normal family meals May always helped out with the fetching and carrying and never expected to be waited on, but for this occasion her father had employed some local girls as waitresses. Under Maria's supervision the service proceeded smoothly, but May constantly had to suppress the urge to get up and clear the empty dishes or fetch something from the kitchen. As the meal progressed, however, she began to relax and enjoy chatting to the people on either side of her. The ages of the guests varied, as might be expected, but the senior members had been given the positions of honour to her left and right, or beside her father who presided at the other end of the table. But she couldn't help her eyes being drawn to the middle of the table, where the younger guests were seated, and in particular to a young man who belonged to one of the German families; she could not remember which. He had blond hair and a nose and chin chiselled with almost classical precision, and she found her gaze returning to him so often that she had to take herself to task. 'You are engaged to be married! You have no business eyeing another man ...' Or was she engaged, in reality?

One convention of European society was still observed, and when the meal was over the men sat back and lit cigars, and May led the ladies back into the house and seated them in the drawing room. Most of them knew each other well from previous social gatherings and they chatted easily, but May was still a novelty and she found herself being eagerly questioned, not so much about herself as about what was happening in England. Was it true that the Queen was still in deep mourning for Prince Albert and was very rarely seen in public? What was all this about a Reform Act that allowed ordinary men to vote? What were the latest fashions? Only the last question was one she felt herself competent to answer. It was a relief when a violin struck up outside and the ladies rose as one and headed for the windows.

'Oh, music! Who is that playing?'

'It's Patrick O'Dowd. He's brilliant on his fiddle. Should you like to go and listen?'

'Oh yes! Let us join the gentlemen. They shouldn't have all the fun.'

Outside, the men had left the table and were strolling in the garden. Patrick was perched on a stool in the centre of a group of younger people, including Gus.

'Come on, Kitty! Dance for us!' Gus begged. Then to the others, 'You should see how they dance. Feet twinkling and the rest of them almost still. Show them, Kitty!'

After the request had been repeated in different voices, Kitty and her sister stood up and began to dance, to an accompaniment of 'oohs' and 'ahs' and finally loud applause. Then someone else produced an accordion and Patrick struck up a reel and other people began to dance. When the reel was finished a contingent of the Germans took over to demonstrate their own style of dancing, with much knee and foot slapping. After that, someone said, 'Can't we have something we can all dance to?' and the accordionist began to play a waltz.

May was watching from the margins of the group, content that everyone seemed to be enjoying themselves. She was taken by surprise when a voice just behind her said, 'Miss Lavender, may I have the pleasure of this dance?' It was the German boy she had been watching earlier, and close up he was even more handsome than she had thought.

Disconcerted, she stammered, 'Oh no, I don't dance. I never learned how.'

'Really?' His expression suggested that he did not believe her.

'Yes, really. I wasn't ... I didn't grow up among people who thought that was important.'

'What a shame! Dancing is a great pleasure. But it's not too late to learn. I can teach you.'

His manner was serious and his look seemed to suggest that he was truly concerned that she should not be deprived of one of life's pleasures. She felt it would be impolite to refuse. He led her a little away from the rest and put his arm round her waist. A shiver of mixed surprise and pleasure ran through her nerves and she almost pulled away.

'Like this,' he said, taking her hand in his free one. 'Now, your hand on my shoulder. So! Now we step: one, two, three, one, two, three. There, you see? We are dancing.'

And so they were, to May's surprise. She had discovered when she was walking out with James that she loved music of any kind, and now something in her responded to the rhythms of the waltz. She forgot how strange it seemed to have a stranger's arm around her waist and began to enjoy herself.

After that, one or two of the other young men came to ask her to dance and she found herself learning the movements of the cotillion and the polonaise. But when another waltz struck up, her German partner claimed her again.

'It's very silly of me,' she confessed, 'but I don't remember your name.'

He smiled at her. 'Why should you, among so many? It's Anton, Anton Schloer. My father owns the St Nicholas vineyard, which runs beside your father's land.'

Guests were beginning to drift away and May excused herself to say goodbye to them. Finally, everyone had departed, leaving her to survey the garden littered with cigar butts and empty glasses. She was collecting them up when her father came out of the house.

'Leave them! We'll clear it all up in the morning.' He stretched and yawned. 'I don't know about you, my dear, but I'm ready for bed.'

May realised for the first time that she was very tired.

'Yes, you're right,' she agreed.

He put his hand on her shoulder. 'I was proud of you tonight. You look beautiful and no man could ask for a better hostess. Did you enjoy yourself?'

May was surprised to find that the answer came very easily. 'Yes, Papa. I did.'

'Good.' He kissed her forehead and went back into the house.

Gus came round from the stable yard. 'Ah, sis! I saw you dancing. Glad to see you haven't quite decided to join a nunnery.'

'I don't know what you mean!' she protested.

'Well, I was beginning to think you'd lost all interest in the opposite sex.'

'That's not ... I mean ...' she stammered to a halt.

'He's a good bloke, Anton. You could do a lot worse.'

'Don't be ridiculous. It was just a couple of dances.'

'So far, but who knows?'

'Oh, leave off, Gus! I don't want to talk about it.'

'You're not still pining after that toffee-nosed solicitor chap, are you?' he demanded.

'I'm not pining after anyone!' she snapped. 'Mind your own business, Gus. I'm going to bed.'

Freshfields
Rutherglen,
Victoria
July 1st 1868

Dear Patty,

I was so pleased to get your letter, with your wonderful news. I remember you made me a cake for my birthday last year. It was absolutely delicious, although I know you had to scrounge the ingredients from whatever you could find in the store room! I'm sure all the things you are baking now will be even better, and I'm so proud of you. You really deserve a lucky break. I wish I could visit Freeman's, just to take tea in your new tea shop.

I promised to write and tell you more about my new life here. It's hard to know where to begin. Australia is so different from anything I ever knew before and I feel that I am different too. When I think of myself in the orphanage or when I worked for Mrs Freeman, scrubbing and polishing from dawn to midnight, I can hardly believe that was the same person. The fact is, I am a lady of leisure, or I could be, if I wanted to. I don't want to, though, and I do my best to make myself useful, but we have a housekeeper, Maria, who is a wonderful cook and terribly efficient, so all I can do is help out where I can. My father and Gus are busy all the time with the vineyard, but there is nothing I can do to help there. I sometimes think I should like to go back to making hats, but I don't think my father would approve of that.

I have taken up painting again. Do you remember, James encouraged me to try, back in Liverpool? And I do get a great deal of pleasure from it. There are so many marvellous things here to paint. The animals are extraordinary, and they are much less shy than most of the wild animals in England. Kangaroos will not stay still while you sketch them, of course, but there are lovely little creatures called koala bears who just sit in the eucalyptus trees all day and hardly move at all. They are not really bears, but they have the same sort of round cuddly look as teddy bears. My favourite subjects are the birds. I have never seen so many brilliantly coloured birds. There are different kinds of parrots, with red and blue or orange and green and yellow feathers, and tiny little fairy wrens with glistening blue breasts. We have a lake at the end of our property and on that there are kingfishers, which flash by so quickly that they look like a streak of blue lightening, and cormorants that stand stock still holding their wings out to dry in the sun, and black swans – yes, black ones. This is 'down under', of course. So it's not surprising that things are a bit topsy-turvy!

So, let me tell you a bit about Rutherglen itself. It is only here because gold was found here about ten years ago in what was called the Wahgunyah gold rush. It didn't last long, and now most of the gold has gone, but by then people had settled here and found other things to do. There is a river called the Indigo Creek and the soil is very fertile, so apart from vineyards there are market gardens growing all sorts of fruit and vegetables that I had never seen in Liverpool. They are also growing tobacco round here, and we have a flour mill and a brewery and several hotels. People have set up all sorts of businesses to supply the needs of the people who have settled here, so we have a draper's shop and a blacksmith, and of course a butcher and a general store that sells almost anything you could ever need.

There are other towns nearby too. Beechworth is the main one. It has a post office and banks and a court house and a police station and a hospital.

Did I tell you that Gus has a sweetheart? She's an Irish girl called Kitty, who came out with her family on the same ship as he did. In fact, I think that is the main reason why he decided to come to Australia. Her father is a cobbler and bootmaker, and has set up in business in Chiltern. Gus rides over to see them whenever he can get away. He has taken to riding a horse as if he was born to it!

It may seem odd to you that so many of the towns have English names. I suppose it was because when the first settlers arrived this part of Australia reminded them of home. There is one quite amusing story about how Rutherglen got its name. There is a man called John Wallace, a Scotsman who owns a chain of hotels called Star Hotels. When he opened one here this place still didn't have a name. From what I have been told, a group of men were gathered in the bar and the subject came up and someone suggested that if Mr Wallace would 'shout' everyone a drink he could call it whatever he liked. (Out here, to shout someone means to give them something without paying for it.) So he bought them all a beer and called the place after the town where he was born in Scotland. I think that is rather charming, don't you?

We have quite a good social life here. There are dances most weekends in the local hotels and parties on the various wine estates. Everyone mixes very easily here and there is none of the snobbery we have in England. No one cares where you come from or who your family are, or whether you are a professional or in trade – though I have heard it said that in Melbourne people who came out here of their own accord look down on those who were transported, like my father. Luckily that doesn't seem to apply here. I have been learning to dance, and I quite enjoy it but there is a problem. There are a great many unmarried men here and few single women, so I never lack for dancing partners, but I know some of them would like to be more than that. I try not to give them expectations that can never be realised but I'm afraid they are beginning to think me very cold and stand-offish. I haven't told anyone about James, not even Papa. I truly believe he will keep his promise and come to join me when he is able, but sometimes I wonder why he should give up the comfortable life he could have in Liverpool and risk

*starting again in an unknown country. If anything hap-
pened, and he did not come, I couldn't bear everyone
knowing and feeling sorry for me. Gus knew him, back
in Liverpool of course, but he never really approved of
me walking out with him and I think now he believes
it is all over. But going back to the men who ask me to
dance – I cannot say I am engaged, because in truth
we never were, so I cannot explain why I try to keep
my distance. Gus gets annoyed with me sometimes. He
thinks I am missing the chance of a good marriage.
I wish James could be here! Everything would be so
much simpler then.*

*I really must stop going on about my problems. The
fact is I am one of the luckiest people alive and I should
be grateful. And I am – truly!*

*Write as soon as you can and tell me how your won-
derful new venture is going. How does it feel to be in
charge, and not having to take orders from anyone else?*

*With love from,
May*

Chapter 4

Liverpool, October 1868

Patty looked at herself in the small mirror fixed to the wall at the end of the dormitory she shared with the other single girls employed by Freeman's. She pinched her cheeks and bit her lips to bring some colour to them. Once, years ago, she had described her face to May as being like a bun with a couple of currants stuck in for eyes. That wasn't quite true anymore. She was eighteen now and maturity had made her nose and cheekbones more pronounced. Her eyelashes had thickened, so that her eyes looked larger, but it was true she would never be a beauty by any conventional standards. Nevertheless, she did have redeeming features, she thought. Her skin was clear and unblemished and several years of good food had transformed her once scrawny figure. It could now be described as 'voluptuous', she decided. She liked that word. She had come across it in a ladies' magazine and had had to ask one of the girls who worked on the shop floor what it meant.

She hitched her corset, to expose a little more cleavage above the neck of her dress, adjusted her bonnet and turned to the others behind her.

'Ready, girls?'

There was a chorus of assent and they all clattered down the uncarpeted back stairs towards the street. There were five of them; Lucy was one and the other three were sales girls. Normally, the better educated and more sophisticated girls who came into direct contact with customers on the shop floor looked down on those who worked behind the scenes, the cooks and kitchen maids and seamstresses and others, whose work was nevertheless as vital to the success of the store as their own. They made an exception, however, for Patty, now that she was manageress of the tea shop and she had insisted on bringing Lucy with her.

At the street door, five young men waited for them. They were also employees, who worked in the gentlemen's outfitting department and lived in, like the girls. Patty had soon discovered that one of the good things about no longer having to cook the evening meal and clear up afterwards was that she was free to go out in the evening and tonight they were going to The Eagle, a tiny pub just behind the Royal Alexandra Theatre in Lime Street. Once there, they settled in a corner of the saloon, the boys bought glasses of ale and the girls ordered either port and lemon or ginger beer. The atmosphere was cosily convivial and Patty settled back in her seat with a sigh of contentment.

'Hey, Patty!' One of the boys nudged her elbow. 'There's a fellow over there giving you the eye.'

Patty looked across to the bar. A man had followed them in and taken a stool at the bar and now he had swung round and was staring in her direction. He was about thirty, she guessed, with light-brown hair slicked back and parted in the centre, and a neat moustache that curled downwards, framing full lips. He was wearing checked trousers in the latest fashion with the new, shorter jacket, a waistcoat and a rather flamboyant cerise cravat. There was something about him that seemed familiar but she couldn't recall where she had seen him before.

'He's a bit smart for this place, isn't he?' Lucy murmured in Patty's ear. 'Looks like he'd be more at home in a gentleman's club.'

Seeing them looking in his direction, the young man got off his stool and came over. 'Ladies,' he said with a small bow, and then, almost as an afterthought, 'and gents. Do you mind if I join you?' He made an expansive gesture with one hand, which finished by indicating his own chest. 'Percy Dubarry, at your service. Now, let me buy you all a drink. What's your pleasure, ladies?'

His eyes were focused on Patty and her first instinct was to refuse, but that seemed rude so she said, 'I'll have a small port and lemon, please.'

Percy took the others' orders and went back to the bar. When they all had their drinks he surveyed the bench where the girls were sitting. 'Mind if I squeeze in?' he said, and inserted himself neatly between Patty and Lucy. Patty found his hip and thigh uncomfortably close to her own.

'What's your name?' he asked Lucy and she told him with a simper. 'How about you?' he turned his gaze on Patty.

'Patty Jenkins,' she responded.

'And what do you do, Patty?' he asked.

'I work for Freeman's, the department store.'

'Do you?' He sounded impressed. 'What as?'

'I'm in charge of the tea shop. That is, I make all the cakes and other things.'

'No, really? I was in there the other day. You must be a good cook. The cakes were first-rate.'

'I thought I had seen you before,' Patty said. 'I was surprised to see a young gentleman there on his own.'

'Why? Isn't a fellow entitled to a nice cup of tea and a piece of cake if he fancies it?'

'Well, yes, of course,' Patty responded, feeling slightly awkward. 'It's just, it was unusual, that's all.'

After that Percy turned his attention to Lucy and the conversation became general. Percy had a way of focusing on people as if he was really interested in what they had to say and before long the slight uneasiness, which in the case of the young men in the group bordered on resentment, was dissipated.

When Patty said, 'It's time we were getting back,' he said, 'Already? The night is young. I thought we might go on to somewhere we could have a dance.'

'Sorry,' Patty replied. 'We have to be back by ten o'clock, or we get into trouble with Mrs Stevens, the matron.'

'Back by ten!' he exclaimed. 'What is this, some kind of institution?'

'We live in at the store,' Patty explained, feeling rather nettled by his tone. 'We have to be up at six, so it makes sense to be in bed at a reasonable time. Now—' she got to her feet '—if you'll excuse us ...'

'I'll walk you back,' he said.

'There's no need. It's only a few steps, and we've got the other gentlemen with us.'

'It will be my pleasure,' he said, undeterred.

Outside the pub he offered Patty his arm. 'You know what I was thinking, when I first saw you in that bar?' he said.

'What?'

'I was wondering what a lovely girl like you was doing out on her own.'

'I wasn't on my own,' Patty said, feeling herself blush.

'I mean, not with a feller of your own. Don't tell me that one of these boys is your beau?'

'No, they're not. I mean, they are just friends, people I work with.'

'So, you're not walking out with anyone?'

'No ... not at the moment.'

He pressed her arm against his side and she felt a frisson of pleasure. He was very much better looking than any of the others, and he was a proper man, not a boy like them. She felt suddenly proud to be on his arm.

'Would you walk out with me?'

'With you? I don't know you.'

'You could get to know me.'

She glanced sideways at him. He seemed to be serious.

'Why would you want to walk out with me? Why me?'

'Because I think you are the best-looking girl I've seen in a long time.'

She giggled. 'Oh, don't be silly! I'm nothing special.'

'Oh, but you are, Patty Jenkins, queen of the tea table,' he said, with a laugh.

They had reached the alleyway leading to the back of Freeman's and the others were disappearing down it.

'What do you say?' he asked. 'Can I see you again?'

'I suppose so, if you want to.'

He smiled down at her. 'I'll come and call for you tomorrow. What time do you get off?'

'About six o'clock, when the shop shuts.'

'I'll be here then.'

The next day he was there as he'd promised and he took her to a restaurant. Patty did not tell him that she had never eaten in a restaurant before, but when she was in service at Speke the butler and the housekeeper had insisted on proper table manners and she had copied the other servants. Now she watched covertly to see what other diners were doing and felt reasonably confident that she had not disgraced herself. They ate asparagus and steak, things she had seen taken up to the dining room for the rich people but had never tasted before, and Percy insisted on buying a bottle of wine. She did not like the taste of it much and he drank most of the bottle, but the little she did have made her feel pleasantly woozy.

When he walked her back to the shop the autumn breeze felt softer on her face and the lights in the shop windows seemed brighter than she remembered. In the alleyway he drew her close to him and kissed her and that broke the spell. Her only intimate experience with men had been far more brutal than Percy's eager kiss but still his touch repelled her. She broke away and muttered something about 'we mustn't ... I don't ... sorry. Look, I've got to go in, or I'll be in trouble.'

He did not seem put out. He pressed her hand and said, 'Don't worry. I'll see you again soon. Goodnight.'

She thought, as she got ready for bed, that she would never see him again, but two nights later he was waiting for her again. This time he took her to a different place. It was a restaurant, again, but much more crowded and there was a small orchestra at one side and a dance floor. At the far end was a doorway leading to another room, and when it opened she saw through a haze of cigar smoke men sitting round tables, playing cards. Some of the women seemed, to her, rather gaudily dressed and were often in the company of much older men. Memories of the worst months of her life rose in her mind.

'Those women,' she queried. 'Are they … ?'

'Hostesses, that's all,' he said reassuringly. 'Just here to dance with men who don't have a partner. Come on, let's have a dance ourselves.'

As he led her onto the floor Patty was grateful for another thing she had learned while she was at Speke. At Christmas there was a servants' ball, when the grand ballroom was thrown open to all the staff and the lords and ladies danced with them – only, of course, with carefully selected upper servants – but that left the rest to enjoy a rare opportunity for gaiety. Afraid that she would be shown up as ignorant she had turned to the one person who had shown her any friendship, Robin the stable boy, and begged him to teach her. He had shown her how to dance the waltz and the polka, which was the sensation of the moment, and explained the intricacies of the Roger de Coverley and the cotillion. It had come at a price, of course. After the ball was over he had dragged her out to the stable yard, pushed her against the wall and thrust his tongue down her throat and his hand up her skirt. She had sworn then that she would never dance with a man again, but Percy was different. He took her onto the dance floor and held her quite decorously as they waltzed. He was, she decided, a real gentleman. That evening, when he took her home, he did not try to kiss her.

A few days later she was clearing up after the tea shop had closed when one of the waitresses put her head round the kitchen door.

'There's a fellow upstairs asking for you.'

'What sort of a fellow?'

'Dapper sort of gent. Says his name's Percy. Says you will know him.'

'Yes, I know him,' Patty agreed. 'But I can't think what he wants with me.'

Percy was standing in the almost empty tea shop, chatting amiably to Miss Winterton, the lady who had been brought in to run the business side of the enterprise.

'Ah, here she is!' he exclaimed. 'The queen of cakes!'

'It seems your fame is spreading,' Miss Winterton said archly. 'Mr Dubarry has come specially to sample your creations.'

'Oh,' said Patty, flustered, 'really?'

'I must get on,' Miss Winterton said. 'I've got to cash up. I'll leave you to entertain the gentleman.'

'Why did you ask them to call me up,' Patty asked, as the other woman moved away.

'I just wanted to tell you in person how much I enjoyed your baking.'

'I'm glad,' she said. 'But you could have told me next time you take me out.'

'Tell you what I liked best? Those gingerbread ladies. That's a real stroke of genius, making them to look like the models.'

'Yes, they are very popular,' Patty agreed.

He leaned towards her. 'Don't suppose you've got one or two left over, have you?'

'Well ...' Patty hesitated.

'Look, I'm not asking for myself. There's a family I know. Father was killed in an accident on the docks, mother takes in washing to make ends meet, three little 'uns. I do what I can, but it's never enough. Those children never taste anything sweet from one year's end to the next. Most of the time they have to make do on bread and scrape. They'd give their right hands for one of your gingerbread ladies.'

'Wait here,' Patty said.

She ran down to the kitchen and collected half a dozen of the gingerbread figures. She had intended them for herself and the two girls who helped, but this was obviously a better cause. She wrapped them in a napkin and took them back to where Percy was waiting.

'Bless you!' he exclaimed. 'It'll be a red letter day for those children. I can't wait to see their little faces when I give them these. I'll tell them to remember you in their prayers tonight.'

When he had gone Patty smiled to herself. She wished she could see the children's faces, too, but it was a pleasure just to imagine it. Thinking back to her own childhood in the workhouse, she had never actually gone hungry but she remembered how she and the other children had longed for the taste of something sweet.

Two mornings later she had just taken a batch of gingerbread ladies out of the oven when there was a knock at the door that opened directly from her small section of the kitchen onto the basement area behind the store. Opening it, she found Percy with a woman, whose ragged shawl and haggard face proclaimed her poverty.

'This is Agnes,' Percy said. 'It was her children you gave the gingerbread ladies to. She wants to thank you in person.'

'Yes, miss,' the woman confirmed. 'I'm that grateful to you. I could never afford to give the little 'uns a treat like that. They loved every mouthful. My little Bobby broke his in half to save it for another day. He slept with it under his pillow, in case one of the others took it in the night.'

'You see?' Percy said. 'Doesn't it feel good to be able to give so much pleasure to children who have so little?' He paused and sniffed the scent of ginger and sugar coming from the kitchen. 'I don't suppose you could spare a few more?'

Patty looked at the woman's face and saw the look of hope quickly succeeded by fatalistic resignation. She glanced at the kitchen clock. There was time to bake a fresh batch, just. Maisie's mother had come round that morning to say that her daughter had a bad cold and could not come to work, and Patty had just sent Lucy to the store cupboard to fetch more flour, so she was alone. She picked up the empty flour bag and quickly shovelled the entire batch of a dozen into it.

'Here.' She held it out to Agnes. 'Don't tell anyone, for goodness sake. And don't let them eat them all at once. Keep a couple for yourself.'

'Oh, miss!' the woman exclaimed. 'I don't know what to say. Thank you! The bairns will think they've died and gone to heaven.'

'Well done, Patty!' Percy said. 'You're a lady, and no mistake.'

She did not see Percy again for a week or two and when he called for her next he explained that he had had to go away on business. For the first time it occurred to her to ask how he earned his living.

'What sort of business, Percy?'

He shrugged and smiled. 'Oh, this and that. Buying and selling. You have to make your money wherever you can in this city.'

Over the next weeks he appeared at irregular intervals to invite her to accompany him to a restaurant, or a dance hall. His favourite place was the one where they had first danced together, which he jokingly called his 'club'. Wherever they went, he seemed to be well-known and was warmly greeted, but he never introduced Patty or accepted the invitations to join other groups. She found their relationship puzzling. The other girls in the dormitory had taken to referring to Percy as 'your feller' and seemed to assume that in the course of time they would be engaged; yet apart from that first time he had never attempted to kiss her again. It was not what she assumed a romantic relationship would be like at all.

Once she said to him, 'I don't know what you see in me. I'm not half as pretty as some of these other girls.'

'Ah,' he said with a wink, 'beauty's only skin deep, they say. You've got something about you. You've got what they call personality.'

'Have I?' Patty felt a swell of pride. 'Really?'

'Tell you what, though,' he said. 'You don't make the best of yourself. Why don't you get yourself a new dress? Something a bit swanky, so I can show you off.'

Patty had never thought of going into the ladies' fashion department of Freeman's as a customer. Her pay rise had allowed her to save a little money, so she thought she could probably afford to buy a dress, but at some only half-realised level she had the idea that such clothes were not intended for 'the likes of her'. But the suggestion that Percy did not feel she was well enough dressed to mix with his friends was enough to prompt her into action.

Next morning she plucked up her courage and braved the superior stare of Miss Clarke, the manageress.

'Patty? Is there something you need?'

Patty swallowed. 'Please, I'd like to try on a dress.'

'A dress? Which dress did you have in mind?'

'That yellow one, over there.'

'The yellow silk with the black lace?'

'Yes, please.'

'It's quite expensive, you know.'

'Yes, I know. But I've saved a bit of money from my wages.'

Miss Clarke looked at her for a moment and Patty was afraid that she was going to refuse. She had been right all along. Girls like her were not supposed to wear dresses from the ladies' fashion department. But then the manageress's face softened.

'Miss Brown? Here, please.'

A young woman obeyed the summons.

'Patty here would like to try on the yellow silk. Will you assist, please.' She paused and ran her eyes over Patty. 'The next size up, I think.'

Patty followed Miss Brown into a changing cubicle and allowed her to help her into the dress. Even with the larger size she had to pull her stays as tight as she could bear before the buttons would do up, but when she was finally squeezed into it the assistant looked her up and down and said, 'You know, that really suits you.'

Coming out of the cubicle she found Miss Clarke waiting. She nodded approvingly. 'I think that does very nicely on you. And you're in luck. I have just realised the sale price of that dress has been reduced.'

'Oh!' Patty said. 'How much is it now?'

Miss Clarke named a price. Even with the reduction it was almost more than she could afford, but she bought it anyway.

That evening Percy greeted her with an appreciative whistle.

'Well, you're a sight for sore eyes, and no mistake.' He offered her his arm with a little bow. 'Shall we go, my lady?'

He still did not introduce her to his friends, but for the first time she felt equal to the other women on the dance floor – no longer the poor relation. She began to take more interest in her appearance and soon felt that one new dress was not enough. She knew it would be a long time before she could afford another one, so she began to haunt the room where the seamstresses worked. Ready-made dresses were a novelty still and most ladies preferred to have clothes made for them and Freeman's offered that facility as well. Patty found that she could beg off-cuts of fabric – but never enough to make a dress, and anyway she knew she did not have the skill to create one herself. But she did fashion a little black velvet cape to wear over the yellow dress and some white lace ruffles to add to the plain dark blue dress she had been given when she went to work for Freeman's. She ventured into the millinery department, too, hoping to pick up some ribbon or some flowers to trim a bonnet. But the milliner in charge now was not the cheery Nan Driscoll but the martinet Miss Jones. Patty remembered how much May had disliked her new boss and she soon understood why. The suggestion that there might be some unwanted trimmings leftover was dismissed out of hand.

'We do not waste anything in this department. It's no good you coming scrounging here.'

On her way out, Patty noticed a black feather lying apparently discarded on one of the tables. Without pausing for thought she swept it into her hand and hid it under her apron.

Returning to the common room with her booty, she was delighted to find a letter addressed to her with an Australian post mark.

Freshfields
Rutherglen,
Victoria
July 25th 1868

Dear Patty,

You will be surprised to get another letter so soon, but I have some news that I know will interest you. Do you remember the little girl we used to call Angel? I used to look after her as a baby in the workhouse, but then she was adopted by a Mr and Mrs McBride. They did not want anyone to know their child had come from the workhouse so they made up a story that she was his brother's child and had been born in Ireland.

You are probably wondering why I am bringing all this up again now. Well, I have just received a letter from James, dated last May. An extraordinary thing has happened. A man called Richard Kean walked into the office of the solicitor James works for and asked for help to trace his daughter. He left her at the workhouse because he was destitute and was leaving for South Africa to find work. Having made a good living, he had come back to claim her, but the workhouse supervisor would not tell him who had adopted her. James guessed from his description that it might be the child I called Angel. So he has turned detective! He has been to Ireland, to the village her adoptive parents told everyone she had come from but found no trace of anyone called McBride or any child being baptised there who might be Angel. So the whole story is obviously a lie.

Mr Kean naturally wanted to see her, but she has been sent away to school and no one knows where, so when James wrote they were waiting for her to come home for the summer holidays.

Of course, it may all come to nothing. Angel may not be his daughter after all and, even if he believes she is, I do not know how he can prove it. But I should like to think of her reunited with her real father. I'm sure she was not happy with the McBrides. Well, I shall just have to be patient and wait for James's next letter.

I hope you are well and the tea shop continues to go well. I'm sure it must be a great success. You haven't told me much about yourself in your letter. Have you got a beau? I bet you can have your pick now you're a manageress! How is Mr Carton treating you these days? I know he used to bully you. I should think he's had to change his tune a bit. Quite right, too.

Write soon. I'm longing to hear all the gossip.

Love,
May

Chapter 5

Rutherglen, October 1868

It was race day, and the entire population of Rutherglen was in a ferment of excitement. The atmosphere at Freshfields was particularly frenetic, as George Lavender had been co-opted into the Rutherglen Jockey Club, the group of leading citizens whose job it was to choose a site for the meeting and make the necessary arrangements. To add to the tension, Gus had insisted on entering his black gelding, Storm, and proposed to ride him himself.

'You don't stand a chance,' his father told him. 'If it was just local people you might, just, though I doubt it against horses like Wallace Chambers' Gladiator. But people will come from up-country and they are serious breeders. You haven't seen some of these thorough-breds run. Against them any of our beasts will look like carthorses.'

'You've never ridden in a race, Gus,' May said. 'You don't know what you're letting yourself in for.'

'I've raced Storm against some of the other fellows, out on the road,' Gus said obstinately. 'I know what I'm doing.'

May and her father had given up the argument and concentrated on practical arrangements for the day. They had invited a number of other local people to join them and May and Maria were busy packing a picnic to satisfy a dozen large appetites. As soon as it was ready May hurried upstairs to change her dress and put on her most attractive bonnet, since she had been told that this was one of the occasions in the year when everyone was expected to appear in all their finery. By the time she came down again, Maria and the two boys who were employed to look after the stables, together with their Chinese gardener, had loaded the hampers of food and the magnums of wine onto a wagon, and they all set off for the stretch of land that had been chosen for the meeting.

There was no permanent structure, although there was talk of one day building a stand for the spectators and stables for the visiting horses. At present there was only a track, marked out by tapes, and some marquees to provide shade. A special area near the finishing post was set aside for members of the jockey club and their families. May supervised the unloading of the provisions and their storage in a corner of the marquee, then she and Maria spread a rug on the grass and settled down to watch the passing crowd. On the far side of the track a paddock had been created for the horses and their riders and a number of local men were engaged in either exercising their mounts or putting finishing touched to their appearance with grooming brushes and polishing cloths. As May watched, a horsebox drawn by two dray horses arrived.

'That'll be one of the squatters from up-country, bringing his thoroughbred to race,' Maria said.

'I don't understand that term,' May said. 'I thought a squatter was someone who was occupying a house that didn't belong to them.'

'Well, I suppose the fact is that when those families first moved onto the land, it didn't belong to them. They brought their sheep and their cattle over from New South Wales and just marked out territory for themselves. In the end the government realised they could never get rid of them, so laws have been brought in allowing them to lease the land, or sometimes even buy it. Most of them have huge runs with hundreds of head of sheep and cattle, so they are very well off.'

More horseboxes arrived, and May saw glossy animals being led out of them and tethered under the trees. Gus appeared, his brows drawn down in an expression May remembered from their childhood days, whenever he had conceived the idea that someone had insulted him or treated him unfairly.

'Those damn squatters!' he muttered.

'Really, Gus,' she protested, 'you shouldn't use words like that.'

'Why not?' he demanded irritably. 'No one worries about language like that out here.'

Her father patted her arm. 'I'm afraid he's right, May. You have to remember that most of us come from pretty rough backgrounds, where that sort of language – and worse – was quite normal. All the same, Gus—' he turned to his son '—you shouldn't swear in front of ladies, and that includes your sister.'

'Sorry,' he mumbled, then more loudly, 'but it's not fair. Those chaps shouldn't be allowed to bring their thoroughbreds here to race against local people. We don't stand a chance against horses like that.'

'Isn't that what I told you?' his father said. 'I'm afraid horse racing is becoming big business. The Victoria Racing Club is beginning to lay down rules and regulations, and little local races like this will probably soon be a thing of the past. Soon the only people who can be involved are the ones with the money to import stallions from abroad and breed horses specifically to race.'

'We've got money,' Gus said. 'Why can't we breed our own horses?'

'Well, for one thing, because we don't know the first thing about it,' his father responded with a laugh.

'We could learn.' May recognised the obstinate set of her brother's chin and knew that this was something he would not easily let drop.

'Yes, well,' their father said easily, 'you learn enough to convince me that it won't be a waste of money and I'll think about it.'

Their guests had arrived, and May and Maria set out the picnic. Gus looked around at the rest of the gathering.

'Where's Kitty? Her dad promised to bring her.'

'They'll be here soon, I expect,' May said. 'It's quite a long drive from Chiltern.'

'You should see those horses, May,' Gus said. 'They are the most beautiful creatures. Why don't you come over to the paddock with me and I'll show you? We've still got half an hour before the first race.'

'I don't know,' May said. She had had very little experience of horses and they made her nervous.

'Oh, come on! They won't hurt you,' he said.

She saw that he would be annoyed if she refused so she nodded and put aside her glass of lemonade. 'Very well, then, if I must.'

He stretched out his hand and pulled her to her feet and they strolled around the track to the paddock. As they approached they were greeted by Anton Schloer, who was holding the reins of a tall grey horse. He clicked his heels together and made a little bow.

'Good afternoon, Miss Lavender. I am glad to see that you have come to support us.'

Over the last months Anton had become a regular visitor to Freshfields. Ostensibly it was because he and Gus were friends, but he always took every opportunity to spend time with May. He carried her easel when she went to the lake to paint and sat with her, discussing the wildlife they saw. At the local dances he was always the first to ask her to dance and did his best to monopolise her attention. She enjoyed his company and his manner was always correct, even formal, but she knew that he was hoping for some indication from her that she was prepared to take the relationship further. She felt she was being unfair and longed to be able to explain her position, but without telling him, and her family, about James that was impossible. Her dilemma was complicated by the fact that Gus made no secret of his approval of a potential match and was puzzled and irritated by her reluctance.

She smiled and gave Anton her hand. 'I don't think my support is going to be much use to you. I know nothing at all about horses or horse racing.'

'But we are not experts either,' he said. 'And seeing the competition, I do not think either of us stand much chance of winning a race. Is it not so, Gus?'

'Not today,' Gus agreed. 'Not until we take a leaf out of the opposition's book.'

'Oh, and how do you propose to do that?'

'I'm not sure, yet. But I'll find a way.' He indicated a dark chestnut horse that was being led past them by a groom. 'Look at that! Look at the muscles in his hocks and the depth of his chest. That's what I'd be looking for.'

'Well, well! A farmer with an eye for horseflesh! That's a new one!'

The speaker had come up behind them. He was a young man, perhaps in his mid-twenties, May guessed, with dark, slightly unruly hair and wide-spaced brown eyes fringed with thick lashes. She took this in, in the first seconds of the encounter, with a sudden jolt, as if she had missed her step on the grass.

Gus flushed angrily. 'I'm not a farmer. I'm a wine grower.'

The man lifted dark brows. 'There is a difference?'

Gus squared up to him. 'Are you looking for a fight?'

It was Anton who stepped between them. 'Whether farmers or vignerons, we know better than to behave in this way in the presence of a lady.'

The newcomer's eyes went from Anton to May, and stayed focused on her face. 'Forgive me, you are quite right. I should mind my manners. Please accept my apologies. My name is Rudolph Marshall. May I know yours?'

May glanced at her brother, who was still glowering, and knew that it was up to her to maintain the peace. 'I am May Lavender, and this is my brother Augustus. This gentleman is Anton Schloer.'

Marshall nodded to Gus and then to Anton. 'Pleased to meet you, gentlemen. Forgive me if I offended you just now. I was surprised, that is all, to hear you speak in such perceptive terms about my horse.'

'He's yours?' Gus said, with a change of tone.

Marshall moved to pat the neck of the horse. 'Yes, he's mine. This is Excalibur – the winner of your three-thirty race. I can guarantee that.'

'He is a splendid animal,' Anton said. 'I am glad that my race is the two-thirty, so I shall not be running against him.'

'And you?' Marshall turned to Gus. 'Do you also ride today?'

'In the two-thirty, also,' Gus said.

'Then I wish you both the best of luck.' He offered his hand to May. 'Miss Lavender. I'm delighted to make your acquaintance; I hope we may meet again – after the race perhaps?'

'I ...' she hesitated, taken by surprise. 'I don't expect so.'

'Oh? I am disappointed. Perhaps then, you will give me that flower you are wearing, to stick in my cap to bring me luck?'

May swallowed hard. Behind her back she could sense Gus bristling and the thought came to her that she need not be bound by his disapproval. She was wearing a small sprig of wattle pinned to her collar, the golden yellow of which complimented the blue of her dress. She unpinned it and handed it to Marshall.

'Here you are. I hope it does bring you luck.'

'I'm quite sure it will.' He raised the blooms to his nose, bowed and turned away to take the reins of his horse.

'What did you do that for?' Gus demanded, as he moved off. 'You don't want to encourage that sort.'

'What do you mean, that sort?'

'He's one of the squattocracy. We don't mix with his type.'

'The what?' Her laughter burst out at the name.

'It's a mixture of squatters and aristocracy. It means they're at the top of the heap, or they like to think they are. Like the lords and dukes and such like back in England.'

'I don't see how they can think that,' May said, puzzled. 'I mean, what gives them the right?'

'What gives the barons back in England the right?' he countered.

'Well, they inherited it.'

'And that makes it right for them to own half the country and treat the rest of us like dirt?'

'I never said that. And I don't see what it has to do with these squatters. What right do they have to think themselves so superior?'

'The same thing. They own great swathes of the land and that means they have great pots of money.'

'We have money, now. Well, Papa does.'

'Not like them. We'll never be as rich as they are.'

'Well, anyway, I don't see why I shouldn't be polite to that man. He seemed quite pleasant.'

'He's a condescending b ... I won't say the word. You know what I mean.'

Anton had stood quietly by during this exchange. Now he said, 'We should perhaps give Marshall the benefit of the doubt. He did apologise for his bad manners to begin with.'

May smiled at him. 'Thank you, Anton.' On an impulse she added, 'I'm sorry I haven't got another flower to give to you for luck.'

He bent his head gallantly. 'Just the wish from you is good enough.'

'Oh, I have had enough of all this rubbish,' Gus said. 'Come on, Anton. We need to get ready.'

May walked back to the marquee feeling a strange mixture of excitement and embarrassment. Whatever had possessed her to give that strange man her flower? It had been more than just an impulse to defy her brother. What did he say his horse was called? Excalibur, that was it. A faint recollection flickered through her mind and then took shape. She was back in Mrs Kelly's needlework classes at the workhouse and Mrs Kelly was reading aloud to them while they sewed. She had a big book full of pictures of knights in armour and ladies in beautiful flowing dresses. That memory triggered another. James had taken her to an art gallery and they had looked at pictures by artists he had called the Pre-Raphaelites. Some of those showed similar images. She had told him about Mrs Kelly's book and that had led him to talk about the legend of King Arthur and the medieval cult of chivalry. It was James who had told her that sometimes when a knight was riding in a tourney he would ask his lady for a favour to wear in his helmet, to show that he fought in her honour. She realised with a small shiver that it was that recollection that had prompted her to respond to Rudolph Marshall's request and she felt guilty, as if she had shared something with him that rightfully belonged to James.

Back at the marquee she found that Kitty and her family had arrived, and before long the first race was announced and everyone crowded forward to the edge of the course. May and Kitty edged their way through the crowd to stand as close as they could to the tape.

'Do you think Gus stands a chance?' Kitty asked.

'I really don't know,' May answered. 'I think it depends on whether any of the horses the squatters have brought are in the race.'

'Oh, they won't be running in this one,' Kitty said. 'The prize money is not big enough. They'll save themselves for the three-thirty.'

'You seem to know more about it than I do,' May said.

'Oh—' Kitty flicked her dark hair back over her shoulders with a shrug '—my da's very keen on the horses. It's the Irish tradition, you know. We all love anything to do with horses.'

'Gus wants to start breeding thoroughbreds,' May told her.

'Does he now? Well, if he does, my da will be more than ready to give any advice he can. Oh, look! They're lining up at the start.'

The course was roughly oval in shape and the starting line was away to May's right. Craning her neck, she made out the back of Gus's big black and Anton's grey, but beyond that she could not recognise any of the others. The starter dropped his flag and the horses leapt forward so closely bunched together that it was impossible to say who was leading. But by the time they came round the bend at the far end of the track the field had spread out and she saw that three horses were ahead of the rest. One she recognised as Gladiator, the horse her father had predicted would win, another she could not name and the third was Gus's Storm. By now everyone was jumping up and down and yelling encouragement to their chosen riders, and May found herself jumping and yelling with the rest.

'Come on, Gus! Come on, Storm!'

Beside her Kitty was screaming the same. The horses thundered towards them.

'He's right there! He could win! Come on, Gus!' Kitty yelled.

At the winning post, it was Gladiator who was half a length ahead, but Gus came in second, punching the air in celebration.

May headed back to the marquee with a sense of relief. Gus would be in a much better mood now.

'Well, this calls for a celebration,' her father said. 'Who's for a glass of wine?'

Some of the group opted for beer and May stuck to lemonade. She had tried to like the wine her father was so proud of, but the fact was she found it made her mouth feel dry and her head feel dizzy. They were all drinking when Gus re-joined them, sweating but triumphant.

'Second, eh?' he exclaimed. 'Not bad for a beginner.'

'Very well done!' his father said. 'Congratulations.'

Kitty stood on tiptoe and kissed his cheek, with a boldness that May found slightly surprising. Patrick O'Dowd clapped him on the back and said, 'We'll make a champion jockey of you yet.'

May kissed him in her turn. 'I'm so glad for you, Gus. Well done.'

No one had any great interest in the outcome of the next race but when the runners in the three-thirty began to line up May felt her pulse quicken. Gus got to his feet.

'Let's see how your toffee-nosed squatter gets on, shall we?'

'He's not mine!' May protested, feeling the colour rise in her cheeks. Nevertheless, she followed her brother and Kitty to the side of the track.

'What does he mean – your squatter?' Kitty asked.

'Oh, nothing really. It's just a joke. We spoke to him earlier, before you got here.'

Gus had elbowed his way to the front of the crowd but May hung back. She did not want to seem too interested. This time she did not jump up and down and yell, but she still felt a thrill when she saw her sprig of wattle on the cap of the winner.

'Well,' Gus conceded, 'that horse can certainly run. I wouldn't mind riding something as fast as that.'

The races were over but the pleasures of the day were not finished. There was to be a hog roast, followed by dancing. May helped Maria pack the remains of the picnic onto the wagon and rode back to the house with her, glad of the chance to wash her face and change her dress. When she got back to the race course the sun was setting and the smell of roasting pork brought the saliva to her mouth. Lanterns had been strung in the trees at the edge of the field and beneath them there was a cheerful crowd, eating and drinking and chatting to friends and neighbours, some celebrating their winnings, others trying to forget their losses. A makeshift dance floor had been created by nailing sawn planks to a framework and very soon the band struck up. It was made up of an odd selection of instruments, played with varying expertise by local people, with Patrick O'Dowd taking a leading part on his fiddle.

As soon as the first dance was announced, Anton claimed May as his partner and succeeded in fending off potential rivals until she was out of breath and her feet were hurting and she insisted that she must sit the next one out. He went off to fetch them both a drink, and May sank down on one of the folding chairs that were placed around the floor.

'Miss Lavender, at last! I thought I was never going to get a chance to return this.'

Rudolph Marshall bent towards her and held out a wilted sprig of wattle. She looked up in surprise.

'Really, there was no need for that! It's dying anyway.'

'I know.' He grinned. 'But it gives me an excuse to speak to you, and thank you for bringing me luck.'

'I don't think luck had anything to do with it,' she said. 'The best horse and rider won.' But she found herself smiling back at him.

Gus appeared at her other side. 'Still here, Marshall? I thought you'd be on your way home by now.'

'And miss the chance of paying my respects to your sister? And also congratulating you. Am I right in thinking this was the first time you had ridden in a proper race? You did very well to come in second. That's a nice-looking gelding you were riding.'

'Not as nice as your thoroughbred,' Gus said. 'Congratulations on your win, by the way.'

May could see from her brother's face that he was torn between his instinctive antagonism towards what he termed the squattocracy and his new-found interest in horse racing. The interest won.

'Did you buy him, or did you breed him yourself?'

'We bred him,' Marshall replied. 'My father has always been interested, and five years ago we bought in an English thoroughbred stallion called Galahad and a couple of brood mares. Excalibur is one of the first colts they produced.'

'Galahad, Excalibur,' May repeated. 'They are all names from the legend of King Arthur, aren't they?'

'Ah.' He looked at her with a new spark of interest. 'You know the stories?'

She blushed and dropped her eyes. 'Not really. But someone I know told me about them.'

'Well,' he said, 'it wasn't something I had taken an interest in until we got Galahad. I wanted to know where the name came from and it seemed a good idea to base the names of our stud around the legends. We have a filly called Guinevere, who looks quite promising.'

'Do you keep all the horses you breed?' Gus cut into the conversation.

'Not all, no. We keep the most promising looking ones and sell the others on.'

'I see ...' May could see that Gus was longing to ask the price, but was afraid it would be far out of his reach.

The band struck up a waltz and Marshall held out his hand to May. 'May I have the pleasure?'

She heard Gus make a sound, as if he wanted to intervene, but she gave Marshall her hand and allowed him to lead her onto the dance floor. As they reached it, she saw Anton coming back with a glass in either hand and saw him frown in annoyance. Then Marshall put his arm round her waist and whirled her into the dance. This was a new experience. Anton had taught her to dance, practising the steps with her until she felt confident enough to dance in public. As with everything else, his teaching had been formal and correct, but she realised now that there was something stiff in the way he moved. By contrast, her new partner seemed to flow with the music, as if carried along by its current. She felt herself respond in a similar way and began to enjoy herself.

'Tell me, Miss Lavender,' he said. 'Why have I not seen you before?'

'Oh, I have not been here long,' she replied. 'I only came out just before Christmas.'

'Came out from where?'

'From Liverpool. I ... I grew up there.' It occurred to her that she was at risk of having to explain what she had been doing and who she had been living with. To change the subject she said, 'Please call me May. Miss Lavender sounds so formal.'

'With great pleasure,' he agreed, 'as long as you call me Rudi.'

'Not Rudolph?'

'No, I don't care for Rudolph.'

'Very well, Rudi it shall be,' she said.

When the dance ended he led her back to where Anton was waiting, his lips pursed in a disapproving pout.

'I have your lemonade here,' he said. 'I thought you were thirsty.'

'Thank you, Anton,' she responded, taking the glass with her warmest smile. 'I am.'

She sat down and took a long drink, aware that over her head eyes were meeting in an unspoken challenge. She sighed inwardly. She was tired of being the prize in a struggle for male dominance and longed more than ever for James to arrive to claim her as his own.

Gus re-joined them with Kitty on his arm. Marshall turned to greet him.

'I was thinking. We have a little colt that might interest you – if you're serious about getting into thoroughbred racing. He's only a yearling, but I think he has a lot of potential. Why don't you come up to the station some time and look him over? Perhaps you could bring May with you.'

'Isn't it a long way?' May asked.

'No! We're an hour's ride west, fronting onto the Ovens River. Come and see, why don't you? You'll be very welcome.'

May looked at Gus, who was still struggling to reconcile opposing impulses.

'I'll talk to my pa,' he said finally. 'See if he can spare me for a day.'

'Excellent! The homestead's called Eskmere. Anyone will direct you.'

May went to bed that night subject to much the same confusion of emotions as her brother, though for different reasons. There was something dangerous about Rudi Marshall, something she sensed but could not put her finger on. It had to do with the way she had felt when they danced together; with the way his eyes met hers when they mentioned the Arthurian legends; with the annoyance she had felt with the rivalry between him and Anton. At the same time, there was a kind of defiance in her; a refusal to be confined and manipulated by men, whether by Gus or Anton or Rudi. And underneath it all was the question, 'what would James want me to do?' She turned over and buried her face in the pillow. 'Oh, James, James! I wish you were here!'

On the morning after the races it seemed that some benevolent deity, unable to fully grant her prayer, had nonetheless provided a small compensation in the shape of a letter. Post had to be collected from the general store in town and May had taken that duty on herself. It meant that when a letter arrived from James she could read it in private without having to explain it to the rest of the family. As soon as she could she found a quiet spot down by the lake and devoured his words.

The letter was full of expressions of love and his longing to be with her. By the time she had finished it she was able to think of the competition between Rudi and Anton as an amusing diversion, no more then that.

Chapter 6

Liverpool, November to December 1868

Patty did not see Percy for a while. She missed their outings together. The dinners and the dancing had brought some glamour into her life, something she had never experienced before. Then one day he reappeared, as before with no explanation for his absence, and invited her out to dinner. As he walked her home from his favourite restaurant, he said, 'You know, I keep thinking about those little children you gave the gingerbread ladies to. There are dozens, no hundreds of others like them in the city.'

'I can't feed them all with gingerbread,' she said.

'No, of course you can't. But we could do something for some of them. You could make a few extra, couldn't you?'

Patty looked at him, with a sudden sense of anxiety. 'Look here, Percy. I can't keep giving them away. They're not mine to give.

'Whose are they, then?'

'Well, they belong to the shop. I suppose to Mr Freeman, really.'

'Do you think he'd miss a few gingerbread ladies?'

'No, of course not. But the ingredients cost money, you know. When I give them to you they can't be sold in the shop. So I'd be stealing, really.'

He cocked his head on one side and grinned at her. 'Have you ever heard of Robin Hood?'

''Course I have.'

'Well, you know what he did.'

'He stole from the rich to give to the poor.'

'Well then?' He lifted his eyebrows. 'When you think how the well-off people live, I reckon the food they waste every day would feed six poor families.'

Patty remembered the food that had been sent back from the dining room of the Big House and fed to the pigs. She thought that the same was probably not true of the Freeman household, but it was also sure that no one went short there. And Percy was right when he said that Mr Freeman would not miss a few cakes. She looked at him.

'Very well. Come to the kitchen tomorrow, after we close.'

Next day she deliberately left a batch of gingerbread in the oven slightly too long, so they came out singed at the edges.

'Oh, look at that!' she exclaimed. 'Maisie, why didn't you warn me they were burning?'

'I though you was watching them,' the girl returned with a hint of indignation.

'We can't serve them like that,' Patty said. 'I'll have to make another batch.'

'I'd eat 'em,' Maisie said.

'Well, here, have one,' Patty replied, feeling guilty. 'Take one for Lucy, too.'

Maisie went off with the two gingerbread figures and Patty put the rest to one side. Once they were cool, and no one was looking, she slid them into a bag and hid them under the shelf.

'What happened to the burnt gingerbreads?' Maisie asked later.

'Oh, I threw them away. They really weren't up to standard.'

After her two assistants had gone Percy knocked at the door and Patty handed him the bag.

'Good girl!' he said, and winked at her. 'Do good by stealth, isn't that what the Bible says?'

'Is it?' Patty responded.

'There will be some happy faces tomorrow, I can tell you,' he said.

After that, Patty got into the habit of making slightly more of the gingerbread ladies than were required in the tea room. She took them up and laid them on the serving table with the other cakes and when she returned later to collect any leftovers she put them into a bag and hid them until Percy came to collect them.

'I don't know,' Maisie said one day. 'We seem to be making more of those than ever, but there are never any leftover these days.'

'They're very popular,' Patty said with a shrug.

Christmas was approaching and the weather turned cold. Patty found that her velvet cape was not sufficient to keep her warm on her outings with Percy, and her hands were so cold that she had to resort to wearing a pair of shabby woollen mittens. One day, going to collect the leftovers, she noticed a pair of elegant lady's kid gloves on the serving table.

'What are these doing here?' she asked.

'Someone must have left them by accident. I'll take them up to lost property,' Miss Winterton said.

'I'll take them,' Patty volunteered.

'Oh, will you? That would be very helpful. Thanks.'

As soon as she was out of sight, Patty slipped the gloves into the pocket of her apron. After all, she reasoned, the owner of gloves like that must have half a dozen like them at home.

There remained the problem of the cape. Patty wandered through the fashion department, hoping to see something she might be able to afford. She saw exactly what she wanted. It was made of heavy red wool with a collar of black fur, but when she asked the price it was far beyond her means.

She found Miss Clarke and asked, 'I suppose there's no chance of a reduction on the red wool cloak?'

The manageress shook her head. 'Not on that one, I'm afraid.'

'Then, is there any chance I could buy it now and pay you out of my next month's wages?'

'Certainly not! How would I square my accounts at the end of the month if I did that?' Miss Clarke looked at her severely. 'You shouldn't get into the habit of buying things you can't afford, Patty. That's the way to end up in debt, and before you know it the debts will have mounted up so that you have no chance of ever paying them off. Believe me, I've seen it happen. Come back next month and I'll see what I can do for you – but it probably won't be that cloak. That's far too expensive.'

Patty went away, but she could not banish the image of the cloak from her mind's eye. Percy was taking her out that evening and he had indicated that it was going to be a special occasion. It was bitterly cold outside and she would freeze in that little black velvet cape. The only alternative was her shabby old coat, with the frayed hem and the stain on the sleeve. She could not possibly wear that. She asked around among the girls to see if anyone could lend her the money, but they were all saving up for Christmas and her requests fell on deaf ears.

As she cleared up in the kitchen later an idea came to her. With a little help from Lucy she dressed herself in the yellow silk, ready to go out.

'Thanks, luv. You get along now. You don't want to miss your supper.'

Everyone was in the canteen, eating the evening meal, so no one saw Patty slip quietly down the back stairs to the first floor and into the fashion department through the door she had used to serve that first tea party. The large room was dark and silent but a gleam of moonlight from an upper window showed her that it was not empty. The mannequins used to display the clothes stood around, shadowy shapes that might well have been human. Patty stood still, her heart hammering. For a minute she was convinced that there were real people among the shapes; that perhaps someone was hiding, watching for just such an interloper as herself. After a moment she forced herself to think rationally. There was no one here. She could borrow the cloak and have it back before any-one came in next morning. She crept forward, feeling her way past the inert figures. She remembered exactly where the cloak was and very soon she felt the soft fur under her fingers. She lifted the garment carefully clear of the mannequin and wrapped it round her own shoulders. It was wonderfully warm. Suddenly she had an overpowering sense that at any second someone would step out from behind one of the figures with a lamp and catch her, and she had to quell her rising panic and force herself to move carefully, so as not to knock one of them over. At last she reached the door and closed it behind her. Then it was easy to run down the empty staircase to where Percy was waiting for her in the alleyway.

'That's my girl,' he said. 'You look fantastic. Off we go.'

That night he accepted the invitation of one of his friend to join their group. They were a jolly bunch, all out to get into the spirit of Christmas. When Patty asked for her usual port and lemon Percy said, 'Come on! That's an old lady's tipple. I'll get you a proper drink.'

The drink had a pleasant fruity flavour, a mix of sugar and sharpness, and it left a warm sensation in her stomach.

'Ooh, that's nice,' she said. 'What is it?'

'It's called a gimlet,' he said. 'Officers on board ships drink it for their health. It's mostly lime juice, you see. Stops them getting scurvy.'

He bought her two more the same over the next couple of hours and she began to enjoy herself. She had thought the group rather rowdy at first, but soon she was laughing and calling out like the rest of them. She danced twice with Percy and twice with two different men, but on the last dance, a polka, she suddenly felt her legs were no longer under her control and she had to ask her partner to take her back to their table.

A vague anxiety that had been nagging at the back of her mind came to the surface. 'Percy, what time is it?'

He took out his pocket watch. 'Twenty to eleven.'

'What? It can't be! Percy, you know I have to be back by half past ten. I'll be locked out!'

Senior staff, of which she was now one, were allowed an extra half-hour's grace to return to the store. Percy had frequently complained about this restriction on the evening's entertainment but he had never let her miss the deadline before. He looked at his watch again, with an expression of irritation.

'It's damned ridiculous. You're a grown-up woman. Why are you still living in that prison?'

She had never heard him swear before and it shocked her. 'It's not a prison. Anyway, where else could I live?'

'I dunno.' He looked at her. 'We'll have to think of something. There are ways …'

For an instant she thought that he might be on the brink of the proposal she both feared and hoped for, but instead he got to his feet.

'Come on, let's get you back to the penitentiary.'

'Don't call it that,' she protested, but he was already taking his leave of the others and holding out her cloak for her. The sight of it made her stomach clench in shock.

'Oh, dear Lord! The cloak!'

'What about it?'

'Never mind. Just get me back as quick as you can.'

They took a hansom cab but by the time they reached the store the clock on St John's Church was striking eleven. With a last desperate hope Patty tried the door.

'It's locked. Now what am I going to do?'

He shrugged. 'You'll have to knock, I suppose. There must be someone still awake.'

'You don't understand!' She was on the verge of tears. 'I borrowed this cloak, from the fashion department. Nobody knows I've got it. I need to sneak it back before anyone comes in in the morning.'

'Well, what's to stop you doing that, once you're inside?'

'If Mrs Watkins lets me in she'll see it. She knows I haven't got anything like this.'

He thought a moment. 'Turn it inside out. In the lamp-light she won't know the difference.' He took the cloak from round her shoulders and swiftly reversed it. 'I'll tuck the collar inside, so it doesn't show. Now, knock! I'm not standing here in the cold all night.'

The lining of the cloak was black and Patty hoped that in dim light it would not look very different from the one she normally wore. She tapped on the door.

'Not like that!' Percy said. 'You'll never wake anyone like that. Here, let me.'

He stepped forward and thumped on the door, sending echoes bouncing down the alleyway. Lamplight flickered through an upstairs window.

'There you are,' he said. 'I'm off. Won't do any good me being here.'

'Percy ...' she protested. But he had already melted into the shadows.

A voice above her head called querulously, 'Who's there? What do you want?'

Patty lifted her face. 'Please, ma'am, it's me, Patty. I forgot the time.'

She heard an indistinct mutter of annoyance and the lamplight moved away from the window. Footsteps clacked on the stairs and the lock rattled. The door opened revealing Mrs Watkins in her nightclothes.

'Whatever do you mean, coming back at this hour of the night? You know the rules. Well, come on, come in. I'm not standing here all night.'

Patty pulled the cloak close around her and sidled past her. As she set foot on the stairs she heard Mrs Watkins sniff.

'Have you been drinking?'

'No, not really. Just lime juice,' Patty said, heading up the stairs.

'Huh! Lime juice with something added. I can smell it on you. No wonder you're late. Mr Freeman will have to be told about this.'

Patty turned and looked back at her. 'Oh no! Please, Mrs Watkins. Don't bother Mr Freeman with this. I won't do it again, I promise.'

'You had better not!' was the grim reply.

The dormitory was in darkness and the eight girls she shared it with were all asleep. Patty stood still just inside the door until she heard Mrs Watkins close the door of her own room. She made herself wait until she had counted to a hundred, then she cautiously peered out. The staircase and the corridor were dark and silent. She took off her shoes, folded the cloak over her arm and crept down the stairs to the first floor. Her head was still muzzy and her legs felt weak. She realised that whatever it was Percy had given her to drink was much stronger than she was used to. Very carefully she opened the door into the fashion department. The mannequins still stood, silent figures on guard against intruders, it seemed to her. The moon had gone behind a cloud, so it was darker than before and she had to feel her way across the room, and each time she touched one of the unmoving figures she had the feeling that a hand might reach out and grab hold of her. To add to her misery, she could no longer remember exactly where the mannequin stood from which she had taken the cloak. She felt first one, then another, trying to recall what had been underneath the cloak. Panic began to surge up inside her, like a rising tide, and in her desperate hunt she knocked into one of the figures and sent it sprawling. She was sobbing now, silent, strangulated paroxysms. Fumbling, she succeeded in righting the fallen model. This was it, surely? This was where the cloak had been. She unfolded it and spread it over the rigid shoulders. Then she turned and stumbled back to the door and up the stairs to her bed.

Patty woke with a headache and a terrible sense that something was very wrong. She was unable to eat breakfast, prompting suggestions from her colleagues that she must be sickening for something. She was beginning preparations for that day's baking when the messenger boy came into the kitchen and told her that Mr Freeman wanted her in his office.

As she made her way there, she told herself that Mrs Watkins must have acted on her threat. It would be about her lateness the night before, and the fact that she had had a couple of drinks. Nothing to do with borrowing the cloak. She had put it back, hadn't she? Why should anyone be any the wiser?

Her hopes were dashed as soon as she entered the room. Mr Freeman was sitting behind his desk with a stern expression and standing on either side of him were Mrs Watkins and Miss Clarke.

Patty bobbed a curtsy and folded her hands demurely. 'You sent for me, sir?'

'I did. I have been given some very disturbing facts this morning. I take it that you do not deny that you returned half an hour late last night and had to wake Mrs Watkins to be let in?'

'No, sir. I'm very sorry, sir. I've told Mrs Watkins that it won't happen again.'

'Is it true also that you had been drinking?'

'I ... I suppose it is, sir. I didn't know what it was. Percy – Mr Dubarry – told me it was just lime juice.'

'From what I gather, it was probably mixed with gin. Mr Dubarry had no business giving you that without warning you of the possible consequences. I would suggest that you would be wise to have nothing further to do with a man like that.' He folded his hands on the desk and fixed his eyes on her. 'Such things might be put down to inexperience and possible excused, but unfortunately there is a much more serious matter to be dealt with. Miss Clarke tells me you asked to buy a very expensive cloak and when it proved too much for you means you wanted to be allowed to take it and pay from your next month's salary. Is that correct?'

Patty's fingernails were digging into her palms. 'Yes, sir.'

He turned to the woman on his right. 'Miss Clarke, will you repeat what you told me you found when you entered the department this morning?'

Miss Clarke's lips were drawn in a tight line, so that her voice sounded thin and clipped. 'Someone had obviously been in overnight. One of the models had been displaced, and the hat it was wearing was on the floor. The cloak, the one that Patty had asked about, was on the wrong mannequin. It was crumpled and smelt strongly of alcohol and cigar smoke.'

Mr Freeman's expression was sterner than ever. 'Patty, did you borrow that cloak and wear it last night?'

Tears were running down Patty's cheeks. 'Yes, sir, I did. I never meant it to be damaged. I thought I could put it back and no one would ever know.'

'Why did you do it? You must have known it was wrong.'

'I ... I needed something warm to wear. I've only got a little velvet cape, or my old coat. I can't go out dancing in that. It ...' the words burst from her ' ... it doesn't seem fair that some ladies have all those clothes, and I have to shiver.'

For a moment Mr Freeman said nothing, but Patty thought she saw a hint of compassion in his eyes. Eventually he said, 'What you have done would be ample grounds for dismissal. You do understand that?'

'Yes, sir. But don't turn me away, please! I've nowhere else to go. I'll do anything you want. I'll pay for the cloak. You can take it out of my wages. I'll never do anything like that again, I swear!'

There was a long silence. At length Mr Freeman said, 'I shall have to think long and hard about this, Patty. You have betrayed the trust I had in you, and there will have to be a reckoning of some sort. For now, you had better go back to your kitchen and get on with your work.'

'Oh yes! Yes, I will. Thank you. Thank you!'

'Don't thank me yet, Patty. I still have to make up my mind if you can be allowed to continue here. I will let you know in due course.'

Patty went through the rest of the day in a daze. Her head was throbbing and she felt sick with fear. Somehow the cakes and biscuits were baked and sent up to the tea room. Her two colleagues were puzzled and concerned, but she snapped at them to mind their own business, so they left her to get on with the work without further questions. Eventually the day came to an end and she was able to retreat to the common room. A letter was waiting for her. Her first reaction was to throw it aside. What interest could it have for her, under the circumstances? But in the end she took it to a chair by the window and slit open the envelope.

> *Freshfields*
> *Rutheglen,*
> *Victoria*
> *October 15th 1868*

Dear Patty,

I had a letter from James yesterday with some sad news. His mother passed away in August. Of course, it was not unexpected and James says it was a merciful release in the end. She was in great pain. The terrible thing is, my first thought was that James is now free to come to Australia. He has to wait for his final examinations, of course, but that is only a matter of months. He could be here by March or April. I suppose I should feel guilty, but I cannot. After all, as he said, it was a mercy in the end. It just relieves my mind of the idea that he might agree to marry someone else, just to please his mother, but he tells me that right at the end she changed her mind and gave us her blessing. That is a wonderful comfort to both of us.

He told me something else that I find much more disturbing. You remember in my last letter I told you how someone had turned up who might be Angel's real father? They were waiting for her to come home from school, so he could see her. Now it turns out she was sent away to a convent school in Ireland and she has run away. It happened several months ago and no one has seen or heard anything about her whereabouts. Of course, James's letter is dated August 3rd and by now she may have been found, but I can't bear the thought of what may have happened to her. The poor little mite is only eight years old, after all. There is one small comfort. The police have searched and her father – I mean Mr Kean – has been to Ireland and searched himself, and no body has been found. So it is possible that someone has taken her in and is looking after her. But for what purpose? We both know what terrible things can happen to children who have no one to protect them. I can't stop thinking about it, but there's nothing I can do.

I'm sorry to send you such a gloomy letter. I should be feeling happy, because James is free now. He says he still loves me and longs to be with me, and I believe him. But I still have to wait another six months before he can get here. We've been apart for a year now, but it seems much longer and waiting gets harder and harder.

I hope everything is going well for you. Send me some happy news to cheer me up!

With love,
May

Chapter 7

Rutherglen, November 1868

At first sight, May was slightly disappointed by the Eskmere homestead. After Gus's characterisation of the owner as 'squattocracy', she had expected something grander, more like some of the big houses she had seen in the Toxteth area of Liverpool; more like, in fact, the house where Angel had lived with her adoptive parents – tall, stucco-fronted, with imposing doorways flanked by columns. Instead, she saw a long, low building with a gabled roof and a veranda running all round it, much like her father's house in Rutherglen. But as the pony trap swept up the drive she saw that it was considerably larger and set in an extensive garden running down to the banks of a river and planted with shade trees. To the rear, she could see a block of wooden outbuildings set round an inner courtyard. In a paddock to her left five horses were grazing, two of them full grown, one smaller and two long-legged foals.

Rudolph Marshall came down the steps of the veranda as Gus drew the trap to a halt. He held up his hand to help May down and she felt a fresh shiver of excitement as she took it. There was something inside her that responded to his sparkling eyes and wide smile and would not be suppressed.

'I'm delighted you decided to accept my invitation,' he said. 'Welcome to Eskmere.'

'Thank you,' she responded, unable to think of any pleasantries to add.

Gus had descended from the trap and he and Rudolph shook hands. If their host was aware of something guarded in his manner, he did not show it. A boy had followed Rudolph out and now stood by the pony's head.

'Ben here will take the pony round to the stables and see him fed and watered,' Rudolph said. 'Come inside, out of the heat.'

He led them through a wide hall and out to the shaded veranda at the rear. Here a table was set with glasses and jugs, beer for the men, lemonade for May. His eyes met May's as he handed her a glass.

'I hope you didn't find the journey too tiring.'

'No, not at all,' she answered. 'The countryside is lovely at this time of year, isn't it? Still so green. But it was hot. I'm glad to sit in the shade.'

An older man came out of the stable block and crossed the lawn towards them. It was obvious at a glance that he was Rudolph's father. He had the same luxuriant dark hair, complemented in his case by sideburns and a neatly trimmed moustache, and the same lithe, athletic movements. Rudolph introduced them and he shook May's hand with a warm smile.

'Well, Rudi didn't exaggerate.'

'I'm sorry?' she queried.

'He told me he'd met a very beautiful young lady.'

May dropped her eyes and blushed.

Mr Marshall turned to Gus. 'And you are the young man who is interested in breeding thoroughbreds.'

'I like the idea,' Gus said, 'and I admire your Excalibur. But it probably isn't a practical proposition.'

'Well, don't be put off too easily,' the older man responded. 'Rudi says you ride well. With the right horse, you could be a winner.'

May saw her brother colour in his turn. 'I don't know about that,' he mumbled, but she could tell that the compliment had further disarmed his suspicions.

'Why don't we put him up on Sir Lancelot, let him get the feel of it?' Rudolph suggested.

'Yes, why not?' his father agreed. He looked at Gus. 'Lancelot is one of our promising youngsters. He's only a three year old, but we've been training him since he was a foal. Would you like to try him?'

'If ... if you think ...' Gus stuttered and then recovered himself. 'Yes, I should like that.'

May looked at him in some alarm. 'Are you sure? I mean, you've never ridden a horse like that.'

'Don't worry,' Rudolph reassured her. 'Lancelot has no vices, and we'll take care of him.'

'If you're rested, we could stroll down to the stables and I'll introduce you,' Mr Marshall said.

'Whenever you're ready,' Gus said. May kicked herself mentally, knowing that her doubt had been enough to make him determined to prove himself.

As they walked down towards the stables Rudolph offered her his arm. 'Don't worry about your brother. I wouldn't have suggested it if I didn't think he was up to it.'

They reached the stable block and he led her through an archway into a yard. Along one side there was a row of loose boxes, and the heads of four horses were visible over the half-doors. As Mr Marshall and Gus walked in, all of them whickered in greeting.

'Why do they make that noise?' May asked nervously.

'Just saying hello.' He smiled. 'And asking if we happen to have a titbit in our pockets for them.'

Mr Marshall led Gus to a stable where a white horse snorted and ducked his head. 'This is Lancelot. Takes after his sire, the grey over there.' He nodded to the stable in the corner. 'That's Galahad.'

The boy, Ben, was forking manure out of a vacant stall. Marshall called to him.

'Ben, bring me Lancelot's tack, will you?'

Gus was stroking the horse's neck and peering over the door at the rest of his body. 'He's got good hocks, like Excalibur.'

Marshall led the horse out and soon he and Gus were deep in conversation about his finer points. May began to wish she had stayed in the house.

Rudi said, 'Come over here and look at this mare. Her name is Guinevere.' He led her to a stall where a pale chestnut horse stood. 'Pretty, isn't she?'

'Yes,' May agreed. 'But I think I like white horses best.'

'Not white,' he corrected. 'We call them grey. Very few horses are pure white. I think this mare would make a perfect lady's mount. Would you like to try her?'

'Oh, I can't ride,' May said.

'No? But you must learn. It's a great sport. Both my sisters rode. I could teach you.'

She shook her head. 'No, thank you. I really don't want to.'

He looked at her with his head on one side, and she sensed a challenge, but when she did not respond he said, 'It's your choice, of course.'

The grey horse was saddled now and Marshall said, 'Right you are, Gus. Up you go!'

Gus put his foot in the stirrup and swung himself into the saddle. Rudolph opened a gate on the far side of the yard and they went out into a dusty, fenced area behind.

'This is our schooling yard,' Marshall said. 'Take him round a few times and see how you get on.'

May watched her brother anxiously as he first walked, then trotted the horse round the enclosure. Marshall stood in the centre, occasionally calling out an instruction. Gus rode in a figure of eight, then tried a canter. Halting in the middle of the school, his face glowing, he exclaimed, 'He's so willing! You only have to give the lightest touch on the reins.'

'You've got good hands,' Marshall said. 'You know how to keep them still and not interfere with his mouth. Well done.'

May discovered that Rudi had left her side. Now he reappeared, mounted on Excalibur.

'How about it, Gus? Are you up for a race?'

'Oh no!' May put her hand to her throat. The three men took no notice.

'Why not?' Marshall said. 'It'll be good for both of them to open up. What about it, Gus?'

May could tell that her brother was nervous, but she knew he would never back down from a challenge.

'Yes, great idea!' he said. 'Where?'

'We've got a practice track out there,' Marshall told him. 'This way.'

The track was marked out with tapes and was roughly oval, much like the one at Rutherglen. As soon as the horses sat foot on it, they began to fidget, prancing and side-stepping and snorting.

'Shorten up your stirrups,' Marshall told Gus. 'Here, I'll give you a hand.'

When he had finished Rudi called out, 'Start and finish here, by this post. Right, Gus?'

'Right!' Gus sounded breathless.

'Away you go then!' Marshall called, and both horses shot forwards.

May watched with her heart in her mouth. The sheer speed terrified her. Excalibur had started in the lead but Gus's horse soon closed the gap so that they were almost neck and neck. They disappeared from view behind a slight rise in the land, but when they came in sight she was relieved to see that Gus was still in the saddle and only a few yards behind. As they came closer she could see him urging Lancelot on and when they reached the finish his horse's nose was level with Rudi's stirrup. Their momentum carried them on past May and their host and for a moment May thought that Gus was not going to be able to stop, but he got his mount under control and came back to them, flushed and panting but with an expression of sheer, unadulterated joy such as she had never seen on his face before.

'That was fantastic! It was like flying! Thank you, sir. It's the best thing I've ever done.'

'I'm glad you enjoyed it,' Marshall returned.

A bell rang from the house. 'Time for dinner,' Marshall said. 'Rudi, will you show May where she can have a wash and refresh herself? I'll take Gus to the dunny.'

Rudi took her to a bedroom at the end of a passageway. 'I'm afraid we haven't got round to installing modern plumbing,' he said. 'But there's water here and a you-know-what. I hope that will suffice.'

May assured him it would but it struck her as amusing that even in Nan Driscoll's little house in Liverpool, where she had lodged until a year ago, there had been a water closet, something that did not exist in these grander surroundings. She was glad that her father had installed modern plumbing. She used the chamber pot, washed her hands and face and made her way back to the veranda, where a table was laid for the meal. Eskmere might lack modern facilities, but it certainly did not fall short in food; though in common with many of the households she had visited there was, perhaps, a lack of imagination. Plain roast meat, in large quantities, with boiled potatoes seemed to be the regular menu. May felt glad for Maria's Spanish influence in her own kitchen. Such thoughts did not, however, disturb the three men, who tucked into the roast mutton with relish.

When the meal was over the men lit cigars – a habit Gus had only recently acquired – and May retired again to the bedroom. When she returned Marshall said, 'Well, perhaps we'd better have a look at that yearling you are interested in, eh, Gus?'

Gus rose to his feet eagerly, but Rudi said, 'I think May has had enough of hearing us talk about horses. Perhaps you'd like a stroll by the river, May. It's cool under the trees and there is usually a breeze off the water.'

'That sounds lovely,' she agreed, without considering that it meant some time alone with him.

Gus and Marshall went off together and Rudi gave her his arm and led her through the garden to the edge of the river. It was bordered by the trees the locals called she-oaks, though they had no resemblance to any oak tree that

May remembered seeing on her outings to Birkenhead Park with James. The river flowed clear and sparkling and as he had promised there was a light breeze.

'Why are they called she-oaks?' she asked.

'Because of the noise they make when the wind blows,' he answered. 'Listen.'

She understood them. The trees did not have leaves, as she knew them, but had long wispy branches that hung down in clusters, and the wind moving through them produced a gentle hushing sound.

'Oh, now I see,' she said.

'The proper name is casuarina,' he told her, 'but I prefer she-oak.'

'Have you lived here all your life?' she asked.

'Oh, yes. I was born here,' he said.

To make conversation, she said, 'Are you and your father ... do you have any other family?'

'My mother died when I was quite small,' he said. 'I have two sisters, older than me, but they are not here. One of them married a doctor and lives in Melbourne. The younger one, Bella, went back to England to do the Season and stayed on to be a companion to my maiden aunt.'

May had only the vaguest idea what 'doing the season' entailed, but she did not like to ask. 'You must miss them,' she said.

'Yes, we do. But the life out here doesn't suit everyone, especially ladies. Do you think it would suit you, to live on an up-country station like this?'

'I don't know,' May responded. 'I have had so little experience of life in Australia. But to my mind, it is much more enjoyable than life back in England.'

'Really?' He checked his steps for a moment and looked into her face. 'You don't feel deprived of the delights of society?'

She sensed that she was on shaky ground. The last thing she wanted was an inquest into her former life. 'I miss the concerts,' she said after a moment. 'But on the other hand, the weather is much better here.'

'You are fond of music?'

'Yes, very. Are you?'

'My older sister, the one in Melbourne, plays the piano. I used to enjoy listening to her. Of course, there are concerts in Melbourne, you know. Tell you what, maybe I could take you to one.'

Now she was on even more dangerous territory. The idea of going to a concert with Rudi was too appealing for her own comfort. She reminded herself that soon she might be able to go to one with James, but the prospect felt so distant that it seemed to belong to another life altogether.

'Oh, Melbourne is too far,' she said. 'It would not be practical.'

'If only they would bring the railway through,' he said. 'There's always talk about it, but nothing gets done.'

'Have you ever been to England?' she asked.

'Oh yes. I was sent back to school there,' he said. 'Harrow.'

Something about the way he said it made her feel she should recognise the name, but it meant nothing to her.

'Did you like it?'

'England, or school?'

'Both, I suppose.'

'School was bearable, enjoyable sometimes. But I always longed to be back here. I missed the wide open spaces – and the weather.'

'I can understand that,' she said, smiling.

'Tell me about Liverpool. I never went there.'

She hesitated, wondering how much she could say without revealing too much about her own life there. 'It's a great port. Ships from all over the world are coming and going all the time. And that has made some people very rich. Some of them have chosen to spend their money on beautiful buildings, as grand as any you might find in London. There is one, St George's Hall, in the centre of the city, which has a floor made up of mosaic tiles. The designs are wonderful and specialist terrazzo workers had to be brought over from Italy to execute them.'

The memory brought a second image flashing before her mind's eye – a dark-haired, black-eyed youth. Armando, with whom she once thought she was in love. She had to make an effort to recall her attention to what her current companion was saying.

'Have you travelled much, in England?'

'No, very little.'

They strolled in silence for a few minutes. Then he said, 'Do you know why this place is called Eskmere?'

'No. Is it named after somewhere in England – somewhere that means a lot to you or your father?'

'You might say that. My grandfather is Lord Eskmere.'

May gasped. So what her father had told her about the squattocracy was correct. Aloud she said, 'Oh, really?'

'My father is the younger son, needless to say. When Grandpapa dies it is Uncle William who will inherit the title – and the land that goes with it.'

'And your father gets nothing? That doesn't seem fair.'

'It's the law of primogeniture – the firstborn son inherits everything. But someone told Pa that there was land out here, just waiting for someone to lay claim to it. So we came here.'

'I see. And you're glad about that?'

'Oh yes. It was the best decision he could have made.'

They walked on in silence for a while. Then he said, 'But here's the thing – Uncle Will is married but he has only daughters, and they can't inherit because the estate is entailed.'

'What does that mean?'

'It means it can only be passed down through the male line. So, when Uncle Will dies the next in line is my father – if he is still alive.'

'And if he is not?'

'The title and the estate passes to me.' He stopped suddenly and looked into her face. 'How do you fancy being Lady Eskmere?'

She stared at him in silence for a moment. Then she laughed. 'You are not serious.'

He continued to look at her, his head tilted in a way she was coming recognise. 'I could be, given a little encouragement.'

She turned away, towards the house. 'Don't be silly. It's out of the question. I think we should go back now. Gus and I will have to be starting back soon.'

He said nothing, but took her arm and walked her back the way they had come.

They found Gus and Mr Marshall in the paddock, admiring the smaller of the horses she had seen when they arrived. Close up, she could see that it was young, its slender legs seeming a little too long for its body, but already with muscles rippling beneath the sleek hide.

'Look, May!' Gus hailed her. 'Isn't he a beauty?'

The colt was a bright, glossy brown with a darker mane and tail, and a white mark down the front of its face. Dark-lined ears twitched alertly as she approached, and the colt whickered softly.

'His name is Merlin,' Gus said. 'But I'd call him Lightning, from that white blaze on his nose.'

It was true that the white mark did look like a streak of lightning, but May said, 'Merlin was the great wizard, wasn't he? It's a magical name.'

'Thoroughbreds sometimes have two names,' Mr Marshall said. 'The stud name they are registered under and what we call a stable name, often something easier to say. This little fellow is registered as Merlin, but if you want to call him Lightning when he's at home, that's up to you.'

'Do you mean …?' May queried, looking at her brother.

'I'm going to try to persuade Father to buy him,' Gus said. 'Mr Marshall thinks he's got a great future.'

'But you don't know anything about training race-horses,' May objected.

'I can learn. Kitty's father knows a lot about it. He'll help me.'

'We can help, too,' Rudi said. 'I should like to see how he develops.'

May looked from him to her brother. She knew how determined Gus could be when he set his heart on something, and she could see that Rudi was keen to establish a connection that would give him an excuse for visiting them. She had a feeling that she was being – not driven exactly – but gently nudged in a direction she did not want to take.

'No hurry to decide,' Marshall said easily. 'I'm not in a rush to sell him. Let me know when you and your father have made up your minds.'

They took their leave soon afterwards and on the journey Gus could talk of nothing but the merits of the colt and the great future he saw for him, and for them, if he was theirs. May listened with half an ear. One question repeated itself over and over again in her head. 'How do you fancy being Lady Eskmere?'

Chapter 8

Liverpool, December 1868

'Come in, Patty. Take a seat. This gentleman wants to ask you a few questions.'

Patty had not been surprised to receive a summons to Mr Freeman's office. She had been expecting, and dreading, it ever since their last interview. But she was taken aback by the presence of a second man, a stranger. She sat down, as instructed, and the stranger leant towards her.

'I am Inspector Vane, of the city police. Tell me, do you know a man called Percy Barry?'

'Dubarry,' she corrected. 'His name's Dubarry.'

'That's what he likes to call himself, but you can take it from me his real name is Barry. Now, answer my question.'

Patty shifted in her seat. This new development was more frightening than her expected interview with her employer about the borrowed cloak. 'Yes, I know him.'

'You have been walking out with him for some time, I gather.'

'For a few months, yes.'

The inspector reached into an inner pocket and withdrew something wrapped in a white handkerchief. 'Do you recognise this?'

He unfolded the wrapping and showed her a gingerbread lady.

Patty caught her breath. 'It's one of mine. I mean, I make them. How did you get it?'

'That is a good question,' the inspector said, 'but I will answer it later. Did you give this to Percy Barry?'

'Yes.' Patty swallowed hard. She was beginning to feel sick.

'Am I right in thinking that you have given him quite a number of these over recent months?'

'Yes.' Her voice was husky and her throat felt constricted.

'Patty?' It was Mr Freeman's voice. 'You have been giving this man property belonging to the store? Whatever possessed you?'

'He said it was for the poor children, children who never get anything nice to eat. He brought a woman to see me, a mother who couldn't afford to give her children any treats. She was so grateful, it made me want to cry to see it.'

'But it hasn't just been a few cakes, here and there, has it?' the inspector said. 'What did you think was happening to them all?'

'He was giving them to poor families. He said … he said it was like Robin Hood, robbing the rich to give to the poor.'

She heard Mr Freeman give a deep sigh. The inspector held the gingerbread out to her.

'Shall I tell you how I came by this?'

'Yes, please.' Her voice came out as a squeak.

'I took it from a child who was being held in a house of ill-repute. Do you know what I mean by that?'

'I … I think so.'

'There are men in this city – indeed all over the world – who have the most depraved tastes. Men who do not wish to have sexual congress with grown women but who prefer children. Little girls and sometimes little boys. Your friend Percy was in the business of satisfying those tastes. And do you know how he won the trust of these children? He offered them your gingerbreads. He is known around the slums of the city as 'the gingerbread man'. What do you think of that?'

Patty gazed at him through the tears that almost blinded her. 'I didn't know … I swear I didn't know.'

There was a silence, broken only by her sobs. At length the inspector said, 'I believe you. Barry is an expert con man. You are not the first girl he's bamboozled into helping him. I don't think you can be held responsible for the use these delicacies were put to. But you have taken property that rightly belongs to your employer, and you will have to answer to him for that. I leave it to him to decide if he wishes to press charges.' He got up.

'I have got the information I require, sir. I shall leave the rest to your good judgement. Good day to you.'

'One thing,' Mr Freeman said. 'What has happened to this vile man?'

'Oh, he's safely behind bars. He will come to trial in due course and receive a sentence, I don't doubt, commensurate with the foulness of his crime.'

'And the children?'

'Returned to their families – those that have them. The others will have to go to the orphanage in the workhouse.'

'I don't understand how the parents did not do something. Where did they think the children were?'

'Oh, Barry spun them a yarn about finding work for them, or apprenticeships. To be honest with you, I think some of them did not ask too many questions. One less mouth to feed, you know?'

Freeman heaved another sigh. 'We live in a wicked world, Inspector.'

'We do indeed,' the inspector agreed. 'And I must get back to trying to right at least some of the wrongs. Good day to you, sir.'

'Good day.' Mr Freeman ushered him out of the room and returned to sit behind his desk. Patty saw that he had gone pale.

'Patty, how could you betray my trust like this?'

She swallowed another sob. 'I'm sorry, sir. I truly am. But I didn't know ... I didn't know what he was using them for.'

'No,' he said sadly. 'I do believe that. But the fact is that you allowed yourself to be persuaded by this man into actions that you must have known were wrong. It is not just the gingerbreads. There is the whole business of the borrowed cloak. Your infatuation with this ... this monster ... has turned you from an honest, reliable girl into ... into a criminal.'

'Oh no, sir! Don't say that!' she begged.

'What else can I call it? You knew that those cakes were not yours, but you gave them away. Have you been baking extra, to supply that man?'

Patty hung her head and could not answer.

'I take your silence for assent. And now you see what has happened? A newspaper reporter has got hold of the story. See, here?' He leaned over his desk and thrust a copy of the local paper in front of her. Through her tears she made out the headline: FORGET THE PIED PIPER. IT IS THE GINGERBREAD MAN WHO IS STEALING OUR CHILDREN.

'The whole sordid story is here,' Freeman went on. 'The reporter specifically identifies the cakes as having come from this store. You have dragged the whole reputation of Freeman's through the mud.'

Patty could only shake her head and repeat, 'I'm sorry. I'm so sorry.'

Freeman sat back and said in a quieter tone, 'I rescued you once, Patty. When May Lavender found you working as a prostitute and tried to hide you, I sent you to that house where women like you had a chance to rehabilitate themselves. And when you seemed to have proved that you were ready to take a different course I gave you a job here in the kitchen. I promoted you, put you in a position of trust, a position where you earned a good deal of respect. You had a good salary, good prospects. And how have you repaid me?'

Patty was silent.

'You understand what this means?' Freeman asked.

She lifted her head and gazed at him, unable to respond.

'I cannot let you stay here. I cannot employ someone who has so completely lost my trust. I will not press charges against you. I do not wish to see you in prison. But you will have to go. You understand that?'

Patty shook her head wildly. 'No, sir! No! Please don't sack me. I'll do anything. I'll work for nothing, if you just let me stay.'

He shook his head sadly. 'No, Patty. There is no way out of this. You must leave.'

'But where will I go? I've got nowhere.'

'You should have thought of that before you let yourself be led down a path you knew was wrong. You cannot just blame that man. You have your own moral compass. You may say, it was just a few cakes, Mr Freeman can afford to lose them. But that is not the point. You have shown yourself to be capable of dishonesty. You cannot be trusted. So you must go.'

'Give me a few days, sir, please,' she begged, 'till I can find somewhere else.'

He shook his head again. 'No, you must go at once.'

'But what about the tea room? Who's going to bake the cakes for this afternoon?'

'The tea room will be shut down, as from today. I cannot have the general public coming in to gawp. Its reputation as a safe, respectable place for ladies to meet is destroyed. Now, you must go up to the dormitory and collect your possessions and then you must leave. I shall inform Mrs Wilkins of the situation and she will see you off the premises.' He stood up. 'Goodbye, Patty. I shall pray for you. I shall pray that you may find a way to redeem yourself and make up for the damage you have done. Now, go.'

Patty stood at the end of the alleyway leading to the staff entrance with a paper parcel containing all her worldly goods at her feet. She had not been allowed to speak to any of the other staff, even to say goodbye. For a long time she stood motionless, unable to think what to do or where to go. Her world had come tumbling down about her ears and she was too shocked to make sense of it. Only the thought that very soon the store would close for the midday meal and some of her colleagues might come out and find her standing there forced her to move. Even then, she wandered without direction, her feet dragging. It was cold. A bitter wind was blowing off the Mersey, cutting through her worn coat. She'd had no appetite for breakfast and now her stomach was empty. In her pocket was a purse containing a few pennies, all she had saved from her wages. The rest had been spent on small adornments for her evenings out with Percy.

Where could she go? She would have to find another job. Cooking was her only skill, but she knew no respectable household would take her without a reference. Perhaps there might be a small restaurant or public house that would not be so choosy, but she knew very well that there were dozens, hundreds even, of other girls tramping the streets looking for work. Why would anyone take her on in preference to them? There were bound to be questions asked about why she had been dismissed, and what could she say that would not immediately put an end to her chances?

Without her conscious volition, her feet had carried her back along the route she had followed in such a hurry two evenings earlier and she found herself standing outside the place Percy had called 'the club'. It occurred to her that one of the few people who knew her was the manager, who had always greeted Percy as an honoured guest. The idea of associating herself with anything connected to him was repellent, but a restaurant must need cooks. No other place would take her without a reference, but her instinct was that this establishment did not abide by the normal rules. At least, it would be warm inside and maybe they would give her something to eat, if nothing else.

The main door from the street was shut but there was a passageway at the side that she guessed must lead to the staff entrance. She walked down it and found a door.

The paint was flaking and it looked as if it bore no relation to the smart frontage on the street, but she tried it
and was immediately met by the smell of cooking. Her
stomach rose and saliva filled her mouth, making her
feel nauseous and hungry at the same time. She moved
forward and saw an open door, leading into the kitchen.
Several men were at work there and one, wearing a
chef's hat, saw her and came over.

'What do you want? This is a private entrance, not for
customers.'

'I know,' Patty said. She took a deep breath. 'I want
to speak to the manager.'

He looked at her suspiciously. 'If you've come to
make a complaint ...'

'No!' she said quickly. 'No, I'm looking for a job.'

'A job, eh?' His eyes raked her from head to toe.
'Very well. Through that door and the office is on your
left. The boss is in there.'

Patty followed his instructions and tapped on the
inner door.

'Bugger off, I'm busy,' said a voice from inside.

She almost turned and ran, but desperation gave
her courage. She pushed to door open and looked in.
'Please, sir. I'm looking for work.'

The manager looked up from his desk and scowled at
her. 'Who sent you here? There are no vacancies ...' He
broke off and peered at her. 'Don't I know you?'

'Yes. I ... came here ... I used to come here with ...
Mr Dubarry.'

'Ahh!' The manager's expression suggested that that explained a good deal. He got up and came round his desk. 'I read the paper. Bad business. But what's it got to do with you?'

'I ... I made the gingerbreads.'

'I see. Lost your position, have you?'

Patty nodded, unable to speak.

'And now you want me to take you on?'

'Please! I'll do anything. I'm a good cook. I can do most things, not just cakes.'

He was looking her up and down in a way she found uncomfortable. 'Take your coat off. Let's have a look at you.'

She shrugged off the coat. Underneath it she wore a simple brown skirt with a green blouse, the clothes she wore when she was off-duty. She had not been allowed to keep the blue dress issued to all Freeman's staff and apart from the yellow silk it was all she had.

'Hmm,' he said. 'You're a buxom lass, aren't you? Well, that's no problem. Men like something they can get hold of. You want to work here?'

'Yes! Yes, please.'

'Very well. You can start tonight.'

'Tonight! Really? Oh, that's wonderful. I'm ever so grateful.' She hesitated. 'I don't suppose I could live in, could I?'

''Course you can. You'll have a room of your own. A nice one. I'll get one of the girls to show you later. What's your name, by the way?'

'Patty. Patty Jenkins.'

'How do you do, Patty? Have you still got that yellow silk dress I saw you wearing when you came here with Percy?'

'Yes, why?'

'Never mind. Have you had any dinner?'

'No, no I haven't.'

'Go back to the kitchen and tell Chef he's to give you something to eat. I'll call for you later.'

'I can't tell you how grateful I am!' she said.

He smiled at her. 'That's all right. Glad to help. I'll see you soon.'

Patty went back to the kitchen and relayed the message.

'Taken you on, has he?' the chef said. 'I thought he might.'

'He hasn't told me what he wants me to do,' Patty said. 'But I suppose that's up to you.'

'Me? Oh no. The boss will tell you what your job is. Nothing to do with me.'

That struck Patty as odd, but all that mattered at that moment was that a good plateful of scrambled eggs was put in front of her. She was warm, and tonight she would have a place to sleep.

She had finished eating and was beginning to feel drowsy when a woman put her head round the door. 'You Patty?'

'Yes.' Patty scrambled to her feet.

'Come with me.'

Patty followed her through to the restaurant, which was still closed, and then to the door through which she remembered seeing some of the diners disappearing, with some of the glamorously dressed young women Percy called hostesses. Beyond that was a flight of stairs leading to a corridor. The woman pushed open a door and said, 'This is you.'

It was the nicest bedroom Patty had ever seen. There was a big bed covered with a purple velvet bedspread, a couple of armchairs, a washstand with a porcelain basin and ewer on it and a small table with a mirror. Purple velvet curtains hid the windows.

'Oh!' Patty exclaimed. 'Is this really for me? Just for me?'

'Well, when you finish it will be,' the woman said. 'My name's Dolly, by the way. Now, have you got all the necessary? If you need anything let me know.'

'When do I start work?' Patty asked.

'Seven o'clock. Boss says to wear the yellow silk.'

'Yellow silk? To work in the kitchen?'

'You're not working in the kitchen. You're front of house, my duck.'

'Doing what?'

'Being nice to the gentlemen, of course. Didn't he tell you?'

'No. Do you mean I'm to be a … hostess?'

'Yeah, that's what we call them. Now, you can do what you like till this evening. I should have a rest if I was you. You'll be busy later.'

She went out, closing the door behind her.

Patty slumped down on one of the chairs and understood for the first time what was happening. How could she have been so stupid? She had seen the women going through that door with their escorts. That door led to the stairs and the stairs led to rooms like this one. She should have known what was going on. She had known, really, but she had chosen not to think about it. Now she was one of them.

She remembered the weeks she had spent on the street, before May had rescued her; the hasty, furtive couplings in alleyways or dark corners; the coarse hands mauling her; the stink of sweat and bad breath. She had loathed it, and loathed herself for submitting to it. Now she was going to have to do it all over again. But this would be different, she told herself. At least there was a soft bed to lie on, instead of cold stone pressing into her back with every thrust. And the clients were ... well, if not gentlemen, at least reasonably clean and decently dressed. She would have a roof over her head, and food.

She had watched the other women, laughing and chatting with the men, eating and drinking with them. They seemed to be enjoying themselves. The idea of what happened when they got upstairs was repellent, but perhaps it was a price worth paying. Anyway, what choice did she have? The alternative would be to go back to the workhouse but the memory of her childhood there sent a shudder through her body. She remembered how the governor had chosen her, above May, to be sent to work in the great house. How could she go back there and admit what a mess she had made of her life? How could she bear to be shut up again inside those forbidding walls? Anything was better than that.

She took off her boots and lay down on the bed. She thought she might allow herself to have a good cry, but discovered that she was too exhausted. After a while, she drifted into an uneasy doze. She was awakened by her door banging open. A girl came in with a mug in either hand.

'Hey there! Brought you a cuppa. Thought you could probably do with one.'

Patty sat up, rubbing the back of her hand across her eyes. She thought she had seen the girl before, in the restaurant, but she looked very different now. Her hair was tied back in a rough plait and she was wearing a loose robe that revealed her bare legs as she walked.

'You're new, aren't you?' she asked.

Patty nodded.

'I'm Josie. But down there—' with a jerk of her head towards the door '—I'm Elvira. What do they call you?'

'Patty.'

'Pleased to meet you, Patty. You done this before?'

'Sort of. Not for a long time.'

'It's not so bad, considering.' Josie looked round the room. 'You got a dress to wear?'

Patty looked at the parcel, which she had dropped unopened on the floor. 'In there.'

'In here?' Josie picked up the parcel and pulled off the string. The yellow silk spilled out onto the carpet. 'Blimey! This is in a bit of a state. You better hang it up, try and get some of the creases out before the boss sees you.' She looked from the dress to Patty. 'I've seen you before, ain't I?'

'I used to come here, with ... with a man.'

'Oh, right! Dropped you, has he?'

'Yes, you could say that.'

'Hey, you're not ... are you ... you know. In the family way?'

'No, no I'm not.'

'That's good.' The girl hesitated for a moment, looking round. 'Better get yourself ready. I'll drop by in a bit, give you a hand if you like.' She came over to the bed. 'Cheer up. We girls look after each other. And the blokes aren't too bad, most of them. Just make sure he washes his John Thomas before he gets started. Right?'

'Right,' Patty mumbled.

When the door had closed behind Josie she got up and shook out the yellow dress. It was very creased, but there was nothing she could do about that. Outside in the corridor she could hear voices, women calling to each other, doors opening and closing. Her fellow hostesses coming to work. She poured water into the ewer and splashed her face. Then she got out the few toiletries she possessed and dragged a comb through her hair and coiled it into a bun at the back of her head. Putting on the dress was more of a problem. It buttoned down the back and always before she had got Maisie or Lucy to fastened them for her. To do it for herself was virtually impossible. She was still wrestling with it when there was a tap on the door and Josie reappeared, looking very different.

She was wearing a rose pink dress and her hair was dressed in ringlets hanging to her shoulders, and there was something about her face that made her eyes look larger and her skin look more creamy. She looked Patty up and down and clicked her tongue.

'Oh, you'll never do like this! Here, let me help.' She fastened the remaining buttons and then said, 'Sit here and let me do something to your hair.'

Patty sat as instructed, in front of the table with the mirror, and Josie unfastened her hair and redid most of it in two thick plaits, which she coiled on either side of Patty's head. The remainder she also made into plaits, looping them round in front of her ears to join with the rest. 'There, that's a bit more fashionable,' she said. 'Now, sit still a minute while I fetch something.'

She was back a moment later with a small case of polished wood, which, when opened, displayed a small array of glass jars.

'What is all this?' Patty asked.

'Have you never used cosmetics?' Josie asked.

'No ... I—' Patty stopped. She had been about to say that only fallen women painted their faces.

'They are a woman's best friend,' Josie asserted. 'Now, let's see ... some Cream of Roses first to smooth your skin, then a touch of rouge and some lip salve. It's got something called alkanet in it, to make them look redder.' She dabbed and smoothed at Patty's face for a few minutes and stood back. 'Yes, that's better, isn't it?'

Patty looked at herself. The face that looked back was not exactly pretty, but the roses and cream complexion and the full, red lips did give it a certain allure. It was like looking at a different person. She had a sudden feeling that she had stepped aside and allowed someone else to inhabit her body. It made what she was about to do easier.

'Stand up and let's have a look at you,' Josie said. She gazed for a moment and then nodded. 'That dress needs ironing, but we can't do that tonight. It will have to do for now. Apart from that ... not bad. Not bad at all. You ought to have a working name, like me. Got any ideas?'

Patty shook her head.

'Let's think. Something posh and romantic sounding. I know. How about Griselda?'

'If you think so,' Patty agreed. It helped to strengthen the feeling that it was not her but another girl who was about to sell herself.

'Come on,' Josie said. 'We're due downstairs and the boss doesn't like to be kept waiting.'

Down in the restaurant Patty lined up with half a dozen others and the manager walked along the line, examining each one. When he got to Patty he said, 'Hmm. Polish up quite nicely, don't you? I thought you might. But for Pete's sake get that dress ironed before tomorrow. Now just remember this. You're here to make the gentlemen feel happy, and the more they drink the happier they get. If they offer to buy you a drink, you ask for champagne. Got it? Right, get yourselves something to eat. You won't have a chance later.'

In the kitchen they were served with a good meal, simpler than what was on offer in the restaurant but ample and tasty. The other girls proved to be a friendly crowd and chatted easily to Patty but no one asked how she came to be in the same position as they were. She got the impression that it was not something any of them wanted to discuss. All too soon, Dolly appeared and shooed them all out.

'Time to work, ladies!'

In the restaurant the doors were opened and people began to come in, just a few at first but then in greater numbers. There were parties of friends, like the ones Percy had introduced her to, and some couples, but the majority of the clients were men, either alone or in twos and threes.

Patty whispered to Josie, 'I don't know what to do!'

'Look for anyone who is on his own, and go and ask if he would like to buy you a drink. Or one of them might call you over. Just remember, the more champagne they order the better the boss will be pleased.'

The guests were studying the menu and ordering food and the other girls began to circulate around the room, pausing to exchange greetings and jokes with the men. Patty noticed a middle aged, slightly corpulent man sitting on his own. She took a deep breath, braced herself and went over to him.

'Good evening, sir. Would you like me to join you?'

He looked her over and grinned. 'Well, you're a juicy little morsel, aren't you? What do they call you?'

'P ... Griselda,' Patty said.

'Sit down, my dear. What can I get you to drink?'

'Champagne, please,' Patty said.

A waiter was already hovering near with a bottle in an ice bucket and very quickly Patty found a glass in her hand.

'Well, here's to you, my lovely,' her companion said, raising his glass.

'Cheers,' she responded, and took a sip.

She had never tasted champagne before and she did not much like it. It was sour, to her taste, but it seemed very easy to swallow. She would have preferred the taste of the drink Percy had given her, the one he called a gimlet, but she remembered the effect that had had on her. This champagne seemed much less dangerous and she emptied her glass quite quickly.

'That's the way, drink up!' her companion said. 'Let's have another bottle.'

The manager would be pleased with that, she thought, and allowed him to refill her glass again. Over the course of the second bottle he told her that his name was Alfred and he was a commercial traveller, which meant that he was away from home a good deal and had to spend many evenings alone. He was glad to have some jolly company.

Eventually he said, 'Well, I think I'm ready for a little lie down. Shall we go upstairs?'

When she got up, she had some difficulty in getting her balance and she had to focus hard on the doorway leading to the stairs to keep moving in that direction. She managed to remember which room was hers and as soon as they got inside he began unbuttoning her dress.

'Oh, I do like to unwrap a nice little parcel,' he chortled, as it fell to her feet. 'Now let's have these stays off.'

When he had got down to her shift she thought he would stop but he pulled that over her head and stood looking at her, panting slightly. She had never expected to be naked. In her previous encounters her skirt had been heaved up, sometimes her bodice yanked down, but she had never had to take them off and it had always been dark. Now she felt horribly exposed. She put one arm across her breasts, the other in front of her thighs, but he pulled them away and unbuttoned his trousers.

'Now then, that's enough of that. No need for modesty here.'

And at that he picked her up bodily and deposited her on the bed and fell on top of her. He was inside her almost at once and she cried out in pain. She was not a virgin, but it had been years since the last occasion and she was dry. He took no notice, but to her relief it was all over very quickly. He hauled himself off her with a grunt, fastened his trousers and threw some coins onto the dressing table. Then, without a word, he was gone.

Patty pulled the sheet over herself and curled up. It was over and at least he hadn't knocked her about. Perhaps she could sleep now.

A few minutes later her door banged open and Dolly appeared. 'What do you think you're doing, madam? This isn't a rest home, you know.'

Patty struggled to sit up. Her head was going round. 'Please, the gentleman's gone. He got what he wanted. The money's on the table.'

'There are plenty more like him downstairs,' Dolly said. 'You're not done yet, my girl. It's barely ten o'clock. Now get yourself dressed and get downstairs.'

She had to go through it all again twice before the evening was over and the restaurant closed its doors. One was with a man who was so drunk she thought he was not going to be capable of performing, but who kept rubbing himself and trying again until he finally succeeded. The third man wanted her to sit on his lap and let him caress her breasts while she sang a lullaby. She disliked that one more than the others.

Over the next week or two these encounters began to seem like normal routine. She learned to close her mind to what was happening. It was Griselda who was having to endure these unpleasant things, not Patty. There were compensations. The rest of the girls were friendly and there was a spirit of camaraderie among them. They never talked about their former lives or what had brought them to where they were now, and no one asked Patty for her story. They remembered seeing her with Percy, but they never read the papers so they knew nothing about his activities and she was able to hide her shame at her part in them.

They all slept late and around mid-morning a maid brought up a tray of breakfast for each of them. After that, the rest of the day was their own. The wages were good, and most of them went out to look round the shops and spend their money. Patty went with them and bought herself a new skirt and blouse for daytime, but she was careful never to go near Freeman's. The yellow silk, sponged and ironed, sufficed for the evening. Josie showed her where to buy cosmetics and she learned to apply them herself, adding extra touches to enhance the Griselda face that she put on every evening.

There were times when she wondered if the old Patty would disappear and Griselda would take over. Some of the girls were looking forward to Christmas, but she found it impossible to think ahead, even by a few days. She could see nothing in the future that offered a prospect of change. All she could do was live each day as it came.

The end came suddenly, much sooner than she could have imagined. One evening a man she had not met before asked her to perform an act that she found so repulsive that she refused. He was a big man, rough-mannered in spite of his smart clothes. He grabbed her by the hair and forced her to her knees.

'You don't say no to me, bitch! Do it!'

'Please, I can't! I can't do that. I won't!'

'You what? Do you think you can get away with that? I'm paying you, and you'll do what I tell you.'

'No, please,' she begged. 'I'll do all the usual things. I'll give you a good time. Just not that!'

'That is what I'm paying you for,' he said. 'Now do it! Last chance!'

She shook her head, beginning to weep.

The blow knocked her down and made her ears ring. Before she could get up he grabbed her hair again and banged her head repeatedly on the floor. She fought him desperately, trying to pull his hands away, and when that failed she twisted her head and bit his wrist. He screamed at her in fury and slapped her face, twice. Then he started kicking her and that was when she lost consciousness.

Chapter 9

Rutherglen, Christmas 1868

This was the second Christmas May had spent in Australia but she could not get used to the idea that here it happened in high summer. The residents of Rutherglen were, nevertheless, determined to celebrate it in the traditional manner, which varied according to their countries of origin. This year May and her family, together with the rest of the household, were invited to spend the day with the Schloers. It was a prospect that she viewed with some alarm, as Anton's attentions had become increasingly pressing over recent months. There was nothing she could do about that, however. To refuse the invitation would be the height of discourtesy and deprive her family of an enjoyable occasion.

On Christmas morning they exchanged presents over the breakfast table. May had sent away to Melbourne for a pair of fine kid gloves for her father and an elegant cravat for Gus. For Maria, she had painted a portrait of Pedro, and for Pedro one of Maria. Both of them had shown great interest in her artistic efforts and, though she did not consider herself in any way an expert at portraiture, she knew it was something that would please them both.

On her plate that morning was a small package addressed to her in her father's handwriting. Opened, it revealed a beautiful opal pendant on a gold chain. On Gus's plate was an envelope inscribed 'For Merlin' and he let out a yell of delight when he opened it to find a cheque to cover the sum Mr Marshall required for the colt. Pedro gave him a head collar of fine leather and Maria a saddle-cloth embroidered with his initials. For May, there was a chemise of fine linen edged with lace and delicately embroidered with a design of white roses and, from Pedro, earrings to match the pendant. As a final gesture, May revealed a picture she had painted of Freshfields with all of them sitting on the veranda.

Breakfast over, and the morning chores out of the way, it was time to get ready to leave for the Schloers' house. May had another new dress, this time of peacock-blue silk. When her father had suggested it she had demurred at the extravagance, but he had pointed out that all the other ladies would have new clothes for the festivities and he wanted her to be a credit to him, so she had given way.

As they entered the main hall of the Schloers' house they all stopped with exclamations of wonder. A tall pine tree stood in the centre of the room, it's branches decked with ribbons and paper flowers and apples and pieces of gingerbread wrapped in gold paper, all illuminated by dozens of candles. May had seen Christmas trees before. Mr Freeman had adopted the new fashion and had used them to decorate the shop windows the year before she left England, but she had never seen anything as magnificent as this.

Herr Schloer stood in front of the tree to greet them and then they were conducted through to the veranda at the back of the house where Frau Schloer waited with Anton and his three sisters. Gifts were exchanged and then there was a bang as a bottle of champagne was opened.

'Not our own production, sadly,' Herr Schloer said. 'The climate here does not lend itself to the cultivation of the Pinot Noir grape, but we shall sample some of our own vintage later.'

The glasses were passed round and a toast was drunk, but May only sipped at her wine. She was just beginning to appreciate some of her father's red wines, and this light, fizzy drink was enjoyable in the summer heat, but she knew very well what would happen if she drank much and she felt she needed to keep her wits about her today.

Other guests arrived, amongst them the O'Dowd family, and soon they were all seated around a long table. There was a spicy beef soup to start with and then a huge roast goose was placed ceremonially in front of Herr Schloer. It was accompanied by slices of spicy sausage and potato dumplings and sauerkraut. May was happy to eat something other than the regular dish of roast mutton, which was the staple diet of most of their neighbours, but she found the whole meal too heavy for such a warm day. It was a relief when as an alternative to the plum pudding there was a dish of raspberries and cream.

After the meal the guests settled back in long chairs and the men lit cigars. Some started to play cards. Anton's youngest sisters were ten and twelve years old, and there were several other children among the guests and May found herself co-opted to organise games for them. She found this ironic, having never been allowed to play and join in sports as a child herself, but she entered into the spirit of the day. They played hide and seek and blind man's bluff, and then someone produced a cricket bat and a ball and Anton and Gus were lured away from the adults to organise the game.

Tea was served as the sun sank lower and then Patrick O'Dowd struck up on his fiddle and was soon joined by another guest on the accordion and the dancing began. This was the part of the festivities May had been dreading. Anton had been on his best behaviour, dividing his attention between his father's guests, but now he came towards her with a proprietary air and led her onto the impromptu dance floor in the middle of the lawn. She managed to escape once or twice when other young men among the guests asked her to dance, but as soon as she remarked that she was tired he made that an excuse to lead her away into the shadow of a rose arbour where there was a seat.

'You are looking more beautiful than ever tonight,' he told her.

'Thank you. But I'm not sure that is true. I'm so hot, I'm sure I must be purple in the face.'

'Oh, believe me, it is! You are a little flushed, it is true, but it suits you.'

He took hold of her hand and leaned towards her. He was breathing a little more heavily than could be accounted for by their recent exercise on the dance floor. She knew what was coming but felt impotent to prevent it. His lips as they met hers were dry and slightly roughened by exposure to the sun. It was not the first time she had been kissed. She had a vivid memory of passionate kisses exchanged in shop doorways with Armando, and, more precious to her, of being kissed by James. Those kisses had inflamed her blood, sending surges of desire through her body. This one left her cold. She wanted to draw back but some sense of indebtedness prevented her. He had been kind to her, and he was obviously fond of her; she felt that perhaps she owed him some return. She endured the kiss as long as she could, but when his pressure on her lips became more urgent she put her hand on his shoulder and pushed him away.

'No, Anton. It's not ... we shouldn't ...'

To her surprise he sat back without protest. 'No, you are quite right. This is not the correct way to behave. Forgive me.'

'There's nothing to forgive. But perhaps we should go back to the others now?'

For the rest of the evening he behaved impeccably, even permitting other men to dance with her without protest, and by the time they were ready to leave, May had come to the conclusion that he had at last taken the hint and realised that there was no possibility of a closer relationship between them.

Next day, when May returned from the lake, where she had been sketching, Maria said, 'Anton was here earlier.'

'Oh? Did you tell him where I was?'

'Yes, but he said he had not come to see you. He had business to discuss with your father.'

'Oh well, that's all right then.'

That evening she was sitting on the veranda, enjoying the cooler air and trying to read by the light of an oil lamp, when her father came and sat beside her.

'May, there's something I need to discuss with you and I don't quite know how to begin.'

She looked at him anxiously. His expression was serious but not angry. If anything he looked slightly embarrassed.

'Is something wrong?' she asked.

'No, not wrong. It's just that I've never had to do this before. It's not something I ever expected.'

'Have I done something to upset you?'

'No! No, it's nothing like that.'

'Well, then …'

He cleared his throat. 'Young Schloer came to see me today.'

'Oh yes, Maria told me. What did he want?'

'You. He wants to marry you. He came to ask my permission to propose to you.'

'Oh no!' She gazed at her father in anguish. 'Papa, I don't want to marry Anton. Please, don't ask me to.'

He looked surprised but not annoyed. 'My dear girl, if you don't want to marry the fellow, no one is going to make you. But I thought you liked him. You danced with him all evening, more or less.'

'I do that because he gets angry if I dance with other boys. He seems to feel he has some rights over me.'

'Well, he doesn't, so he can forget that.'

'What did you say to him?'

'I said it was entirely up to you who you married, so he should ask you. I left you to fend for yourself years ago, and you seem to have done a pretty good job of it, so I've no right to put my oar in.' He paused and drew on his cigar thoughtfully. 'It seems a pity, though.'

'Why?'

'Well, for one thing, there are not so many young men around – not ones I would call suitable. And then ... the Schloers' land runs beside ours. Anton is the only son. One day he will inherit and if you did decide to marry him that would unite the two estates.'

'Does that matter?'

'It's not vital, but from a commercial point of view it would be a good thing. These vines are still young. They don't produce at their full capacity yet. We produce some very good quality wines, but the quantity is small.'

'Is the vineyard in trouble?'

'No, no. Not yet, at least. But things are changing. The gold is all but exhausted. Yields are so small that people are beginning to move away. So we shall have to look for new markets. That means Melbourne – perhaps even exporting. But as you know, to do that we have to send the wine by riverboat to Echuca and then onwards by rail. If only the railway came through here, it would be so much cheaper, but there's no sign of that yet. If we were moving larger quantities it would work out cheaper. The larger vineyards have the advantage there.'

'So it would help if our land was joined with the Schloers'?'

'Yes, it would.'

May was silent for a few minutes. It was clear that her father would like her to marry Anton. And there was still no certainty that James would keep his promise and come to join her. Marriage to Anton would be bearable. He was kind-hearted, reliable – and he loved her. She had no wish to end up as an old maid.

She looked at her father. 'Give me a little time, Papa. In – say, six months? – I may feel differently. Is that acceptable?'

'My dear girl, whatever you decide to do is acceptable to me. I would never push you to do anything you did not want to do. When you are ready, you can tell me if you have changed your mind. And if Anton tries to hurry you, refer him to me. Understand?'

May got up from her chair and knelt at his side. 'Dear Papa! I'm so lucky to have such an understanding father. Thank you!'

She kissed his cheek and he put his arm round her and held her close for a moment.

'You don't have to thank me for anything. All I want is to make up to you for all the years you spent in that damn orphanage and after.'

'You've done that already,' she told him. 'I am very happy here and I don't want for anything. But will you do one thing for me? Will you speak to Anton, and tell him I need more time to decide? He will take it better from you.'

'Of course,' her father said. 'If that's what you want, that's what I'll do.'

Gus, when he heard about her decision, was not so understanding.

'Anton says you've turned him down! What's wrong with you?'

'What do you mean, what's wrong with me? I just don't want to marry Anton – or not yet anyway.'

'And you expect him to wait around until you make up your mind?'

'Only for a few months.'

'Why? What is going to change in a few months?' May said nothing and he went on, 'You're not the only pebble on the beach, you know? One day Anton will inherit the vineyard. There are plenty of girls who would see him as a very good catch.'

'Then they are welcome to him, if that's what he decides.'

'Are you determined to be an old maid, then? Oh, wait a minute! I know what you're waiting for.' May stared at him. Could he possibly have read her mind? 'You're hoping that Rudi Marshall is going to propose to you, aren't you? You fancy being a member of the squattocracy. Dream on! Men like that marry their own kind, not girls like you.'

'That is not it!' she exclaimed. 'I never even thought of marrying Rudi.'

'Then why won't you marry Anton?'

'Because I'm not in love with him.'

'Oh, that's just romantic nonsense.'

She gasped. 'How can you say that, Gus? You are in love with Kitty. Why else did you follow her to Australia? Why else did you leave me all alone to come here, if not for love?'

He looked into her face and she saw that her words had struck home. He reached out and touched her hand. 'Sorry, sis. I'm being a selfish pig. I'd like to see you married to Anton because he's my friend, but if you don't want to, that's up to you. Just don't wait too long. There isn't going to be a fairy prince on a white horse, like you used to talk to me about when we were little.'

'I know that, Gus,' she said. 'I'm not waiting for that. Just give me a bit of time.'

Next day Gus rode over to Eskmere to finalise the purchase of the colt Merlin and came back to tell them that they were all invited to see in the New Year with the Marshalls. Accordingly, on New Year's Eve, they dressed in their best again and drove there in the pony trap, Gus riding beside them on Storm to make space for Pedro and Maria. They were greeted warmly and introduced to the members of two other squatter families, all of whom had emigrated from England. The dinner was lavish and the mood convivial, aided by generous quantities of local wine, including, May was glad to see, some of Freshfields' best vintages.

At one point, conversation turned to more serious matters.

'We could be in for some trouble in the next few months,' Andrew Marshall said. 'The tension between the squatters and the selectors is getting worse.'

May knew what the term meant. In an effort to prevent even larger areas being squatted, the government had allowed ordinary men and women, some of them transported prisoners who had served their sentence like her father, to 'select' an area of land on which to set up a small farm. Unfortunately, they had to make their selection without the benefit of a survey and some of them were now finding it hard to make a living. It was different for her father. Having struck gold he had been able to purchase the land he chose, rather than relying on luck in the selection process.

'What is the problem?' George Lavender asked.

'Some of them feel that we squatters have deliberately made it impossible for them to select viable holdings, by denying them land with good access to water, for example. That may well be true, in some cases. Others just don't have the skills, or the capital, to make a go of their holdings. As a result, we now have an under-class of discontented people who feel that we owe them something and who are prepared to take it by force if necessary.'

'These bushrangers have been around for a good few years now,' someone pointed out. 'It's nothing new.'

'I know,' Marshall said. 'But with characters like Frederick Ward, who calls himself Captain Thunderbolt, and Benjamin Hall committing armed robbery, appar-ently at will, none of us are safe. And in my opinion it's only going to get worse.'

'Come on, Father,' Rudi said, 'this isn't the right sort of talk for an evening like this. You're frightening the ladies. We're here to enjoy ourselves.'

'You're right,' Andrew said. 'I apologise. Let's adjourn, shall we? Mrs Fisher, would you care to lead the ladies into the drawing room?'

In the drawing room there was the usual casual chat-ter, while ladies took their turn to discreetly withdraw and avail themselves of the chamber pots in one of the bedrooms. Then, after a suitable pause, Mrs Fisher, as the senior lady present, suggested they might re-join the gentlemen. Outside the gathering broke up into small groups to stroll around the garden admiring the carefully tended plants and shrubs. Gus and some of the younger men headed for the paddock to admire Merlin. There were two other young women among the guests and May had watched them making eyes at Rudi all through dinner and they were both now intent on claiming his attention, but he came to May's side and said, 'Will you walk with me, please, and protect me from those harpies?'

She laughed. 'I'm sure you are perfectly capable of protecting yourself – and it's not very kind to call them harpies.'

'Oh, but they are!' he said, taking her arm. 'I know the type. They will strip the flesh off a man's body if you give them half a chance. Shall we go down to the river?'

A small thrill of danger ran through May's nerves, but she ignored it. 'If you like.'

As they walked she said, 'Tell me about these bushrangers your father mentioned. I've never heard of them before.'

'Some of them are escaped convicts, some just men who have lost everything and turned to robbery as a way to make a living. One or two have just been crazy. There was Mad Dog Morgan who once shot a policeman just for saying hello. Then there was Black Douglas Russell. He was a brute. He preyed on diggers coming and going from the goldfields at Bendigo. He was captured when the miners burned down his camp, must be more than ten years ago now.'

'Are some of them still at large?'

'That one who calls himself Captain Thunderbolt is still around. He's been credited with several armed hold-ups over the last few years.' He squeezed her arm. 'But you don't need to worry. He's after bigger fish than us – gold shipments and the like. And several of his gang have been rounded up recently.'

They had reached the river bank and turned to stroll under the shade of the she-oaks. He said, 'Let's not talk of violence and robbery, this is a celebration, a special day.'

'Yes,' she agreed. 'Let's forget about them.'

They walked in silence for a while and when they came to the spot where they had stopped on the previous occasion he came to a standstill.

'Beautiful!' he said,

'Yes,' she agreed, gazing at the dappled sunlight reflecting on the water. Then she turned and realised that he was looking at her. Before she could speak or do anything to deflect him, he put his arms round her, drew her close and kissed her. This was very different from Anton's kiss. This set her pulse racing and turned her body liquid with desire. It was a long time since she had felt like that. For a moment she let herself give in to her natural instincts, then she pulled back and broke away.

'No, Rudi!' She was breathless and shaking. 'No, we really shouldn't ...'

He kept hold of her but made no attempt to renew the kiss. 'I know. I know. But I wanted you to understand how I feel.' He was panting too, but she saw him make an effort to control himself. 'You remember what I said to you the last time you were here – about being Lady Eskmere?'

'I thought you were joking.'

'I was – in a way. But now I can't stop thinking about it. Would you ... could you ... consider it?'

She drew back out of his grip. 'It's impossible.'

'Why?'

She should have said, 'Because I am already promised to someone else,' but something prevented her. Instead she said, 'For one thing, English society would never accept me as the wife of a baron.'

'Why not?'

'Think about it, Rudi! Can you imagine those ladies and gentlemen accepting the daughter of a man who was transported for smuggling into their society?'

'They need not know. As far as they are concerned, you are the daughter of a successful wine grower.'

She gave a small, dry laugh. 'I don't know if they would find that any better.' She sighed, suddenly weary of having to revisit these old arguments. 'But I'm serious, Rudi. I'm not qualified to mix in that sort of society. I haven't had the right sort of education. I can read and write and add up, but that is about all. I don't have any of the accomplishments expected of a young lady. I can't play an instrument, or sing, or speak a foreign language ...'

'You paint,' he said. 'Gus told me you did a painting of Freshfields and all the family as a Christmas present.'

'Oh, that. Yes, I dabble a bit. But that isn't enough. I just wouldn't fit in to that sort of society.'

'Then we won't live in England. Why would I want to live in that chilly, grey climate with those chilly, grey people? We'll stay here. No one worries about the sort of thing you're talking about here.'

'But you would have land, an estate, and a house in England.'

'I'll let the house to wealthy Americans and get a land agent in to manage the estate.' He stopped and threw up his hands in a self-mocking gesture. 'Why are we arguing about this? I may never inherit the title. And even if I do it won't be for years. What I should be asking you is, would you consider being plain Mrs Rudolph Marshall?'

She drew a sharp inward breath and bit her lips. This was the moment to give him a definite 'no', but somehow the word stuck in her throat. Instead she said, 'Rudi, we hardly know each other. We've met, what, three times? I can't give you an answer on such a short acquaintance.'

'No,' he said and paused, nodding to himself in confirmation. 'You're right, of course. I shouldn't try to rush you. I'm afraid that's a fault of mine. When I see something I want I go hell-for-leather for it. Forgive me. Let's just agree to go on meeting. And when you feel ready you can give me your answer.'

'Well,' she responded, 'it looks as if we are bound to meet quite frequently. I know Gus wants your advice about training Merlin.'

He grinned suddenly. 'Why do you think I persuaded my father to let him have the colt at a knock-down price?'

She looked at him, seeing him suddenly in a different light. 'You mean, that wasn't the proper price?'

'Well, put it this way. He would have fetched a lot more to the right customer.'

'And you persuaded your father to accept a loss – why?'

'So that I would have a reason to call on you often, of course.'

'I see.' She thought for a moment. 'I think we should go back to the others now.'

It was not practical for the party to continue until midnight, in order to see the New Year in. Eskmere was a large property by local standards but it did not have enough rooms to accommodate all the guests and no one wanted to have to drive home in the dark. So shortly after they re-joined the others people began making their farewells.

Jogging home in the pony trap as the light faded May tried to make sense of her confused impulses. It is not often, she thought, with a flicker of humour, that a girl gets two proposals of marriage within a week. But the fact was that she now had two young men hanging on her decision, a decision that was almost certainly going to be 'no'. If it had been another woman, she would have condemned her as a shameless flirt. With a sudden pang of guilt she asked herself what James would think of the situation. He would be mortified by the discovery that she had so little faith in his promises. If you truly loved him, she told herself, you would trust him and wait for him. And if in the end something prevented him from coming to join you, you would resign yourself to the life of an old maid. But she could not silence the nagging doubt. It was over a year now since they had last seen each other. She knew that in that time she had changed greatly. She was no longer the timid girl she had been. She was self-reliant, confident in her own abilities, in spite of what she had said to Rudi. And he would have changed, too, though perhaps not so much. What if they found, when they met again, that they were no longer in love? The questions went round and round in her mind, without finding any solution.

Back at Freshfields, her father opened a bottle of his best vintage and as the clock on the mantelpiece struck twelve he raised his glass.

'Here's to 1869, my dears. May it bring us all our hearts' desires.'

Chapter 10

Liverpool, Christmas 1868

Patty opened her eyes. Above her was a blank white-ness and somewhere nearby a choir was singing 'Hark the Herald Angels Sing'. So this, she thought, is what heaven is like. But she was surprised that her head and body still throbbed with pain.

A face framed by a white cap came into her field of vision.

'Ah, you're awake. Are you thirsty?'

'Yes.' Her throat was so dry that the word came out as a croak.

A strong arm was slid under her shoulders and a cup was held to her lips. 'Sip carefully, now. Not too much at once.'

When she had drunk some water she was laid back on the pillows. She took in the figure of the person leaning over her. Spotless white cap and apron over a plain brown dress – a nurse then. She turned her head with difficulty and looked to one side. There was a long row of beds made up with clean white sheets and bright floral bedspreads. Not heaven, after all. A hospital.

'Where am I?' she whispered.

'You are in the infirmary, dear.'

'The infirmary? Where?'

'It's part of the workhouse, officially. But we work quite independently.'

Patty frowned. There was something here that did not fit. 'This isn't the workhouse infirmary.'

'Why do you say that?'

'It doesn't look like this. It's dirty, and it smells.'

'Have you been here before?'

'I grew up in the workhouse. I was sent to the infirmary when I had scarlet fever.'

'Ah, that explains it. Things have changed here a lot since those days, so I am told. I only came to work here six months ago.'

'Why can I hear singing?'

'It's Christmas Day. You didn't know? Some charitable ladies have organised a choir to come and sing to the patients.' The nurse took hold of Patty's wrist and felt her pulse. 'That's better. But you should rest now. Don't talk any more.'

She moved away and Patty saw her lean over another bed. She closed her eyes and tried to think. Her head was bandaged and her face felt swollen. How had she got here? What had happened to make her head ache so, and gave her a sharp pain in her ribs when she took a breath? The last thing she remembered was sitting in a crowded room, where there was a lot of laughter and chatter. Where had that been? What had she been doing there? She could find no answers and after a while she drifted into a doze.

She was woken by someone else leaning over the bed. An older face this time, but the same kindly expression.

'Do you feel able to answer a few questions?'

She wanted to say no and be left alone, but that would be rude. 'Yes,' she whispered.

'Can you tell me your name?'

'Grisel ... no, that's wrong. It's Patty. Patty Jenkins.' Where had that other name come from?

'How do you do, Patty? I'm Sister Robinson. Nurse Peters tells me you think you have been here before.'

'Yes, when I was a child.'

'And you grew up in the workhouse. Is that right?'

'Yes.'

'So, are you an orphan?'

'Yes.'

'Is there anyone you would like us to contact? You are not wearing a ring, so I assume you are not married. Is there anyone else – your employer perhaps?'

Patty wrestled with the effort of remembering. There had been someone ... Then it came back to her. She had been sacked. She shook her head.

'No, there's no one.' She peered up into the other woman's face. 'How did I get here?'

'You were found lying on the pavement when the porter opened up in the morning. Someone has obviously attacked you. You have been quite badly beaten. When you feel up to it I will send for the police.'

'No!' Patty was beginning to get glimpses of the past twenty-four hours and something told her she should not involve the police. 'No, I don't want that.'

'Who was it, Patty? Was it someone you know?'

She started to shake her head and stopped because it hurt too much. 'No ... no.'

'Don't worry. We won't call them if you don't want us to. Just try to relax.' Her head was raised again and a cup put to her lips. 'Drink this. It will take away the pain.'

The drink was bitter and Patty gagged briefly, but she managed to finish it and once again sank into sleep.

When she woke next time a trolley was being pushed along the middle of the ward and she could smell food. A young girl who was not in nurses' uniform helped her to sit up and put a tray with a plate of stew on her lap. She ate some but she was not hungry and it was a relief when the girl came to take the plate away. Patty lay back and looked at the ceiling, so surprisingly clean and white compared with her memory. Something had happened to her, something bad. What was it? Then, like a curtain being lifted, it came to her; the man who had asked her to do that revolting act; his voice shouting at her, then nothing. Had he hit her? He must have done. But that had been in her room at the club. How had she got here? Left outside the doors in the middle of the night ... Bit by bit she pieced together the rest of the story; the inspector's revelations about Percy's betrayal of her trust; her sacking from Freeman's; the 'work' she had done at the club. At length she understood. The man had beaten her unconscious and someone had found her – one of the other girls, probably. The manager would not have wanted to call a doctor, or the police, for obvious reasons. So they had brought her here under cover of darkness and left her. It was a heartless thing to do, but she understood the reason. The manager was breaking the law and could be accused of living off immoral earnings. As for the girls, they could be heavily fined. It was wicked, the way the women always got the blame, she thought, but that was the way of the world.

Next day the nurse who had first spoken to her came to her bedside with a tray of ointment and bandages.

'I'm going to replace the dressing on your head and I've got an unguent that will help to take the ache out of those nasty bruises.'

She undid the bandage and Patty winced as the dressing was removed. 'Why ...' she began. 'What is wrong with my head?'

'You've got a nasty cut but the doctor stitched it while you were still unconscious. It's healing up nicely.' She paused. 'It looks as though someone kicked you there, and again in your ribs. Sister says you don't want to involve the police. Are you sure?'

'Yes, I'm sure.' Patty had realised that the people who would suffer most if the police were involved would be the girls she had come to regard as friends. If the club was closed down they would have to resort to working on the street, which was far more dangerous. The man who had attacked her had told her his name was Jack, but she knew no more and that was probably a false name anyway. The manager might know who he was, but he would not tell anyone.

The nurse was smearing something on a dressing. To change the subject Patty asked, 'What is that?'

'It's a herbal ointment, special to the infirmary. I've got another one here to help your bruises.'

'Why is it special to the infirmary?'

'It was made by one of the nurses, Sister Latimer. Her mother was from Jamaica and she taught her how to make medicines from herbs. Some of the doctors don't really approve but the fact is they work.'

Patty thought back. 'I remember someone who worked here when I was a child. She was black, but she wasn't a nurse. Her name was Dora, I think.'

'You knew her? What a coincidence! But that would be before she went away to London to train, of course. When she came back she was fully qualified. Everyone said she was a brilliant nurse. I've heard some of the old hands say she should have been Lady Superintendent.'

'Is she here?' Patty asked.

'No. She got married, only just over a month ago, and they went to live in Jamaica. You should have seen the wedding! The little chapel here was packed and all sorts of important people came, as well as the staff here – and all the children from the orphanage. That was her special request.'

'Was she the one who got this place cleaned up, like it is now?'

'No. That was Sister Jones. She was brought up from London by a gentleman called Mr Rathbone, a philanthropic gentleman who saw that this placed needed something radical done. He got in touch with Miss Nightingale and got her to send Nurse Jones and a team to work here. That was before my time, of course. You will appreciate the difference better than I can, if you were in here as a child.'

'It's certainly different,' Patty agreed. 'It was horrible before.'

Later that day Patty was able to get out of bed and on the following day a doctor came and examined her.

'Well,' he said, 'the wound on the head is healing up nicely and the bruising is going down. I think you're ready to leave.'

'Leave?' Patty said, with a sudden surge of panic. 'Where can I go?'

'You don't have a home to go to?'

'No, I don't.'

He regarded her doubtfully for a moment, then said, 'Well, in that case I think you need to talk to Mrs Court.'

'Who is that?' Patty asked.

'She is the Lady Superintendent of the workhouse, not the infirmary. If you are destitute you will probably have to stay here.'

He moved on to examine another patient, leaving Patty to come to terms with this new twist in her life's story. 'Destitute'? Was that what she was? She had no home, no job, no prospect of getting one. He was right. So was that to be her fate, brought up here, only to end up back again?

An hour later a small boy came in with a message. She was to go to the superintendent's office. She said goodbye to Nurse Peters, who wished her luck, and followed him out into the workhouse proper. At once she was in a familiar place. The tall, grey buildings and the narrow lanes between them had not changed since she left at the age of fourteen. Even the smell was the same, a mixture of old cabbage and dirty clothes. The boy left her at a door labelled Female Superintendent. She knocked and was told to enter. A woman in a severe black dress sat at a desk. Patty realised that she remembered her from her childhood, though she had forgotten her name.

The superintendent looked up at her. 'Patty Jenkins? Yes, I remember you. You were a good girl and we thought you would do well. That was why we chose you to go to Speke Hall when they were looking for a scullery maid. There were several girls who would have been glad of the chance to work in such a grand house. You were the lucky one. But it seems you have lost your position.'

Patty felt like telling her that far from being lucky she had been condemned to a life of unrelenting drudgery, put upon and taken advantage of by all the other servants who were above her in the pecking order. But she sensed that it would not help her case now to seem ungrateful, so she said nothing.

'What happened?' Mrs Court asked. 'Have you been dismissed?'

'That was years ago, ma'am,' Patty found herself reverting to the manners and mode of address of her childhood. 'I wasn't there long.'

'Why?'

'Cook caught me eating some of the pie that had been sent back from the dining room. She said it was theft.'

'What made you do a thing like that? You must have known it was wrong.'

'I was hungry. I never got enough to eat.'

The superintendent looked hard at her for a moment and then made a note in the file on her desk. 'So what have you been doing since?'

Patty decided to slide over the period before May came to her rescue, when she had worked as a prostitute. 'I've been working at Freeman's Department Store, in the kitchen.'

'Freeman's?' Mrs Court looked slightly less forbidding. 'I used to go there quite often to take tea in the tea room. I don't suppose you had anything to do with that, did you?'

'If you please, ma'am, I was in charge of it. I made all the cakes and pastries.'

'You did?'

'Yes, ma'am. I ... I'm quite a good pastry cook.'

'If you made all those delicious cakes you must be. But it suddenly closed down. There was some kind of scandal. I read about it in the newspaper.' She frowned for a moment, then looked at Patty with a sudden expression of horror. 'I remember now! Don't tell me you were the one who made the gingerbread ladies.'

Patty drooped her head. 'I did, ma'am. But I didn't know what that terrible man was using them for. He told me he was giving them away to poor children, as a treat.'

'And is that why you lost your job?'

'Yes, ma'am.'

Mrs Court said nothing for a moment, then she sighed. 'Well, you are not the first to be led astray by an unscrupulous man, and I don't suppose you will be the last. I suppose you have been living on your savings since then?' Patty let her silence be taken for assent. 'And you have nothing left now?'

'No, ma'am.'

'You must have earned a good salary. Has it all been spent?'

'Every penny, ma'am.'

'And have you nowhere to live?'

'No, ma'am. I used to live in at Freeman's.'

'So where have you been staying since you left?'

Patty bit her lip. She had talked herself into a tricky situation. She had already decided that she would tell no one about her time at the club. 'Cheap lodgings, ma'am. But I had to leave when my money ran out.'

'And then you were attacked in the street and left half dead on our doorstep. Were you soliciting?'

Patty hung her head. 'A girl has to keep body and soul together somehow.'

Mrs Court sighed again and shook her head. 'It makes me sad to think that you have sunk so low. I had good hopes of you. Is there any chance that you might find another position, as a cook?'

'Not without a character, ma'am.'

'No, you are right, of course. Well, you have no money and nowhere to live, so we shall have to take you in. You had better start work in the kitchen here. They are always glad of an extra hand.' She made another note in the file and looked up. 'Very well, that will be all.'

Out of habit Patty made a small curtsy. 'Thank you, ma'am.'

Out in the narrow street she leaned against the wall, suddenly overcome with a sense of hopelessness. She had spent all her childhood within these grey walls. She had had a few short years of freedom, a brief sample of a better life, and now she was back again and she might have to spend the rest of her life here. The prospect was bleak indeed.

After a few moments she straightened up and squared her shoulders. 'I will not stay here,' she told herself. 'Somehow I will find a way out of this place. I will make a new life for myself, and I will never let myself be used and duped by a man again.'

In the huge kitchen, six or seven women were at
work. The steam from great vats of stew made it hard
to see across the room, and there was an overpowering smell of cabbage and onions. It was lobscouse day.
Patty hesitated for a few minutes, uncertain who to
address herself to. Then an older woman saw her and
came over.

'Want something?'

'Please, I've been told to come and help out here.'

'New, are you?'

'Yes, well – sort of. I grew up here.'

The woman peered at her. 'Thought your face was
familiar. What's your name?'

'Patty.'

'What you doing back here again? No, don't tell me.
I can see the bruises. Some man beaten you up and then
chucked you out, has he?'

'More or less,' Patty agreed.

'You'd better go and help Vera over there. She's a
nice girl. You'll get on with her.'

A young woman was chopping onions at a table a short
distance away and something about her appearance set
her apart from the others. Although she was dressed in
the plain blue dress, white cap and apron issued to all the
female paupers she wore it tidily, as if she still had some
pride in her appearance and her dark hair was pinned up
neatly in a bun.

Patty went over to her and said, 'Good morning. I've
been sent to help you.'

The woman looked up and Patty saw that her eyes were red and her cheeks were wet. 'I'll be grateful for any help peeling these wretched onions. I can hardly see what I'm doing for the tears.'

'I know how it feels,' Patty said. 'Give me a knife.'

They worked in silence until the heap of onions had all been peeled and chopped and one of the other cooks came over and took them to throw them into one of the pans. The young woman rubbed the back of her arm across her eyes and said, 'Phew! Thank goodness that's done.' She turned her eyes to Patty. 'I'm sorry. I'm forgetting my manners. I'm Vera Aston. How do you do?'

Her speech was more refined than that of most of the inmates, and her accent was not the typical Liverpool scouse. It had a country burr. Patty guessed she came from a village in Lancashire somewhere.

'My name's Patty,' she responded. 'Patty Jenkins.'

'Pleased to meet you,' Vera said. She looked at Patty's face. 'I can see you've been in the wars. Are you feeling well enough to work?'

'I've got a bit of a headache,' Patty confessed. 'But I can carry on.'

They worked side by side until the meal had been cooked and served. Looking at the long tables, men on one side of the room, women on the other, Patty felt a gloomy familiarity, but it was the sight of the children, with their pinched faces and bony arms and legs, that really caught at her throat.

'Poor mites!' Vera said. 'It must be horrible to grow up here.'

Patty said nothing. She was not yet ready to confide her story to this new acquaintance, but she was intrigued to know how a woman like Vera came to be in the same predicament.

It was two days before either of them felt like broaching the subject. They were sitting in the kitchen after the midday meal had been cleared away and washed up. It was a slack time, before the preparations for supper began, but the kitchen was warm, which was more than could be said for the rest of the workhouse. Officially they were peeling potatoes for the evening soup but there was no urgency and most of the other women had left so it was quiet for once.

Patty said, 'You're not from round here, are you? You don't speak like one of us.'

'No,' Vera agreed. 'I grew up in a little village called Winwick. It's about halfway between Liverpool and Manchester.'

'Oh,' Patty said, not sure how to proceed. 'That sounds nice.'

'Yes, it was. It's a bit of a backwater, I suppose, compared to a city like this. Not much going on. But it suited me and I loved the countryside all round.'

There was a silence. Then Vera said, 'I suppose you're wondering how I came to be here.'

'Well, yes,' Patty admitted. 'But you don't have to tell me if you don't want to.'

'There's no reason why I should hide it,' Vera said. 'None of it was my fault.' She threw the potato she had been peeling into the pot and picked up another one. 'I came to the city looking for work.'

'Oh?' Patty hesitated. 'No offence, but you don't seem like a lady who has to work for her living.'

Vera gave a brief, bitter laugh. 'I would have agreed with you once. My grandfather was well off. He owned a factory making machinery for the cotton mills in Manchester. When he died, he left the factory jointly to his two sons, my father and my uncle Wilfred. My father had no interest in the factory. He was fascinated by this new science of geology and spent his time picking up rocks and hunting for fossils, so he offered to sell his share to his brother. Wilfred agreed, and we moved away from Manchester to Winwick. That was when I was about five years old. But Wilfred was a wastrel. He was a gambler and he let the business go to rack and ruin. Then, when I was ten, there was a disastrous fire and the factory burnt down. That was bad enough, but then we discovered that he had not paid the insurance premium, so there was nothing left. A couple of weeks later he hanged himself.'

'Oh, how terrible!' Patty said.

'I suppose it was, but I didn't feel it affected me really. Father and Wilfred did not get on very well, so we hadn't seen much of him. And Father said there was no need for us to worry because his share of the money was invested and was giving us a good income.' She paused, gazing unseeing at the part-peeled potato in her hand. 'Then, when I was twelve, my mother died in childbed. I didn't know it at the time but she'd had two miscarriages before that and the doctors had said she should not have more children, so that is why I was the only one. But these things happen, don't they?'

'That's very sad for you,' Patty said. It seemed the right thing to say, but at the back of her mind was the thought, 'at least you had a mother for twelve years.'

'After that,' Vera went on, 'I had to keep house for my father. That's why none of this—' she gestured round at the kitchen '—is strange to me. We didn't keep a servant, except for a woman who came in daily to clean, so I learned to cook and deal with the tradesmen and generally manage things. I was quite happy doing that, but as the years went by Father became more and more vague and forgetful. He would go out in the morning and be brought back by one of the local farmers who had found him wandering, not able to find his way home. Sometimes he thought I was Mother and called me by her name. I asked the local doctor for help but he just said, 'it happens as people get older. They become forgetful.' Then, last April he announced that he was going to Lyme in Dorset to look for fossils. I tried to dissuade him but he was determined. He was never a man to listen to arguments. A week later I heard he had been killed by a rock fall while he was digging in the cliff.'

'Oh no!'

'When the solicitor came to look at his affairs he discovered that the company father had invested in had gone to the wall and lost all our money. Since then, we had been living on what Father could borrow. He had mortgaged the house and when I could not keep up the repayments the company repossessed it. I had to sell the furniture and everything else to pay off his creditors. When it was all done, I was left with nothing but the clothes I stood up in.'

'That's terrible! Patty said. 'Was there no one to help you?'

'No. Uncle Wilfred was my father's only close relation and he had no family, which was a mercy under the circumstances. So I had no aunts or cousins to turn to and Father was never very sociable so we had no close friends in the village. I looked for work locally, hoping someone would take me on as a governess or a house-keeper. I have had a reasonable education at least. My mother saw to that and after she died my father liked to talk to me about his interest in geology. It's surprising how much you can learn about history and geography from that. But no one needed me, so I thought I would try my luck here. I did think of going to Manchester and looking for work in one of the mills but my mother had told me such dreadful stories about conditions there that I couldn't face it. I thought, in a rich city like Liverpool, there must be people who need a governess or a house-keeper. I didn't understand that without references no one will take you on.'

'Oh, I know all about that,' Patty said.

'I tramped the streets day after day, knocking on doors and being turned away,' Vera said. 'And of course the longer it went on the shabbier and dirtier I looked, so it became harder and harder to convince anyone. I even tried to get work as a scullery maid, but they told me I was too well educated for that. I suppose they thought I wouldn't be prepared to work hard enough – or I would upset the other servants.'

'So what happened in the end?' Patty asked.

'I started to beg in the street. Sometimes men offered me money to go with them, but I couldn't bear the thought of that. It was getting colder and colder and sometimes I didn't eat for days. In the end I must have collapsed. Someone found me unconscious in an alley-way and brought me here.' She looked around her. 'At least here it's warm and you get enough to eat. It's not so bad. But I'm not staying here. One day I'm going to find a way of supporting myself so I can leave.'

'That's exactly what I promised myself when I found myself here,' Patty said.

Vera looked at her. 'Well, I've told you my story. Now it's your turn.'

So Patty repeated more or less the same story as that she had given Mrs Court, except that Vera had never heard of the scandal surrounding the tea room and her part in it, so she just said she had been dismissed for giving some of the cakes she made to someone who promised to pass them on to poor children. But in one respect she was more honest. She felt she owed it to Vera, in view of what she had said about refusing the offers of men.

'I'm not as strong as you. I did go with men, for a while after I lost my job. Until one of them beat me up and left me on the doorstep here.'

'So that's what happened,' Vera said gently. 'I wondered. You poor thing!'

Neither of them spoke for a few minutes. Then Patty said, 'You said you were determined not to stay here. What would you really like to do, if it was possible?'

'I ... don't know,' Vera said slowly. 'I suppose what every woman wants is a husband and a family.'

'Not me!' Patty said firmly. 'I've had enough of men. I never want to be at the beck and call of a man, to be dependent on one for every little thing. I want a job where I can be my own mistress.'

'What sort of thing were you thinking of?' Vera asked.

Patty considered for a moment and out of the blue an idea came to her.

'I know what I would really like, but of course it isn't possible,' she said. 'I should love to have my own tea shop. Nothing big or flashy, just a little place where ladies could come and drink tea and eat my cakes.'

'That doesn't sound too much to aim for,' Vera said. 'From what you've told me, you more or less ran the tea shop at Freeman's, so why shouldn't you do it again?'

'Because to start something like that you need money,' Patty said. 'No one is going to give you a place and the equipment you need.'

'Then you have to find a way to build up some capital,' Vera said.

'In this place?' Patty responded.

'It must be possible ...' Vera said thoughtfully. She looked at Patty. 'Would you consider going into partnership?'

'Who with?'

'Me. Think about it. You can make wonderful cakes. I can do plain cooking and I'm a good organiser. I know how to deal with tradesmen, manage money, that sort of thing. You would need someone to take care of the business side. What do you think?'

'I think it sounds a wonderful idea, if only we had the money,' Patty said.

'Well, we shall have to find a way to make it. We might have to do it in stages. Perhaps we can find work of some kind so we can save up.' She dropped the knife she was holding and grasped Patty's hand. 'I know we've only known each other for a couple of days, but I feel we can be good friends. What do you think?'

Patty looked at her with a sudden pricking of tears at the back of her eyes. 'If you can bear to be friends with what some people call a "fallen woman".'

Vera smiled. 'When I was little and fell over, my mother would say, "Are you badly hurt?" and if I said I wasn't she'd say, "Well, don't sit there whinging. Pick yourself up."'

'Oh, that's wonderful!' The tears were spilling down Patty's cheeks now but she smiled back at Vera. 'Let's make that our motto. Don't sit there …'

'Whinging,' Vera joined in. 'Pick yourself up.'

Chapter 11

Rutherglen, February 1869

One day in late February, May walked into Rutherglen, as she usually did, to collect the post. The worst of the summer heat was over and all round her the vines were heavy with grapes. Soon it would be time for the vendange. She took the small bundle of mail and glanced through it and her heart gave a sudden thump and then speeded up as she recognised James's writing. She managed to thank the post mistress politely and walked out of the post office as if nothing unusual had happened, but she had calculated that James must have taken his last examination before Christmas, so there would no longer be any reason for him to remain in Liverpool. The moment for him to make a decision had arrived and this letter was the result.

She seated herself on a bench in the shade of the veranda of the Star Hotel and slid her finger under the flap of the envelope. The letter was shorter than usual. She read it through twice. Then she jumped up and began to run in the direction of home. After a few strides she pulled herself together and forced herself to proceed at a more decorous pace. This news was not something to be blurted out to the first person she met. It needed to be delivered at a suitable time and place.

May succeeded in behaving normally until the family gathered at the table on the veranda for the midday dinner. When they were eating dessert she put down her knife and said, 'I have something to tell you all.'

Her father and Gus and Pedro looked up with mild curiosity. Only Maria, with intuitive understanding, caught her breath and raised a hand to her heart.

'I am engaged to be married,' May said.

Reactions round the table ranged from surprise to satisfaction at a prediction confirmed.

'You've seen the sense of what I told you and changed you mind about marrying Anton,' her father said.

'No, sorry, Papa. It's not that.'

'My God, you've managed to hook Rudi Marshall!' Gus exclaimed.

May gave him a look of reproof. A year at sea followed by months associating with men who had grown up in some of the rougher neighbourhoods in England before finding themselves transported to Australia had swept away any inhibitions he might once have had about blasphemy.

'No, Gus,' she said. 'It's not Rudi, either. It could have been. He asked me if I fancied being Lady Eskmere one day, but I told him I didn't think that would work.'

'Then who the devil is it?' Her father normally watched his language in the presence of ladies but this was too much.

'You haven't met him, Papa. His name is James Breckenridge. We walked out together in England before I came here.'

'You're not going back to England?' Surprise had turned to concern.

'No, Papa. James is coming here. He is already on his way.'

'But I thought he'd thrown you over,' Gus said, 'and that was why you were happy to come out at such short notice.'

'No, he didn't throw me over,' May said with a hint of irritation. 'In fact it was the other way round. I realised that marriage for us simply would not work at that time.'

'Why not?' her father asked. 'Who is this fellow?'

'He is the son of a lady I used to make hats for. When we met, he was an articled clerk in a solicitor's office. By now, he will be a fully qualified solicitor.'

'A pen-pushing lawyer who can argue both ends against the middle,' her father said disparagingly. May remembered with misgiving that he had no reason to be fond of English justice. 'So why do you say your marriage wouldn't work?'

May's initial euphoria was beginning to evaporate as she understood that it was not going to be as easy as she had expected to reconcile him to the prospect of this unknown future son-in-law.

'You remember what English society is like, Papa. How rigid the divisions are between the working classes and the people who think they are a cut above that – the professionals, the doctors, the lawyers, people like that.'

'So this man thinks you're not good enough for him?' Her father's tone was becoming steadily more belligerent.

'No, that's just it! He loves me. We love each other. But if we were in England people would never accept a milliner's apprentice who was brought up in the workhouse as a suitable wife for a successful solicitor. It could ruin his career. And his mother was against the idea. She wanted him to marry a suitable young lady from his own class. He wanted us to get married anyway but I realised that if we did I should have to spend my life trying to pretend to fit in and being afraid all the time that someone would find out the truth. And that was when I got your letter, Gus, and the ticket for the steamer. It seemed like the perfect solution. But I had to act quickly because the ship left in two days. I wrote to James, telling him where I was going and why. I thought that by the time he got the letter the ship would have sailed. But it must have been delivered very early, because just as we were pulling away from the quay he appeared on the dockside. He shouted across to me, begging me to come back, but of course by then it was impossible. So I shouted back that, if he really loved me, he should follow me. And he promised he would.'

'He's taken his time about it,' her father grunted.

'That's not his fault. I realised as soon as I said it that he couldn't come straight away. For one thing, his mother was very ill and not expected to live much longer. He's the only child. He couldn't leave her alone at a time like that.'

'Of course he couldn't,' Maria murmured sympathetically.

May threw her a grateful look. 'And there was something else. He had nearly finished his articles but he had one more year to go and one final examination to take. It would have been foolish to give that up and fail to get his qualification.' She looked at her father. 'He was adamant that he wouldn't come until he felt he could establish himself in a decent career and support a wife and family. He didn't want to seem to be relying on your generosity.'

'Well, that's something in his favour,' her father grudgingly admitted. 'So what's changed now?'

'His mother died about six months ago, and now he has taken his final exam, so he's free to leave. Please, Papa, give him a chance. He's throwing up an absolutely solid prospect of a comfortable future with people he knows in order to come out to a country he knows nothing of, except what I have told him in my letters. And he did so much for me. I might have lost my position at Freeman's if it wasn't for him. He found out I love music, so he took me to concerts and I heard music I would never have heard otherwise. He saw that I had a talent for design and he took me to art galleries and encouraged me to paint. I was really uneducated and he gave me books to read. Being with him gave me the confidence to go to places and try things I would never have dared to do before.' She met her father's gaze. 'I wouldn't have been able to fit in here, and act as your hostess at dinner parties with people like the Schloers, if it wasn't for James.'

'Hmm.' Her father turned to Gus. 'You've met the fellow. What do you think of him?'

May watched her brother and saw the familiar conflict in his expression between his natural good nature and his suspicion of anyone who seemed to stand above him in the social hierarchy.

'You owe James a lot, Gus. If it hadn't been for him, you would have gone to jail, instead of getting that job with White Star Line.'

'How's that?' her father asked.

Gus looked uncomfortable. 'I got into a scrap with bloke who was harassing a ... a young lady I knew. He turned on me, but then he went to the police and told them I'd set on him and he was a gent, so of course they believed him. I was accused of affray and told to appear before the magistrate.'

'As it happened,' May took up the tale, 'I'd recently met James. His mother had come to pick up a hat and he'd come to escort her home. She'd told me he was studying to be a solicitor so I called at her house and asked James for his help. He'd said at first that there was nothing he could do because he wasn't qualified to speak in court, but then he'd changed his mind.'

'Because he'd taken a shine to you,' her brother put in with a glint of mischief.

'Just as well he had,' she retorted. 'Gus was unemployed except for casual work on the docks. James said that if he had the prospect of a proper job we might be able to persuade the magistrate that he would lose it if he went to jail, and it would be better for everyone if he was working rather than hanging round the streets. So we spoke to Mr Freeman, who was always so good to me, and he persuaded the chairman of the White Star Line to offer Gus a position as a clerk. Then James persuaded his boss, Mr Weaver, to speak for him when he came up in court and he got him off. So you do owe him a debt, Gus.'

'I suppose I do,' Gus conceded.

'Never mind that for the moment,' her father said. 'I want to know what he's like as a man.'

Gus considered for a moment. 'He's a decent enough sort. A bit of a toff, but he doesn't give himself airs.'

'Good enough for our May?'

There was a brief hesitation. 'Yeah, I suppose so. She thinks so anyway.'

'He's a good man, Father,' May said. 'I know you'll like him when you meet him.'

'Well, as long as he is going to make you happy, I suppose that's good enough for me,' her father said.

She got up and moved round the table to kiss him in the cheek. 'Thank you, Papa.'

'So you have been waiting for him all this time?' Maria said. 'How romantic! And you never mentioned him.'

'That's another thing,' her father said. 'Why haven't we heard about all this before?'

May sat down again. 'It's hard to explain. I never felt quite sure that it would really happen, and I didn't want to talk about it in case something went wrong. It's not that I didn't trust James to keep his word, but a year is a long time and so much could happen – an accident, an illness. I suppose it was a sort of superstition, that if I told everyone what I was waiting for it would be bad luck.'

'I understand that,' Maria said.

'What I don't understand is,' her father went on, 'why did you leave young Anton hanging around when you had no intention of accepting him?'

'If you remember, Papa, it was your idea that I should wait a while. And then, I thought that if something did go wrong ...'

'You'd have someone to fall back on?'

May hung her head. 'It sounds bad if you put it like that, but yes, I suppose that was at the back of my mind.'

'And Rudi Marshall, too?' Gus asked.

May felt herself blush, but she nodded.

'I see, hedging your bets, were you?' A gleam of amusement shone in her father's eyes. 'Well, maybe that's no bad thing. But you're going to have to make it right with both of them now.'

'Yes, I will,' May promised.

'So when is this James character going to arrive?'

May reached into a pocket and produced a small wad of letters. Opening one she said, 'This was written on December twelfth and he says he has booked his passage on a ship sailing on December twenty-third – but he doesn't say when she is due to dock in Melbourne.'

'That isn't very helpful.'

'No, but he was writing in a hurry. He had to arrange the sale of his mother's house and put all his affairs in order, so he had a lot to think about.'

'Mr Croft will know,' Gus said. 'He will have the list of all the arrivals over the next month, so he knows when to expect people at his hotel.'

Croft's Hotel was where Gus had been kindly received on his first visit to Melbourne as part of the crew of the *Shenandoah* and had found a job on his return.

'Telegraph to him and ask if he can give us a date,' Mr Lavender said.

'I should like to be there when James arrives,' May said. 'I think he will be disappointed if I'm not there to greet him. Do you mind, Papa?'

'You're free to come and go as you please, my dear. If you want to make the journey, I shan't stop you.'

'I'll go with her,' Gus said unexpectedly. 'If you don't need me for a day or two.'

'Good idea. I'd be happier knowing she wasn't travelling alone. You'd better book a couple of rooms at Crofts – and one for James.'

'We need more than that,' May said. 'He's not travelling alone.'

Her father looked suspicious. 'He's not bringing a crowd of aunts and cousins and hangers-on, is he?'

'No, he's not. But he is bringing me a bridesmaid and his best man.'

'How's that, then?'

'It's a bit of a long story,' May said. 'You remember I said it was because of James I didn't get the sack from Freeman's? This all happened while you were still on the *Shenandoah*, Gus. But it starts when I was still in the workhouse. I used to help out in the nursery and one day I found that a little child, not quite two years old, we reckoned, had been left on the doorstep during the night. She was the prettiest little thing, with blonde curls and blue eyes, and I called her Angel. She had obviously been well cared for up till then, but you can imagine how unhappy she was, suddenly finding herself among all those strangers with no mama or papa.'

'Poor little mite!' Maria exclaimed.

'She cried all the time, and the women looking after the nursery couldn't put up with her, so I looked after her, whenever I could. She was quiet with me and when I walked in she used to call, 'May-me! May-me!' I loved that little girl! Then one day I went to the nursery and she wasn't there, and they told me she had been adopted, but they wouldn't say who by. I was heartbroken. The only thing she had left behind was an old rag doll that was found with her and she was absolutely devoted to. So I kept it as a souvenir. Then, years later, when I was working at Freeman's this woman came in, an Irish woman called Mrs McBride, and she had Angel with her. Of course, she was much older, about six by then, but I knew her at once and I called to her and held out my arms. I think she knew me, but Mrs McBride was furious. She sent Angel out of the room and told me I was being presumptuous. Of course, I realised later, she was ashamed that she had found Angel in the workhouse and didn't want anyone to know. She and her husband had cooked up some tale about Angel being his brother's child, born in Ireland. I didn't like Mrs McBride. She was rude and pushy and expected to be served before anyone else. But she complained about me to Mr Freeman and he made me write a letter of apology. Well, that gave me the address, so the next Sunday afternoon I went there and hung around until Angel came out with her nursemaid. I followed them to the park and when the nursemaid was busy chatting to some others I called Angel and gave her back her rag doll. I wanted to talk to her, to find out if she was happy, but she just grabbed the doll and ran back to her nursemaid. Somehow Mrs McBride must have found out it was me who gave it to her and she went to Mr Freeman and said if I wasn't sacked she would never buy another hat from Freeman's. I was telling Mrs Breckenridge about it and that was when James came to pick her up. He suggested that his mother should get all her friends to write to Mr Freeman and say that, if I was sacked, they would never buy their hats there. So he saw that sacking me would be worse for business than annoying Mrs MacBride and he kept me on. But of course I never dared go near Angel again and I thought that would be the end of the story.'

'But it isn't?' Maria said.

'I don't see where this is getting us,' her father put in.

'I'm coming to that. A few months ago I had a letter from James. He told me that a man had come into the solicitor's office where he worked and told him he was looking for a child he had left on the workhouse doorstep years before. That sounds a terrible thing to do but it seems his wife had died and left him with the little girl and he was destitute. He had a chance of a job in South Africa but he couldn't take the child with him. From his description James guessed that the child might be the one I had called Angel so he started to investigate, but before he got very far he discovered that the McBrides had sent her to Ireland, to a boarding school, but she had run away and disappeared.'

'Oh no!' Maria exclaimed. 'That's terrible! That poor child!'

'That's exactly how I felt,' May said. 'Night after night after I read that I lay awake wondering what had happened to her.'

'But I don't see what this has to do with the present situation,' her father said. 'I thought you said James was bringing her with him.'

'He is,' May told him with a smile. 'She has been found. I haven't got the full story yet, but it seems she was taken in by some gypsies and somehow ended up with a company of travelling music hall artistes. James says she has a remarkable singing voice for a child of her age. They brought her to Liverpool and somehow James and Mr Kean found her. There was some kind of confrontation with her adoptive parents but they managed to get her away, and now they are all coming here. Oh, and they are bringing a girl called Lizzie as her nursemaid.'

'I thought you said he wasn't bringing a lot of hangers-on,' her father said.

'They are not "hangers-on", if you mean they are going to expect you to support them,' May replied. 'Mr Kean is a mining engineer and he feels sure he can find work in this area. Angel and her nursemaid will live with him. But can we put them up until they get settled?'

'I don't see how. This house is big but now you and Gus are here there is only one spare bedroom. Kean and the women will have to take rooms at the Star for the time being.'

May sighed. 'Yes, I suppose you're right. I'm sure they will understand.'

'And what about you?' Maria asked. 'When are you planning to get married?'

'As soon as it can be arranged,' May said.

'Hold your horses!' Her father stubbed out the cigar he had been smoking. 'I haven't met this fellow yet. When I have, and if I think he's a suitable husband for my daughter, then we'll talk about weddings.'

'But . . .' May began to object.

'No buts! You may have had to plough your own furrow for most of your life but I'm still your father and you are still under age. You don't marry unless I say so.'

May was about to argue but Maria laid a hand on her arm and shook her head warningly. May took the hint and lowered her eyes. 'Very well, Papa. But I can go to Melbourne to meet him?'

'As long as Gus goes with you. I'll leave you to telegraph Croft's and book rooms. Now, I must get back to work. Come on, Gus.'

He stomped off with Gus and May turned to Maria. 'I thought he'd agreed . . .'

'I know,' she said soothingly. 'But it's come as a shock. He only found you and your brother a few months ago and now it looks as if he is going to lose you. He needs time to get used to the idea.

'He isn't going to lose me . . .' May began, but then it struck her that once she and James were married she would no longer live here at Freshfields. Life was going to change again. It would take some getting used to for all of them.

'He'll come round,' Maria assured her. 'Now, why don't you go to the post office and telegraph to Mr Croft and find out when the ship is due to dock?'

May threw off her momentary doubts and smiled. 'Yes, why don't I do that?'

Ten days later, she stood with Gus on the quayside in Melbourne harbour and watched the steamer carrying James and the others ease its way into its berth. She had dressed in the pale-green silk and bought a new bonnet, which she had decorated herself with white silk roses and green ribbons. As the gangplank was lowered she started to tremble. It had been such a long time. Would she even recognise James? Would he recognise her?

Gus reached out and squeezed her hand. 'Stop worrying, sis. You look a real beaut. He'll be knocked out when he sees you.'

May watched the passengers streaming down the gangplank and at first she could see no one who looked familiar. A terrible suspicion seized her. Perhaps he had changed his mind at the last moment. Perhaps instead of bringing him the ship brought a letter, explaining that he had had second thoughts. Then, suddenly, there he was, almost at the foot of the gangplank, looking exactly as she remembered him. How had she not seen him before? He stepped onto the quay and stood looking around him. He could not be sure she was there to meet him. He was wondering where he should go next.

May hastened forward, pulling Gus after her. 'James! James! Over here!'

He heard her and turned. In a few breathless seconds they covered the ground between them and then both stopped, suddenly at a loss. May had thought she would throw herself into his arms, but she felt suddenly shy. For a moment they stared at each other in silence. Then he said,

'May! At last! It's wonderful to see you.'

She swallowed and blinked back tears of joy. 'I'm so glad you're here. It's been such a long time.'

'Yes.' He seemed at a loss for words. 'How are you?'

She regained her composure. 'I'm very well, thank you. And you?'

'Very fit, thanks.'

There was a pause and she turned to her brother. 'James, you remember Gus, don't you?'

'Of course!' He shook Gus's hand. 'By George, you've changed a bit since I last saw you! The climate out here must suit you.'

'It does,' Gus agreed. 'It's good to see you again.'

James looked round. 'See who I have brought with me?' and May became aware of a tall, fair-bearded man standing behind him with a young woman holding the hand of little girl. She dropped to her knees and held out her arms. 'Angel? Do you remember me?'

The child stepped forward but not into her embrace. 'I think so,' she said composedly. 'But my name is really Amy.'

'Of course.' May straightened up. 'I must try to remember that – but I'm afraid I shall always think of you as Angel.'

'I don't mind,' the little girl said. 'I've had lots of names. I was Angelina once, but I don't like that. Then I was Maeve, when I was in Ireland.'

'Maeve?'

'It means a song thrush.'

'May,' James said, 'can I introduce Richard Kean, Amy's father?'

Kean offered his hand, a trifle shamefacedly. 'I am afraid you must think me a very heartless creature, to have left Amy as I did.'

May took his hand. 'No. I understand something of the circumstances. And I can hardly blame you, I ended up in the workhouse because my own father was unable to look after me. And if things had turned out otherwise, I should never have known Angel – I mean Amy.'

'Well, I'm delighted to meet you at last,' Richard said. 'James has told me so much about you.' He turned to the young woman. 'This is Elizabeth Findlay. She looks after Amy – and after me, when she gets a chance. Lizzie, this is May Lavender.'

May held out her hand. 'How do you do?'

Lizzie made a small curtsy. 'Please to meet you, ma'am.'

'Oh, goodness!' May exclaimed. 'You don't need to call me ma'am. There was a time when my position in the ranks of servants would have been far below yours.'

'This is May's brother, Gus,' James said. 'He's the lad who sailed on the *Shenandoah*, if you remember.'

'Of course!' Richard shook Gus's hand. 'I should like to hear more about that when we have a chance.'

'Willingly.' May could see from her brother's expression that he was pleased and flattered that this was how he was remembered, rather than as the boy who might have ended up in jail if it had not been for James's good offices.

She looked around at the little group and recalled her duties as hostess. 'You must all be tired. We've booked rooms for you at a local hotel. Shall I show you the way?'

James met her eyes and she saw tenderness vying with amusement. Then he offered his arm. 'Please, lead on.'

The little procession, followed by a couple of porters carrying the baggage, wound its way through the streets to Croft's Hotel.

'Mr and Mrs Croft were very kind to Gus the first time he came to Melbourne and they've been our friends ever since,' May explained as they walked.

And as friends they were welcomed. Mr Croft personally showed them to the rooms reserved for them and then said, 'When you are ready, please join my wife and myself in the drawing room for a cup of tea.'

Over tea the conversation ranged over the usual topics: the highs and lows of the long voyage, first impressions of Melbourne and so on. Mrs Croft recalled how her daughter Victoria had found Gus, then a boy of fourteen, sitting in the street, having been persuaded by his shipmates to drink too much rum, and brought him home with her. Gus told the visitors how on his second visit Mr Croft had given him a job as his receptionist and how, on one memorable day, the father whom he believed 'lost at sea' had walked into the hotel to book a room.

May said little, but she watched with fascination how Angel/Amy responded to any questions with almost adult composure. The little girl was a lovely as she remembered, with her blonde curls and her blue eyes, but she wondered what had happened to her in the intervening years to make her so self-assured.

The one thing May longed for was a chance to talk to James alone, but there seemed little chance of that, until he said, 'Mrs Croft, I'm intrigued by some of the exotic plants in your garden. May I go and take a closer look?'

'Of course,' their hostess replied with perfect tact. 'Perhaps May would like to show you round.'

May probably knew less about the plants than she did, but she was more than ready to seize the opportunity. She and James strolled together until they were well away from the house and sheltered by a trellis covered by a bower vine, a creeper with glossy green leaves and delicate white flowers. There they stopped by mutual, unspoken consent and looked at each other.

James said, 'I don't know what to say. You take my breath away.'

'What do you mean?'

'I just marvel at the change in you.'

'Change?' She felt a sudden stab of alarm. 'Have I changed?'

He smiled and the look in his eyes reassured her. 'Oh yes! I said goodbye to a girl, a milliner's apprentice whose beauty and intelligence captivated me but who still did not know her own power. Now I have just met a grown woman who has come into her own, self-confident and at ease – and more beautiful than ever.'

May swallowed hard. 'Oh, James! If you could only see inside my head! I'm not confident at all. I'm shaking like a jelly.'

'Why?'

'Why? Because I have longed for you for such a long time and I've been terrified that you wouldn't come, or that if you did you might find that it was all a mistake. It's not a mistake, is it?'

He took her in his arms then and held her close. 'No, my darling girl! It's not a mistake. I've had my misgivings too, but now I know it's the best thing I have ever done in my life.'

She drew back enough to look into his face. 'You're sure?'

'Quite sure – as long as you feel the same.'

'I do! I didn't know how I would feel when I finally saw you again, but as soon as I did I knew nothing had changed. And I haven't changed, either.'

'Oh, but you have,' he murmured. 'But only for the better. You are like a bud that has opened into a wonderful flower.

She looked into his eyes and breathed a long sigh of relief. 'Oh, darling! I love you so much.'

He kissed her then and eighteen months of waiting and wondering dissolved into joy.

Chapter 12

Liverpool, April 1869

Patty and Vera were sitting together in a corner of one of the many small courtyards that linked the various sections of the workhouse, enjoying the warmth of some early spring sunshine. A bucket of the inevitable potatoes was at their feet but they were cherishing a rare moment of idleness. Joyce, one of the older women who worked in the kitchen, who was with them, looked up at the sound of approaching voices.

'Hey up! Better look busy. We've got visitors.'

All three of them fell to peeling potatoes as if their lives depended on it, but squinting up without raising her head Patty saw the governor and Mrs Court escorting a well-dressed middle-aged man and a younger woman across the courtyard and into the kitchen.

'I wonder who they are,' Vera said as the little party disappeared.

'Couple of busy bodies come to poke their noses in,' Joyce said. 'Some of them fancy a bit of slumming so they can go home and feel smug because they're not like us.'

Shortly the group reappeared and Patty saw them descend the steps leading to the children's classrooms, which were situated under the chapel. She felt a little shiver of fear at the memory of those rooms, even at this distance in time. Her recollections of her days there were not happy. She knew that Miss Bale, who had terrorised her as a child, was still in charge of the girls. She had seen her escorting her class into the dining hall at meal times, but had been careful to keep out of her way in case she was recognised. She wondered what the young lady visitor would make of what she saw. Of course, Miss Bale was good at putting on a show. She would have one of the brighter, more amenable girls stand up and recite her seven times tables, or exhibit her handwriting. And if the lady spoke to any of the others none of them would dare tell her how much a stroke of the ruler hurt on cold, thin hands or how often they were forced to miss a meal to redo work that was not up to Miss Bale's exacting standards. The teacher's revenge afterwards was not something any of them would wish to contemplate.

The visitors emerged and it seemed to Patty that the lady's expression was less sanguine that it had been. She was earnestly questioning Mrs Court who was murmuring reassuring responses. As they headed back towards the governor's office they were confronted by a bizarre vision: an old lady, gaunt and grey-haired, sporting a bonnet that had once been the height of fashion but was now filthy and battered, the ribbons and flowers that decorated it now tattered and limp. In addition to this, she clutched around her narrow shoulders a silk shawl, stained and fraying at the edges.

'Oh lawks!' Joyce exclaimed, with suppressed hilarity. 'It's Mad Nelly. I wonder what they'll make of her.'

The old woman approached the visitors and made a curtsy. 'Good day to you, sir and madam. Delighted to make your acquaintance.' Her cracked voice still retained some element of sophistication.

Mrs Court stepped forward. 'Now, Nelly …'

'You will be acquainted with my papa, Sir John, of course,' the old lady continued. 'Please inform him that I am waiting for him to take me home.'

The two visitors looked at each other in consternation. Mrs Court took the old woman's arm. 'This is your home, Nelly. Now don't bother the lady and gentleman any more.' She began to urge her back in the direction she had come from.

The governor turned to his guests apologetically. 'I am sorry you were troubled. It is a sad case. I believe it is something the medical men term "delusions of grandeur". Now, if you would care to return to my house, my wife will be happy to offer you tea.'

The party moved off and Joyce let go a suppressed cackle of laughter. 'She's a caution, isn't she?'

'I think it's sad,' Patty said. 'Poor old girl!'

'You don't think it could be true, do you?' Vera asked. 'That she really has got wealthy relations somewhere?'

''Course not!' Joyce said. 'How could she have ended up in here if she had?'

The following afternoon a small girl came to inform Patty that she was wanted in Mrs Court's office. Her immediate reaction was to wonder what minor regulation she had infringed. She had a dread of being removed from her job in the kitchen, where she felt more or less at ease, and sent to another area, such as the dreaded oakum-picking shed. She knocked nervously on the office door and the superintendent looked up from her desk.

'Ah, Patty. I have a job for you.'

Patty's heart sank. 'Please, ma'am, I don't know what I've done wrong, but please don't take me out of the kitchen.'

'Done wrong?' Mrs Court looked puzzled. 'What makes you think that?'

'Nothing,' Patty mumbled in confusion. 'I just thought ...'

'Oh, never mind,' Mrs Court interrupted. 'Just sit down and listen.'

Patty sat.

'You saw the visitors who came round yesterday?'

'Yes, ma'am.' A dreadful thought struck her. Had the lady been one of her customers at the tea shop? Had she been recognised? Perhaps the strangers were on a formal visit of inspection and felt that she was being insufficiently punished for her part in the scandal.

Mrs Court was continuing to speak. 'The gentleman is Sir Basil Fanshawe. He is a wealthy shipping merchant and a member of the Vestry, which is responsible for the running of the workhouse.'

Patty's sense of impending doom increased.

'The lady is Miss Helena Thornton. They are soon to be married. It seems that Miss Thornton was interested to see round a place to which her future husband gives his time and authority. It came, I am afraid, as something of a shock to her.'

I bet it did! Patty thought. Most of the gentry have no idea what goes on in places like this.

Mrs Court went on. 'She was particularly disturbed by the children and she feels she wishes to do something to make their lives a little more cheerful. Apparently she asked one little girl what she missed most about her old home and the child replied "the cakes my mum used to make when one of us had a birthday". When Miss Thornton inquired what sort of cakes they were, the child said "ones with currants in them".' The superintendent drew a breath and expelled it in a sigh of impatience. 'So Miss Thornton has decided that every child between the ages of five and fourteen should be given a piece of cake next Sunday afternoon, to celebrate her engagement to Sir Basil. The governor feels that, rather than buy cakes in from a local baker, they should be made on the premises. Miss Thornton has given the money to provide the necessary ingredients and it has been left to me to arrange the baking. Naturally,

I immediately thought of you. There are fifty-four children of the prescribed age. Can you produce cakes for that number by next Sunday? It is only two days away.'

It took Patty a few seconds to absorb this unexpected turn of events. Then she said, 'Of course I can. I'm used to cooking for a lot of people. That is … if I can get hold of the ingredients.'

'I have already said that Miss Thornton has left money to pay for them. You had better make a list of what you need and I will send someone out for them. No, on second thoughts, it will be better for you to go yourself. I will arrange for someone to escort you to a suitable shop. Will tomorrow morning be soon enough?'

'Tomorrow, yes.' It was unbelievable. She was being treated as if she was on equal terms with the superintendent, as if things were being arranged for her convenience. Her mind was already busy with recipes, and with the practicalities of what she was being asked to do. 'I'll need time in the kitchen, the use of the oven, without being interfered with.'

'I have thought about that. There are a few hours between serving dinner and preparing the supper. Will that be long enough?'

'It should be. When are the children going to be given this cake?'

'At four o'clock. Oh, I forgot to say, Miss Thornton is going to be present herself to hand it out.'

Of course she is! Patty thought. Wouldn't want to miss the chance of playing Lady Bountiful!

Aloud she said, 'I'll have to bake tomorrow, then. It won't matter. If it is to be a fruit cake it will keep perfectly well till the next day.'

'Excellent!' Mrs Court said. 'You get on with making your list and I'll see there is someone to go with you tomorrow.'

'There's one thing,' Patty said. 'I'll need an assistant. You will not object if Vera comes with me?'

'No, no. I think that is a good choice. Vera is a very sensible young woman.'

'Oh, and I'll need paper and a pencil, if I'm going to make a list.'

'Of course. I should have thought of that.' Mrs Court took two sheets of writing paper from a folder on her desk and handed them to Patty with a pencil. 'Will this be sufficient?'

'Yes, thank you.'

'Well then.' Mrs Court got up, indicating that the interview was over. She held Patty's gaze for a moment. 'We have the opportunity to make a good impression on someone who will soon be in a position of influence, where the workhouse is concerned. It is very important that Miss Thornton is not disappointed.'

Patty returned her look. 'It's important that the children are not disappointed, too. It's them I'll be thinking of while I'm cooking.'

Back in the kitchen she relayed the gist of the conversation to Vera.

'It's a tall order, at such short notice,' Vera said. 'Can you do it?'

''Course I can, with your help.'

'Oh, you can count on that.' Vera smiled. 'I think it's really kind of Miss Thornton to arrange a treat like this.'

'Is it?' Patty said. 'She'll get her reward, playing the charitable lady with everyone looking up to her and thanking her for her generosity. I don't suppose she'll even notice the hole in her pocket. That sort of thing comes easy to some people.'

Vera put her head on one side and frowned. 'I never thought of you as being so cynical. As I see it, Miss Thornton saw how poor the children's lives are and wanted to bring a little cheer into them. I think we should applaud her for that.'

Patty rubbed a hand over her face. 'Perhaps you're right. We should give her the benefit of the doubt, I suppose.'

'We must try not to see the worst in people,' Vera said.

'We both have reason to expect the worst,' Patty said. 'But you're right. It doesn't help to always look on the dark side. And the children will be pleased, whoever pays for the cakes.'

'Exactly,' Vera said. 'So let's get busy. What are you going to need?'

By supper time Patty had her list and next morning one of the wardresses arrived to escort her and Vera into the city. Patty was careful not to choose any of the shops from which Freeman's had bought their goods, in case she was recognised, but it was a joy just to go into a grocer's and smell the familiar odours of spices and dried fruits. The wardress had a purse with the money but it was Vera who carefully noted down the prices against Patty's list.

When they had everything on it she added it up and said, 'There's money over. Are you sure we have enough of everything?'

'Easily,' Patty said. 'I've worked it all out. What shall we do with the rest? We can't give it back.'

'I have an idea,' Vera said. 'We could ice the cakes, that would make them extra special.'

So they added icing sugar to the list and then, again at Vera's suggestion, some cochineal to colour it.

Back in the kitchen at the workhouse Patty set to work and with Vera's help the first batch of cakes were soon in the oven. Patty had had the presence of mind to add several bun tins to her list, knowing that no such things had ever been required there before. When they were cool Vera set to work icing them while Patty got on with the next batch.

'I've had a thought,' Vera announced.

'What now?'

'This whole thing is supposed to be in celebration of Helena Thornton's engagement to Sir Basil Fanshawe, isn't it?

'That's what Mrs C. told me.'

'Suppose we were to decorate each cake with their initials in pink icing.'

'That's a lot of extra work.'

'But it would make it clear to the children why they are being given them.'

'They won't ask why,' Patty said. 'They'll just ask for more – which they won't get.'

'I know that,' Vera said. 'That's not the point.'

'So what is?'

'You did say Miss Thornton is coming to hand them out in person, didn't you?'

'Yes.'

'If she sees that we have taken the extra trouble, as a compliment to her and Sir Basil, it will make a good impression, don't you think?'

'I suppose so. But I can't see why we should bother. Chances are we shall never set eyes on either of them again.'

'Think about it! If we are ever going to achieve our ambition of having our own shop, we shall need all the help we can get. Sir Basil is on the Vestry committee. If we can make a good impression on him, he might help us one day.'

'I don't see how.'

'Nor do I, at the moment. But it can't hurt to have an important man on our side. And one day, if ... *when* we open our shop, Miss Thornton, or Lady Helena as she will be then, might be one of our first patrons.'

Patty stopped dolloping spoonfuls of mixture into tins and looked at her friend. 'You're right. I would never have thought that far ahead. You're much cleverer than me, Vera.'

'No, I'm not. We just have different talents, that's all. That's why it will be so good for us to work together.'

Patty reached out to touch her arm, then saw that her hand was covered in flour and drew it back. 'I'm that glad I met you.'

Vera smiled at her. 'Me, too.'

It took a long time to add the combined HB initials on every cake, but when they had finished Patty looked them over with satisfaction. 'I'd have been happy to serve those in Freeman's tea shop, if I was still there.'

'You'll be serving them in your own shop one day,' Vera promised.

'Taste one,' Patty said. 'I made a few extra.'

They sampled the cakes in silence, relishing the sweetness after so many days of bland, unappealing food. As they were storing them away ready for the following day a figure appeared in the doorway.

'I wonder if I could trouble you for one of your cakes?' said a quavering voice.

Patty looked round to see the gaunt outline of Mad Nelly supporting herself with one hand on the door jamb.

'Now then, Nelly,' Vera said. 'These are for the children, not for everyone else.'

'You were eating one,' the old woman pointed out.

'Yes, but we cooked them,' Vera said, slightly embarrassed.

'Oh, come on,' Patty said. 'We can spare one more. Here you are, Nelly.'

A bony hand shot out and the cake was rapidly crammed into the toothless mouth. Nelly chewed and swallowed and licked her lips. 'Thank you. That was kind.' A pause. Then, 'And my name is Eleanor.'

Patty smiled at her. 'As you wish, Eleanor. Now, off you go. And don't tell anyone else, will you.'

The old woman drew herself up. 'A lady knows when to be discreet.'

As the door closed behind her Vera said, 'I wonder where she learned to speak like that.'

'My guess is she was in service in a great house somewhere and picked it up from listening to the gentry,' Patty said. 'There were a few like that when I was at Speke Hall, parlourmaids and footmen, trying to make out they were a cut above the rest of us.'

The next afternoon Patty and Vera set out their cakes in the dining hall, making them look as attractive as they could on the chipped dinner plates. Patty knew they would be greeted with delight by the children, but she could not suppress a twinge of nervousness about Miss Thornton's reaction. Beside the kind of confectionery she was used to, these must look very unexciting, she thought. The children filed in, with a suppressed hum of anticipation, and took their places on the long benches.

They were all on their best behaviour. No one wanted to miss a treat like this.

When they were all assembled, the governor and Mrs Court escorted Miss Thornton to the top of the room, where Patty and Vera waited. When she saw the cakes Helena gave a little gasp and clasped her hands in front to her face.

'Oh, how pretty you've made them! And you've put our initials on them. What a lovely idea!' She looked at the governor. 'Who is responsible for these?'

The governor puffed out his chest as if he had made the cakes with his own hands. 'They were produced here, in our own kitchens, I am happy to say.'

Mrs Court stepped forward. 'They were made by these two young women, Miss Thornton. May I present Patty Jenkins and Vera Aston?'

To Patty's surprise Helena held out her hand. 'I'm delighted to meet you. And thank you for making my little idea turn out so well.'

Patty briefly touched the outstretched hand and curtsied. 'Honoured, ma'am.'

Helena shook hands with Vera, too. Then Patty offered one of the less cracked plates, on which she had carefully arranged three of the cakes.

'Will you try one, ma'am?'

'Oh, I don't know. I should not wish to deprive one of the children. But they do look tempting.'

'It's all right, ma'am,' Patty said. 'I made enough to go round.'

'Oh, well, in that case …' Helena took a cake and bit into it. Behind her, Patty could almost hear the communal sucking in of saliva from the watching children. 'It's delicious!' Helena declared. 'Beautifully baked.'

Patty offered the other two cakes to the governor and Mrs Court and they ate them with appreciative murmurs. Helena turned to look at the long rows of boys and girls.

'Now, shall we let the children have theirs?'

'Would you like them to come up one by one, so they can thank you properly?' the governor asked.

'Oh, no! That would mean some of them would have to wait such a long time,' was the reply. 'Why don't we just pass the cakes along the tables?'

'Beg pardon, ma'am,' Patty said. 'I think that way there might be none left by the time the plate got to the end.'

'I see what you mean,' Helena said. 'Well, perhaps you could help me to hand them out. If I take one side of the girls' table and you take the other, perhaps Mrs Court and Miss Aston could do the same with the boys.'

Patty saw Mrs Court's eyebrows go up at Vera being called 'Miss Aston' but she said nothing and Helena was already making her way down the table with a plate in her hand. Patty followed her example. Eager hands reached out and young voices repeated again and again, 'thank you, ma'am'. Some of the children ate their cakes in two or three bites, as if afraid that they might be snatched away from them. Others nibbled slowly, savouring the taste, trying to make the pleasure last as long as possible. Apart from the words of thanks, no one spoke, but after a few minutes there was a kind of collective sigh, a mixture of satisfaction and regret.

When all the cakes had been handed out and they returned to the top table Patty saw to her amazement that there were tears in Helena's eyes.

'Poor little mites. It was such a small thing. Did it really mean so much to them?'

'Oh yes, ma'am,' Patty said. 'They'll remember today for months.'

'You speak as if you knew how they feel.'

'I do, ma'am. You see, I grew up here.'

'You did? But you have not spent your whole life here, surely?'

'Oh no, ma'am.' Patty was wishing she had not spoken. 'No, I left when I was fourteen. I ... I've had a few jobs since then but ...'

'But you lost the last one and could not find another? I'm amazed. I should think many people would be glad to employ someone with your talent for baking.'

The conversation was ended, to Patty's relief, by the governor. 'Well, Miss Thornton, as you can see the children are all very grateful for your kind thought. Now, perhaps we should adjourn to my house for tea?'

Helena nodded and turned to Patty and Vera. 'Thank you again. I know it must have been a lot of extra work. I really appreciate your efforts – and I shall not forget, any more than the children will.'

When she had gone, and the children were filing out of the hall, Vera said, 'What did I tell you? We've made a good impression, and one day that may come in very useful.'

A few days later, in a pause in the normal work of preparing supper, Vera said, 'I've got a new idea.'

Patty looked up. It had been a long day and she was tired, and Vera's ideas usually meant extra work. 'What now?'

'The cakes went down really well, didn't they?'

'Yes. But it was a once in a blue moon thing. It won't happen again.'

'Not like that, of course. But listen, we get paid a few pence every week for our work in the kitchen. If we pool our resources, by the time the next Thursday we are allowed out on comes round we should have enough to buy the ingredients to make maybe a dozen buns. They don't have to be anything elaborate, like the cakes we made for the children. There are lots of people who would be happy to pay a penny for a sweet bun.'

'I suppose so,' Patty said cautiously. 'But will we be allowed to do it?'

'Who would know? We shall not be using any of the stuff supplied by the management. And no one who enjoys the buns is going to let on.'

'But I don't see the point,' Patty said. 'Why are we doing it?'

'So we make a profit. And by the next month, we can buy enough to make twice as many. Do you see where I'm going?'

'I'm no good at adding up,' Patty said. 'I always got my sums wrong when I was in Miss Bale's class. But I don't see the point, if we are always going to spend any profit we make on ingredients for the next month.'

'But there will come a point when we don't have to do that. We can buy enough flour and butter and what not for two dozen buns and have money left over – and that we can save. See?'

'I think so,' Patty said. 'But why are we doing it?'

'Because we've already agreed that if we are going to start a business of our own we need capital.'

'But it will take months – years – to save enough for that.'

'Maybe. But which is better, to save for five years so we can get out of this place – or to make up our minds that we're going to be here for the rest of our lives?' Vera asked.

Patty summoned up a weary smile. 'You win. You're right as usual.' She reached out and caught hold of Vera's hand. 'I'm so lucky I've got you for a friend.'

Vera squeezed her hand in return. 'The feeling's mutual.'

As spring turned to summer it was clear that Vera's plan was working. On the Friday after the monthly exit day there was always a queue outside the kitchen door of women ready with their pennies for one of Patty's cakes, and soon they were able to set aside some of the money. It was a very small amount, which Vera kept concealed in a jar labelled Dried Fruit, under a bag of currants, but for both of them it represented hope for the future. Every month, also, when the queue had dispersed one gaunt figure hung on in the doorway. Mad Nelly was too frail and unreliable to be set to work, so she never had any money, but Patty always kept back one cake to give to her.

On the third Thursday in June the two friends were ready as usual to set out for the shops. As they stepped out of the gate, Patty saw a familiar figure waiting.

'Lucy! Whatever are you doing here?'

The girl rushed forward and threw her arms around Patty. 'Oh, Patty! I'm so sorry! So sorry!'

'Sorry for what?' Patty asked, holding her off to look into her face.

'To see you here. Someone told me you were, but I couldn't believe them. It's not fair!'

'Maybe it is, maybe it isn't,' Patty said. 'Who told you I was here?'

'Susan. We grew up here together, but she's younger than me so she's still here. We sometimes meet up on these Thursdays, when I can get away. You chose me to come and work at Freeman's and I've never forgotten that and I'll always be grateful. So when Sue said she'd seen you here I had to come and see you. But it's all wrong! You shouldn't be here.'

'Listen, Lucy,' Patty said, taking hold of her arm. 'I made a stupid mistake. I let a man talk me into something I knew was wrong and now I'm paying for it. Just don't let the same thing happen to you.'

'I won't,' Lucy promised. 'I'll try not to.' She delved into a pocket in her skirt. 'Oh, look, I nearly forgot. This came for you. I've been keeping it till I could come and see you.'

She held out an envelope. Patty took it with a sudden lift of her heart. It was postmarked Australia.

Freshfields
Rutherglen,
Victoria
April 3rd 1869

Dear Patty,

I am married! James and I were wed on March 20th at St Stephen's Church here in Rutherglen. He arrived here in February, just as he promised, and life has been a wonderful whirl since then. He was determined to set himself up in his own career as soon as possible and our first thought was that he might apply to one of the established solicitors' practices in Beechworth to see if they would take him as a partner. I was not really happy with this idea as Beechworth is several hours' drive from here and it would mean I could not see my father and Gus as often as I would wish to. But then Father pointed out that anyone in this area who needs the services of a lawyer also has to make a long drive to Beechworth, as there is no one closer, so he suggested that James should set up on his own account in Rutherglen. So he has rented a couple of rooms above the draper's shop and almost as soon as he put up his brass plate he had his first client! It now looks as though he will soon have a thriving practice.

At present we are living at Freshfields, but we have purchased a plot of land not far away, overlooking the lake, and we are having a house of our own built there.

For the first time in my life I shall have a home of my own and it means I can still see the rest of my family every day, so it is the ideal solution.

You can imagine how busy we have been in the last few weeks, what with planning our new home and preparing for the wedding but somehow it all got done and the great day arrived – a day I have so often dreamed of and which I was afraid might never happen.

Of course, one important thing I needed to arrange was my wedding gown. I know that white is now the fashionable colour, since the Queen wore it for her wedding, but I decided that a white gown would not have any practical use afterwards, so I chose a beautiful cream silk. There is a woman in the nearby town of Chiltern who is a skilled dressmaker and has made several dresses for me since I arrived here. We designed the dress between us. It is Empire style, with a short train and a neckline trimmed with a deep fringe of cream lace. The waist and the back of the dress are ornamented with bows of pale lavender-blue ribbon and I made myself a bonnet trimmed with flowers in the same colour. My little bridesmaid wore a dress of the same blue with a circlet of lavender and white flowers on her hair.

Oh yes! I must explain about my bridesmaid. Can you believe it was Angel? If anyone had told me when I was holding her on my knee in the nursery at the workhouse that one day she would be my bridesmaid, I should have thought it was a fairy tale! But let me explain how it came about. You will remember that I told you in one

*of my letters that her real father had turned up out of
the blue at the solicitor's office where James worked
and asked for their help in finding her, but when they
enquired they discovered that she had been sent away
to school in Ireland and had run away and no one knew
where she was. Well, she has had a most extraordinary
time. She was taken in by some gypsies and then liter-
ally sold to a company of travelling music hall perform-
ers. Did I mention before that she has a most beautiful
singing voice? It seems she became quite the star of
the show and all was going well until the company was
invited to perform in Liverpool. Angel's face was on
all the bill boards and her adoptive father saw it and
actually kidnapped her from the theatre, but James and
Richard (that's her father) saw it too and somehow managed to get her away. Richard and James have become
fast friends, in fact he acted as James's best man. He
is a mining engineer and is convinced that it will not
be difficult for him to find work here so he decided to
bring Angel – I mean Amy – and her nursemaid/govern-
ess, a delightful young woman called Lizzie Findlay, to
Australia with James.*

*Amy is a remarkable child. She is only nine years
old but she is so self-possessed that you would think
she was much older. I suppose after her experiences in
Ireland that is not surprising. But she can also be quite
wilful and likes to get her own way. There has been
some discussion about her education. Richard feels she
should go to the local school and learn to mix with other*

children, but I am afraid that she will find it hard to fit in. She learned a lot at her convent school, although she was only there for a short time, and he and Lizzie have been teaching her on the long voyage out, and I fancy she is far beyond the standard of most of the local children of her own age. It is a problem, but I suppose I must leave it to her father and not interfere. The one thing we all agree on is that she must be allowed to develop her amazing talent for singing, though how that is to be managed is another question.

Well, I think that is all my news for now. It seems to be a long time since I heard from you. I expect you are very busy managing the tea shop. I'm so glad Mr Freeman recognised what a wonderful cook you are and gave you that chance. He has always done so much for both of us. Please give him my regards when you see him. And write soon!

With love from your old friend,
May

Chapter 13

Liverpool, August 1869

'Gov'nor wants you.

'Who, me?'

'Both of you.'

Patty and Vera exchanged glances. 'Now what?' Vera asked.

'He's probably found out about our little scheme and wants to stop us.'

'That's not fair!' Vera exclaimed.

They arrived at the governor's office ready to face another injustice at the hands of authority, but he greeted them with a smile – as far as that could be deduced from among the thicket of whiskers that decorated his face.

'Ah, my two bakers! Come in, come in. I have an opportunity for you.'

'Sir?'

'You did very well with the cakes for Miss Thornton. Now I have an idea that will give you a chance to show your skills to a wider audience. You will not have met my daughter, Catherine, of course ...'

You're hardly likely to have introduced her to a couple of paupers, Patty thought.

Aloud she said simply, 'No, sir.'

'She has been away in France, to complete her education,' the governor went on. 'She returned yesterday and tomorrow is her birthday. She will be seventeen. My wife and I have decided to give a small party to celebrate it and to introduce her to society. Nothing too grand. A tea party for about forty people. And it occurred to me that this would be a very good opportunity for you two to demonstrate your culinary skills.'

You old cheapskate! Patty thought. What you really mean is, you can see a way of entertaining your friends on the cheap.

Vera asked, 'What exactly did you have in mind, sir?'

'Nothing elaborate. Some sandwiches, sausage rolls perhaps, scones and cakes. And a birthday cake, of course.' He looked at Patty. 'Something special, with icing perhaps and decorations.'

'When do you want this to happen?' Vera, always practical, asked.

'On Saturday, a week tomorrow.'

Vera caught Patty's eye. 'That means a good deal of extra work, for both of us,' she said. 'Do you propose to give us some form of remuneration?'

'Remuneration?' The governor's bushy eyebrows disappeared into his shaggy hair. 'You are here to work.

This is a workhouse. You are expected to earn your keep.'

Patty touched Vera's sleeve and gave her a warning look. Anything that could be interpreted as insubordination could bring down the governor's wrath on their heads and result in punishment.

Vera, however, was not to be deterred. 'We do that already, in the kitchen, sir. You are asking us to do something over and beyond our normal duties. I thought you might regard it as just to reward our efforts in some way.'

'Ah, reward your efforts, yes, well ...' He could see a way of agreeing without losing face. 'If what you provide comes up to expectations, you may be sure that some recognition of your work will be forthcoming. And I shall, of course, provide you with any funds required for the purchase of ingredients.'

Vera looked at Patty, who said, 'We'll do our best for you, sir.'

Back in the kitchen she said angrily, 'That mean old devil! He could afford to bring in caterers. He just wants to do it on the cheap.'

'That's obvious,' Vera agreed. 'But there's something in what he said about an opportunity.'

'What do you mean?'

'Well, I don't know who he plans to invite to this party, but they will be people of some standing, presumably. If we can impress them – well, who knows where it might lead.'

'If they think I'm going to work my fingers to the bone to feed their guests for no extra outlay on their side, they can think again,' Patty said. 'I'll do it this once, but I'm not going to let the governor lend me out to his friends as a cheap cook.'

'No, of course not,' Vera said. 'I'm talking about getting out of here, permanently.'

'You think someone might help us to get the backing we need for the tea shop?'

'You never know. I think it's worth pulling out all the stops to put on the best show we can manage,' Vera said.

The governor's eyebrows shot up again when Patty presented him with a list of necessary provisions, but he handed over the money and this time they were allowed to go out unsupervised to buy them. Vera sought, and was granted, an interview with the governor's wife and came back having arranged details of seating arrangements, dishes, plates, cups, saucers, napkins and other requisites. Patty chewed her pencil and trawled her memory for recipes. Most of the choices were simple enough: cakes and pastries she had made many times for sale in the tea shop. The thing that gave her most trouble was the birthday cake. Should it be a fruit cake, or a sponge? The governor wanted something spectacular ... of course! A Savoy cake! The perfect centrepiece for the table.

During the Friday and the Saturday morning of the following week Patty and Vera worked non-stop. Vera revealed a hitherto unsuspected talent for making bread, so Patty delegated the sandwiches to her, while she concentrated on the sweet things. There were scones and chocolate cakes and the ever popular Victoria sponge and little fairy cakes flavoured with cinnamon. The only thing she did not make was gingerbread. As soon as the midday meal was over, they enlisted the aid of two of the porters to carry the whole lot to the governor's house, which was adjacent to the workhouse itself. It was a pleasant, double-fronted building with sash windows, set in an extensive garden. The weather was fine and a marquee had been erected on the lawn, with long tables spread with white cloths. The governor's wife was already there, chivvying a maid servant who was laying plates and cups and saucers. Patty and Vera set out the dishes of delicacies and then Patty placed the Savoy cake in the centre of the top table and removed the cloth which covered it. The sugar coating had set perfectly and Patty had adorned it with candied rose petals and crystallised fruit so that it glowed in the sunlight that filtered in through the canvas.

The governor's wife clapped her hands and exclaimed, 'Oh, now that is perfect! How clever of you.'

The visitors were beginning to arrive and Patty and Vera stationed themselves behind the tea urn, ready to serve.

'Oh, look!' Vera murmured. 'Miss Thornton is here, with Sir Basil.'

'She'll be Lady Helena now, won't she?' Patty asked.

'I don't see a wedding ring,' Vera replied, 'so I suppose they are not married yet.'

Catherine, the governor's daughter, arrived, in an over-elaborate pink dress that clashed with her tawny hair. The guests filed past her, offering gifts and good wishes, and took their places at the tables. Vera and the maid servant handed out cups of tea, which Patty dispensed, and the sandwiches and cakes began to disappear.

'I hope we've made enough,' Vera whispered.

'There should be,' Patty responded, 'unless none of them have eaten dinner.'

'Everyone's admiring your Savoy cake,' Vera told her.

To Patty's relief, before the table had been completely cleared, the governor rose and made a short speech and then Catherine cut the cake. As they handed the plates round she heard snatches of conversation.

'What a beautiful cake! I wonder where it came from.'

'I heard someone say it was made here, by one of the women in workhouse.'

'No! I don't believe it!'

'Really, that's what I was told …'

After that, the party began to break up and the guests stood around chatting. To her surprise, Patty saw Helena Thornton approaching.

'Miss Jenkins, and Miss Aston, we meet again.'

'Yes, ma'am.'

'You have really excelled yourselves today. Is all this your work?'

'Yes, ma'am.'

'Even the Savoy cake?'

'Yes, ma'am.'

'That was all Patty's,' Vera put in. 'She's a brilliant pastry chef.'

'She is indeed.' Helena paused. 'I can't help thinking … No, never mind.'

'Helena?' Sir Basil called from the other side of the marquee.

She looked round and then turned to smile at Patty and Vera. 'I must see what he wants. I'm delighted to have met you both again. Goodbye.'

'I wonder what she was going to say,' Vera mused.

'Never mind that,' Patty said. 'We've got this lot to clear up.'

When everything had been washed and tidied away Vera sat down to work out what they had spent.

'There's five shillings and threepence halfpenny left-over from what the governor gave us,' she said.

Patty looked at her. 'You sure?'

'Oh yes.'

'I mean, would the old man know, if it was only say … three shillings.'

'Are you suggesting we should keep some of it?'

'You were the one who said we should be – what's the word? – remunerated.'

Vera shook her head. 'Not like this. That would be dishonest.'

Patty felt herself blush. 'Yes, of course it would. I was only joking.'

Next morning they went to the governor's office after church and handed over the surplus money.

'An excellent effort yesterday,' he commented. 'Everyone was full of praise for what we had achieved.'

'We?' Patty queried mentally.

'I'm glad you were satisfied, sir,' Vera said primly. And waited.

There was a long pause. The governor looked up from counting the money. 'Ah ... yes. The question of reward ... a job well done is its own satisfaction, is it not?'

Neither of the women spoke.

'Yes, quite, but the Bible tells us the labourer is worthy of his hire. Here ...' He pushed two shilling pieces across the table.

Vera scooped them up. 'Thank you, sir.'

Outside Vera gave a small laugh. 'Well, it's better than nothing. It would have taken us a couple of months to accumulate this much.'

'It's still an awful long way off what we need, though,' Patty said.

Vera squeezed her arm. 'Never mind. Who knows what might come along next?'

She was answered surprisingly rapidly. Two days later they were again summoned to the governor's office.

'Now what?' Patty muttered. 'If he wants me to make his daughter's wedding cake he will have to pay me the same as he'd pay a baker.'

'I think it's bit early for that,' Vera said with a chuckle.

They were surprised to find Helena Thornton with the governor. She smiled at them both and said, 'I'm so glad to see you again.'

'Miss Thornton has a suggestion to put to you,' the governor said gruffly. 'It is not one that I can fully endorse, but I must bow to her judgement.' He turned to his guest. 'Miss Thornton?'

'As you know,' Helena said, 'I am about to be married to Sir Basil Fanshawe. The wedding will take place on September the first. We are having a house built on the other side of the river, not far from Birkenhead. It is a pleasant, rural location away from the soot and smoke of the city and now that the ferry service is so frequent it will be easy for Sir Basil to travel to and from his office every day. Hitherto Sir Basil has not needed a separate establishment. He has lived in a bachelor apartment in the city with just a man servant to attend to his needs, but now we shall, of course, need staff to run the new house. Sir Basil has appointed as housekeeper an elderly lady, Miss Eliza Banks, who used to be his nurse when he was a small boy. She has since had several other positions but is now of an age where she finds the care of small children too demanding, and Sir Basil feels an obligation to see that she does not want in her old age.' Helena smiled but gave a small gesture that suggested that, although she accepted her finance's motives, she was not entirely happy about the outcome. 'But the fact is that I do not believe that she is capable of the work involved in running a household, either. So I have decided that what is needed is a young, energetic woman as under-housekeeper, to fulfil those duties which are beyond Miss Banks's strength.' She paused and looked from Vera to Patty. 'We do not want a large establishment. Both Sir Basil and I prefer a quiet life. But I shall, of course, need a cook. I have seen that you are capable, between you, of organising and catering for an event like the party the other day. I am offering you the posts of under-housekeeper and cook. What do you say?'

Patty and Vera stared at her and then at each other, bereft of words. Then Vera said, 'You do know, ma'am, that we have no references.'

The governor cleared his throat. 'I have already pointed out that fact to Miss Thornton.'

Helena rearranged her gloves in her lap and leaned forward slightly. 'Let me explain something. Sir Basil and I are both interested in social progress. We feel that there are a great many injustices in the way society operates at present. It seems to me that your present … situation … is an example of that injustice, and one which I can go some way towards remedying. I am not offering you charity. I am offering you both jobs, which will allow you to return to an independent life. And do not think that I am doing it because I think I can get your services for less than what I would have to pay on the open market. The question of wages can be settled later but you will not find Sir Basil ungenerous. Will you accept?'

'Of course we will!' There was a catch in Vera's voice which was close to tears. 'I can't thank you enough for the opportunity, ma'am. And I promise you won't regret it.'

Helena turned her eyes to Patty, but she did not reply at once. She was struggling with the demands of her conscience. At last she said, 'Ma'am, might I speak to you in private?'

Helena looked surprised but nodded at once. 'Of course.' She turned to the governor. 'I wonder ... could we ... ?'

The governor was plainly not pleased at being asked to vacate his own office, but he hauled himself to his feet and said gruffly, 'Of course. We shall be outside when you are ready.'

He waved Vera out ahead of him and closed the door. Helena turned to Patty.

'Why don't you sit down? There is no need to stand on ceremony.'

Patty lowered herself onto the chair she indicated, twisting her hands in her apron as she tried to order her thoughts.

'Now,' Helena said gently, 'what is it that is troubling you?'

In broken sentences Patty explained why she had been dismissed from her first position at Speke Hall, and described her brief time on the streets and her rescue by May. She told Helena how Mr Freeman had helped her and given her a job and the circumstances that had led to her being dismissed again. Finally she confessed how she had earned her living afterwards, until a brutal beating had brought that to an end. By the time she finished her cheeks were wet with tears.

Helena leaned forward and laid her hand on Patty's. 'You poor creature! I had no idea. What a life you have had! Brought up here as an orphan, half-starved in your first job, and then to have to resort to that ... that terrible life to keep yourself alive. But you overcame all that! You worked yourself up to a position of responsibility and trust. I admire that! And then to lose it all because of the criminal machinations of that horrible man! I can't begin to imagine all that you have suffered. But in spite of everything, you can still produce those delicious cakes that gave so much pleasure to those poor children. You still have your skills and there is nothing in what you have told me to be ashamed of.'

'But ...' Patty murmured, 'but I am ashamed – of what I let men do to me.'

'The shame is theirs!' Helena said firmly. 'And society's, that you were forced to stoop to that to keep body and soul together.' She stood up. 'Nothing of what you have told me makes me want to change my mind. If you will come and cook for me and for my future husband, we shall think ourselves fortunate.' She smiled and held out her hand. 'Do we have a deal?'

Patty rubbed her hand on her apron and swallowed. 'Oh yes, ma'am. If you still want me, I'll come and work for you, and be grateful for the chance.'

The house that Sir Basil had built for his bride was called Avalon. It stood at the end of a leafy lane on the slopes of Bidston Hill, a few miles outside the town of Birkenhead. It was built of red brick with a central section flanked by two wings surmounted by tall gables. It stood alone, the land around it, still raw and bare from recent clearing, sloping away towards the distant Mersey estuary. To Patty, it looked like something out of a fairy tale.

In the weeks between their interview with Helena Thornton and their first sight of the house she had felt she was living in a dream world. A dressmaker had arrived at the workhouse to take her measurements, and Vera's, and a few days later boxes had been delivered containing, for each of them, two black dresses, one slightly finer and more elaborate than the other, two white aprons, one plain for working, the other trimmed with lace for special occasions, two mob caps similarly differentiated, a black woollen cape lined with crimson silk and stays and cotton chemises to go underneath. Patty was reminded of the uniform she had worn while working at Freeman's, though these were better quality. She remembered, too, with a shudder, the yellow silk and the fur-lined cloak that had led her into so much trouble. She had no wish for such finery now. Vera's reaction was rather different. Looking at herself when the dressmaker came for a final fitting, she had made a small grimace and commented that she had never thought to see herself in a servant's dress.

That morning they had been collected in a hansom cab and driven down to the pier head where the ferry was waiting. Patty had never ventured across the Mersey and as the boat pulled out into mid-stream it felt as if she was going into foreign territory. On the far side a smart pony trap was waiting for them, driven by a lad who introduced himself as Barney. He had sandy hair and freckles and a smile so wide it seemed to split his face from ear to ear – and an accent that was pure Liverpool scouse. Patty stared around her as he drove them through Birkenhead; around a square lined with elegant houses, some of them not yet quite completed; up a long, straight road past an imposing gateway that opened into an area of wide lawns and flowerbeds rich with autumn colour.

'What's in there?' she asked.

'That's the park,' he replied.

'Who's it belong to?'

'Us. Well, the town, but anyone can use it.'

'Really?'

'Yes, honest! You should go and take a stroll round one day.'

Leaving the railings bordering the park behind they were out in the countryside. There were fields where cows and horses grazed. Patty knew what cows were because she had seen pictures outside the dairies in the city. She was less sure about smaller creatures covered in grey wool.

'They're sheep,' Vera said, in surprise. 'Surely you've seen sheep before?'

'Not many sheep in Liverpool,' Patty said.

Vera stretched her arms. 'Oh, isn't it wonderful to be out in the open air again. I'd almost forgotten how beautiful the countryside is at this time of year. Just look at that beech tree.'

'What tree?'

'Over there, with the leaves all golden in the sunlight.' Vera turned her gaze on Patty with a kind of wonderment. 'You don't know the country at all, do you?'

'Never been there,' Patty said.

Vera leaned over and patted her hand. 'Don't worry. I'll teach you the names of the trees and the birds – and the animals. I grew up in countryside like this. You'll soon feel at home.'

Patty had grave doubts about that, but she said nothing. Now, standing outside the house that would be her home for the foreseeable future she felt even more out of her depth.

The front door opened and an elderly woman dressed in grey came down the steps to meet them. Her plump body gave the impression of struggling to break free of its restraining corset and her severely parted white hair framed a round, red-cheeked face. Her eyes were a faded blue, but they surveyed Vera and Patty with a sharp, critical gaze.

'So, you are the two workhouse girls. Which is which?'

Beside her, Patty sensed Vera draw herself straighter. She spoke in the polished tones which she had sometimes tried to roughen in the company of the other women in the workhouse.

'Good morning. My name is Vera Aston. How do you do?'

If the older woman was taken aback, she did not show it. 'And you?' she said, looking at Patty.

Under the gaze of those sharp eyes Patty could not muster the same confidence. Old habits of deference asserted themselves. 'If you please, ma'am, I'm Patty Jenkins.'

'Very good. I am Nanny Banks. I nursed Sir Basil as a child and now I am housekeeper here. You may call me Miss Banks. Come along, this way. I will show you around.' She started up the steps and Patty and Vera followed. Over her shoulder Nanny Banks said, 'The house is empty at the moment, as you know. Sir Basil and Lady Helena are still in Italy on their honeymoon. We have two weeks to get everything straight, ready for them to move in.'

She opened the imposing front door, which was set in a stone surround ending in a pointed arch and flanked by two stained glass windows, one of which depicted a knight in armour and the other a beautiful lady in a long, flowing gown. This led into a large hall, which stretched the full depth of the building. An arched ceiling supported by rafters towered above their heads and a broad staircase of polished wood led up to a galleried landing. Passages went off on either side, into the two wings. Miss Banks took the right hand one. Double doors, carved with patterns of fruit and flowers, opened onto a big room facing the back of the house. Large windows looked out to what would one day be, Patty supposed, a garden, and the other walls were papered in a design of twisting branches from which hung oranges and lemons. There was no furniture and a smell of new paint and wallpaper paste hung in the air.

'This will be the dining room,' Miss Banks informed them.

'The wallpaper is ... unusual,' Vera ventured.

Miss Banks sniffed. 'It's some new-fangled idea of Sir Basil's. All the designs are by a man called William Morris, or his friends. I can't say I approve, but who am I to criticise?'

Two doors on the other side of the passage, facing the front of the house, were designated as the billiard room and the library. On the far side of the hall, corresponding to the dining room, was the drawing room, papered with a complex design of blue flowers and twining greenery. The rooms at the front on this side were to be the morning room and the music room. The morning room had paper in a cheerful design of birds against a golden trellis, but in the music room one whole wall was painted a glowing turquoise blue. Patty gazed around in fascination. She had never seen rooms so full of colour.

Upstairs there were five bedrooms and a modern bathroom and two WCs, and a suite of interconnected rooms designated optimistically as 'the nursery'. On the top floor, under the sloping gable roofs, were the servants' rooms. Women above the right hand wing, men above the left.

'There's only young Barney at the moment,' Miss Banks announced, 'but of course Mr Charles, Sir Basil's man, will sleep there when they get back.'

Miss Banks had a bedroom and a sitting room, with a fireplace in which a fire had been lit although the September day was warm. Vera and Patty each had a room of their own, and there was another for Lady Helena's personal maid, who would return with her mistress. These rooms were the only ones furnished at the present. Patty looked round hers. There was a bed, with a comfortable mattress and a bright patchwork coverlet; a rag rug on the floor; a washstand and a chest of drawers and a hanging rail in one corner. She had to bend to look out of the window, which was situated under the eaves, but when she did so she caught her breath. She could see across the garden and over the tops of the trees that hemmed it in, clear away to the roofs of Birkenhead and the broad estuary of the Mersey and beyond that the roofs and smoking chimneys of Liverpool. She had never known an outlook so vast and for a moment it gave her a feeling of vertigo, as if she might be drawn out of the window and into the void beyond.

There was no more time to contemplate it. Miss Banks was at the door.

'Leave your things, and I'll show you the kitchen. You'll be wanting to get to work. The men will be wanting their dinner.'

The reference to 'the men' puzzled Patty. So far she had seen no one who fitted that description, with the possible exception of Barney, but she followed the housekeeper down the back stairs without question. The kitchen was in a semi-basement, but because the house was built on a sloping site it had large windows looking out onto a yard with outbuildings beyond. There was a big range, which was already alight, and a modern gas cooker. Copper pots and pans hung on the walls and a large deal table occupied the centre of the room.

'You'll be familiar with one of these contraptions, I suppose.' Miss Banks indicted the cooker with an expression that suggested she regarded it with grave suspicion. Patty was happy to agree that she was, since Mr Freeman had had one installed in the department store's kitchen.

On either side of the passageway leading to the kitchen there were two doors, one labelled 'Housekeeper – Private' and the other 'Butler – Private'. Miss Banks nodded from one to the other.

'My office – and Mr Charles will have the use of the other.'

Patty and Vera exchanged glances at the possessive note in the old woman's voice.

Leading off the kitchen was a spacious larder and beyond that was the laundry and the boiler room. Here the mystery that had puzzled Patty was at least partly resolved. A big man with a weather-beaten face and hair greying at the temples straightened up from tending the boiler and nodded at Miss Banks with just enough respect to establish his own independent status.

'It's going fine now, ma'am. You'll have plenty of hot water.'

'Thank you.' The housekeeper turned to Patty. 'This is Jackson, gardener and handyman. He doesn't live in but has a cottage on the estate. Mrs Jackson will come in to clean, with another woman from the village, but they aren't here today. And Mrs Jackson's daughter, Iris, will come as kitchen maid if you think she will suit. Mrs Jackson will bring her up to see you later on. Jackson, this is Miss Patty Jenkins, our new cook, and this—' indicating Vera '—is Miss Aston, under-housekeeper.'

Jackson nodded in greeting. 'Pleased to meet you, ladies.'

'Now,' Miss Banks turned back to the kitchen, 'you'd better make a start. Jackson's son, Danny, helps out and they will eat their dinner with us. So there will be the three of us, plus them and Barney. Dinner at twelve-thirty prompt. You'll find provisions in the larder. I ordered what I thought suitable for today but of course you will want to order whatever else you require when the grocer's boy calls in tomorrow.' She looked around the kitchen and then at Patty. 'Is that all clear? Good. I'll let you get on, then.' She turned to Vera. 'Come into my office and we will discuss your duties.'

Patty noticed that the tour of the house had left the old woman breathless and wheezing. She caught Vera's eye and saw that the same thought was in both their minds. Miss Banks might be keen to establish her status as housekeeper, but it was clear who was going to do most of the work.

Patty looked at the big clock on the wall. Eleven o'clock. She had an hour and a half to produce dinner for six people. For the first time she fully understood the challenges posed by her new job. She had been used to working in a variety of kitchens, from the fine food produced at Speke Hall through to the large scale catering involved in feeding the staff at Freeman's and the meagre and unvarying diet of the workhouse. But she had never been in total charge, except in her own limited realm of the tea shop. Now she had not only to devise menus to satisfy her fellow staff members but soon to cater for the more rarefied tastes of her new employers, whatever they might be. Tomorrow the grocer's boy would call and she would have to work out what to order for the days ahead. She had never had so much responsibility and it was a daunting prospect.

She took a deep breath and forced her mind back to the task at hand. She looked in the larder and saw to her relief that Miss Banks had ordered a large ham. There were potatoes in a sack and onions hanging from a hook and a dozen eggs and a basket of apples. She rolled up her sleeves and set to work. At twelve-thirty the six of them sat down to onion soup, ham, eggs and fried potatoes and apple crumble with custard.

When he had finished eating, Jackson pushed back his chair and gave an appreciative sigh.

'By 'eck, Miss Patty, those are the best ham and eggs I've eaten since Mr Vyner forced old Pendleton to close the Ring o'Bells. Famous, he was, for his ham and eggs. Folks used to come from miles around just to try them.'

'Who is Mr Vyner?' Vera asked.

'Lord of the Manor. I daresay you'll come across him before long. Sir Basil will want to entertain him, I expect.'

'And the Ring o'Bells was the local inn, I suppose. Why did it have to close?'

'Ah, well now. The story was it was used by smugglers. I don't know how true that was.'

'Smugglers?' Vera's eyes sparkled. 'How exciting!'

Miss Banks's face made her disapproval clear. 'I see nothing exciting about breaking the law.'

Vera caught Patty's eye and then lowered her gaze demurely. 'No, sorry.'

The following days were filled with a bustle of activity, as the house was prepared for the arrival of the master and mistress. There was paintwork to be washed and floors to be swept and polished and windows to be cleaned. Then furniture started to arrive. There were Persian rugs to be laid and curtains in complex floral designs to complement the wallpapers to be hung. Easy chairs and a chaise longue were placed in the drawing room, and in the dining room there was a table in a beautiful wood, which Patty was told was walnut, and chairs with ebony rungs and cane seats, together with a dresser inlaid with an elaborate design in different coloured wood. A grand piano was manoeuvred into the music room and a billiard table into the room on the opposite side of the house, and a huge four-poster bed with embroidered drapes was installed in the master bedroom. More and more, to Patty's eyes, the house began to resemble something out of a fairy tale.

After that, the household goods began to arrive. There were crates of china and glass, boxes of books, canteens of silver cutlery. All had to be unpacked, washed or polished and set in the proper places.

As they emptied yet another crate of fine glassware Patty looked at Vera.

'They can't need all these, can they? I don't even know what half of them are for.'

'Nor do I,' her friend confessed. 'But it seems they are necessary – at least, that's what Sir Basil and Lady Helena believe.'

'I reckon the cost of this one crate would keep a poor family for a month,' Patty said.

'Longer than that,' Vera agreed. 'It doesn't seem right, does it?'

'I suppose that's just the way things are meant to be,' Patty said with a sigh. 'You know, like it says in the hymn, "The rich man is his castle, the poor man at his gate".'

'Hmpph!' Vera responded. 'That may be what the rich people like to believe. I'm not sure it's what God intended.'

Patty often had to leave the unpacking to Vera and Mabel Jackson and her friend Doris, who came in from the village to help out, so that she could head for the kitchen to prepare food for the regular staff plus the various workmen who came and went. She spent anxious hours chewing her pencil and trying to work out what she needed to order from the grocer and the baker and the butcher when their errand boys came to call. Here she discovered an ally. If she found she had forgotten something vital, Barney was always ready to put the pony into the shafts of the trap and go into Birkenhead to buy what she needed. Iris Jackson was a help, too. She was a big-boned girl, taking after her father, and inclined to be clumsy, but she had a cheerful nature and took everything in her stride. Patty found her easy-going attitude a useful counterbalance to her own nervousness. It was hard work, but somehow there was always food on the table when it was required.

At the end of the two weeks the house was ready to receive the master and mistress on their return from their honeymoon. Barney harnessed the horses to the carriage and set off to meet them, and the Vera and Patty and Miss Banks put on their best dresses and their lace-trimmed aprons and caps ready to receive them.

Chapter 14

Bidston, Wirral, September 1869

'Basil, it's wonderful! It's exactly how I imagined it!' Helena had been all over the house and now she stood in the lofty hallway with her hands clasped under her chin in delight.

'I'm very glad to hear it,' her husband responded with a smile.

Sir Basil was good-looking man with nut-brown hair, parted in the centre, and a neat beard and moustache. Slightly above medium height, he had the athletic build of a sportsman and his face was tanned from exposure to the Italian sun. Patty guessed that he was some years older than his new bride, perhaps in his early thirties, but together they made an attractive couple. Helena was blonde and willowy, with wide violet eyes and, contrary to her husband's bronzed complexion, her skin, carefully protected from the sun, was roses and cream. To judge from the way they looked at each other, theirs was a genuine love match.

He turned to Miss Banks, who had accompanied them on their tour of the house. 'You've done wonders, Nanny. Thank you.'

The old woman glowed with pleasure. 'I'm glad you're satisfied, sir.'

'I think all the staff deserve our congratulations,' Helena said. 'I'm sure it has been a team effort.'

'Of course,' Sir Basil agreed.

Later that evening, when Iris had gone home and Vera was closeted with Miss Banks, Helena came into the kitchen. Patty had just sat down with a cup of tea and she jumped to her feet in surprise.

'Oh, ma'am! Was there something you wanted? You should have rung.'

'And make you run upstairs, when I'm perfectly capable of walking down?' Helena said. 'Anyway, all I wanted was to congratulate you on the dinner. It was excellent.'

Patty breathed a sigh of relief. She had agonised over the menu for days, until Miss Banks had let fall the remark that Sir Basil liked simple food, well cooked. 'None of your fancy foreign concoctions,' was how she had put it. Then Jackson had come in with a pair of trout a friend had caught in the River Dee and the butcher had provided some fillet steak that he promised was so tender a toothless babe could eat it, and Patty's problems were solved.

She bobbed a curtsy. 'I'm pleased it was satisfactory, ma'am.'

To her surprise, Helena sat down at the kitchen table. 'Do sit down, Patty. There's no need for this sort of formality. I know our stations in life are different, but I should like to think we can be friends.'

Patty slid into her chair. The idea seemed far-fetched to her. The world simply did not work like that. But she had no wish to argue.

'Now,' Helena said, 'for the future. Sir Basil will go back to his office tomorrow and he will have something to eat at his club at midday. So we will adopt the new fashion of dining in the evening. I think seven o'clock would be convenient. I do not require a large meal in the middle of the day as well. Just a light luncheon. Some soup, perhaps, and a salad or an omelette.'

'Very good, ma'am,' Patty said, her mind running over this new schedule. It would work well, she thought. It would allow her to concentrate on the dinner for the staff in the morning and give her the afternoon to prepare something more elaborate for the gentry in the evening, and the midday soup would do for her employer as well.

'But I shall want afternoon tea,' Helena went on. 'I am looking forward to sampling some more of your delicious cakes.'

'Of course, ma'am,' Patty agreed. It meant more work but she was glad to be able to show off her greatest skill.

'That reminds me,' Helena said. 'On Wednesday I have invited some lady friends to visit. There will be four of them. We are going out for a walk first. There is something I want to show them. But then we shall all want tea. I'd like you to make a special effort for that. I have told them all what a wonderful pastry cook you are.'

'Very good, ma'am.'

Patty hesitated. There was a question that had been nagging at her for some time and now seemed as good a time as any to voice it. 'Begging your pardon, ma'am, and not wishing to presume, can I ask you something?'

'Of course you can. You really don't have to worry about being presumptuous. I've told you, I want you to think of me as a friend. What is you want to ask?'

'I was just wondering, ma'am, what Sir Basil's business is. Only him being a ... a titled gentleman, I thought he wouldn't need to work.'

'Ah, I understand,' Helena said. 'Yes, it does puzzle people sometimes. It's like this. He never expected to inherit the title. He had an elder brother who would naturally succeed when his father died. Basil expected to have to make his own way in the world. The idea of a career in the military did not appeal to him – and he is certainly not fitted for the church. So he decided to try his hand in business. He came to Liverpool and joined a firm of shipping agents. He did well, and now he owns a fleet of ships that carry goods from all over the world.' Her eyes sparkled with pleasure. 'I love to see them coming and going, and learn where they have been and what cargo they carry. It's romantic, don't you think?'

Patty thought, romantic or not, it obviously paid very well.

'But you were wondering about the title,' Helena continued. 'Basil's brother was killed in a riding accident ten years ago. So when his father died, Basil inherited the baronetcy. But he had a life here. He had no wish to go and bury himself in the country. So he sold the land and rented the house out to a rich American. And I'm very glad he did. I should hate to be cooped up in a country manor with no one to talk to but farmer's wives. This house suits me very well. It's a lovely situation and we are away from the soot and the smells, but close enough for friends to visit or for us to go to the theatre or a concert.' She checked herself with a laugh. 'Listen to me, rambling on. I'm interrupting your well-earned rest. Have I answered your question?'

'Oh yes, ma'am,' Patty responded. 'And thank you.'

'Then I must get back to my husband. He will be wondering what I am doing all this time.' She got up. 'Goodnight, Patty.'

'Goodnight, ma'am.'

As well as the master and mistress, the household had increased by two more servants. Mr Charles, Sir Basil's manservant, was a slightly built, fair-haired man with what Vera described as 'an almost perfect Greek profile'. That meant nothing to Patty, but he was undeniably good-looking. He was clean-shaven except for a small moustache and, although Patty guessed that he was not much younger than Sir Basil, he had a youthful, almost boyish look. His actions were neat and precise, and his manner of speaking was reserved, almost to the point of rudeness. Vera wondered whether Charles was his first name or his surname, but when she asked his reply, through pursed lips, was, 'That is the name by which I wish to be known in this household.'

Dulcie, the lady's maid, was a very different character. Dark-haired and vivacious, she chattered away in a voice slightly tinged with the accent of North Wales, where she had grown up. The two of them had, however, certain points in common. One was that both were plainly devoted to their respective master and mistress, and the other that they both had a firm conviction of their position in the hierarchy of the household – a position that debarred them from taking on any work not immediately related to the service of that master or mistress.

The four ladies duly arrived and they all set out at once for their walk. They returned flushed with excitement. Vera met them in the hall and relieved them of their wraps, then conducted them to the drawing room where Patty was ready to serve tea. Charles had gone to Liverpool with his master, and Dulcie had made it clear that she did expect to act the role of parlourmaid, so Vera and Patty carried out those duties between them.

As Vera handed round cups and plates, the excited conversation continued.

'I would never have believed it!' one exclaimed. 'Such an ancient relic right on our doorstep, and I had never heard of it.'

'I know,' Helena responded. 'I thought at first that the local people were making fun of me. But then Jackson, our gardener, took me up there and showed me.'

'Viking, they think?' queried another. 'What makes them say that?'

'I looked it up in the encyclopaedia. This whole area was occupied by the Vikings from around nine hundred. They say it's a depiction of the Viking sun goddess.'

Patty was only half listening as she dispensed sandwiches and slices of cake, but she could see that Vera was agog with curiosity. When the four ladies were climbing into the coach to be driven back to the ferry she whispered, 'I wonder what they were talking about.'

'Ask Lady Helena,' Patty said. 'She doesn't mind you asking questions.'

So when Helena returned from seeing her friends off Vera said, 'May I ask you something, Lady Helena?' (Patty had noticed that she rarely called their employer 'ma'am'.)

'Of course,' was the reply.

'I couldn't help overhearing the conversation at tea time. I'm wondering what it was that you had shown them that they were so excited about.'

'Oh, yes. I suppose it must have sounded rather mysterious if you did not know what we're discussing. There's a rock carving up on the hill. It seems to show a woman's figure with outstretched arms and a halo of sunbeams at her feet.'

'Oh, I should love to see that!' Vera said. 'Can you tell me how to find it?'

Lady Helena's brow creased. 'It's not easy to direct someone – but if you are really interested I will take you.'

'Would you? That would be most kind!'

'Would you like to come, Patty?' Helena asked.

Patty hesitated. She really had no idea what they were talking about, but the idea of going out walking with her employer, as if they were social equals, seemed rather shocking. 'Yes, I suppose so, ma'am,' she muttered eventually.

'Tomorrow?' Lady Helena said. 'Perhaps after the luncheon has been cleared away. I suppose you must have a little free time before you have to start preparing the dinner. We should only be gone for an hour.'

'That would be perfect,' Vera said, without pausing to consult Patty. 'Thank you, Lady Helena.'

'Not at all. I'm pleased to find that you are interested in such things.' She moved away and then turned back. 'Oh, and Patty, the tea was delightful, as always. We have decided to make it a regular occasion, every Wednesday afternoon.'

As they washed up after the midday meal the next afternoon, Vera kept urging Patty to hurry.

'We mustn't keep Lady Helena waiting, when she's putting herself out for our benefit,' she said.

'I don't know what you're so excited about,' Patty grumbled. 'Me, I'd rather take the weight off my feet for an hour or so.'

'Oh, come along!' Vera exclaimed. 'Don't be such a stick-in-the-mud. This will be really interesting. And it's a lovely afternoon for a walk.'

She was right there. They were enjoying an Indian summer. The sun shone, but the heat was gentle, the sky a softer, paler blue than in mid-summer and there was a light breeze. They walked at first through woodland, where the trees had shed their leaves in a golden carpet that rustled as they walked. Patty trod it suspiciously at first. Used to city streets, she had misgivings about what might be concealed beneath.

Vera, by contrast, kicked up the leaves with the glee of a child and exclaimed, 'Oh, it's so good to be out in the country. I have missed this!'

'You have lived in the country, then?' Lady Helena queried.

'Oh yes. I grew up there. I only came to the city when … well, about a year ago.'

'I grew up in the country, too,' Helena said. 'I should not want to live there permanently but I feel we have the best of both worlds here.'

They walked on, Vera and Helena engaged in an animated discussion of the contrasting advantages of the country life versus the city, chatting more like friends than mistress and servant. Vera seemed to know the names of all the trees and to be able to identify the birds that hopped ahead of them or flew up as they approached. After a while the tall trees were replaced by smaller ones which grew more sparsely and Patty found herself picking her way over uneven slabs of rock – sandstone, Vera called it. Prickly bushes grew on either side of the path, covered in yellow flowers.

'That's gorse,' Vera said. 'There's an old country saying that "when the gorse is not in flower, kissing is out of fashion".'

Helena laughed. 'Because gorse flowers all year round, of course.'

It took Patty a moment to catch up. 'Oh,' she said eventually

The path grew steeper and Patty began to pant. Country walking, she decided, was a vastly over-rated pastime. Then, quite suddenly, the ground levelled out into an open clearing and there in front of them was a tall structure with four huge sails, which rotated slowly in the breeze.

'Is that a windmill?' she asked.

Helena smiled at her. 'You've never seen one before?'

'No.'

'Well, don't go too close. Even in a light wind like this those sails can be dangerous. The miller before the present one was killed when he came out of the wrong door and was struck by one. There's a story that once a pedlar had tied his donkey to one of them and when the miller released the brake and the sails started to revolve the donkey was whisked up into the air.'

'No, really?'

'Well, that's what they say.'

A door opened and a large man in a floury apron appeared. Helena called cheerfully, 'Good day, Mr Youds,' and he responded with a respectful, 'Good day to you, ma'am.'

'We are going to look at the sun goddess,' Helena said.

'Ah, now there's a sight. Strange to think people were carving these rocks all that time ago.'

'Yes, isn't it. But Bidston seems to have so many ancient stories associated with it. I heard that people say one of King Arthur's knights came here, bringing the Holy Grail.'

'Aye, so they say. And Joseph of Arimathea too. Him that gave his own tomb for Our Lord to be buried in.'

'I wonder, could it be true?'

'Who knows? There's many a tale of goings on on this hill. Maybe some of them are true.'

'Ah well,' Helena said, 'at least the sun goddess is evidence that ancient people were here. We had better be on our way. Good day to you.'

As they walked on Vera said, 'Is there really a connection with King Arthur?'

'They say Sir Gawain came here. I'd love to think it was true. That's why the house is called Avalon.'

'I'm sorry. I don't understand.'

'It's the island where Arthur was taken after his last battle. It means the island of apples, and the land where the house is built was once an apple orchard, so it seemed appropriate.'

'Is that why you have those two figures in the stained glass either side of the front door?'

'Yes. They are supposed to be Sir Lancelot and Queen Guinevere. They were designed by the artist Edward Burne-Jones. Ah, we are nearly there.'

A little further on the ground fell away on either side and Patty saw that they were standing on a high ridge. To her right was a view of the Mersey estuary and the Liverpool skyline, much like the one she had from her bedroom window, but more extensive. To her left another vertiginous prospect revealed green fields and the estuary of another river, and beyond that in the blue distance the hazy outline of distant hills.

'That's the River Dee,' Helena said, 'and those are the mountains of North Wales.'

Patty felt slightly dizzy. She told herself that she was out of breath from the climb, but the fact was that after growing up in the city, where her view was always bounded by high walls, this vast panorama made her feel queasy.

Helena led them across the ridge to another clearing.

'There!' she said. 'There she is, the sun goddess.'

At first Patty could only see a flat sandstone slab; then she began to make out the crude outline of a woman etched into the stone. At her feet, lines radiated like spokes in a wheel.

'That is a symbol of the sun,' Helena said, 'Her head is pointed in the direction that the sun sets on midsummer's day.'

'And did you say it was carved by the Vikings?' Vera asked.

'That's what scholars believe. Or perhaps it would be more accurate to say the Norse Irish, but they were of Viking descent, of course.'

'Who were the Vikings?' Patty asked.

A look flashed between Vera and Helena and Patty understood that she had revealed an unexpected depth of ignorance. She felt herself flush with embarrassment.

Helena answered kindly, 'They were a warlike people from Scandinavia. They came in their longboats and attacked eastern England and Ireland. Then some of them came across the Irish sea and settled here, on the Wirral. That was a long time ago. About nine hundred years.'

'Oh,' Patty said humbly. 'Thank you.'

As they walked home Vera said, 'I wish my father could have seen that. He would have been fascinated.'

'Your father was a historian?' Helena queried.

'He was a palaeontologist. His main interest was in fossils. But that carving would have excited him.'

'A palaeontologist? How interesting! Tell me, did he agree with the theories about the earth being far older than we ever thought?'

262

'Oh yes. He said it must be millions of years old. Some of the fossils he found were of creatures that lived long before men ever walked the earth.'

'Indeed! So he discussed these things with you?'

'After my mother died he had no one else to talk to. He was not much given to society.'

'You were very fortunate. So many men believe women to be incapable of comprehending such things. Was he familiar with the work of Mr Darwin?'

'He had his book, *On the Origin of Species*.'

'And did he agree with him, that humans were not created in their present state, but evolved slowly from lower forms of life?'

'He said it fitted with what he had learned from the fossil record.'

'Fascinating! So we really could be descended from the apes?'

'In some way, yes. At least, that seems to be the way scholars are interpreting the evidence.'

'Just a minute!' Patty stopped walking and faced them. Here was something she did know about and was quite certain of. 'That can't be right. God created Adam, the first man, and then Eve, in the garden of Eden. The Bible tells us so.'

Once again she saw Helena and Vera exchange glances. They looked uneasy, as if she was a tricky problem they had to solve.

Helena said, 'Modern scholars – some of them – are beginning to think that the Bible stories were made up to explain things that were too mysterious for ancient people to understand.'

'You mean, you don't think the Bible is the Word of God?'

'Not – not all of it, no.'

Patty looked at Vera for confirmation.

'The problem is,' Vera said, 'that what we are learning from the fossil record is that creation cannot have happened in the way the Bible describes it, in six days. It took much, much longer than that. And Mr Darwin's work shows that creatures of all kinds did not just spring to life fully formed. They evolved slowly from more primitive forms. And that is true for human beings too.'

Patty gazed from one to the other for a few moments longer. If she was to believe what they said, the whole bedrock of her universe, everything she had been taught in the workhouse chapel and in the schoolroom below it, was unreliable.

'Of course,' Helena said, 'there are many people who refuse to believe the new theories. Eminent churchmen have argued bitterly against them and denounced Darwin as an atheist.'

'But you believe him?'

'I think the evidence is in his favour, yes.'

'I see.' Patty turned and began to plod in the direction of the house. Somewhere in the centre of her being she felt a weight, a deep, slow-burning anger at the system that had left her so ignorant, so incapable of making her own decisions on matters like this. And she was aware of a yawning, hitherto unsuspected, gulf between her own education and Vera's.

Outwardly, nothing changed in the daily routine of running the house and Vera showed no sign that she harboured any contempt for Patty's ignorance, or pitied her lack of education. But Patty could not dismiss a nagging worry that her friend was making a terrible mistake. She had been taught all her life that the Bible was the word of God and to question it would be a sin. She believed that if you obeyed the Commandments, said your prayers and confessed your sins, you could be redeemed and that in the end you would be received into heaven, where there was no poverty or sickness but only eternal joy. She had been taught to accept her place in the world and to regard misfortune and suffering as part of God's plan, to try her faith and purge her soul. Now it seemed all that was thrown into question. She did not know what to believe, but she was very much afraid that Vera was committing the sin of pride in her own intellect and would eventually be punished for it.

Her misgivings received added weight the following Sunday. The whole household was expected to attend matins and they duly trooped off to St Oswald's, the parish church, in their Sunday best. That particular Sunday, the vicar chose as the subject for his sermon the Creation story and delivered a forceful diatribe against the ungodly ideas being perpetrated by Mr Darwin and his supporters. As they left the church Patty looked at the faces of Sir Basil and Lady Helena, but she could detect no embarrassment or unease as they exchanged pleasantries with the local gentry. She wondered if Sir Basil shared his wife's heretical beliefs or not.

'You see?' she said to Vera as they walked back to the house. 'This man, Darwin or whatever you call him, has got it all wrong. The vicar says so.'

Vera glanced sideways at her. 'I'm afraid I have more faith in Mr Darwin's intellect than the vicar's.'

After that, Patty decided to leave the subject alone.

At mealtimes, Vera made it her project to draw out Mr Charles, Sir Basil's valet. She questioned him about his recent experiences with his master and mistress in Italy and at last received some response. It transpired that he had taken great pleasure in the art they had seen and he talked with enthusiasm about the glories of paintings by Raphael and sculptures by Michelangelo. It meant nothing to Patty, but Vera seemed at least to recognise the names and made encouraging comments. When she tried to change the subject, however, to the ladies and the Italian fashions, his face closed up again.

'It's not a topic I feel qualified to remark upon,' he said, with a return of his normal prissy manner.

'I don't know why you bother,' Patty said to Vera later. 'He's a miserable so-and-so.'

'I don't think he's miserable, exactly,' Vera said. 'But I don't think he knows how to behave with women. I imagine he has no sisters, and went to a boy's boarding school and since then his life has revolved around Sir

Basil's, which seems to have been divided between his office and his gentleman's club.'

'Well, Sir Basil met Lady Helena somewhere,' Patty pointed out. 'He must have had some social life.'

'True. But I suppose at social events the men servants probably stuck together and didn't have much to do with the women. He certainly doesn't make any attempt to be pleasant to Dulcie. Anyway, I'm determined to humanise him.'

She persisted in her attempts and was rewarded by the occasional smile and even once or twice by a laugh. Patty, observing this, was struck by a sudden misgiving.

'Vera, you are flirting with him.'

'Flirting? No, I'm not. I'm just trying to be friendly.'

'No, you're flirting.'

A mischievous smile crossed Vera's face. 'Well, so what if I am? Where's the harm?'

'Harm? You might give him the wrong idea.'

'Rubbish. I'm sure he's immune to any such suggestion.'

Patty put down the dish she was drying and sat down opposite her friend. 'Listen, I don't know much, but I do know about men – more than you do; a lot more. You can't lead them on and not expect some kind of – well, a response.'

'So? Perhaps I want a response.'

A cold hand gripped Patty's heart. 'You don't mean what I think you mean, do you? You're not hoping he'll fall for you?'

'Well, why not?'

'Why not? Vera, you can't marry a man like that.'

'Why can't I? What do you mean by a man like that?'

'He's not good enough for you.'

'I don't know.' Vera seemed to consider the prospect. 'One day he will probably be promoted to butler, and when Nanny finally retires I shall be housekeeper. Butler and housekeeper have a certain position in a household, a respectable place. I could do worse.'

'You couldn't!' Patty said passionately. 'You're worth much more than that.'

'Am I? So what should I be aiming for?'

'I don't know. Someone well educated, a professional gentleman.'

Vera shrugged. 'I don't see much likelihood of my meeting a "professional gentleman" who will want to whisk me away from my humble situation and set me up as a lady, do you?'

'So would you really settle for Mr Charles?'

'He is very good-looking, you know.'

Patty was close to tears. 'And what about us? What about our dreams, our plan to own our own teashop? Have you forgotten that?'

Vera gave a sudden laugh and leaned across the table to grasp her hand. 'Oh dear, Patty. It's so easy to lead you up the garden path! Of course I've no intention of marrying Charles – even if he ever thought of me like that, which I doubt. Don't worry! Our plans are still the same. I was only teasing you.'

'Oh, were you?' Patty swallowed and rubbed her hand across her face. 'Thank goodness for that.'

Vera squeezed her fingers, her eyes troubled. 'I've upset you. I'm so sorry. I really didn't mean to. But the whole idea of me and Charles ...' she suppressed a giggle. 'It was just so ridiculous I couldn't resist having you on.'

'Well, please don't do it again,' Patty said.

'I won't.' Vera's expression became more serious. 'But don't you want to marry one day? Don't you want a home of your own, children, all that?'

'Not me!' Patty said with emphasis. 'I've had enough of men to last me a lifetime.'

Later that evening, as a distraction from the confusing events of the last few days, she took refuge in writing a much-overdue letter to May in Australia.

Avalon
Bidston,
Wirral
October 2nd 1869

Dear May,

I'm so happy to know you and James are married. You had to wait such a long time but I'm sure you will have a wonderful future together.

I'm very sorry that it has been such a long time since I wrote to you. I've had a difficult time lately but things are looking up now. I lost my job at Freeman's. It was my own stupid fault. I let a man take me in. He was a real con man but I should have known better. Things were hard for a while and I ended up back in the workhouse for a few months. Can you believe it? I thought I'd turned my back on that years ago.

But I had a bit of luck. I am now working as a cook for a gentleman, who owns a lot of ships, and his wife. They have only just got married and he has built a beautiful house here in Bidston. It's a tiny village close to Birkenhead. I'd never even been this side of the river before and this place is right out in the country, so it feels a bit strange, but I'm getting used to it. Lady Helena, my new missus, is very nice and treats servants like human beings, which makes a nice change!

Another good thing is that I made friends with a girl called Vera in the workhouse and she is working here as well, as under housekeeper. You probably think it's funny that someone like Lady Helena should want to employ two girls from that place, but she has ideas about how unfair society is and wants to make a difference. Pity there aren't more like her!

She has some funny ideas about other things too, like this thing called evoltution. I'm not sure if that's the right spelling. Vera seems to understand her and they chatter on about fossils and a man called Darwin. It's all above my head, so I let them get on with it.

It must be lovely for you, having Angel with you. What a turn around that is! I hope she is settling down well in Australia. I expect it all seems a bit strange to her but at least she's with people who love her now.

Well, that will have to do for now. Please write and let me know how married life is suiting you. I'll try not to be so long answering this time.

Your friend,
Patty

Chapter 15

Rutherglen, November 1869

'I won't go! I hate it there. And they hate me!'

May sighed as she looked at the flushed face and the tumbled golden curls. This had been brewing for some days now and she knew from experience that once the child worked herself into this state it would be hard to persuade her out of it. She raised her eyes to Lizzie Findlay, who stood behind the irate figure.

Lizzie lifted her shoulders helplessly. 'I've tried, but short of throwing her over my shoulder and carting her bodily to the school I don't know what else to do.'

May lowered herself to her knees to bring her face level with the little girl's – not such an easy operation now that she was six months' pregnant.

'Listen, Angel ...'

'My name's Amy! Not Angel.'

'I'm sorry. I've always thought of you as Angel and it's hard to change, you know. But please listen to me.

Your papa wants you to go to school. He knows that that is the best thing for you, so you can grow up to be an educated young lady.'

'I want my papa!' The small face crumpled. 'If he was here he wouldn't make me go to that horrible school. He loves me!'

'We all love you, darling. You know we do. We just want the best for you, and right now that means going to school.'

'But it's horrible there. The other children laugh at me. They make fun of the way I talk. They call me Little Miss Pom.'

May looked over Amy's head to Lizzie and sighed. There was no arguing with the fact that Amy's manner and speech were completely different from that of most of the other children in the local school, most of whose parents had either been transported as criminals or had come to Australia to escape abject poverty in the homeland. Families that had come voluntarily, like the wine growers who were friends with her father, either educated their children at home or sent them away to boarding school.

'And Miss Clark's cruel. She caned Freddy Watson on his bottom and Joan Fitch on her hands.'

'Why?'

'Freddy was talking in class, and Joan Fitch got her spellings wrong.'

'Oh dear!'

'They're all stupid. I won't learn anything there. I know more than them already. I know more than Miss Clark does.'

'Oh, now, I don't think that can be true.'

'It is! Miss Clark doesn't know a word of French, and I've read books she's never even heard of.'

That was probably true, May reflected. Amy had spent less than a year at the convent school in Ireland to which she had been sent by her adoptive parents, but in that time she had been introduced to subjects that would be regarded as quite unnecessary at the Rutherglen elementary school. And before that she had been under the charge of a sequence of governesses, of whom Lizzie had been the last and most successful.

'The thing is, Amy—' May suppressed a groan as she straightened up '—education isn't just about how much you know. It's about learning to get on with people, too. You need to be with boys and girls your own age. Don't you have any friends?'

'I wouldn't be friends with any of them. They're horrible.'

'I'm sure they aren't, really. You're a bit different, and they don't quite know how to take you, but if you show them that you want to join in, play the same games and so on, they'll get used to you very quickly.'

'They won't let me play. The girls laugh at me and say I'll get my pretty clothes dirty. The boys pull my hair. If you make me go back there, I'll run away. I've done it before, you know.'

May took hold of her shoulders. 'Don't even think of doing that! This is not Ireland. You wouldn't last a day out there in the bush. There are poisonous snakes and spiders everywhere – and some very dangerous men, too. Amy, promise me you won't do anything so foolish.'

Amy began to sob. 'But I can't bear it there. Please don't make me go.'

May looked around her for a chair, then sat and drew the weeping child onto her lap.

'Listen. I will come with you this morning and I will talk to Miss Clark and see if there is some way she can help. And I will write to your papa and tell him how unhappy you are and ask him if there is some other solution he can think of.'

Amy's tears subsided to snuffles. 'When is Papa coming back?'

'I hope he will be here for Christmas.'

'Why couldn't I go with him?'

'Because he is working in a mine in a very out-of-the-way place, where he doesn't have a nice house like this to live in, and it's very hot and there are no ladies there to look after you. You wouldn't like it. But we hope soon he will find a better job, in a nicer place, where he can settle down, and then you and Lizzie will be able to join him. And perhaps there will be a school there that you will like better. But he will be very worried and unhappy if I have to write to him and tell him you are refusing to go to school.' She drew Amy's head away from her shoulder and wiped her wet cheeks with her handkerchief. 'I always thought, you know, that you were such a brave girl, going on the stage in front of all those people. That must have been very frightening.'

'That was different,' Amy said. 'I was performing, pretending to be someone else.'

'Then can't you pretend at school? Pretend you don't care if they tease you. If they see they can't upset you, they'll stop doing it.'

'Do you think so?'

'I'm sure of it. You need to show them how brave you can be. They will respect you for that. And I shall be able to tell your papa, and he will be proud of you.'

Amy sniffed and rubbed her hand over her face. 'All right. I'll try. But I won't stay there for ever. Papa will have to find somewhere else, somewhere better.'

'I'm sure he will do his best,' May said. 'Now, go and wash your face and let Lizzie comb your hair. Then we will all walk up to the school together.'

In the single classroom at the school they found the pupils working at sums that were written up on the blackboard. Several of them looked up as they entered and sniggers and nudges passed from one to another.

May bent and whispered in Amy's ear. 'Pretend you are just walking on to the stage.'

To her relief Amy straightened her shoulders, lifted her head and walked across the room to her desk, without glancing at the other children. She sat down, opened her satchel, took out her pencil case and started to work.

Miss Clark was sitting at a desk on a slightly raised podium. She was very young, no older than she was herself, May thought. The school had only been open for a year and from what May had heard, it had not been easy to find a teacher. In the end, the school board had appointed a young woman whose only training had been as a pupil teacher in a school in Beechworth. Glancing around the room, May sympathised with her unenviable position. The class consisted of around thirty children, whose ages varied from five-year-olds to boys and girls on the brink of puberty. Many of those, she knew from local gossip, resented the law that confined them to the classroom, when they could have been out earning a living or helping their families on the farm or in the shop.

May approached the podium and murmured, 'I'm sorry to interrupt your lesson, Miss Clark, but I wonder if we could have a few words in private.'

The young woman looked at her with a tinge of alarm in her expression, but she said, 'Of course. Just a minute, please.'

She stood up and looked around the room. 'You are to continue with your work in silence. Mary Peters, I am putting you in charge. If anyone speaks, write their name on the blackboard and I will deal with them when I come back.'

The girl she had named got up with a smirk of satisfaction and moved to stand in front of the class. Miss Clark led May out into the entrance passage, where Lizzie was waiting.

'Now—' her voice betrayed her anxiety '—what seems to be the problem?'

'You will have noticed that Amy came to school late this morning.'

'Yes. Normally that would mean a detention.'

'Please don't do that in this case. The fact is that we are having the greatest difficulty in persuading her to come to school at all. She is very unhappy here and I am wondering if you can help in any way.'

'I don't see how. Amy makes no effort to fit in. She does not seem to want to join in any of the other children's games.'

'That may be because she doesn't know how. You see, she has had very little chance to mix with children her own age. For most of her early life she was taught at home, and her adoptive mother did not encourage her to play with other children.'

'I understood she had been to boarding school before her father brought her here.'

'Yes, but that was only for a short time, and it was a convent school. I would imagine that the sort of games the girl played there were ... well, more sedate. She is not used to the kind of rough and tumble that the boys and girls here enjoy.'

'You mean she thinks of herself as too much of a lady.'

'No, that's not what I intended to say.'

'It's the impression she gives.'

'I think it's ... a kind of defence. She doesn't know what to do, so she prefers to stand back. And she says some of the others are unkind if she tries to join in. They laugh at her and the boys pull her hair.'

'Some of them can be a bit rough, I have to admit. But boys will be boys, you know. Amy needs to learn to stand up for herself.'

'I thought that part of what any school was supposed to teach was consideration for others.'

Miss Clark wriggled her shoulders. 'That is all very well. I can preach at them, but you can't change human nature.'

May felt they were getting nowhere and changed tack. 'What about her work? She's a bright child. Does she do well in class?'

'She hardly speaks in lessons, except …'

'Except?'

'She has once or twice corrected me over matters of grammar. The fact is, she seems to have altogether too high an opinion of herself.'

'Oh dear!' May exchanged an exasperated glance with Lizzie. 'I'll speak to her and tell her that is not the way to behave. But please, in return, can you try to persuade some of the other children to make friends with her? You might present it perhaps as their good deed for the day? A Christian act?'

'I can try.' The response was grudging. 'But Amy has to make an effort, too. She has to stop behaving as if she's too good for us.'

'I'll talk to her. And thank you for talking to me. I can appreciate you have enough problems on your hands without this. I won't take up any more of your time.' May turned away, feeling dispirited. Then a thought struck her. 'Do the children have music lessons?'

'We've no piano, and I can't sing.'

'What about art?'

'Drawing is part of the curriculum, but we don't have much time to spare for it. It's all I can do to get the basics of reading and writing and arithmetic into their heads.'

'Yes, I can understand that,' May said. 'Well, thank you again. Good day.'

As she and Lizzie made for the door they heard Miss Clark's voice raised in furious tones. 'Three names on the blackboard! Right! Mary, fetch the cane.'

'Well, that didn't get us far,' Lizzie commented, as they walked home.

'No, it didn't,' May agreed.

'Strikes me that Miss Clark's useless. Can't change human nature! What sort of an attitude is that?'

'I think the poor woman is completely overwhelmed,' May said. 'I can't help feeling sorry for her. I wouldn't want to be in her shoes.'

'That's all very well, but what do we do about Amy?'

'I wonder if it would help if I invited one or two of the girls to tea.'

'It might, I suppose. But which ones?'

'I'd have to ask Amy if there is anyone she thinks she might like.'

'It seems to me that that school is the wrong place for her. I'd rather have her back at home and teach her myself.'

'You may be right, but Richard was very keen for her to learn to mix.' May sighed and wiped the sweat from her face. The November heat was more trying than ever in her pregnant state. 'I'll talk to James when he comes home for dinner. Maybe he'll have some ideas.'

*

James walked the half mile from his office to his home in the languid midday heat. He had chosen to retain his rooms above the draper's shop for business purposes, partly because it was a central location where it was easy for clients and potential clients to find him, but mainly because he liked the feeling that at the end of that half mile there was sanctuary away from any concerns connected with his work, a small, private paradise containing his wife and, soon, his child. That it also contained Amy and Lizzie Findlay he regarded as a bonus, if a temporary one.

Lake House was built on a parcel of land purchased from May's father, overlooking Lake Moodemere. He and May had designed it together. It was double-fronted and surrounded by a wide veranda, to give it shelter from the sun, like most houses in the area. At the front of the house two rooms led off from either side of the central entrance hall. One was designated as the 'music room' because it contained a piano, and the other as the 'library' because it contained a desk and shelves holding several books, but this room also doubled as May's studio, where she kept her painting materials.

At the back of the house a long sitting room looked out onto the veranda and the lake beyond. There were four bedrooms upstairs. Apart from the master bedroom, two were currently occupied by Amy and Lizzie and the third, which had a communicating door with the master bedroom, was furnished as the nursery. The kitchen and scullery were set off to one side. On the long rear veranda there was a dining table and chairs and several cushioned rocking chairs where he could relax after his meal with a cigar. To James's eyes, it was idyllic.

Reaching home that day, he found that the atmosphere was not as relaxed as he had grown to expect. Lizzie was clattering dishes in the kitchen and May was setting the table with a worried frown on her face. She looked up as he appeared and gave him a smile but he sensed at once that something was wrong.

'Cheer up, my love,' he said, kissing her. 'I don't know what the problem is but I'm sure we can sort it out.'

'I hope so,' she said, leaning her head against his shoulder. 'But at the moment I can't see how.'

As briefly as she could she outlined the scene with Amy earlier that morning and the response of the schoolteacher to her approaches.

'I can't blame Miss Clark,' she finished. 'The poor woman is obviously at her wits end trying to cope with those children and get some basic knowledge into their heads. The last thing she needs is a problem with Amy.'

'Where is Amy now?' James asked. The school day started early and finished a dinner time.

'Sitting in her room, sulking,' May said. 'She's convinced that we are all trying to make her life miserable.'

Lizzie came in carrying a dish of chicken baked with aubergines and peppers, a recipe May had learned from Maria, and Betsy followed with potatoes and green beans. James took his place at the head of the table and the three women seated themselves on either side. The organisation of the household was less hierarchical than James had been used to in England, and sometimes he felt a little uncomfortable with it. In England he and his mother had been attended by a cook and a parlourmaid, both of them trusted and valued servants, but they would never have dreamed of sitting down to eat with the master and mistress.

May, however, having been at the bottom of the pyramid herself, was determined not to inflict the same humiliation on anyone else. Lizzie, whose position as a governess had raised her slightly above the rank of servant but had still meant she was regarded as a social inferior by her British employers, was keenly aware of the difference and grateful for it. Betsy, by contrast, had never regarded herself as a servant of any sort. After

May's marriage to James she had agreed to come in every morning to help out, but in her mind she was doing them a favour and it made no difference that she was paid for it.

When they were setting up their household, James had wanted a larger establishment. He had suggested they should employ a cook and, at the very least, a maid-of-all-work who would live in and attend to all the chores, but May had insisted that she liked to cook and would not be comfortable sitting back and being waited on, so he had reluctantly agreed, telling himself that once they had children May would have her hands full and raise no further objections to the employment of more help. For the time being, while Lizzie was living with them at least, May could manage very well with only Betsy, plus a Mr and Mrs Jones who came in three times a week to clean and do any heavy work and look after the garden. They had no need for a stable boy since they kept no horses. Neither of them were keen riders, and when a horse or a pony and trap were needed they could always borrow from May's father.

There was one empty place at the table. 'Isn't Amy coming down for her dinner?' James asked.

'I told you, she's shut herself in her room.'

'Well, that can't be allowed. It's dinner time and she should be here. Lizzie, will you fetch her, please?'

Lizzie made to rise but May reached a hand across the table. 'Let her be, James, please. She's finding life rather difficult at the moment. She'll eat when she's hungry and if we try to force her she will resist much longer.'

She was proved right when a few minutes later the door opened and Amy slid into her seat at the table. James opened his mouth to speak, but May caught his eye and shook her head. She served out a helping of the chicken and Amy set to with a good appetite.

Later, when James had gone back to his office, Amy said, 'I want to go riding on Snowflake. Can I?'

Snowflake was her chief delight. Richard had kept his promise and bought her a pure white pony and they were all impressed by her ease and confidence in the saddle, the product of the teaching she had had when she lived with the family of Irish tinkers and horse-traders who had taken her in when she'd run away from school.

'Yes, of course you can,' May said. 'I'll walk up to the house with you. I want to talk to Grandpappy George.'

George Lavender was, of course, no relation by blood to Amy, but she had no grandparents of her own and when, out of the blue, she had christened him Grandpappy, no one had objected. They strolled the short distance to Freshfields together and then Amy went off happily to saddle up while May went into the large, cool 'cellar' where the finished wines were stored. It was not a true cellar, but the thick stone walls and the thatched roof kept the summer heat at bay. She found her father and his partner Pedro supervising the packing of casks ready for shipment to Melbourne.

They chatted for a while, her father voicing his regular complaint about the difficulty of transporting the wine and the delay in bringing the railway to Rutherglen.

At length, May asked, 'Where's Gus?'

Her father snorted. 'That boy? Out with his damned horse, of course. I could kill Rudolph Marshall for selling him that colt. Ever since he got him he's lost all interest in the vineyard and wants to spend all his time exercising the animal.'

'You bought Merlin for him,' May pointed out.

'More fool me!' her father responded. 'Ever since he got him he's had only one thought in his head, to win the big race at the next meeting.'

'Oh dear,' May murmured. 'But you know Gus. Once he gets an idea into his head … Maybe, if he does well in the race he'll be satisfied and get back to work.'

'He'd better!' her father said.

May wandered out into the yard. The mention of Rudolph Marshall had stirred a twinge of discomfort in her mind. In the flurry of excitement around James's arrival and the preparations for their wedding she had almost forgotten her flirtations with him and with Anton. Flirtations they were, she had to admit to herself, and Anton at least had got the wrong impression of her intentions, though she had never made any kind of commitment to either of them.

She had realised that before she was married she must speak to both of them and try to make things right. When Anton had asked for her hand she had left it to her father to explain that she needed more time and she'd been tempted to leave it to him to break the news of her engagement, but that, she told herself, was the coward's way out. So she asked her father instead to invite Anton over and then to leave them alone. It was clear from Anton's expression that he was anticipating a very different message, but when she explained to him that she was to marry an 'old friend' from England he took refuge in Teutonic formality and declared that in that case, of course, he would not press his suit. It distressed her to think that she had made him miserable, but within a few days he was courting a girl called Magda, the daughter of another German family who had settled in the area, and showing no symptoms of a broken heart.

With Rudolph it had been easier. Gus had already told him about James's arrival and he'd come to see her to wish her well. There were no hard feelings, he'd insisted, and he hoped they could remain friends. The hardest part of all had been confessing to James but he had clasped her hands and exclaimed, 'Oh what a relief! At least I'm not the only one.' And he had told her how close he had come to finding himself committed, almost by accident, to a girl called Prudence, who he had known since they were children. It was a relief to admit the doubts and fears that had beset her during their year apart and reassuring to discover that he had suffered in the same way.

Well, that had cleared the air and she had thought it would all be plain sailing from now on. It seemed she had been mistaken. As if she didn't have enough to worry about with Amy, now she had to mediate between her father and her brother. The sound of hooves drew her eyes to the track leading to the yard and, in spite of her worries, she found herself smiling. Coming towards her were two riders, one on a tall, bright bay horse, the other on a small white pony, jogging to keep up with the long stride of its companion. The rider on the big horse was leaning down, apparently in close conversation with the small girl beside him, whose face was eagerly raised towards him. May had worried a little that Gus might resent the attention she gave to Amy, but they had become good friends, almost like sister and brother.

The two rode into the yard and Gus swung down from his mount and lifted Amy down from hers.

'Good day, sis,' he said, kissing May. 'How's the mother-to-be?'

'Hot,' May told him. 'How's Merlin?'

'He's coming on in leaps and bounds! Rudi wouldn't let me enter him for the first meeting of the season, but I'll have him ready for the big race at the last meeting in February, you wait and see.'

May looked at the horse. In a few months he had grown from a leggy colt into a sleek, powerfully muscled animal. 'He looks splendid,' she said. Amy had taken her pony back to his stall and was out of earshot, so she went on, 'But Gus, you mustn't spend all your time with him, you know. I think Papa is getting rather impatient with you.'

'Oh, he'll come round when we start winning races,' Gus said carelessly. 'But listen, Amy's been telling me that the other children are giving her a hard time at school.'

'Yes, I know,' May said. 'I've already been to see Miss Clark to see if anything can be done to improve things.'

'And was she any help?'

May sighed. 'Not really. I think she's got her hands full as it is.'

'I've been telling Amy she should take things into her own hands. She's got to stand up for herself, give as good as she gets. If one of the boys pulls her hair she should kick him in the shins – or somewhere where it will hurt him more.'

May looked at her brother and was suddenly taken back ten years, to the small, pugnacious boy she remembered in the workhouse, always in trouble, always bruised and battered from taking on boys bigger than himself. 'Oh, you mustn't tell her that, Gus! It will only get her into worse trouble.'

'It's the only way!' he insisted. 'They'll respect her for it in the long run.'

That evening, when Amy had gone to bed, May sat down with her husband and Lizzie.

'We really need to find an answer to Amy's problems,' she said. 'I hate to think of her being so unhappy.'

James put down his cigar. 'I suppose it's not surprising after the rackety life she's led that she is finding it hard to settle down. Going from being a star on the music hall stage to being an ordinary schoolgirl must be hard. But she has to understand that education is important.'

'I think,' Lizzie ventured, 'that part of the trouble is, she doesn't feel she is learning anything. I've seen the work she brings home and most of it is far below her standard. She says she knows more than the teacher, and in some ways I think she's right.'

'Really? May said. 'I know she says that, but is it true?'

'I suppose,' James said, 'in some ways that is our fault. Richard was so keen that she should catch up on the schooling she was missing during that long voyage out here that we instituted a programme of lessons. I did my best with history and geography, Lizzie took on English literature, and Richard taught her maths and some elementary science – oh, and the first officer on the ship gave her an introduction to navigation and basic astronomy.'

'The ship had a very good library,' Lizzie put in, 'and we read our way through a lot of it together. Amy has probably read books that many adults will never have read.'

'Good heavens!' May exclaimed. 'I had no idea of all that. No wonder she isn't impressed with anything Miss Clark can teach her. But couldn't we go back to that regime? I know you haven't time to spend with her now, James, but the Chiltern Athenaeum has a lending library and I'm sure with their help Lizzie could cover history and geography as well as English and I could teach her to draw and sew. She has her music lessons already with Mrs Franklyn. Isn't that enough for a young girl to learn?'

'Perhaps you're right,' James said, 'but I wish we could consult Richard. He was adamant that what she needed more than anything was to learn to mix with children her own age. And that seems to be the thing she is finding most difficult. I'll write to him tomorrow and tell him what the situation is and ask what he wants us to do. But until then I think she must just soldier on and try to fit in.'

Next day May put one of her own ideas into practice.

'Amy, how would you like to invite one or two of the girls from school to tea?'

From Amy's expression, she might have suggested inviting a couple of poisonous snakes to tea. 'Why would I want to do that? They're all horrible.'

'I'm sure they can't really be as bad as you think. There must be one or two, at least, who would be friendly if you gave them a chance. Try to think. Who are the girls who don't join in when the others tease you?'

After some further encouragement Amy came up with three names. 'But they won't come,' she added with certainty.

'We'll see,' May said.

At the end of school the following day, May met the children as they came out. 'Which are the three girls you mentioned?' she asked.

Amy pointed them out and May approached the first one, whom she recognised as the daughter of the woman who worked as a seamstress, making and mending clothes for the local people.

'It's Wilma, isn't it?'

The girl looked at her suspiciously. 'Yes?'

'I was wondering if you and one or two of the others would like to come to tea with Amy, tomorrow afternoon. I've written a note you can give to your mother, inviting you, so she knows it's true. Please will you give it to her?'

'S'pose so,' the girl muttered, casting a glance round her at her fellow pupils.

'I'm going to ask Susan and Chrissy, too, so you won't be the only one,' May assured her.

She delivered the other notes and saw consternation on the faces of all three girls. She was seized with foreboding that the idea was doomed to failure but she said brightly, 'We'll expect you tomorrow afternoon, about three o'clock.' Then she added, as an afterthought, 'There will be strawberries and cream for tea, and I'm going to make a cake.'

'They won't come,' Amy reiterated. Then, in a change of tone that bordered on panic, 'What'll we do, if they do come.'

'We'll find things to do, don't worry about that,' May assured her.

Next day she and Lizzie busied themselves with baking and making sandwiches, and devising games that the girls might play.

When Amy came home for dinner May asked, 'Well, are they coming?'

Amy shrugged. 'Don't know. Don't expect so.'

A few minutes after three o'clock the three girls, faces scrubbed and in their best dresses, appeared at the door. May, delighted by the success of her initiative, welcomed them in and seated them round the table on the veranda with Amy. She and Lizzie hovered, offering sandwiches and slices of cake, trying to encourage the conversation, but it was hard going. Amy, to do her credit, did her best to play her part as hostess, but her politeness only seemed to point up the differences between her and the other girls. All three were plainly over-awed by the situation. Susan and Chrissy, May learned, both came from families of small farmers, 'selectors' who struggled to scrape a living from the poor land they were given. Wilma, the eldest, came from a slightly less poverty-stricken background but May knew that her widowed mother still had to work hard to make a living. For all three of them, to be invited into the home of a professional man like James, a home full of what seemed to them undreamed of luxury, was intimidating. May knew from her own experience how they must be feeling and did her best to put them at their ease, but with little success. Susan and Chrissy were simply dumbstruck, while May sensed in Wilma a suppressed resentment. One thing, however, was clearly appreciated, and that was the food, and as the plates were emptied May felt a slight thawing of the atmosphere.

'How about some games?' she asked brightly.

'What sort of games?' Wilma asked.

'I spy with my little eye,' Lizzie offered, 'something beginning with "p".'

'Plate,' said Wilma.

'Well done! Your turn ...'

This kept the party going for a while, and once the table was cleared Lizzie suggested Blindman's Buff. It was impossible for anyone to stand on their dignity when blindfolded and Amy forgot her pose of sophistication and joined in. Soon they were all giggling. Then May said, 'Shall we play hide-and-seek?'

Finding they were at liberty to explore the house for hiding places the girls accepted with alacrity; then just as the game was beginning to pall Chrissy came out onto the veranda to ask, 'Is that a piano in there?'

'Yes, it is,' May said. 'Would you like to play it?'

The girl shook her head. 'Don't know how.'

'Amy can play the piano,' May said. 'Would you like her to play something for you?'

Chrissy and Susan looked at each other, then said in unison, 'Yes, please.'

They all moved into the music room and Amy seated herself at the piano. For a moment May wondered if this had been a mistake on her part and Amy would take the opportunity to show off, but she chose Haydn's German Dance, a piece with a jolly rhythm that got Chrissy and Susan jigging happily.

'Play it again!' Susan demanded when it finished, and Amy obliged.

'I wish I could do that,' Chrissy said when it was over. 'How do you know how?'

'I go to piano lessons with Mrs Franklyn, in Chiltern.'

'Oh. Does it take a long time to learn?'

'Years. And you have to practice every day.'

'Oh.' The disappointment was plain on the little girl's face.

'Amy,' May said, 'couldn't you teach Chrissy something very simple, so she can play?'

'All right.' Amy moved along the piano stool. 'You come and sit here.'

Over the next few minutes she taught the other girl to play the simple tune of Baa Baa Black Sheep. Then Susan wanted to try in her turn. Only Wilma hung back and as soon as Susan had played the tune she cut in with, 'We ought to go now. My ma will be wanting me home.'

The other two followed her lead but with perceptible reluctance and at the door their thanks to May had the ring of genuine gratitude.

May turned to Amy as they disappeared along the road. 'Well done, darling. You behaved perfectly. And they're not so bad, are they?'

'Susan and Chrissy are all right, I suppose,' Amy conceded.

'So do you think you can be friends now?'

'Maybe. It'll be different at school, I expect.'

'Well, perhaps not. We'll have to see, won't we?'

When Amy came home the next day May greeted her eagerly. 'Well? Was it any better at school today?'

Amy wrinkled her nose. 'A bit. Wilma was telling everyone I'm a show-off because I played the piano. But Chrissy and Susan talked to me at break time – and Chrissy told her brother to leave me alone.'

'Well, that's a start, isn't it? Perhaps things will get better from now on.'

Amy shrugged. 'Maybe.'

Chapter 16

Bidston, Wirral, November 1869

Vera came into the kitchen one evening carrying a magazine.

'Look what Lady Helena has lent me,' she said, laying it on the table.

Patty peered at the front page. '*The Englishwoman's Review*. What is it, a fashion magazine?'

'No, something much more important than that. It's trying to make people – well, women particularly – aware of how badly we are treated by society.'

'Well, I could tell them something about that,' Patty said. 'I don't need a magazine to do it.'

'Yes, quite, but this is intended for a much wider audience. Women like us know what it is like to be at the bottom of the heap. This is aimed at all women, even the well-off ones. For example, there's an article here about married women's property. Did you know that if we marry, everything we own belongs to our husbands and not to us?'

'That wouldn't make any difference to me,' Patty said. 'I don't own much except the clothes I stand up in, and he'd be welcome to those if he wanted them.'

'No, be serious. For women who do have some property, maybe money that has been left to them by a relative, or even money that have earned by their own efforts, all that becomes their husband's property, to do as he likes with.'

'So,' Patty said, thinking, 'say we managed one day to start our tea shop, and then one of us married, her share of the shop and her earnings would belong to her husband.'

'Exactly.'

'And if he turned out to be a wrong 'un, a gambler say, he could spend all her money and leave her with nothing.'

'Yes. And it happens to women all the time. You should read the article. Women and children left destitute because the husband has spent all their money, or gone off with another woman.'

'That doesn't seem right.'

'It's not right. The lady who wrote the article here—' she leafed through the pages '—yes, here it is. She's called Millicent Fawcett. She tells how one day a pickpocket stole her purse. He was caught and when he came up in court he was charged not with stealing *her* money, but money belonging to her husband. It made her realise how unjust the law is.'

'Suppose it happened to one of us, or any unmarried woman. Who would they say the money belonged to then?'

'Oh, that would be different. It explains it here. An unmarried woman, or a widow, is what they call … where is it … yes, here. Legally she is a *femme sole,* so her property belongs to her. But once she's married, she stops existing as a woman in her own right. She is just part of her husband. Like it says in the marriage service, man and wife are 'one flesh', so they are seen as one person.'

'Well, that settles it. I'm never getting married.' Patty put the last dish she was drying down with a clatter.

'It's all very well to say that. But what about all the women who are married already?'

'Nothing I can do about them, is there?'

'That's just it. Lady Helena and her friends think there is something to be done. There's going to be a petition to parliament asking for a change in the law.'

'I can't see that happening,' Patty said. 'The MPs are all men, aren't they? So why should they worry?'

'There are some of them who can see how unjust the law is. There's a man … what was his name? … yes, John Stuart Mill. He is trying to get a bill through parliament.'

'So what has Lady Helena got to say about it?'

'She thinks we should go and lobby our MP and persuade him to back the bill.'

'Us? He's not going to listen to us.'

'Not just us. Lady Helena and her friends are planning to do it, but she suggested we should join them.'

'What, go to London?'

'No. The MP for Birkenhead is Mr John Laird, the head of the ship-building firm. He lives not far from here, in Hamilton Square, and he divides his time between there and London. Lady Helena has found out that he's at home this week, so she has made an appointment to see him tomorrow. She's arranged to meet up with the other ladies and all go together. And she thinks we should go with them.'

Patty shook her head. 'Count me out. I wouldn't know what to say. You go, if you like. I'll stay here and stick to cooking. Sir Basil will want his dinner at the usual time, whatever her ladyship is up to.'

Vera was not deterred, and next day she joined Lady Helena in the coach heading for Birkenhead. She arrived back as Patty was putting on the kettle for afternoon tea.

'Well?' Patty asked.

'Oh, I don't think it did much good. Mr Laird was very polite. He listened to what Lady Helena and the others had to say but he didn't promise anything. I got the impression that he is much more interested in the Navy estimates. You know, how much money the government is going to spend on ships.'

'Well, that was a wasted afternoon, then,' Patty said.

'I don't know. Lady Helena says that at least we've put the idea that something is wrong into his head. Maybe if it comes to a vote he'll remember.'

Milk and eggs for the household came from one of the local farms. Each morning a churn of milk was left at the gate and Jackson brought it up to the still room, where it could be kept cool until needed. Twice a week a boy came to the kitchen door with a dozen eggs. He was a cheery lad with a thatch of straw-coloured hair and a face already roughened by exposure to wind and sun. His name was Jerry. Patty liked him and usually found him a small titbit in the shape of one of yesterday's scones or a currant bun.

One morning he said, 'You ought to have a cat, missus.'

'A cat? What do I want with a cat?'

'Keep the mice down. I bet you got mice all over the place. Place like this, you should have a cat.'

Patty gave him a shrewd look. 'So why are you suddenly so keen for me to have a cat?'

He grinned. 'Our Flossie's just had kittens. Five of them, there are. We'll keep a couple but the rest will have to be drowned unless someone'll take them.'

'Drowned? That's terrible!'

'It's what has to be done, else we'll all be overrun with cats.' His voice took on a wheedling tone. 'You could take one, maybe two. Why don't you come down to the farm and choose the one you like best?'

Patty thought for a moment. 'I suppose a cat doesn't need a lot of feeding ... and you're right, there are mice in the still room ...'

'Won't need feeding at all, if there's plenty of mice,' he assured her.

'I'll think about it,' Patty said.

Vera, when consulted, shrugged indifferently. 'I prefer dogs to cats, but if you want one I don't see why not.'

Jackson declared it to be an excellent idea. 'I can't think why we haven't got one already. Every house needs a good mouser.'

Miss Banks put up no objection, so the matter was decided.

On Sundays the main meal was served at midday, with a light supper later on, so Patty had a couple of hours off in the afternoon. The next Sunday, she walked down to Yewtree Farm. She had seen most of the local farmers and their families in church and over the weeks she had developed a nodding acquaintance with most of them, though she had never done more than pass the time of day. She had seen Jerry with his family and more than once had found her eyes drawn to his father. He was what was commonly described as 'a fine figure of a man'; tall and broad shouldered, with the same straw-coloured hair as his son, though more neatly kept, and well-trimmed beard. Patty had noticed that he was accompanied by four children plus a babe in arms, but there was no sign of his wife. He seemed very young to have such a large family.

She had never entered a farmyard before and when she reached the gate she almost turned back. The weather had turned wet in the last week and, although the rain had stopped, the yard was slick with mud. Chickens were scratching and clucking underfoot and a pig stood up on its hind legs to peer over the edge of the sty. The smell of manure was all pervasive. A large dog rushed out of a kennel, barking, and was brought up sharp when it reached the end of its chain. While she hesitated, the back door of the farmhouse opened and Jerry's father appeared.

'Don't let old Rover worry you, miss,' he called. 'Come right in. You're quite safe.'

Patty lifted her skirt and picked her way awkwardly over the muddy cobbles. The farmer held the door wide and ushered her into what was obviously the kitchen. A girl of about twelve was sitting on the floor, playing with the baby. There was no sign of Jerry or the other children.

'Welcome to Yewtree Farm,' the farmer said. 'You're from the new house, aren't you? I know you by sight, but we've never been introduced. I'm Gregory Armitage.'

'How do you do?' Patty responded. 'I'm Patty Jenkins.'

He offered her a hand large enough to swallow both hers, but its clasp was surprisingly gentle. 'Our Jerry's been telling me you might take one of our kittens. Is that right?'

'I thought I might, but I don't know much about cats.'

'There's not a lot to know,' he said with a chuckle. 'Cats mostly look after themselves. Come and have a look and see if there's one that takes your fancy.'

He led her through to a small room, where a wooden crate lined with a bit of old blanket served as a bed for a big, black cat. Curled up round her were five kittens of assorted colours. Gregory stooped and spoke softly, reassuringly, to the mother and gently lifted one of them out. Its coat was dappled tan and brown and it had a black tip to its tail.

'Here,' he said, holding it out to Patty.

Gingerly she took hold of the little creature. It was warm and soft and vibrantly alive.

Gregory said, 'Do you want a male or a female?'

'Oh, I don't know. Which is best?'

'Well, if you have a female you'll be having litters of your own to deal with in a very short time.'

'Oh. Perhaps I'd better have a male, then.'

Gregory dipped into the basket again and lifted out a black kitten. 'This here's a boy. Maybe he'll suit you.'

Patty put the first cat down and took the black one, but it squirmed round in her hand and escaped. 'He doesn't seem to like me.'

'Take no notice of that. Here, how about this little feller?'

This one was black with four white feet and a white patch between its ears, and when Patty took hold of him he curled up in her hands and began to purr. 'This one!' she said. 'I'd like this one, please.'

'He's yours,' Gregory said. 'But they're all too young to leave their mother yet. You'll have to wait a week or two. But why don't you come down when you can and get to know them?'

The other kittens were stalking around the floor on unsteady legs. Patty watched, enchanted. 'Yes, I'd love to do that, if you're sure I won't be in the way.'

'You'll be welcome any time,' Gregory assured her.

From outside Patty heard the sound of lowing, hooves on the cobbles and boys' voices.

'Ah,' Gregory said. 'That's the herd coming in to be milked. You'll have to excuse me for a while.'

'I'd better be getting back,' Patty said.

'No, stay a while. Daisy will be glad to have a bit of female company, and we'll have tea shortly. Please stay!'

He left the room and Patty heard him say, 'Make our visitor welcome, Daisy.'

She followed him back into the kitchen and the girl called Daisy scrambled to her feet and bobbed a hasty curtsy. 'Please have a seat, miss.'

Patty was suddenly powerfully reminded of herself at the same age. 'You mustn't curtsy to me,' she told her. 'There's no need. And you can call me Patty.'

Daisy flushed with pleasure. 'Won't you sit down … Patty?'

Patty took the offered chair and at once the baby crawled over to her. 'And who is this?' she asked.

'That's our Rosie,' Daisy said.

'How old is she?'

'Near on a year'

Patty looked round the kitchen. 'What happened to your mother, Daisy?'

'She died birthing Rosie,' the girl said. It was a statement of fact but underneath the practical tone Patty detected a world of loss.

'I'm so sorry. That must make things very difficult for you all. So who looks after Rosie now?'

'I do.'

'All the time?'

'There ain't nobody else to do it.'

The baby had reached Patty's feet and now held up her arms to be lifted. Instinctively Patty responded and took her on her lap. Rosie gurgled happily and mumbled something.

'She likes you,' Daisy said. 'She don't take to everyone that easy.'

'How do you manage?' Patty asked. 'What about school?'

'I had to give up school. There's the boys to look after, not just Rosie.'

'Do you mind?'

Daisy shrugged. 'Not really. I miss seeing my friends every day. I don't care much about the teaching.'

Patty sighed inwardly, remembering how she had come lately to regret her own lack of education. Poor Daisy was condemned to suffer the same loss, though she did not realise it at present.

'So you've got three brothers, is that right?'

'Yes. There's Jerry and Ben and Mickey.'

'Where are they now?'

'Out in the barn, milking.'

'All three of them?'

'The more hands the quicker it gets done.'

Patty hesitated. 'You know, I don't know how you do that.'

Daisy stared at her in disbelief. 'Ain't you never seen a cow being milked?'

'No, I haven't. You see, I've always lived in the city.'

'Want to see?'

'Well, yes. If it's no problem.'

''Course not. Come on.' Daisy lifted the child from Patty's lap and hoisted her onto her hip with practised ease. 'This way.'

Patty followed her out into the yard and then across to a barn. The evening was drawing in and yellow lamplight spilled through the door. Inside it was warm and there was a sound of peaceful munching as the cows chewed their hay, and the hissing of liquid into pails. Daisy led her to the nearest stall, where Jerry sat on a low stool, his hands busy underneath the belly of a cow. It took Patty a moment to understand what he was doing, and then she recoiled in shock. The whole process seemed to her slightly obscene.

'Don't they … the cows … don't they mind having that done to them?'

''Course not. They get really uncomfortable when their udders are full. They'll have been lined up at the gate, waiting for the boys to bring them in so they can be milked.'

'I see,' Patty murmured, wondering if she would ever drink milk again.

Daisy took her back into the kitchen and put a big kettle on the hob. In a while the three boys and their father came in, kicking off muddy boots, and Daisy poured warm water into a bowl for them to wash their hands.

Jerry said, grinning, 'You came for a kitten then? Which one are you having?'

'The little black one with the white feet.'

Jerry went into the other room and came back carrying the kitten. 'This the one?'

'Yes.'

'What are you going to call him?'

'I don't know. I don't know any names for cats.'

'What about Socks? He's got these white socks, see?'

'Socks? Yes, that's good. Come here, Socks.'

Daisy made tea and cut slices of seed cake to go with it. It was so heavy that Patty found it quite difficult to swallow, though Gregory and the boys ate it with apparent relish. When they had all finished, Patty sat stroking the kitten and chatting to the three boys about life on the farm. Gregory looked on, putting in the occasional comment. In the lamplight and the warmth from the big hob the atmosphere was cosy and peaceful and Patty felt more relaxed than she had for days. It was an effort to get to her feet when she knew the time had come when she must get back to Avalon to prepare the evening meal.

'Come whenever you feel like it,' Gregory said. 'You can watch your kitten grow up, and Daisy will be glad of your company, I know.'

Patty put on her coat and said goodbye to the children. Gregory said, 'I'll walk you back to the house.'

'Oh no,' she protested. 'There's really no need.'

'It's getting dark out there,' he replied. 'I wouldn't be happy letting you go on your own.'

As they walked Patty said, 'It must be hard for you, since your wife died.'

'It's not been easy. I won't pretend it has. But we've managed. Young Daisy's done a wonderful job, looking after the babe and cooking for the rest of us.'

'It's a shame she had to leave school,' Patty said.

'Maybe, but there was no help for it. And it seems to me that what she's learned taking care of us is going to be more use to her in years to come than any book-learning.'

Patty felt inclined to agree. It was the practical skills she had picked up while working as a kitchen maid that had led to the career she now enjoyed, but at the same time she was reminded of the sense of inferiority she experienced when Vera talked to Lady Helena about history.

'Perhaps there's room for both,' she murmured. 'But I can see that what Daisy is doing now is more important than school.' Though it was a pity, she reflected, there was no one to teach her how to make a cake.

'You must have married very young,' she said.

'Oh aye.' He gave a rueful grin. 'It were love's young dream all right. I were nineteen and Jeanie were nobbut sixteen years old. But young Jerry were already on the way so that's how it had to be. Not that I regret it. We had fourteen good years together.'

At the gates of Avalon Gregory stopped. 'You'll be safe from here. I'll say goodnight.'

'Won't you come in?' she offered. 'I could make some more tea.'

'Thank you, no. I should get back. It's the babe's bed-time and she can get a bit mardy. Daisy will be glad of some help, I expect.'

'Good night, then,' Patty said, 'and thank you for walking me home.'

'Think nothing of it. Will you come again next Sunday?'

'I'll try, as long as I'm not needed here for some reason.'

She did go again on the following Sunday, and this time she took a cake of her own baking with her.

The Wednesday afternoon tea parties for Lady Helena's friends continued and Patty, dispensing tea from a table at the back of the room, had become quite familiar with them, though they were never formally introduced. Three of them were married but the fourth, who was always addressed rather puzzlingly as Phil, was single. The others were called Elizabeth, Jane and Amelia. One Wednesday, the conversation turned to education.

'Have you read this article in the *Review* by Emily Davies?' Helena asked. 'She writes that it is shameful the way women are denied access to higher education.'

'I totally agree,' the one called Phil put in. 'When I expressed a desire to learn some science my parents were horrified. They actually told me that if I over-taxed my brain like that I would probably end up in a straightjacket.'

'That's terrible!' said Jane. 'But it is true that most of us are taught no more than what will make us accept-able as future wives.'

'But you rebelled against that idea, didn't you, Phil?' Helena said. 'You are the only one amongst us who has actually had the courage to make a career for herself.'

'But you must have taught yourself some science, surely,' Elizabeth put in. 'I mean, to have been given the position of Lady Superintendent at the infirmary, you would have to know about such things.'

Patty almost dropped the tea pot. She had had a fleet-ing impression, once or twice, that she recognised the lady addressed as Phil. Now she recalled a rather aus-tere figure who had passed through the ward while she was there. Without her white cap and starched apron she looked very different, though her manner of dress was still more severe than that of the other ladies, but there could be no doubt that she was the same person. Patty tried to recall whether she had ever spoken to her, but she thought not. She was glad of that. To be recog-nised by someone who knew the whole miserable story of her dismissal from Freeman's and its consequences would have been an unbearable humiliation.

Phil was speaking. 'The only science or mathematics I knew before I went to London to train, I taught myself by borrowing my brothers' books when they came home for the holidays. They were set work to do, mathematical problems to solve and so on. I was better at it than they were and I used to help them, so they didn't let on to my father what I was doing. Apart from that, everything I know I learned while I was at the Nightingale School for nurses.'

'That reminds me,' Jane said. 'I've wanted to ask ever since we first met. I know you were trained in London, and you don't come from this area, so what brought you to Liverpool?'

'I had a good friend called Dora at the training school who came from here. When we all qualified, she came back to work in the infirmary and I was given a post at a London hospital. Agnes Jones was responsible for setting up the whole nursing system at the infirmary, and when she died, Dora should have been appointed Lady Superintendent, but instead she chose to get married. The Vestry, who are in charge of these things, decided that to appoint another nurse already working there might cause trouble, because everyone would know she was their second choice, so they asked Miss Nightingale to send someone from London. I had been here on a visit to Dora, and liked the place, so when a volunteer was asked for I jumped at the chance.'

'Well, we all admire you for what you have achieved,' Helena said. 'But there are so many girls who will never have the chance to do something similar. It should not be such a struggle for girls to get the same education as boys.'

'Well,' Phil said, 'Emily Davies and Barbara Bodichon have taken the first steps, with this college they have set up in Hertfordshire. Perhaps others will follow.'

'But it will be too late for us,' Elizabeth said with a sigh.

'Not necessarily,' Helena said. 'I have an idea that I should like your opinions on. It occurs to me that there must be a great many women, not only people like us with comfortable incomes and a place in society, but ordinary women – farmers' wives and daughters for example – who would be quite capable of learning if they were given the opportunity. It saddens me, when I try to talk to our neighbours after church, or when I visit them when they are sick, to find how limited their horizons are. And they are not stupid. It is just that they have never been given the opportunity to learn more than the absolute basics of reading and writing and reckoning. So I am thinking of instituting a programme of fortnightly lectures and inviting any of the local women to attend.'

'What sort of lectures? Who by?' Phil asked.

'All sorts of things. Astronomy, for example. I mean, we must all have looked up at the stars and wondered what they are and what controls their movements. Philosophy, mathematics, chemistry ... I know virtually nothing about such things. I want to learn and there must be others who could benefit from the chance.'

'What a wonderful idea!' Amelia said.

Phil looked less enthusiastic. 'It's a noble sentiment, but I'm afraid you may be disappointed with the response. In my experience most women are quite satisfied if they know enough to run a household and keep their husbands happy. And men do not want them to be any different.'

'That's very cynical of you, Phil,' Helena protested. 'I'm convinced that there are a lot of women who would be grateful for any opportunity to broaden their horizons beyond their own homes.'

'Well, we shall see,' Phil said. 'But who is going to give these lectures?'

'I thought of applying to the Athenaeum. Sir Basil is a member and he tells me that there are many distinguished people among the membership. I feel sure some of them could be persuaded to come and share their particular knowledge and expertise with us. But, actually, I thought you might be our first lecturer.'

'Me? What do you expect me to talk about?'

'There must be a great many things that you learned at the nursing school which would be of interest. What about this new germ theory that that French scientist has proposed? I saw something in the newspaper about that.'

'That hasn't been proved yet,' Phil said, 'but Pasteur's experiments certainly seem convincing. It'll be a long time before the old men in the medical profession are ready to accept it, though.'

'But you could talk about that, couldn't you?'

'Maybe,' Phil said doubtfully, 'but there might be other more useful things to discuss.'

'Well, I leave that to you. I'm sure whatever you decide to say will be interesting. Will you do it?'

Phil gave a rueful shrug. 'I suppose I shall have to, but I warn you, you may not get many women to attend.'

'We'll see about that,' Helena said.

As Vera remarked to Patty later that evening, once Helena got a bee in her bonnet there was no stopping her. Within a few weeks she had extracted promises from a variety of potential lecturers and had made up a programme designed to last until Christmas. Then, with Vera at her side, she visited every farmhouse and cottage, handing out a list of dates and subjects and persuading the wives and daughters to attend.

'She won't take no for an answer!' Vera said on their return. '"I'm too busy"; "Oh, surely you can find one evening a week" … "My husband won't approve"; "Let me talk to him. I'll persuade him." No excuses accepted.'

No excuses were accepted from members of the household either. Only Nanny Banks was exempt, on the grounds that she would inevitably fall asleep before the lecture was over. Over recent months the old lady had become less and less involved in the management of the household, spending much of her time dozing in her own room. It was the comfortable retirement that Sir Basil had intended for her and no one grudged it to her. Patty and Vera, Mrs Jackson and Iris, and the women who came in to clean, were all co-opted into the audience.

On the evening of the first lecture, the women started to arrive at the front door, where Vera met them and conducted them to the music room, which was deemed the most suitable venue. Some of them made it clear that they were not there of their own free will; others were agog with curiosity or somewhat overwhelmed by being admitted into this grand new house. Helena had decreed that all should be greeted with a cup of tea and a piece of cake, so Patty had her hands full.

As agreed, the first lecture was given by Phil and to Patty's surprise it commanded undivided attention. Phil dealt briefly with the idea that disease was spread by tiny creatures called germs that were only visible under a microscope, and then moved on to the practical care of the sick. She spoke about the importance of complete cleanliness and the benefits of fresh air. She described the best way to deal with wounds and fevers and the danger of drinking contaminated water. Her manner was straightforward and she used plain language that everyone could understand, and at the end she handed out a simple information sheet for the women to take home. They left in a very different mood to the one they had arrived in, and expressed their gratitude to Helena for arranging the talk.

'Don't forget next Wednesday week,' she adjured them. 'Professor Duncan is going to talk about the stars.'

While all this was going on, Patty continued to visit Yewtree Farm, always taking a cake, which was always greeted with delight. On the third occasion, Daisy shyly asked if she would show her how to make cakes like the ones she brought. It was what Patty had been hoping for and from then on her Sunday afternoons were devoted to teaching Daisy, while at the same time keeping little Rosie amused. Gregory always walked her home afterwards and they chatted about life on the farm and her job as a cook, though she always managed to steer the conversation away from her earlier life. He was pleasant company and as the evenings drew in she was glad to have his comforting male presence at her side. She began to look forward to Sunday afternoons as the highlight of her week.

The second lecture was less successful. The eminent astronomer whom Helena had persuaded to give it was used to talking to university students and most of the language he used was incomprehensible to the majority of his audience. When the day approached for the third lecture, billed as The Legacy of Ancient Greece, little notes started to arrive by a variety of messengers, presenting excuses for non-attendance. Patty, for her own part, tried hard to follow what the speaker was talking about but she soon gave up, sat back and closed her eyes and drifted into a pleasant doze. The main drawback of that approach, however, was Vera's enthusiastic interest, which led to an eager discussion of what had been said in the kitchen when everyone else had gone home.

Patty had to confine herself to non-committal grunts in response and change the subject as soon as possible.

It was the fourth lecture in the series, however, that caused the real disruption. This one was entitled 'The Natural History of Creation' and was based on the theories propounded by Charles Darwin. As the talk proceeded the audience became more and more restive, until one woman got to her feet and declared loudly that she was not prepared to listen to this blasphemy any longer. There were cries of agreement from the rest of the audience, followed by a mass walk-out. The next day was a Saturday, which meant that Sir Basil was at home, and he had barely finished his breakfast when Vera announced that the vicar was in the hall and wished to speak with him.

After the vicar had left there were raised voices in the library and then Barney was sent out to deliver notes all around the village to say that future lectures had been cancelled. For a day or two, Lady Helena was unusually subdued.

Chapter 17

Rutherglen, November 1869

Richard replied to James's letter, reiterating his view that Amy must learn to 'rub along' with all sorts of people and 'take the rough with the smooth'. He added that as he could see no alternative they would all have to make the best of what was available. He wrote to Amy as well, telling her to be brave and promising to be back at Christmas with a special present for her.

May followed up on her first initiative by volunteering to go into the school on one morning a week to teach drawing. Her first attempt was frustrated by the discovery that the school was unable to provide either drawing paper or sufficient pencils for the whole class. The next week she took her own supplies and found a mixed reception. Most of the children were only too glad to have a break from the daily routine of spelling tests and multiplication tables, but some of the older boys saw it as an opportunity to lark about, making paper darts and drawing obscene images. After that, with Miss Clark's agreement, she instituted a new regime in which admission to her class was a privilege based on good behaviour. Those excluded would spend their time doing extra maths. From then on the classes proceeded peacefully and May took the opportunity, while the children were sketching, to chat to them about their homes, their hobbies, their hopes for the future and anything else that occurred to her.

In return, they grew in confidence sufficiently to ask her about England and her life there. One day one of the girls remarked that although drawing was enjoyable she could not see that it would ever be useful. May hesitated a moment, then took the plunge.

'Listen. If I had not learned to draw, I would not be here now. I should probably be working as a scullery maid in someone else's house.'

'You, ma'am?' There was a disbelieving laugh.

'It's true,' May said. 'I was once very poor, poorer than any of you, and I had to work as a maid in a house where I had to scrub and sweep from dawn to dusk and never got enough to eat. It was only because the master of the house saw some of my designs and realised I had some talent that I got a position as a milliner's apprentice. And that was how I met Mr Breckenridge.'

'How, miss?' one of the girls asked.

'I used to make hats for his mother.'

There was a silence while they digested this amazing revelation. Then one of them said, 'But your pa's a rich man.'

'He is now. But he wasn't then. But that goes to show that life can change for all of us, if we take the chances we are given – and work hard to make the most of them. So don't miss any chances you get.'

After that Amy reported a change in the other children's attitude towards her.

'Is it true?' one girl had asked. 'Your ma was a poor girl once?'

'She's not my ma. My ma's dead,' she had replied. 'But it's true, yes. 'Course it is.'

The incident set May thinking about how she and James and Amy were perceived in the town. Some of the older inhabitants knew her father's history. He was far from the only one who had survived transportation to make a success of life in Australia. Many of the others, though, must see her as the daughter of a rich man, married to another successful professional gentleman, living a life of ease and luxury. She knew her pupils would have carried her story home with them, and was glad that now they knew the truth – or some of it, at least. She had chosen not to mention her early years in the workhouse.

No one had been told about Amy's early life, either. Her father had decided when they arrived that it would be better for her to start 'with a clean sheet' as he put it. James had argued that she had done nothing to be ashamed of and Richard had countered with the remark that being expelled from her convent school, however excusable the circumstances, was hardly a recommendation. Moreover, her short career on the variety stage might give rise to various preconceptions. So it had been decided to say nothing.

It soon became apparent that this secrecy, too, had its drawbacks. One day Amy came home from school red-eyed and tear-stained. May greeted her with a sinking feeling in her stomach.

'What has happened now, sweetheart?'

'Miss Clark says I'm a liar.'

'Why is she saying that?'

'In class today she asked each of us to stand up and talk for one minute about something we had done that made us feel happy. One of the girls talked about rescuing a kitten that was stuck up a tree, and another one talked about making a birthday cake for her brother, and one of the boys talked about helping a cow to give birth to a calf ...' she wrinkled her nose ' ... I didn't like that. It was disgusting. Then Miss Clark told me to stand up. So I talked about walking onto the stage for the first time, and being really frightened, and then hearing everyone cheering and clapping at the end.'

'So, what was wrong with that?'

'She wanted to know when it had happened, so I told her I was a professional singer, part of a company that performed in music halls in Ireland. And she said she had asked for a true story, not a fantasy. And when I said it was true, she accused me of making it up to make myself seem special. And she sent me to sit outside the door until I was ready to apologise.'

'I hope you didn't!'

'No! Why should I? It's the truth.'

'So what happened?'

'It was home time by then. She said tomorrow I'd have to sit outside until I changed my mind.'

'Oh lord!' May sighed. 'Just as I thought things were really getting better.' She hugged Amy. 'Don't worry, darling. You haven't done anything wrong. I'll go and talk to Miss Clark. She's probably still at the school. I'll go now.'

The way to the school was uphill, and the heat that day was ferocious. By the time she arrived May was sweating and feeling slightly dizzy. The teacher was sitting at her desk, marking papers, and looked up with alarm as May marched in.

'Oh, Mrs Breckenridge! You shouldn't have bothered to come up here in this heat. I suppose Amy has told you about our little disagreement. But I'm sure she will have come to her senses by tomorrow. A vivid imagination is all very well, but she must learn to distinguish fact from fiction.'

May propped herself against one of the desks. 'That is the point, Miss Clark. What Amy told the class was absolutely true. For a few months, a year ago, she did belong to a variety company. You probably don't know it, but she has a really beautiful singing voice and she was more or less the star of the show.'

'Are you sure? It isn't just something she has made up?'

'Of course I'm sure!' May responded irritably. 'I can't go into all the details of why and how, but please take my word for it that it is true.'

'Well, if you say so ...' Miss Clark looked at her doubtfully.

May heaved herself upright. 'So tomorrow, I think you need to apologise to Amy for doubting her.'

'Apologise?'

'Why not? You wanted her to apologise to you. Now the boot is on the other foot.'

'Well, I don't know. I'll have to think ...'

'You do that. I think I need to sit down ...' The feeling of dizziness had grown worse and May found herself swaying on her feet. For a moment her vision darkened and she felt she might fall. Dimly she was aware of Miss Clark holding her up and guiding her into her own chair, then a cup of water was held to her lips.

'I'll call someone,' the teacher was saying.

'No. No need ...' May protested, but realised that she was alone. She closed her eyes and allowed herself to drift into a semi-conscious state.

Her husband's voice roused her. 'May? Darling, are you all right? No, of course you're not. Don't worry. I'm here now. I'll call Dr West.'

May sat up and opened her eyes. 'No, don't do that. I'll be fine in a moment. It was just the heat.'

'Are you sure?'

'Quite sure. Just let me get home.'

He insisted on sending a boy running to Freshfields to ask them to send the trap for her, and flatly refused to let her walk home. Minutes later Gus was there, worried and embarrassed in equal measure, muttering, 'She's not going to pup right here, is she?'

Back in the house, May lay down with a cold compress on her forehead, while Lizzie reassured the two men and got the dinner on the table. Later James tiptoed into the room to ask if she needed anything. When she assured him that all she needed was rest he asked, 'What on earth where you thinking of, trekking up there in the heat of the day?'

She explained what had happened to Amy and her consequent conversation with Miss Clark, and he immediately proposed to go up to the school and give that lady a piece of his mind.

'Don't, dearest,' May pleaded. 'She knows now that she was wrong. But really, you can't blame her for disbelieving Amy's story. It must have sounded quite improbable.'

'I suppose you are right,' he conceded. 'Anyway, I suppose the story is all round the town by now.'

'I expect it is,' May agreed. 'But I'm glad. I feel we have been living under false pretences since we came here – well, not you. You're the genuine article, but Amy and I have both got secrets in our past that mean we are not quite what people take us for.'

'I don't see why that matters. Neither of you have anything to be ashamed of.'

'I'm not ashamed. But that's my point. I grew up in the workhouse and by luck and a bit of hard work I have ended up here. I wake up every morning and I can't quite believe how lucky I am. But I'm not a lady, and I never shall be.'

James bent down and kissed her. 'You're every bit a lady, from the top of your head to the tips of your toes, and it doesn't matter where you grew up. That's what I like about this place. People don't give a damn about where you came from or who your family are. It's what you do that matters.'

'Really, James,' she murmured, 'you're letting the locals corrupt you. Your language is becoming quite coarse.' But she smiled as she said it.

Several weeks passed after that without incident. Amy reported that she was now the object of much curiosity and some admiration, and Lizzie said she could be seen holding court with a little group of friends, all agog to hear tales of her theatrical experiences.

Twice a week Gus drove Amy over to Chiltern for her regular music lessons. It was a duty he accepted willingly, since it allowed him to spend the hour with Kitty. Lizzie usually went with them and sat on Mrs Franklyn's porch, listening as Amy went through her pieces and practised her songs. One evening she came home with a look that suggested she had a problem on her mind.

When Amy had gone to bed, she said, 'Mrs Franklyn asked to speak to me privately this afternoon.'

'Oh, what now?' May asked with a groan. 'Amy hasn't upset her, too, has she?'

'No. It's quite the reverse really,' Lizzie replied. 'She told Amy to go on practising and came to sit with me on the porch. She's very pleased with Amy's progress, but that's part of the problem. She says she can take her on to a higher level with her piano but she really feels she is not qualified to teach her singing.'

'Why not?' May asked. 'Amy sings like a bird. I don't see that she needs much teaching.'

'That's more or less what I said,' Lizzie agreed. 'But it seems it's not that simple. Mrs Franklyn thinks that if she gets the right training she may have a great future ahead of her as a singer.'

'Professionally, you mean?'

'Apparently.'

'But I don't think that's what her father has in mind for her. Is it what she wants, do you think?'

'I don't know. She enjoyed her time with the music hall people, but I don't think it has ever occurred to her that she might go back to it.'

'I'm sure Richard wouldn't like the idea of her racketing about with people like that,' May said.

'I got the impression that that wasn't what was in Mrs Franklyn's mind. She said something about a serious musical career.'

'Does she mean opera? Or oratorio? That kind of thing?'

'I really don't know.'

May cast her mind back to concerts she had attended with James in Liverpool. Sometimes they had featured singers, often singing arias from operas, and she remembered feeling great admiration for them. 'I suppose,' she said doubtfully, 'if it was something like that, something … respectable Richard might allow it. But surely it's far too early to even think about it.'

'What Mrs Franklyn said was that Amy's voice is a precious gift, but if it is overused, or used in the wrong way, it could be spoilt. She says there are techniques that she needs to learn, so that she doesn't damage it.'

'And she can't teach her those techniques?'

'She says she's not qualified to do that. She's a piano teacher, not a singing teacher.'

'Does she know anyone who is?'

'Apparently not. She says the nearest person she can think of is in Melbourne.'

'Melbourne? Well, that's out of the question. It's two days' journey away.'

'Yes, I know.'

'So how did you leave things?'

'She will continue with Amy's lessons as long as we want her to. But she wants us to make enquiries about getting her some proper tuition.'

May sighed. 'Well, we can ask. But if she doesn't know anyone, I don't see that we are likely to find someone.'

Chapter 18

Bidston, Wirral, December 1869

'Isn't it about time you got round to making your Christmas puddings?' Nanny Banks asked, her tone redolent with disapproval. 'You've only got a couple of weeks.'

Patty felt a sudden wave of panic. Of course, the puddings should have been made already, but the weekly lectures and her afternoons at Yewtree Farm had taken so much of her free time that she had simply forgotten how late in the season it was. Added to that, she had only the vaguest idea how to make them. She had seen them being made when she worked at Freeman's but she had never actually been involved and now she had to wrack her memory for the necessary ingredients.

'Oh, don't worry,' she said airily, 'they'll be ready in plenty of time.'

That afternoon she persuaded Barney to harness the trap and drive her into Birkenhead to visit the library. She returned with a hastily copied list and the extra items it required. She stayed up until midnight, while the steam from the kitchen range condensed on the windows in a steady stream.

Next day Lady Helena informed her that Sir Basil's sister and her husband and three children would be spending Christmas at Avalon and her own mother and father had been invited to join them for Christmas dinner. Sitting at the kitchen table she outlined the menus she wanted for each day from Christmas Eve through to two days after Boxing Day. When she had gone, Patty put her head in her hands and almost gave way to tears.

Vera, finding her in that state, wanted to know what was wrong. Patty showed her the list.

'I'll never manage all that. I don't even know what some of those things are. What's a vol au vent, for a start?'

'But I thought you had cooked in a great house,' Vera said. 'Didn't they have food like this?'

'Maybe they did, but I was only the scullery maid. The only things I'm really good at are cakes and pastries, and that's because the pastry chef was kind to me. I've managed so far because Sir Basil likes simple food and Lady Helena doesn't seem to mind what she eats. But now there are going to be all these guests and I don't know how I'm going to cope.'

Vera sat beside her and they went through the menus together. 'Don't worry. I'll do everything I can to help,' she promised. 'We'll manage somehow.'

This time it was Vera who went into town and came back with a copy of Eliza Acton's *Modern Cookery for*

Private Families, borrowed from the library. There followed a frantic two weeks of advance preparation and trial attempts. Patty had just about decided that she would, after all, be able to produce the various dishes as required when Lady Helena looked into the kitchen to remark,

'Oh, Patty, I've invited some of the neighbours in for drinks and mince pies on the morning of Christmas Eve. I think two dozen mince pies should be enough.'

When Iris said she would like to take Christmas Day off to spend with her family, Patty finally broke down. Seeing her sobbing into her apron Iris hastened to fetch her mother and as result the two of them volunteered to help out. The festive season passed in a blur, but somehow all the dishes arrived at table more or less at the required time and were apparently eaten with pleasure – or at least without complaint – and the rest of the household dined well on the leftovers.

Patty was feeling quite pleased with herself when, passing the drawing room with empty plates on the way to the kitchen, she heard Sir Basil's sister in conversation with Helena's mother.

'Wherever does Helena find her staff? That boy, who drove us up from the ferry, for example. He's a nice enough lad, but ... well, a bit of a rough diamond, wouldn't you say?'

'Oh,' said Helena's mother, 'he'll be one of Helena's lame ducks. She has this passion for finding people who are down on their luck and trying to give them a leg up.'

'Well, I'm sure it's very creditable,' the other woman replied, 'but it does seem to make for a rather haphazard household. I mean, it's not just that boy ...'

Sir Basil appeared from the library at that moment and Patty hastened away without hearing any more.

'Is that it?' she asked herself. 'Am I one of her "lame ducks"? Am I only here as an act of charity?'

These gloomy thoughts were put out of her head, at least temporarily, by anticipation of an event to come. Mr Vyner, who was the Lord of the Manor, had invited the whole village to Bidston Hall for a ball on New Year's Eve. In fact, there would be two balls: one for the ladies and gentlemen, and a second for the servants and farm workers. It was a very long time since either Patty or Vera had been to a party, and they were looking forward to the opportunity to dress up for once.

Since starting work at Avalon they had not had any reason to spend much of their salaries and they had both been saving towards their ultimate goal of opening their own shop, but they agreed that they deserved a new dress for the occasion. Vera had chosen a silver-grey brocade, elegant but not too showy, fitting, she felt, her position as housekeeper. Patty had thought long and hard. She wanted nothing reminiscent of the yellow silk that had been her downfall. In the end she had chosen a dark-green velvet with silk ruffles in a lighter a shade. When they came downstairs, ready to leave, they were rewarded by a whistle of appreciation from Barney and a comment from Jackson to the effect that they would outshine all the fine ladies.

The servants' hall had been decorated with swags of holly and ivy and was lit by dozens of candles. The women's dresses made a kaleidoscope of colour, set off by the more sober tones of the men's Sunday best suits. A small band, consisting of fiddles and an accordion, was playing. For a moment Patty was taken back to the first such occasion she had been to, soon after she'd taken up her job at Speke Hall. It was not a happy memory and she pushed it to the back of her mind. She and Vera moved round the room, greeting acquaintances, many of whom had been at Helena's ill-fated lectures; all of them now ready for a break from the daily drudgery of their normal lives. The band struck up the Roger de Coverley and someone touched Patty on the shoulder. She turned to find Gregory Armitage, shaved and spruce in a grey suit with an embroidered waistcoat.

'May I have the honour?' he asked.

'Thank you,' she replied.

He offered her his arm and led her into the dance.

From then on he never left her side, and they danced every dance.

A good supper was laid out for them halfway through the evening, with cider cup in a huge bowl. It looked very tempting but Patty remembered the effects of the gimlet Percy had given her and stuck to lemonade.

As midnight approached the hall grew very hot and her feet started to ache. When Gregory suggested a breath of fresh air she agreed willingly. He led her out into a wide courtyard with a well in the middle. They wandered over to it and perched on the edge.

He said, 'I'm so glad you are here. I was afraid you might not come.'

'Why not?'

'You might think a servants' ball a bit beneath you.'

'Why should I think that?'

'Oh, I don't know. You're a city girl. I expect you've seen much more exciting gatherings than a lot of rustics like us.'

'I don't think of you as rustics,' she said with a laugh. 'And I like the people here much better than a lot of the people I knew in the city.'

'I'm glad to hear you say that,' he murmured. 'Because I like you, Patty Jenkins. Very much indeed.'

He put his arm round her and pulled her towards him. She knew he was going to kiss her and some instinct made her duck out of his grasp and stand up.

'It must be nearly midnight. Let's go back in.'

As they re-entered the hall, the church clock struck the hour. A cheer went up and then everyone joined hands for 'Auld Lang Syne'.

Shouts of 'Happy New Year' rang out, and a banner was unfurled from the rafters: 'BEST WISHES TO ONE AND ALL FOR 1870'.

Gregory wanted to walk her home, but she was relieved to see Barney in the pony trap ready to drive them back.

'Thank you, Gregory, but there's no need,' she said, indicating the trap. There was an awkward pause, then she went on, 'I've enjoyed this evening so much. Thank you for dancing with me.'

'I should thank you, not the other way about,' he said. 'You made the evening for me.'

To Patty's relief Vera appeared out of the crowd and took her arm. 'Come on, Patty. Barney's waiting for us.'

'Yes, coming,' she responded, and offered her hand to Gregory. 'Happy New Year, to you and all the family.'

'And to both of you,' he replied. She could see that he would like to have said more but she turned away quickly to mount the trap.

Chapter 19

Rutherglen, December 1869

Almost the entire population of Rutherglen went to church on Sunday, if not as a matter of religious faith, as a matter of social convention. Most of them attended St Stephen's, whose bell tower had decorated the skyline since it had been built five years previously. The adults went to matins and the children went to Sunday School. After her first few attendances Amy had pronounced that she much preferred that to the religious instruction she had had at the convent school.

'At the convent we had to learn our catechism. It was lots of questions about things I didn't understand and when I asked what it meant, Mother Scholastica got angry with me. She said it was matter of faith and called me a little heathen. But in Sunday School Mrs Swan just reads us stories from the bible and tells us that Jesus loves us.'

November gave way to December and one Sunday Amy re-joined her family with shining eyes. 'We're going to do a nativity play. And I'm the Angel Gabriel.'

'You are?' May said, 'That's wonderful. You see? I always knew you were an angel.'

Amy giggled. 'Not a real angel, silly. Only pretending.'

'I'm sure you will pretend splendidly,' James said. 'But didn't you want to be Mary?'

'Oh no,' Amy assured him. 'Angel Gabriel's a much better part.'

James caught May's eye. 'She has an instinct for the theatrical. There's no doubt about it.'

That evening James remarked, 'One thing I really miss here is the concerts we used to go to back in Liverpool.'

'Oh, so do I!' May agreed. 'Do you remember that wonderful carol concert you took me to at the Philharmonic Hall?'

'Of course I do. It was our first date. I wonder … there must be similar things happening in Melbourne. How do you fancy a few days there?'

'That would be wonderful!'

'Amy would be all right here, with Lizzie to look after her.'

'Of course she would.'

'I'll look into it.'

Next day he came in waving the local paper. 'Melbourne Choral Society are giving the *Messiah* on December the seventeenth. What about it?'

'Oh, yes, please,' May responded. 'I've never heard the Messiah all through.'

'I'll see if I can get tickets.'

As it happened they had been invited to spend the evening at Freshfields, and in the course of the conversation James mentioned their plan.

Maria stared at him. 'Are you mad! May can't go to Melbourne in her condition.'

'I'm expecting a baby,' May protested. 'I'm not ill.'

'Two days, jouncing about in a coach, over these roads? Do you want to lose the baby?'

'Maria's right,' her father said. 'It's too much of a risk.'

James looked at his wife with an expression of contrition. 'May, I'm so sorry! Of course, Maria's right. I was being thoughtless.' Then, seeing her disappointment, he reached out and took her hand. 'Next year. We'll do it next year, I promise.'

May tried to hide her feelings but she had been looking forward so much to the proposed visit and it was hard to have it snatched away again. Over the next days a mood of lassitude crept over her. Christmas celebrations in the mid-summer heat had always felt wrong and suddenly the preparations seemed pointless. She began to spend a good deal of time stretched out on a daybed in the shade of the veranda, dozing or gazing into space. Even Amy's excited accounts of rehearsals for the nativity play failed to rouse her.

James and Lizzie grew increasingly worried, until one evening he came home with a new sparkle in his eyes. 'Listen, my darling. I know you're really disappointed about the concert in Melbourne, but I can offer you a substitute. It won't come up to the same standard, but I still think it's worth doing. We are going to have our own carol concert, here in Rutherglen.'

'How?' May asked, sitting up.

'I've talked to the minister and the other church wardens and they are all enthusiastic about the idea. We'll advertise for volunteers to form a choir. And it seems that they already have one in Chiltern and are preparing their own concert. I thought we could invite them to come and join us. Local people will be glad to put them up for a night afterwards. We can make it a real celebration. What do you think?'

May smiled at him fondly. 'I think it's a wonderful idea – and I know you're doing it mostly for my sake. Thank you, darling.'

'Well,' he said, 'I admit that's why I suggested the idea in the first place, but now the more I think about it the more excited I am. It could be a real community effort and make this Christmas special for a lot of people.'

'There's just a couple of things that occur to me,' May said. 'You will need an accompanist, for a start.'

'I thought we might ask Mrs Franklyn. We could put her up here after every rehearsal.'

'Well, she might do it, I suppose. But there's the other question. Who is going to conduct and be the musical director?'

James looked slightly uncomfortable. 'I've volunteered myself for the job. I know I haven't got any formal training, but I've always loved music and I know a wrong note when I hear one. Do you think I'm being presumptuous?'

May took his hand. 'No, my dear, I don't. If anyone can pull this off it's you. And I'm sorry I've been such a wet blanket lately. I'll help in any way I can.'

James's enthusiasm was catching and very soon almost the entire population of Rutherglen was clamouring to be involved. There was no shortage of volunteers for the choir and though very few of them could read music they all knew the familiar carols by heart. In addition, those from other nationalities brought their own songs and were happy to teach them to the rest, so that very soon the programme included traditional German, Italian and French carols. There was one drawback, however. Mrs Franklyn agreed to play for the concert itself but maintained that it was impossible for her to attend all the rehearsals. She had, she pointed out, her regular pupils to consider.

'But don't worry,' she said. 'Why not ask Amy to play for the rehearsals? She's quite capable of playing, if you can obtain the sheet music.'

Amy was thrilled to be asked to take on the responsibility and, after James had telegraphed an order, packets of music arrived by the next coach. Amy took her new role very seriously and spent every afternoon practising.

When Patrick O'Dowd heard about the concert he got together with the other instrumentalists who normally played when there were dances and they offered to contribute a medley of Christmas music to be played after the actual concert was over. Then someone suggested that the celebrations should finish with a hog roast and the suggestion was adopted with enthusiasm.

James came back from rehearsal one evening and announced. 'I have had an idea.'

'Another one?' May queried with a smile.

'The Sunday School nativity play should be part of the concert. We could have a few carols first, then the play, then finish with more carols. What do you think?'

'I think it's an excellent idea. Have you spoken to Mrs Swan?'

Mrs Swan was the minister's wife, and took charge of the Sunday School as a natural extension of her duties.

'Yes, she's all for it. And listen. It occurred to me that Amy should have a solo as part of her role as the Angel Gabriel. I'm sure we could find a suitable carol.'

'Oh, brilliant! She will be delighted.'

A brief hunt through the sheet music revealed the ideal choice. Amy would sing the carol 'Joy to the World.' Lizzie was tasked with making her costume, about which she had very definite ideas, based on the one she had worn when she appeared as an angel at the climax of her career in the music hall.

'It has to have real feathers on the wings,' she insisted.

Fortunately a local farmer was killing geese ready for Christmas dinners, so there was no shortage.

In the midst of all these preparations James made several further visits to the telegraph office, and the young woman who operated the telegraph was sworn to silence about the content of his messages and the replies. The date for the concert had been set as 18 December, and, a week before, he came home for his dinner looking more triumphant than ever.

'I've got a surprise for you.'

'Oh, what?'

'You know the saying about Mohammed and the mountain?'

'If Mohammed won't come to the mountain, the mountain must come to Mohammed. Why?'

'Well, if May can't come to Melbourne, then Melbourne must come to May.'

May laughed. 'Whatever are you talking about?'

'I've been in touch with a Professor Maxwell at the Faculty of Music and Fine Arts at the university. I suggested that one or two of his more advanced students might like to make their professional debut in Rutherglen – in exchange for bed and board and a small fee. As a result, we can expect two singers, a baritone and a soprano, plus their piano accompanist. They will perform extracts from the *Messiah* and the professor assures me that they are both very accomplished, with a great future ahead of them.'

May stood up and put her arms round his neck. 'Oh, what a lucky girl I am to have such a wonderful husband!'

From then on May was caught up in a flurry of activity. There were beds to be made up for the singers and their accompanist, which necessitated Amy moving in with Lizzie and the nursery being temporarily transformed into a bedroom. There was food to be ordered and prepared as far as was possible in advance. She had resisted any suggestion that she should join the choir, on the pretext that all the standing would be too taxing in her condition, but she was committed to helping with refreshments for the visiting choir from Chiltern and providing a dessert as a contribution to the hog roast. Lizzie took her share of the load but in addition she had to go to Chiltern with Amy, so that she could practise her carol with Mrs Franklyn. Amy, in the midst of all this, remained surprisingly calm, focused on her role as rehearsal pianist and her coming solo.

The singers arrived on the seventeenth. May had been worried that they might be very sophisticated and inclined to look down on this amateur affair in the 'backwoods'. But they turned out to be very unassuming and refreshingly anxious about how their contribution would be received. The members of the Chiltern choir would come on the day of the concert. Letters had gone to Richard, asking if he would be able to return in time but he responded that, although he hoped to be home for Christmas, he could not be sure of when he would be free. On the night of the seventeenth, however, as darkness was drawing in and May and James were entertaining their guests to supper, a single horseman arrived on a sweating steed at the front door.

Betsy, answering the bell, let out a shriek. 'Oh, lordy! It's you, Mr Kean!'

Amy, who was on her way to bed, flew down the stairs. 'Papa! Papa! You're here! I knew you'd come!'

He swept her up into his arms. 'How could I miss such a special occasion?'

Half an hour of happy confusion followed, as Richard was introduced to the guests from Melbourne and an extra place was found for him at the table. Amy forgot about going to bed and no one reminded her. Then the question arose of where he was going to sleep that night. The house was full. But a visit to Freshfields quickly produced an invitation to stay there until the concert was over and the singers and their accompanist had departed.

The next day passed in frantic last-minute preparations. The singers went into the church to rehearse their pieces; the Chiltern choir arrived and were allocated their accommodation at various homes in the town; the fire was started for the hog roast; extra chairs had to brought into the church and arranged to accommodate both the two choirs and the audience. By evening May was feeling exhausted, but she took her place in the front row with a delicious tremor of excitement. It might not be the *Messiah* in its full glory, but this concert would have far more meaning for her.

The programme began with four carols from the combined choirs and May was amazed at how harmonious and full-throated they sounded. They finished with

'Hark the Herald Angels Sing', and then it was the turn of the Sunday School nativity play. It was as everyone had expected, a gaggle of children in a ragbag assortment of costumes, some intently focused on their part, others gazing around in search of parents and friends, some shrinkingly shy, others brashly over-confident. Among them, one figure stood out – Amy, serenely self-possessed in her feathered wings and halo, her golden hair shining in the light from the windows. When her turn came, she spoke her lines with real authority, but it was when she started to sing that a hush fell over the congregation. May tore her eyes away from the small figure, her attention attracted by a movement from the young soprano who was sitting to one side awaiting her turn. She had leaned forward, watching intently, and then May saw her touch the arm of her colleague and a look passed between them. When the song ended, in defiance of convention, the whole audience burst into applause.

Next it was the turn of the professionals and May abandoned herself to sheer delight. The tenor sang 'Comfort ye, my people' and 'Every valley shall be exalted', but it was the soprano aria that went to May's heart: 'He shall feed his sheep, like a shepherd'. When she heard the words 'and gently lead those that are with young' she felt that the whole piece had been specially written for her.

The concert ended with more carols, culminating in 'Oh Come All Ye Faithful'. Then the congregation filed out to find the little band of fiddle, accordion and guitar playing 'The Holly and the Ivy' to lead the way to the paddock where the hog roast was sending savoury aromas into the air.

Everyone was crowding round Amy, congratulating her, and she was the centre of a happy crowd of her fellow actors, most of whom, May noted, were also pupils at the school. She went to join James, who was entertaining the musicians from Melbourne. The soprano, whose name was Stella, turned to her at once.

'Do tell me about the little girl who played the angel. What's her name?'

'Amy Kean,' May said.

'She has the most amazing voice for a child of her age. And such presence! Are her parents here? I'd love to speak to them.'

'Her mother died, a long time ago, but that's her father, over there.'

James, overhearing the conversation, called, 'Richard! Here a moment.'

Hearing the call, Richard made his excuses to the group he had been chatting with and joined them.

'I just wanted to tell you that you have a remarkable little daughter,' Stella said. 'Where does she have her singing lessons?'

'She has piano lessons with Mrs Franklyn, who accompanied the concert,' May put in. 'But she has been saying that she really is not qualified to take Amy's singing lessons any further.'

Richard looked at her. 'Really? That's news to me.'

At that moment the cry went up that the hog roast was about to be served and there was a general movement towards the fire. Richard offered his arm to Stella.

'May I?'

'Thank you.' With a blush she took his arm and he led her to join the queue. They were joined by the tenor and May noticed that for some time all three were in deep conversation.

After the excitement of the concert, and the party that followed, everyone felt a little flat the next day. It was Sunday, but attendance at matins was sparse; clearing up was done lethargically; the visitors from Chiltern departed yawning. James, backed up by Lizzie, insisted that May should spend most of the day with her feet up. By Monday morning, however, things seemed to have returned to normal. The music students were seen onto the Melbourne coach, with expressions of gratitude from both sides, Richard moved back into his room at Lake House and all attention turned towards the preparations for Christmas.

The school term had not ended and Amy went off more happily than ever before, to be greeted, as Lizzie reported, by a small gang of admirers. May sighed with relief at a problem solved, but at mid-morning Amy rushed back into the house, scarlet-faced and weeping and clutching her left hand with her right.

Lizzie caught hold of her. 'Amy? Whatever's wrong?'

'She hit me! Miss Clark. She caned me!'

'She what?' May joined them in the hallway. 'Whatever for?'

'For fighting.' The words came out in gulping sobs.

'Fighting? You were fighting? Who with?'

'Sammy Dawson. It wasn't my fault. He called me a silly show-off. He was laughing at me, saying things like "Where are your wings? Why don't you fly away?" I told him to leave me alone and he said, "Are you going to make me?" and he pulled my hair. Then he pushed me against the wall and tried to put his hand up my skirt, so I did what Gus told me to do. I kicked him.'

'Oh, Gus!' May murmured.

'Then what happened?' Lizzie asked.

'He grabbed my arm and started twisting it. It hurt. So I bit his hand. He let out a yell and Miss Clark came running and pulled me away. She said she wouldn't tolerate fighting and we would both have to be punished.'

Richard had come in from the veranda. 'Come here, Amy.' He took her by the shoulders. 'Who is this boy, Sammy?'

'I know him,' May put in. 'He's a great lout of a boy, twice Amy's size.'

'Has he done things to you before?'

Amy nodded and sniffed. 'He's horrible. He's always teasing and pulling girls' hair.'

'So what did Miss Clark do?'

A small gleam of revengeful satisfaction crossed Amy's face. 'Sammy got six strokes of the cane on his bare bottom, in front of the whole class. Then—' she began to weep again '—then she called me out and said as I had been fighting too I must be punished, and she did this.' She held out a shaking hand on which three purple stripes showed up against the soft flesh.

'The witch!' Lizzie exclaimed. 'That is so unfair!'

Richard held Amy away from him and looked into her face. 'You are quite sure that he started the fight? You didn't kick him just because he was teasing you?'

'No! I told you. He pulled my hair and tried to put his hand up my skirt.'

Richard lifted her hand and touched it gently with his lips. Then he straightened up. 'Right! That settles it. You are never going to set foot in that place again. And I shall go up there right now and tell Miss Clark that.' He turned Amy gently towards Lizzie. 'Look after her. I'll be back shortly.'

The front door opened and they saw him striding away up the drive. Amy said shakily, 'Does he really mean it? I'm not going back?'

'Yes, love. I think he does,' Lizzie reassured her. 'Now, come upstairs and let me bathe your poor hand and wash your face.'

When Richard returned, grim-faced, Lizzie asked, 'Does this mean we are going to teach Amy at home from now?'

'That,' he said, 'is something I shall have to consider very carefully.'

Amy seemed to recover her spirits by dinner time, but that night she roused them all by screaming out in her sleep. When Lizzie and May rushed to her bedside she was squirming in the grip of a nightmare and muttering over and over again, 'Don't beat me, mama. Please don't beat me!'

Lizzie took her in her arms and held her tightly. 'It's all right! It's all right. No one is going to beat you. You're with us now, remember?'

After a little Amy quietened and Lizzie settled her back on her pillow. 'Go to sleep now. You're quite safe. Hush!'

Once the child was asleep again they tiptoed out of the room. May asked, 'Why was she saying that? What was that about her mama?'

'You didn't know? Mrs McBride, her adoptive mother, used to beat her quite often. She believed in the adage "spare the rod and spoil the child". I used to try to protect her but I wasn't always able to. That was why she ran away when she was expelled from the convent. She was terrified what they might do to her when she got home.'

'I had no idea,' May whispered. 'Does Richard know?'

'Oh yes. That's one reason why he reacted so sharply this morning.'

'That poor little girl!' May whispered. 'If I'd known what was happening when we were all back in Liverpool, I'd have killed that woman!'

Lizzie smiled at her. 'Just as well you didn't, then. Come on. Let's get back to bed.'

By next day Amy had apparently forgotten her nightmare, though she still nursed her bandaged left hand in her right and seemed more subdued than usual. But, aided by the fact that for her the Christmas holiday had started early, she soon began to recover her spirits and entered into the preparations. They were all invited to Freshfields for Christmas dinner and after they had eaten there was the usual exchange of gifts. The climax of the afternoon came when Richard, who had slipped out of the room, returned carrying a bundle covered by a towel. The bundle wriggled and revealed itself as a golden Labrador puppy.

Amy came to her feet, her eyes wide with wonder. In a voice scarcely above a whisper she asked, 'Is that for me?'

'Well,' her father said, 'I don't recall promising to buy a puppy dog for anyone else.'

Amy put out a timid hand and touched the golden coat. 'Oh, he's beautiful! Thank you, Papa.'

The puppy turned his head and licked her hand. 'There, he likes you,' Richard said. 'Here, you can hold him.'

He bent and placed the puppy in his daughter's arms and she cradled it joyfully. 'He's so sweet! What is he called?'

'He doesn't have a name yet. What do you want to call him?'

Amy thought for a moment. 'I think I'll call him Sunbeam – Sunny for short. Then I'll have a pony called

Snowflake and a puppy called Sunbeam. That sounds good, doesn't it?'

'Sounds to me,' Gus put in with a laugh, 'like you've got a pet for all seasons.'

There was a general laugh and as it died down Richard said, 'This seems a good moment to tell you all some news I've been keeping back. I was going to say something when I first arrived but there seemed to be rather a lot going on at the time.'

'What news?' George Lavender asked.

'Gold mining is coming back to Rutherglen.'

'No, no,' George said. 'It was all worked out years ago. You're wasting your time there.'

'The easy stuff, that could be got by panning, yes,' Richard responded. 'But I'm talking about deep mining. A survey has been carried out and there seems to be good a prospect of success. I have found half a dozen backers who will put up the money and I propose to start work in the New Year.'

'Risky,' George commented.

'Perhaps. But I have every confidence in the results of the survey.'

'Does that mean that you will be staying here?' James asked.

'Yes, of course.'

'So you won't be going away again, Papa?' Amy asked eagerly.

'That's right. I am going to start looking for a house, or a plot of land to build on, somewhere in this area.'

'You know you and Amy are welcome to stay with us,' James said.

'I know. And I'll be grateful to accept your hospitality until I get settled. But I think it's time Amy and I had a place of our own.'

'Well,' George said, 'charge your glasses, everyone. Let's drink to success in the year to come, for Richard with his new venture and for our vintage of eighteen seventy.'

'To eighteen seventy!' Richard said, and they all drank.

Chapter 20

Bidston, Wirral, January 1870

The failure of her lecture project did not subdue Helena for long. As soon as the household had settled back into its normal routine she announced, 'Well, since my attempts to open up local women's minds to new ideas have fallen on stony ground, I am determined to continue my own education. I have long wanted to know more about the various branches of science, so I am going to concentrate on that. I have employed a tutor, a young man called Paul Sedley. He is a graduate of Cambridge University and has been looking for a position. He will arrive tomorrow. He can sleep in the men's wing. There is an empty room next to Mr Charles's. And he will eat with the rest of the household. I hope you will all make him welcome.'

'Poor man,' Vera said. 'I suppose he was expecting to find a position tutoring someone's children. I should think it will feel a bit odd to find himself teaching a married lady.'

Nanny Banks sniffed. 'It's completely unsuitable, if you ask me. I can't imagine what Sir Basil was thinking of to allow it.'

'Well, I think it's to Lady Helena's credit that she is prepared to embark on something like this when most ladies would be content with paying visits and planning dinner parties,' Vera said. 'And I think it's to Sir Basil's credit that he isn't standing in her way.'

'What does a lady in her position want with science?' Nanny asked. 'It's unnatural, that's what it is.'

'I envy her the opportunity,' Vera said. 'I should love to be able to study such things.'

Paul Sedley was in his early twenties, a slender young man with glasses and soft brown hair that tended to fall across his forehead and had to be constantly pushed back. He was shy and seemed uncertain how he fitted in to the social hierarchy of the household. In many cases this unease was mutual. To the Jackson family he was an exotic creature who should by rights inhabit a completely different sphere, and Patty shared their feelings. Dulcie treated him with suspicion as someone who intruded on the close relationship she had with her mistress and Nanny Banks made no attempt to conceal her disapproval. Vera, however, made it her business to put him at his ease.

A timetable was agreed for Helena's lessons. The first topic of study was to be chemistry. She would spend an hour every morning with Sedley in the library, learning theory, and in the afternoons there would be practical demonstrations. For these, he pointed out, he would need a laboratory, so an empty store room just beyond the boiler room was set aside for this purpose and he went back to Liverpool and returned with several crates in which glassware clinked and metal objects clattered. Vera immediately offered to help him set up his equipment and they both disappeared for the rest of the afternoon.

The atmosphere around the kitchen table at meal times underwent a subtle change. Patty noticed that Vera had given up her attempts to 'humanise' Mr Charles and was now devoting her attention to Paul Sedley.

'The poor chap is so shy!' she said. 'It's the least we can do to try and make him feel at home.'

Charles, conversely, having withstood all Vera's attempts, seemed eager to be friendly with the newcomer, asking him about his time at the university and about what practical demonstrations he planned to make for Lady Helena's benefit. Once they got onto that subject, Sedley's shyness evaporated, and he spoke enthusiastically about his plans.

'Lady Helena has very kindly said that I may use the laboratory to conduct my own researches when she is unable to spare the time to be with me,' he told them. 'I have a whole programme of experiments in mind. But I really need an assistant for some of them.'

Vera and Charles responded simultaneously, offering to help.

'Mr Charles will not be here most of the time,' Vera said pointedly. 'He has to be with Sir Basil all day.'

'And you have your duties here, as housekeeper,' Charles countered. 'Surely they are more than enough to keep you occupied.'

'I am usually free in the afternoon,' she responded. 'And I am very keen to learn.'

'I have some knowledge of the subject already,' Charles said. 'I should not need so much instruction. Perhaps you could postpone your experiments until the evening, when I return from Liverpool?'

Sedley was looking increasingly embarrassed. 'I know Lady Helena expects me to spend most of the afternoons in the laboratory. She will be there herself when circumstances allow. But—' he looked from Vera to Charles '—I am sure there will be times when I shall need to carry on with an experiment into the evening, so …'

'So I shall be happy to help,' Charles said, and he smiled. Patty could not recall ever seeing him smile like that.

From then on Vera spent most of her afternoons in the laboratory and at supper she enthusiastically discussed the outcome of their experiments. She and Sedley were soon on first-name terms, and Patty noticed that she was taking more trouble with her appearance than before. Patty had accused her of flirting with Charles once, but she had far stronger grounds for making the same charge now and she watched them together with increasing unhappiness.

Charles, however, had not given up and with increasing frequency Sedley found it necessary to continue his work into the evening. When Vera offered her help it was made clear to her that she was not needed, and on those occasions she relapsed into a gloomy silence or took herself off to her room to read one of the magazines that Helena passed on to her when she had finished with them.

One day she came to dinner looking smug. 'I asked Lady Helena whether it would be possible for me to attend some of her lessons with Paul. She knows I have been helping out with the practical experiments and I am really keen to understand the theory behind them. Of course, I appreciate that Paul's attention must be entirely on her, but she has agreed that I can sit in and listen.'

As soon as she could get Vera alone Patty said, 'This idea of attending Lady Helena's lessons ... how are you going to get your work done? You are already spending most of the afternoons in the laboratory. If you start to skimp it is bound to be noticed sooner or later, and then there will be trouble.'

'Oh, don't worry,' Vera responded. 'I'll get up extra early – and it's only for one hour after all.'

Over the next weeks Patty saw less and less of her friend. Vera's attention was focused on Paul, and Patty could see that she was falling in love with him, though his own response seemed dubious at best. She worried that Vera was heading for heartbreak, but even if she was mistaken about the outcome, it meant that their plans for the future were in tatters. As the dark days of winter passed she became increasingly depressed.

She had not been to Yewtree Farm since the party on New Year's Eve. She could not explain to herself why she was reluctant to go there. Gregory had made it clear that he was attracted to her and there was no logical reason why she should dislike the idea. He was an attractive man and, as her hopes of owning her own tea shop with Vera's help became more and more illusory, the prospect of marriage to a prosperous farmer had its attractions. And yet something deep inside her rejected the idea and kept her away.

When Jerry came to the door with the eggs she usually contrived to be busy and sent Iris to deal with him, but one day when he knocked Iris was out on an errand and Patty had to answer the door herself.

His face split into a delighted grin at the sight of her. 'Oh, there you are, Miss Patty. We were thinking perhaps you'd been unwell. It's weeks since you came to tea – and Socks is ready for you to take home now.'

'No, I haven't been ill,' Patty said. 'I've just been very busy.'

'Do come!' he begged. 'Our Daisy keeps asking after you. She misses your cookery lessons. We all miss you.'

Patty looked at his eager young face and felt guilty at having disappointed him and his family. Perhaps, she told herself, she had been mistaken about Gregory's intentions. Perhaps he had not been going to kiss her, or if he had perhaps it was just a momentary impulse, born of the heat of the moment and too much cider cup. She smiled at Jerry and said, 'I'll see what I can manage. I'll try to come, if not this Sunday then next.'

In the event, she went on the first Sunday and was received with such warmth that she told herself she had been a fool to stay away. Gregory was his usual, affable self and when he walked her home he made no attempt to kiss her. She decided that her fears had been unfounded.

One morning, when February sunshine gave a hint of spring and snowdrops were coming into flower under the hedges, Vera came into the kitchen, looking pale and shocked.

'Patty, can we go somewhere where we can talk? I don't want the others to overhear.'

'It's all right,' Patty said. 'I've sent Iris home. She's got a streaming cold. And none of the others will be here until dinner time. What is it? What's happened?'

Vera sank down onto one of the benches by the table, 'I've been such a fool! You warned me, but I didn't listen, and now I'm in trouble.'

'What sort of trouble?' Patty asked with misgiving.

'Oh, not that sort of trouble. No chance of that! I'm in trouble with Lady Helena. She called me in to go over the household accounts for last month, and I had clean forgotten to pay the butcher. She had a letter from Mr Spinks, complaining that his bill hadn't been paid, and when we went through the accounts there were several other bills outstanding. I'm afraid I have been so wrapped up in ... well, in the chemistry lessons ... that I'd let things slip. Now, Lady Helena says I must stop going to her lessons and concentrate on my work.'

'Well, she's right, isn't she?' Patty said. 'But it's not so terrible, is it? You will be able to put things straight.'

'It was the way she spoke to me. She said she had given me this job because she felt society had treated me badly and she felt sure that I was capable and ... and honest. Now she thinks I'm ungrateful and unreliable. She said ... she said that Sir Basil has made a few comments about the way the household is being run, and if there are any more complaints she may have to think about finding someone else.'

'Oh Lord!' Patty said. 'You mean, you could lose your job?

Vera nodded and blew her nose on the corner of her apron. 'I've been a fool, Patty. But I won't let it happen again. I've promised Lady Helena and I'll make sure she doesn't have to complain again.'

'And perhaps you need to spend less time with Paul Sedley,' Patty suggested.

'I don't see what that has got to do with it,' Vera snapped. 'I've said I will not go to the lessons in the morning any more, but I can still help out with the experiments in the afternoons.'

'It just seems to me that your mind hasn't been on your work ever since he arrived,' Patty said.

'That's nonsense. I am just taking the opportunity to study things I never had a chance to learn about before. Why shouldn't I?'

'Are you sure that's all there is to it?'

The colour rose in Vera's face. 'I know what this is about. You are jealous, that's what it is.'

'No, I'm not! I just think you are making a bit of a fool of yourself, that's all.'

'Me? Making a fool of myself? What about you and Gregory Armitage? I saw the way you danced with him on New Year's Eve.'

'Why shouldn't I? He's a decent man and we get on well together, but that's all there is to it.'

'Oh, yes?'

'Yes.'

'Well, I get on well with Paul. And why shouldn't I enjoy the company of a man? I haven't taken a vow of celibacy.'

Patty sighed. 'I know, and if you really like Paul I've got no right to object. But I'm not sure he feels the same way about you.'

She saw tears start into Vera's eyes. 'That's a cruel thing to say! You only say that because you want to keep me all to yourself. Well, I've got a right to a life of my own, so you will just have to accept that and keep your opinions to yourself.'

With that, she marched out of the kitchen and slammed the door behind her.

*

362

Sir Basil had been invited to go shooting with some friends and had come back with two brace of pheasants, which were hanging up in the still room. Every time she had to go in there to fetch something Patty's stomach turned over. It was not just the smell, which was getting worse every day; Jackson assured her that was quite normal and birds had to be hung before they could be eaten. The root of her uneasiness was the knowledge that one day she would be asked to cook them and she had no idea how to go about it.

Lady Helena came into the kitchen to say, 'Sir Basil has invited some important guests for dinner on Saturday and he wants you to put on something special. He would like you to cook the pheasants as the main course. There will be six of us. We shall want soup and then fish, then the pheasants and one or two of your delicious puddings. I leave the details to you. I know you will rise to the challenge.'

Jackson agreed to pluck and gut the birds but on Saturday Vera found Patty sitting at the kitchen table with the birds in front of her and her head in her hands. They had been stiff and awkward with each other since their quarrel but now Vera sat down and leaned across the table to touch Patty's arm.

'I'm sorry I snapped at you the other day. I was upset because Lady Helena had hauled me over the coals. Now, what's the problem?'

'These birds,' Patty said. 'Sir Basil wants something special but I don't know what to do with them.'

The Eliza Acton cookery book had had to go back to the library, so there was no help coming from that direction.

Vera said, 'I think you just roast them, don't you?'

'I suppose so,' Patty said doubtfully, 'but I'm not sure how long for.'

'Well, just treat them like you would treat a chicken,' Vera said.

Patty toiled all day in the kitchen. She made a leek and potato soup, and followed it with grilled fillets of sole. As Vera had suggested, she roasted the pheasants, but she was so busy with the other dishes that they were left in the oven rather longer than she intended. They came out looking rather shrunken and dark in colour. There were mashed potatoes to go with them, and a dish of broccoli and she had made a sherry trifle and an apple pie for pudding. Iris was pressed into service to serve the meal and Mrs Jackson came in to help, but it was still a nightmare of juggling to get everything on the table when required.

They had just finished the washing up when they heard the guests leaving. A moment later Sir Basil entered the kitchen. Patty almost dropped the last dish she was drying in shock. There was no doubt from the look on his face that he had not come to congratulate her.

'Put that down and come here,' he ordered. Patty did as he said. 'I wanted very much to impress my guests with tonight's dinner and I am afraid I failed miserably.

The pheasant was so dry and tough it was almost ined-
ible; there was no bread sauce, no game chips, no
redcurrant jelly to go with it. The soup and fish were
acceptable, though unexciting, and your sweet dishes
were well made, but again somewhat pedestrian. And
why was there no savoury to end the meal?'

'Savoury, sir,' Patty mumbled. 'The missis didn't say
anything about that.'

'Have you ever cooked pheasant before?'

'No, sir. I'm sorry it wasn't satisfactory.'

He paused and sighed. 'Patty, I know a little about
your history. Am I right in thinking that you have never
had any formal training as a chef?'

'Training, sir? Only what I learned working in the
kitchen at Freeman's Department Store.'

'So you have never been asked to produce a meal for
a proper dinner party?'

'No, sir, not really.'

'As you well know, I am happy to eat simple food
most of the time but I have been aware before now that
when there is a special occasion you find it difficult to
reach the standard of cooking you would find in most
upper-class houses. I know my wife has the highest
motives in employing you, but I think the time has come
for us to rethink the arrangements. I will let you know
my conclusions in due course. Good night.'

'Goodnight, sir.' She bobbed a curtsy, keeping her
head lowered so that he did not see her tears.

Once again, raised voices were heard in the library the following morning. Patty had slept little and was going about the routine business of preparing the mid-day meal in a state akin to sleep-walking. When the bell indicating that she was wanted in the library jangled she almost jumped out of her skin. Lady Helena rarely used the bell to summon her, preferring to come down to the kitchen herself. With a churning of fear in her guts, Patty presented herself at the library door.

To her relief, Lady Helena was alone. 'Come in, Patty,' she said, her voice gentle.

Patty went to stand in front of her.

'You know that Sir Basil was not happy with the meal you produced last night.'

'Yes, ma'am. And I'm that sorry. I didn't mean to let you down.'

'I know you didn't. But it has made me realise that I am asking too much of you. I took you on because I was impressed by the way you managed to produce such gorgeous cakes and sweetmeats even in the very unprepossessing surroundings of the workhouse, and the way you organised that coming out party – and I have had no grounds for regretting my decision, until now. But now, I'm afraid things will have to change. Sir Basil's business is growing and we shall want to do more entertaining in the future. So he has decided that we need to employ a professional chef, probably a French one.'

Patty swallowed. 'Does that mean you … you're letting me go, ma'am?'

'Good heavens, no! I would not do that to you. Apart from anything else, I couldn't bear not to eat any more of your wonderful pastries. And my friends would never forgive me if they were not on offer when they come to tea. No, what I have decided to do is this: you will stay on as pastry cook, but the new man will be in charge of the rest of the cooking. It will take a good deal of the burden off your shoulders, so I think it will be better for you as well as making sure that we have no more disasters like last night. What do you say?'

'Oh, ma'am!' Patty felt weak at the knees with relief. 'I don't know how to thank you. I'm that sorry to have let you down, and most employers would have sacked me on the spot. It means such a lot to me that you'll let me stay on.'

'And you won't mind working under a new chef?'

'Oh no, ma'am. I'm sure I'll be glad to. I shall be able to learn so much.'

'Then we are agreed. I don't know when the new chef will be appointed. It may take some time to find someone suitable. So until then, you will have to carry on as usual. I am sure we shall not have any reason to complain.'

Chapter 21

In Rutherglen, as soon as the new year celebrations were over, Richard announced that he intended to take Amy to Melbourne for a few days.

'I need to order some equipment for the new mine, and I've promised to buy Amy a couple of new dresses. You don't mind, do you?'

'Of course not,' May replied. 'Amy will be thrilled.'

The pair were back in ten days, Amy showing off a dress that May estimated must have cost more than she herself would have earned in a year in her previous existence as a milliner's apprentice. Richard's expression, too, seemed unusually self-satisfied.

'Well,' he said, when he had washed off the dust of the journey and settled himself with a drink on the veranda, 'Amy's future is settled, at least for the next few years.'

'How?' May asked, in some alarm.

'Are we going to teach her at home?' Lizzie asked.

'No, we are not. She is going to boarding school.'

'Boarding school!' both women exclaimed in unison.

'Let me explain. You remember how impressed Stella Campion was with Amy's voice at the carol concert? She persuaded me that I have a duty to see that such a talent is not lost for want of proper tuition. She promised to speak to Professor Maxwell, at the Department of Music at the university. So I took Amy to see him, and Stella had been as good as her word and obviously made a big impression on him. He asked Amy to sing for him, and then said that she should definitely have lessons from a qualified professional and he offered to arrange for one of his staff to teach her. I pointed out that it would be impossible for her to travel to Melbourne for her lessons and he suggested the school. It's called the Lomond School and it is quite close to the university. The head mistress is a Scotswoman called Miss Fraser and we both took to her at once, didn't we, Amy?'

Amy nodded vigorously.

'She seems a very down-to-earth, sensible woman who believes very strongly that girls should have the same opportunities for education that boys have,' Richard continued. 'The school has a very comprehensive curriculum, including physics and chemistry, which is something I heartily approve of. It also has a strong musical tradition and most of the girls learn one or more instruments. She is perfectly happy for Amy to have leave of absence twice a week to go to her singing lessons at the university, so it seems she will have the best of both worlds. So what do you think? Have I done well?'

'What do you think about it, Amy?' May asked.

Amy's expression was serious. 'I quite enjoyed myself at the convent school, most of the time, except when Mother Mary Andrew got cross with me about the catechism. And I like it that the school is only for girls, so there are no rough boys – and Miss Fraser said they never use corp ... what was it? They never cane people. And I do want to go on with my singing. Of course, it means I'll have to leave Sunny and Snowflake here. But Gus will look after Snowflake, and Papa says he will take care of Sunny, and I'll be able to see them in the holidays. So, yes. I think I want to go.'

May swallowed a lump in her throat. For most of her life she had remembered the baby she had cradled in the nursery at the workhouse and hoped to find her again, and James's news that he was bringing her to live with them had seemed like a miracle. It had been both a joy and a torment to have her for the past nine months – a torment because of her unhappiness at school. Now that seemed to be over and she could see that the new arrangement was the best thing that could happen for Amy, but it would leave a gaping hole in her own life. But then she reminded herself that soon she would have a new young life to care for, a child of her own who would not be whisked away when her back was turned.

'Then that's wonderful, darling. I'm glad you're so happy about it. But we shall miss you here, you know.'

Suddenly Amy cast off her adult seriousness and threw her arms round May. 'I shall miss you, too! But I'll be back in holidays and then I can see my new little baby brother or sister.'

'Not actually your brother or sister,' Lizzie reminded her.

'Well, it feels like it.' Amy said. 'And I'll miss you, too, Lizzie.'

'Will you?' Lizzie said, and abruptly left the room.

Amy left again three days later to start at her new school. May and Lizzie both shed tears as they said goodbye, but after the coach carrying her and Richard to Melbourne had disappeared, May felt a sense of relief. She need no longer worry herself about the little girl's future and she could relax and prepare herself for her coming confinement.

Her peaceful mood did not last long. She was resting on the veranda a few days later when Gus appeared, with an expression on his face that she recognised from their earlier days in Liverpool – a look that combined anxiety and defiance in one dark scowl.

'What's wrong?' she asked. 'Something's happened. Tell me.'

He dropped into a chair beside her, his hands clasped between his knees and his head hanging. 'Pa's threatening to sell Merlin.'

'Oh Gus! Why?'

'He says I'm not pulling my weight at the vineyard because I'm spending too much time with the horse.'

'But I warned you about that months ago. Didn't you listen?'

'It's all very well for you to talk. Training a race horse takes a lot of time. Pa knew when he bought him for me what I wanted to do with him. Now he's saying that even if he wins next month he's going to put him up for auction immediately after the race is over.' He raised a distraught face to her. 'He can't do that! I'll never forgive him if he does. Please, May, you talk to him. He'll listen to you.'

'It's no good me talking to him,' May said. 'You have to change the way you're behaving. You have to show him that the vineyard comes first. Look at it this way. He has built that business up from scratch. It's been a great joy to him to have someone to leave it to, someone who will carry on when he has to give up. Now he's thinking that you don't care. That maybe, when he is not there, you will fritter away everything he's worked for on racehorses.'

'But I wouldn't do that! I want the vineyard to succeed just as much as he does. I just want a few weeks to try to win one race. Then I'll go back to working like before.'

'How can he be sure of that? You have to prove to him where your priorities are.'

'How?'

'You are going to have to put work ahead of training Merlin. You need to be out there, pulling your weight, from the time work starts in the morning till everyone knocks off in the evening. If you need to take Merlin out for a gallop you will have to get up early and do it before work, and if that's not enough you will have to spend your evenings with him. It's the only way, Gus.'

He looked at her gloomily. 'It won't be enough.'

'Well, perhaps not. But Pa is not a man who will go back on his threat lightly. If you want to keep the horse, you have to show that he can trust you with the future of the vineyard.'

Gus sighed deeply. 'All right. I'll do it. I just hope it works.'

'I'm sure it will. Pa loves you, you know. He doesn't want to make you miserable. But he needs to know you understand what is important.'

'Yes, I know.' He was silent for a moment, gazing at the floor. Then he said, 'That's not the only problem. Not the worst one, even.'

'Oh Gus!' She shook her head wearily. 'Now what?'

'Kitty's pregnant. Or she says she is.'

May sat up and stared at him. 'You fool! How could you let that happen?'

'You know how it happens.'

'Don't try to make a joke of it. How could you be so irresponsible?'

He looked up with a flare of anger. 'It's all very well for you. You've got what you wanted – James, the baby, everything.'

'But I had to wait for it. I wasn't stupid enough to get myself into trouble when we were courting, back in Liverpool.'

'But that was just a few months, and then you were here and he was back in England. I've been in love with Kitty since I first met her, back when she and her family were waiting for a place on an emigrant ship. That's what made me sign up to sail with them. That's over two years ago and we've seen each other more or less every day since then. A fellow can only hold himself back so long, you know.'

'Kitty should know better …' May started to say. Then she remembered how much she had wanted to give herself to James when they were courting, and how hard it had been for both of them to hold back. She doubted that her resolve would have held out if they had been together for the same amount of time as Gus and Kitty. 'No, that's not fair. I know it has been hard, for both of you. You should be married.'

'Don't you think I want that? I've asked Patrick O'Dowd to let us marry several times but he always says Kitty's too young. He wants us to wait until she's twenty-one!'

'Well, it looks as if he'll have to change his tune now, doesn't it?' She reached out and took his hand. 'Cheer up. Isn't this what you want? You and Kitty will have to marry now.'

He still looked gloomy. 'I suppose so.'

'It is what you want, isn't it?'

'Yes, of course it is. But it's not so simple. Kitty's mother doesn't think she should marry me, because I'm not a Catholic. It didn't worry Kitty, but her ma's quite religious and she's been frightening her with talk about eternal damnation and I don't know what else. And there's this slimy character called Sean Donnelly sniffing round her. He's got a market garden outside Chiltern and he goes to the Catholic church and makes himself out to be very pious. Kitty's ma wants her to marry him.'

'I shouldn't think he'd want her if she's carrying another man's child.'

'I suppose not. But we've still got her ma to contend with.'

'Don't you think she would rather see her daughter married to you than bearing an illegitimate child?'

'That's what I'm hoping. But it's all a mess. I'm dreading telling Pa about it.'

'He certainly won't take kindly to the idea, on top of everything else. You are going to have to work very, very hard to get back into his good books, Gus.'

'I know that. But what do I do now, sis? Do I tell Pa, or do I talk to Kitty's pa first? Sometimes I think we should just run away and get married somewhere where nobody knows us.'

'Don't you dare! That wouldn't solve anything.' May thought for a moment. 'Listen. Say nothing for now. I'll talk to James when he comes home. It might be best for him to come with you to break the news to Pa. Then all three of you can decide how best to approach Kitty's family. Poor girl! She must be beside herself with worry!'

'Yes, she is. Do you think James will come and talk to Pa with me? I really feel I need someone to back me up.'

'Don't fool yourself, James will be just as cross with you as I am, but he will understand how you feel. We all want this to turn out for the best. And look on the bright side; provided you can convince Pa that you are to be trusted with regards to working in the vineyard, you will be able to offer Kitty a home, and very good prospects. Better than any market gardener could offer. That must weigh in your favour with the O'Dowds.'

Gus got to his feet. 'Thanks, sis. You've made me see things more clearly. And I'll do what you say. I'll work my socks off, if it makes Pa forget about selling Merlin.'

'You've got bigger things to worry about than the horse,' May said severely. But she pulled him down toward her and kissed him affectionately. 'Oh, little brother! What you've put me through over the years! But we always survive, don't we? This will be the same, you'll see.'

James, when informed of the situation, reacted as expected with an outburst of exasperated disgust, but when he had calmed down he admitted with a rueful grin that he could sympathise with Gus's frustration.

'I don't know how long I'd have held out in his situation. It's a good job I didn't have the chance to find out what a passionate woman I was wooing.'

He bent and kissed her and in spite of her advanced state of pregnancy she felt a stirring of desire. It was true. Her sexual urges, once awakened, were powerful. She had discovered that during her short relationship with the Italian Armando, and it was only because of lack of opportunity and the rigid social structure surrounding them, that she had not gone further than passionate kisses. Her courtship with James had been more restrained because they had both been aware of the social divide that separated them, and he had been first surprised and then delighted by her eager response as soon as they were married. For the first weeks afterwards they had made love every night and sometimes during the day as well. It was not surprising, she reflected, that she had fallen pregnant so quickly.

Now she asked, 'Will you go over to Freshfields and help Gus to explain things to Pa? If you are there, it will stop Pa from reacting too violently.'

'Why can't you go?' he asked. 'He's your brother.'

'It seems to me the sort of thing that's best dealt with on a man-to-man basis,' she said. 'Pa won't listen to me if I try to put forward Gus's case, but he respects your legal mind. Please go!'

James went, rather unwillingly, but he returned looking more sanguine. 'Your father has agreed that the marriage must go ahead and he is going to invite Patrick O'Dowd to meet him for a drink at the Star Hotel – neutral territory, if you see what I mean. He thinks they can thrash it out between them, "man to man", as you said.'

'Thank heavens for that,' May said. 'I was afraid there would be a terrible row, and he and Gus might even come to blows. Well done, darling!'

'Well, he came round to my way of thinking eventually,' James said, 'but not before he threatened to horse-whip your brother within an inch of his life. I've never seen Gus look so scared. Mind you, it serves him right. Perhaps the shock has been a good thing for him.'

The meeting between George Lavender and Patrick O'Dowd was arranged for the evening of the following Saturday. James and May joined Gus at Freshfields to await the result. George came back, glowering, and Gus rose unsteadily to his feet to face him.

'Well, you young rapscallion, you're about to get your just desserts,' his father growled. May caught her breath, and Gus visibly paled. 'You can prepare your-self to be wed as soon as the banns can be read,' his father finished.

Gus swayed on his feet and his father clapped him on the shoulder. 'She's a fine lass, lad. You're a lucky dog. But you are going to have to work to keep her. A wife is more of a responsibility than a damned horse!'

'I know,' Gus said breathlessly. 'And I will. But how did you manage to convince her father?'

'I pointed out that he didn't have much alternative, short of turning the girl out of doors with a bastard child to look after. And I made him see the advan-tages. He rather likes the idea that, provided you buckle down, his Kitty will be mistress of Freshfields one day. And I offered him a couple of sweeteners. I said I would pay for the wedding, and make sure the child, whatever it is, has a good education.'

May rose to her feet and went to kiss her father. 'Pa, you are such a kind, generous man. I knew you would make it all come right somehow.'

Gus awkwardly held out his hand. 'I'm truly grateful, sir. And I'll make sure I show it.'

George looked at him for a moment, and then pulled him into a rough embrace. 'Right,' he said, releasing him, 'I think this calls for a drink!'

Lizzie had been unusually quiet since Amy's departure. She helped around the house as usual, taking on more and more of the work as May's pregnancy progressed. She had never been demonstrative, but she had always taken a lively interest in whatever was going on around her. Now she seemed sluggish and depressed. May's enquiries about her health or whether something had happened to upset her were answered with courtesy but evasively and she came to the conclusion that it was simply the fact that she was missing Amy. It was not surprising after all. For the last three years, with inter-missions, Amy had been in her care, and since she had been removed from the McBrides' house they had been together every day. Now she had gone away to school, Lizzie was understandably at a loose end. May tried to make it clear how much she valued her help and com-panionship and endeavoured to interest her in some of her own hobbies. They worked together sewing and knitting baby clothes, but all the time May felt that she had somehow lost Lizzie's confidence.

*

However, unknown to her friend, Lizzie was wrestling with a decision that she did not want to make, but which seemed unavoidable.

The tipping point came when Richard announced that he had purchased a small cottage a few miles out of Rutherglen and was arranging for it to be refurbished and modernised. She waited until he was alone in the library, working on the plans for the new mine. May was resting on the veranda, James was at work and Betsy was busy in the kitchen.

Richard looked up with a distracted air as she entered. 'Yes, Lizzie?'

'May I speak to you for a few moments, please, sir?'

He frowned, surprised at the formality of the address. 'Of course.' He set aside his pen. 'Come and sit down.'

'I'd rather stand, if you don't mind.'

'Whatever is wrong? Has someone upset you?'

'No, it's not that. I'd like to ask you to write a reference for me.'

'A reference?'

'A ... a testimonial. Something to show to a prospective employer.'

'What prospective employer? What are you talking about?'

'No one in particular, at the moment. But there are people advertising.'

'But why? Surely you don't want to leave us.'

'I have to.' Lizzie's voice shook for a moment. 'I don't have any choice.'

'Why not? Aren't you happy here? I thought you were well settled.'

'Here, yes. But you are going to move to a house of your own. I can't live there with you, now Amy's not with us. Me, a single woman; you a widower. It would cause a scandal.'

Richard leaned back in his chair and gazed at her. 'Great heavens! The thought never occurred to me.' He frowned for a moment. 'You wouldn't stay here, with May and James? I'm sure May would value your help after the child is born.'

'It's not them that pays my wages, is it?' Lizzie pointed out. 'And it's a nursemaid they'll need, not a governess.'

Richard was silent for a moment. Then he got up and walked away to stand at the window with his back to her. Lizzie waited, clasping her hands tightly together to stop herself fidgeting. She had nerved herself up to broach the subject and now his silence was testing her control.

After what seemed a long wait he turned back to her and the expression on his face confused her further. It was partly the look of someone who has just seen the solution to a knotty problem, but with that there was a hesitancy, a look of self-doubt. It reminded her of the look on Amy's face when she wanted something very badly but was not sure if she dared ask for it.

'Well,' he said, 'it seems to me the solution is staring us in the face. We must be married.'

'What!' She took an actual step backwards as if he had pushed her.

'Forgive me. That is not the way I should have phrased it.' He hesitated, searching for words. 'The simple fact is, I have just come face-to-face with something I have known deep down for months but chosen to ignore. Ever since you agreed to come with us to rescue Amy from those dreadful McBrides, I have felt drawn to you, but I have put it to the back of my mind as something … I don't know … something unsuitable. Now I have to admit it to myself. I love you. I can't bear the thought of you leaving me. But I know what I am asking is probably repugnant to you. I am at least fifteen years older than you are. Why should you wish to join your life to an old man with a limp?'

'You are not old!' The words burst out unbidden.

'Well, I'm not the handsome gallant you are probably dreaming of.'

'I don't care about that. I'm not dreaming of anyone.'

'Then could you … would you … consider marrying me? I have to warn you that this mining venture may not succeed, though I have every hope that it will. Even if it does not, there are plenty of good jobs for mine managers in Australia. I can promise you a reasonable standard of comfort; a roof over your head, servants if you should wish for them. And Amy will be with us during school holidays.' He put out his hands to her. 'Can you consider it?'

Lizzie put her hands in his. 'It's what I should like more than anything in the world. I don't want servants. I shouldn't mind if there was not much money. I've never been used to that. But I do want to be with you, wherever you are.'

An uncertain smile flickered across his lips. 'Then, the answer is yes?'

'Yes. If you are sure you really want me.'

'I have wanted you for months, but I wouldn't let myself hope. Oh, my dear!'

She raised her face to his and his lips brushed her own. The touch was fleeting; then it came again and lingered. She yielded to the slight pressure and when his tongue slipped between her lips she opened her mouth to him. He drew her close and she felt him hard against her belly, and something long held in abeyance burst in her, like water in an overcharged dam. She had never had any relations with a man, except for a few clumsy fumblings in shop doorways. She felt now she was being swept away and wanted only to let the current take her.

At length he raised his head and looked into her eyes. 'Dear heart, I believe we shall be very happy together.'

'I know we shall,' she answered.

Later, May, when told of this new development, shook her head in surprise. 'But Lizzie, he's years older than you.'

'I know. It doesn't matter.'

'Have you really thought about it? He will be an old man while you are still in your prime.'

Lizzie smiled. 'Then I shall be able to look after him, won't I?'

'And if you have children?'

'I hope we shall.'

'People will think he is their grandfather.'

'What does that matter?' She moved to sit close to her friend. 'The important thing is, he's kind. I know he has never forgiven himself for abandoning Amy as a baby, but he is doing everything he can to make up for it. He's had tragedies in his life. First the accident that broke his leg, then unemployment and poverty, and finally his wife dying just at it seemed that his problems were solved. But he's never been embittered. He deserves some happiness, don't you think?'

'Of course he does. And so do you. Life hasn't been easy for you, either, I know. The point is, will you make each other happy?'

'Yes. I am quite sure of that.'

May took her hand. 'Then I wish you both every good fortune.' She added after a pause, 'Have you thought what Amy may feel about this?'

'Yes, I have, of course. But I can't see that it changes anything for her. She is used to me looking after her, and I'll still be there doing that. It will give her more security, knowing I shall not leave her.'

'I expect you are right,' May said. 'My goodness. It looks as though we have two weddings to prepare for!'

Chapter 22

Ruthglen, February 1870

Lizzie and Richard and Gus and Kitty were married in a joint ceremony at St Stephen's church at the end of February. The date was chosen to coincide with Amy's half-term holiday so she was able to be Lizzie's bridesmaid. When May asked her tentatively how she felt about the wedding she replied, with that precociously adult seriousness with which she greeted important decisions. 'I think it's a very good idea. They will be able to keep each other company now that I am away for so much of the time. In fact, I thought they would do it a long time ago, when we were on the ship. I'm glad they have made up their minds at last.'

That set May's mind at rest on one count, but she had worries regarding the other wedding taking place that day. Patrick O'Dowd had agreed readily enough to the match but May remembered what her brother had told her about Mrs O'Dowd's attitude. She was afraid that

Kitty's mother might refuse to attend the ceremony, or even make some kind of protest during it. In the event, she came and seemed quite content with the marriage. Afterwards, when she had a moment alone with him, she asked Gus how that had been managed.

He grinned. 'Praise the Lord for a Catholic priest with common sense. When Deidre went to ask his advice he quoted that bit in the Bible that says, "it is better to marry than to burn". I've had to agree to have the children baptised in their church, but that's all right. They can make up their own minds what they believe when they are old enough. Kitty's not going to threaten them with hellfire if they don't want to go to church.'

Richard naturally asked James to be his best man, but that left them with a dilemma as to who should give the bride away. George Lavender solved that problem by offering to perform that office. May had another moment of disquiet when Gus announced that Rudolph Marshall was going to be his best man, but a little thought convinced her that it was the obvious choice. In truth, Rudi had taken her decision to marry another man very well, and had not gone back on his promise to help Gus with Merlin's training. The two had become good friends.

The wedding day was clear and bright, with a refreshing hint of autumn in the air. Lizzie wore a simple dress of golden-brown silk and carried a bouquet of gold roses, the last of the season, and Amy was in white with a gold sash. Kitty chose sky blue, which perfectly complemented her dark hair and deep blue eyes. The reception was held at Freshfields, and all the local vineyard owners and their families were invited, as well as some of the townsfolk, and the feasting and dancing went on well into the early hours.

The next day Richard and Lizzie left to spend their honeymoon in Melbourne. Amy travelled with them, eager to show Lizzie her new school and introduce her to her singing teacher. It was clear that she was very happy with her new life and had chattered on about the friends she had made and the new things she was learning, but her chief praise was reserved for Signora Giantonio, her tutor at the University Music School. The signora had once sung at La Scala in Milan and had introduced Amy to the work of Giuseppe Verdi. She had taught her one of Violetta's arias from *La Traviata* and Amy announced proudly, 'Madame says if I work hard and practise every day, one day I may sing the part of Violetta in a real opera company.'

May had looked at Richard to see his reaction to that idea, but he had merely smiled indulgently.

Gus and Kitty did not go away, but moved into Freshfields straight away. Gus said it was because he had too much work to do, but May guessed that the real reason was that he could not bear to be parted from Merlin at this critical stage in his training. He had kept his word and confined the time he spent with the horse to before and after his day's work, but the programme did not appear to have suffered and Rudi had declared that

Merlin was ready for the big race, which would be part of the final meeting of the season in two weeks' time.

Without Lizzie and Richard, as well as Amy, Lake House seemed very empty and quiet. May would have welcomed some company as she anticipated her forthcoming confinement. She knew very little about the process of childbirth. Having lost her mother at a very young age there had been no one to prepare her for what was to come, and her education in the workhouse had certainly never touched on such matters. Her friends at Freeman's had all been single girls and knew very little more than she did, though lurid stories of the agonies involved had gone the rounds. James had insisted on bringing a doctor over from Beechworth to examine her, but when James had suggested that he might attend the birth, the doctor had put the idea aside with a wave of his hand.

'Mrs Bancroft, your local midwife, is very competent. Your wife is a young, healthy woman. There is no reason why there should be any complications.'

Mrs Bancroft had examined her once or twice and declared that she had nothing to worry about. May had remarked hesitantly on one occasion that she had read in the papers that Queen Victoria had used chloroform to ease the pain of childbirth, but the midwife had remarked dismissively that such ideas were all very well for those rich people who had been brought up to expect everything to be easy, but ordinary folks knew that you had to be prepared to suffer what God sent and be grateful.

James was solicitous, but May guessed that he knew less than she did about what was to come and she kept her fears to herself.

The day of the race meeting arrived at last. As always, the whole of Rutherglen turned out to watch, together with people from nearby villages and isolated homesteads. May was tempted to stay at home rather than brave the crowds but she knew that Gus would never forgive her if she missed what he confidently expected to be his great triumph. Richard and Lizzie had returned from Melbourne, both glowing with a happiness that she had never seen before on either of their faces. Together with James, they escorted her to the field and settled her on a chair as close as possible to the finishing line. The early races were run without incident, with winners for the Schloers and several other vineyard owners, but it was the last race that everyone was waiting for. This was where the best horses, many of them bred and trained specifically for racing, would compete.

In the interval before the race, May insisted on going to the paddock where the runners and riders were waiting. Gus was there, leading Merlin round. The horse was tossing his head and gazing around him with flared nostrils, as if sending out a challenge to the other horses. Rudi was there, too, but this time he was not riding Excalibur. Instead, he had entered his as-yet-untried filly, Guinevere, and May knew that Gus was confident of being able to beat her. Most of the rest of the field were known to them all, but there were one or two strangers who had brought horses from distant homesteads. The sun was lowering and the beams lit up the horses' coats so that they glowed ebony and chestnut and gold. All round the paddock powerful muscles glided under sleek hides and sensitive ears twitched this way and that. Kitty came over to where May and James were standing, her eyes alight with excitement.

'Oh, will you look at Merlin! Doesn't he look magnificent?'

May agreed that he did.

'Come and wish them both good luck, will you?' Kitty begged.

May made her way carefully across the paddock and Gus drew his horse to a momentary halt beside her. 'Good luck, my dear,' she said, reaching up to kiss his cheek.

'I've got a good luck charm here, so I know we'll be all right,' he said. 'Kitty found it and kept it for me.' He held up a four-leaved clover.

A horn sounded and Gus turned to the saddle. 'Give me a leg up, will you, James?'

James obliged and the horses began to move off towards the starting line. James took May's arm.

'Come on. Let's get back before someone steals our vantage spot.'

May settled herself and wished she had not eaten a peach at lunchtime. Something seemed to have given her indigestion. The horses lined up. There was a hiatus as one or two of them refused to join the line, or tried to push forward before the starting gun sounded. Then, with a thunder of hooves, they were off. May felt her heartbeat quicken. She knew how much this race meant to her brother and wanted very much to see him triumph.

The race required the horses to cover two laps. The first time they swept past Gus and Merlin were close behind the leader, a grey gelding that none of them had seen before. Rudi on Guinevere was just behind and the rest of the field was strung out over some distance.

'He's well placed,' James said. 'He's letting that grey make the running. You wait, when they come into the last straight he'll make his move.'

May could not see what was happening on the far side of the course, but as the horses came into sight on the last straight section she saw that the grey was still leading but Gus was close by him, Merlin's nose level with the other rider's stirrup. Then she saw her brother lean forward and touch the horse lightly with his whip. Merlin lengthened his stride and swept forward, as if until that moment he had been cruising at half speed. The crowd began to roar and Kitty, who was beside her, jumped to her feet, screaming, 'Come on! Come on!'

The horses were within fifty yards of the finishing line when a dog suddenly appeared from nowhere and hurled itself, barking madly, at Merlin's feet. The horse checked, reared, then plunged forward, throwing Gus over his head. Merlin galloped on, but Gus lay still, his body twisted at an awkward angle. The rest of the field thundered towards him and he disappeared beneath a flurry of flying legs.

Screaming now with terror, Kitty flung herself forwards, narrowly avoiding being mown down by one of the horses bringing up the rear. May rose too and started after her, but a sudden griping pain seized her belly and she doubled over, gasping. Hands grabbed her and raised her, anxious voices demanded to know what was wrong, but she was unable to speak. Then, suddenly, there was a rush of liquid around her thighs and a woman's voice. 'Her waters have broken. She's in labour. Get her away from here.'

She was being lifted, James had his arms round her. 'Gus!' she gasped. 'What's happened? Is Gus all right?'

'Never mind him for the moment,' James said. 'We must get you home.'

'But Gus! I want to see Gus!'

'Yes, yes. All in good time. Forget about him for now.'

Another wave of pain gripped her and she had no breath left to protest. The horizons of her consciousness closed in around her so that all she was aware of was her own body, which seemed to have its own purposes, beyond her control. She was carried, vaguely aware of the transition from sunlight to a cool interior; she was laid on a bed; someone undressed her, who it was she neither knew nor cared. Pain swelled up and then ebbed away, again and again. Lizzie was sponging her face with cool water; other hands groped between her legs. Then the midwife's voice called to her through the mists. 'Push now! Push!'

Her muscles responded; she screamed, and then something slithered out of her and the midwife said, 'Good girl! Well done!'

The pain had gone and somewhere nearby a baby was crying. Mrs Bancroft leaned over her, smiling.

'You have a lovely baby daughter. Look! Do you want to hold her?'

A warm bundle, surprisingly solid and heavy, was laid in her arms and a tiny, wrinkled face looked up at her.

'A girl?' she queried. 'A little girl?'

'Yes. And a fine, healthy babe she is.'

'How wonderful!' May gazed at the child. It seemed incredible that the weight she had carried within her, which she had felt moving and kicking, was now a separate individual with a life of her own. She looked up at the midwife. 'Thank you!'

'No need to thank me. You did most of the work yourself. Nature intended you for a mother, that's plain. Now, let's get you cleaned up. Your husband is longing to see you.'

'Does he know – about the baby.'

'Yes, Lizzie has told him. He'll be here shortly.'

There was more to 'getting cleaned up' than May expected but at last she was propped up on her pillows, her face washed and her hair combed, and James was allowed into the room. He leaned over her and kissed her brow.

'My darling girl. Are you all right?'

'Yes, of course I am. Look! Our daughter.'

He touched the small face with the back of his finger. 'Welcome, little one. What a clever mother you have to make something so amazing.'

'Well, you had a hand in it, too,' she reminded him. Then a memory flashed like lightening across her mind. 'Gus! What has happened to Gus? Is he … is he … ?'

'Gus is fine. He has broken his collar bone but luckily Dr Jackson was among the crowd. He has strapped him up and says he should be fine as long as he takes things easy for a bit.'

'Oh, thank God!' May whispered. 'Thank God!'

'As a matter of fact, he's downstairs – Gus, not God. He refused to go home until he knew you were all right. Do you want me to send him in?'

'Oh yes, please. Silly boy! He should be at home resting.'

'So we told him, but he wouldn't listen. I'll fetch him.'

Gus came in, looking uncharacteristically shy. 'How are you, sis?'

'I'm fine. But you shouldn't be here.'

'I had to wait, till I knew … Is this it?'

'She's a little girl, not an it.'

He touched a small hand that had escaped from the swaddling shawl, and tiny fingers at once gripped his.

'Look at that! She knows how to hang on already. She'll be a horsewoman, wait and see.'

Reminded, May exclaimed, 'Oh, love, I'm so sorry about the race.'

He shook his head. 'No need. We won, really. Merlin came in a whole length ahead of the field, even after that upset. Pity I wasn't on him, but even the judges said that really we should have had the cup. Never mind. There's always next year.'

'Oh dear,' she said with a sigh. 'I suppose there is. But just remember, you're an uncle now and soon you'll be a father. You have responsibilities.'

'I won't forget,' he promised.

'Now you really should go home and rest,' she told him.

'Yes, I will now. And you, too. Take care of yourself.'

'Oh, I'll be taken care of, don't worry about that.'

He kissed her on the cheek and went to the door. She heard him exchange a few words with James and then her husband came back to sit on the edge of the bed.

'My daughter,' he murmured. 'What are we going to call her?'

They had tossed around various names in the months gone by but never finally agreed on one. James thought she should be called after his mother, but Louisa Brackenbridge, in May's mind, was an elderly lady who had been first her patron and then her enemy. She had countered by suggesting her own mother's name, but James did not like the sound of Jane ... plain Jane.

May looked down at the child in her arms and suddenly a vision flashed across her memory – a golden-haired girl dressed as an angel, and a pure, clear voice singing out good tidings.

'Joy,' she said. 'Her name is Joy.'

James put his arms round her and cradled them both. 'That's perfect. Joy she shall be – to us, and everyone who knows her.'

Chapter 23

From the moment M. Antoine entered the kitchen, Patty knew she was not going to be happy working with him. He was a small man with a thick, black beard and small dark eyes that darted to and fro as he prowled round the room, picking things up and putting them down, opening and closing cupboards and muttering what she guessed from his tone were imprecations in his own language.

Finally he turned to face her as she stood with Iris at her side. 'And this is where I am supposed to prepare food? *Mon dieu!*' He spread his arms in a gesture of dismay. '*Alors,* one must proceed somehow. You!' He shot a look at Iris. 'Who are you?'

Iris bobbed a curtsy and answered in a tremulous voice, 'Please, sir, I'm Iris. I'm the kitchen maid.'

'And you?' Antoine turned his gaze on Patty.

She squared her shoulders. She was damned if she was going to curtsy to this ill-mannered little foreigner. 'My name is Patty Jenkins. I am the pastry cook.'

'Pastry cook?' His tone expressed disbelief. 'And where did you train for this?'

'Partly at Speke Hall,' (which was true, if you counted her brief, informal sessions with M. Blanchard), 'and partly at Freeman's Department Store.'

'Department Store?' From the look on his face she might as well have said 'at the zoo'. He sighed theatrically. 'Ah well, for now we must work with what we have. And until today you have been in charge of all the cooking here?'

'Yes, I have.'

'*Mon dieu!* No wonder Sir Basil was prepared to offer me whatever I asked to induce me to come to this … this backwater. Well, we must show him that he made the right decision. So, it is time to prepare the soup for midday. You, girl! Fetch me six onions, and some carrots and peel and chop them. *Alors!* What are you waiting for?' He snapped his fingers. '*Vite! Vite!* Quickly. And you—' he turned to Patty '—you will make me a list, an inventory, of everything you have in your stock cupboards. Then we shall see what is lacking.'

From that day on he made it clear that he regarded Patty as an underling, to be ordered about and relegated to menial jobs. Even when she proposed making some of the sweet dishes she knew were favourites of her employers, her suggestion was countermanded.

'Jam roly-poly? You English and your stodgy puddings! Instead we shall have a tarte aux pommes with crème anglais.'

'I don't know what that is,' Patty said stubbornly.

'Then I shall make it and you shall watch and learn.'

Even when she made cakes for Lady Helena's tea party he insisted on changing her tried-and-tested recipes for one of his own.

His attitude towards Vera was similar. Used to an established hierarchy, he referred always to Nanny Banks in regard to the management of the household, and the old lady, who until then had spent most days dozing by the fire, suddenly felt it necessary to exert her authority, frequently countermanding Vera's instructions to cleaners or tradesmen. She had been in the habit of taking her meals on a tray in her own little sanctum but M. Antoine insisted that she should take the head of the table at meal times. He himself sat at the foot and tutted his disapproval at the table manners of Jackson and his son, Danny. Any jokes or light-hearted comments were met with frowns of disapproval either from him or from Nanny Banks. Only Mr Charles and Paul Sedley were treated with any respect, but they held themselves aloof and the animated discussions about chemical experiments ceased. Vera retreated into injured silence and the once easygoing atmosphere of mutual comradeship was banished.

One result of this was that Jackson and Danny, often accompanied by Barney, took to spending their evenings in the Mother Redcap pub. After one of the earlier occasions, Barney reported that Charles and Paul had been there as well.

'Sat in a corner by themselves,' he said. 'Made it clear they didn't want our company.'

One Monday morning Vera came into the kitchen with a look on her face that made Patty drop the whisk she was using.

'Whatever is wrong? You look as though you've seen a ghost.'

Vera grabbed her wrist. 'I must speak to you. Come into the office, now, please!'

Patty looked round. M. Antoine was leaning over a pot on the stove, stirring it with fierce concentration, and she knew Nanny Banks was closeted with Lady Helena.

'All right, just for a moment. Or I'll get the sharp edge of Antoine's tongue.'

'Never mind that!' Vera said. 'Come on!'

In the privacy of the office she burst into tears. 'Oh, Patty, I've been such a fool! Such a fool!'

'What have you done now?' Patty asked. 'I thought you'd been keeping on top of everything since that last upset.'

'It's not what I've done, or not done. It's what I've been feeling, hoping ... Oh, I don't know what I've been hoping for. But now ...'

'Is this something to do with Paul?'

'I've just seen something so ... I can't tell you. I don't have the words.'

'Seen what? What's happened?'

Vera swallowed and forced back a sob. 'I was changing the bed linen, like I always do on Monday mornings. I thought Charles was with Sir Basil and Paul was getting ready for his lesson with Lady Helena. I went into Charles's room ... I suppose I should have knocked but I thought it was empty. And I saw ... they were ... they were doing something so horrible! I can't describe it.'

Patty stared at her, trying to comprehend. Vague memories of hints and jokes, only half understood, when she worked at Freeman's came back to her as well as what she'd heard from other girls on the street. 'Were they kissing?'

'No, it was worse than that.'

Patty was lost for words, her imagination trying to conceive what Vera had seen. In the end she said, 'I think, I've heard that some men ... prefer other men to women. Perhaps it's good you found out now ...'

'Well, shouldn't I tell Lady Helena? Though I don't think I could bring myself to find the words.'

'Well, what are you going to do, then?'

'I don't know. I haven't thought that far. I just know ... you said I was making a fool of myself. You were right.'

Patty put her arms round her. 'Oh, my dear, I am so sorry. You were right. I suppose I was jealous, a bit. But I could see he wasn't really interested in you. I didn't know why, but now I suppose I do. Really, it's been obvious all along, hasn't it? I'm afraid. He always wanted to be with Charles, not with you.'

'I know! I know!' Vera sobbed. 'But what am I supposed to do now?'

'I don't see what you can do—' A sudden thought came to her. 'Did they see you?'

'I don't think so. They ... Charles had his back to me and Paul ... Paul was – well, he wasn't looking. I only just opened the door and then I closed it very quietly.'

'In that case, can't we just pretend nothing's happened? After all, they aren't doing anyone any harm, are they? I mean, it isn't Paul's fault that you misunderstood his intentions.'

'I can't bear to see him now. How can I look him in the face?'

'I don't see what option you've got. Either we tell Lady Helena and she tells Sir Basil, and they both lose their jobs, or even go to prison. Isn't what they were doing against the law? Or we keep quiet and let them get on with it.'

Vera drew back and lowered herself into a chair. 'If you put it that way ... Perhaps that is the best thing to do. I suppose one day Sir Basil might find out for himself, but that won't be anything to do with me.' She shook her head. 'I don't know what to do for the best.'

'Then do nothing,' Patty said. 'It's the only way, as far as I can see.' She glanced at the door. Beyond the glass panels she could see Antoine moving. 'I must get back. You sit quietly here for a bit, until you feel able to go on. You don't want Nanny Banks complaining that you haven't done your job.'

For the next few days Vera went about her duties like a ghost. As soon as Paul came into the room she found some excuse to be elsewhere and she carried her meals up to her own room, or missed them altogether. Patty made excuses for her, saying she was unwell and hinting at 'women's troubles' when pressed for more details. Patty felt lost herself. Once Vera had been her rock and her guide; now she was in need of counsel and comfort, and Patty had none to give her. That, together with the constant irritation of M. Antoine's behaviour, left her depressed and in need herself of a friendly arm to rely on.

She continued to spend her Sunday afternoons at the farm, but she no longer dared to take a cake. M. Antoine kept a strict record of everything in the store cupboards and she knew that he would have missed the eggs and sugar she needed. It mattered less these days, however, since Daisy had taken her lessons to heart and Gregory made sure that the necessary ingredients were to hand. Patty considered taking him into her confidence about Vera's revelations and asking his advice, but he had taken to asking Jerry to see her home so they were never alone. Then one evening, when the first daffodils were opening, he said, 'Jerry has work to do in the stable. You will not mind if I walk you back, will you?'

Patty felt a frisson of anxiety mingled with pleasure. 'No, of course not.'

As they walked he talked about the coming season and his preparations for it. He had plans to expand his herd. More and more houses were being built in the vicinity and the market for his milk was growing. He spoke with optimism about future prospects.

Some distance from the gate of Avalon he stopped suddenly and turned to face her.

'Patty, I want to ask you something.'

'Oh, yes ...?' She made a movement to continue the walk but he stood between her and the pathway.

'I think you must guess what it is. I have come to know you over these last months and I have seen how Daisy and the boys are with you. They love you, Patty, and so do I. I know you're a town girl and maybe the life of a farmer's wife isn't what you hoped for. But I can offer you a good home and a secure future.' He paused and she said nothing. He went on, 'Maybe you would rather marry someone who does not already have children, but the young ones need you. They need a mother, specially Daisy now she is growing up. And there can still be others, children of our own.' His eyes searched her face. 'I am asking you to marry me, Patty. What do you say?'

She gazed at him mutely. Her mouth was dry and her feelings were in such turmoil that she could find no words for him.

'Come,' he said, 'say yes, and make me the happiest man in the world.'

He reached out and drew her to him. She felt his lips seeking hers, the urgent pressure of his body against her, and, as before, some instinct, some memory not of the mind but of the body, made her jerk away and struggle free.

'No, don't! I can't. Please don't …'

He looked stricken. 'Come, I don't mean to force you. If I have been too eager you must forgive me.'

'I'm sorry!' she panted. 'Really, really sorry. But I can't marry you. I can't marry anyone.'

'What do you mean? You're not wed already, are you, to some fellow who has gone off and left you?'

'No, no. It's not that.' She pulled herself together with an effort and looked at him. 'I'll tell you why, and then you will not want to marry me. I owe you that. Once, not that long ago, I was forced to sell my body to any man who asked. It shames me to say it, but it was the only way to keep from starving.'

He stared at her. 'You were a prostitute?'

'Yes.' She stepped round him. 'Now let me go, and try to forget about me.'

She half ran to the gate of Avalon. When she reached it she looked back. He was standing where she had left him, staring after her like a man waking from a nightmare, unsure what was real and what belonged to the dream.

As soon as she entered the kitchen, M. Antoine began to scold her for being late. There was supper to prepare and for the next hour she was subjected to his frequently snapping fingers and his cries of '*Vite! Vite!*' There was no chance to think about the conversation that had just occurred, no chance to talk to Vera about it. Then the rest of the staff assembled for the meal and by the time it had been eaten, and the dishes had been washed and cleared away, it was bedtime. Patty dragged herself up to the attic rooms and tapped on Vera's door.

Her friend was sitting up in bed with one of Lady Helena's magazines unopened on her lap. She took in Patty's expression and said, 'It's my turn to ask what's happened. You've been distracted all evening. Has something bad happened at the farm? It's not one of the children, is it?'

Patty sat down on the edge of the bed. She felt exhausted, as if her life blood was draining away.

'No, it's not the children. Gregory has proposed to me.'

Vera leaned forward and caught her hand. 'That's wonderful! Why are you looking so down? It's great news.'

Patty shook her head. 'No, it's not. I turned him down.'

'Why? Patty, think! I know you're not happy here anymore. Nor am I. But you are being offered a way out. Gregory's a good man, and he can give you a comfortable home. You like his children, and you will have children of your own as well. It's the perfect answer for you.'

'And what about you?' Patty asked. 'It would leave you on your own here.'

'Never mind about that. I shan't stay, if you leave. I'm sure Lady Helena will give me a reference. I shall look for another position.'

'And what about our plans? Our dream?'

Vera shook her head. 'That's all it is, Patty. All it could ever be. How much have we managed to save since we came to work here? The only money we have spent is on those dresses for the New Year's Eve ball. But even if we hadn't spent that, the sum is so small. It would take us years to save enough to start our own business. You mustn't turn down the chance of a happy life with Gregory just to save that dream.'

Patty shook her head with a sigh. 'That's not why I turned him down.'

'Then why? You like him, don't you?'

'Yes, I do. But I can't ... you know what I did before I ended up in the workhouse. I can't bear to let a man, any man, do those things to me again.'

Vera looked at her sadly. 'Oh, my dear, I am so sorry. I never thought of it like that. But surely, with a man you loved, you could get over that. I don't know Gregory very well, but he strikes me as the sort of man who would not force you.'

'I'm sure you are right,' Patty said. 'But it won't happen. I told him what I did for a living. He won't want me after that. What man would?'

'Did he say that?'

'No. I didn't wait to hear him say it. But it's obvious, isn't it?'

'Not necessarily. If he really loves you ... he might be prepared to forget the past.'

'Even if he was, I can't.' Patty squeezed her eyes shut against her tears. 'I do like him, Vera. But apart from ...

the other thing … I'm not sure I'm suited to being a farmer's wife. I enjoy going there on Sunday afternoons and I like being with Daisy and the little one, but that's not the same as living there all the time, is it?'

'No, that's true,' Vera said. She was silent for a moment. Then she reached out and took Patty's hand. 'It seems to me that we both need to leave this place. It's a shame, because we have been happy here. But I can't face seeing Paul every day, after what I discovered. And it will be hard for you to be near Gregory. Even if you stop going to the farm, you are bound to come across him in church on Sundays and other times. What do you say? Shall we start looking for another position?'

Patty pressed her fingers and then withdrew her hand. 'It will probably work for you. With the sort of reference Lady Helena will give you I'm sure you could get a place as a governess, or lady's companion. But I'm not really qualified to be a cook. Sir Basil found that out. I can manage plain food, but that's not enough.'

'It would be for some people. In a small family, or perhaps an elderly gentleman.'

'It would mean we would not be together, though.'

'Not necessarily. Perhaps we might find a single lady, a widow maybe, who needed a companion and a cook. Or she might have children needing a governess. There must be situations that would suit us both. Come, cheer up! We've both had to start out on unknown paths before, but we have survived. We've been lucky. There's no reason why we shouldn't be lucky again.'

Patty looked at her affectionately. 'You're a good friend, Vera. I don't know where I'd be without you – stuck in the workhouse, probably. If we could find somewhere that would suit us both, it might be the perfect answer.'

'Then tomorrow we start looking,' Vera said. 'Now get some sleep. Goodnight.'

Sir Basil always brought home with him that day's edition of the *Liverpool Daily Courier* and when she had finished reading it Lady Helena passed it on to the staff. Since no one else seemed greatly interested Vera normally commandeered it, so it aroused no curiosity when she and Patty took it up to their rooms after supper. The front page of the paper was devoted to small advertisements, offering items for sale, announcing forthcoming events and listing situations vacant. Every evening they trawled through these, searching for one that would accommodate both of them, but without success. There were several for which Vera alone might have applied, given a good reference from Lady Helena, but none of them also required a cook. Patty began to conclude that in the end they would each have to take whatever came their way.

She dreaded the next Sunday, knowing that she was bound to see Gregory and the children. After the service she tried to get away quickly but he waylaid her.

'Patty, I must talk to you. Come to the farm this afternoon, please!'

She saw the appeal in his open, honest face and could not refuse. 'I'll come, but I don't see what else we have to talk about.'

She kept her word, but as she entered the farmyard she was suddenly aware, as if it was her first visit, of the mud on the cobbles and the smell of dung from the barn and the pigsty.

Gregory was waiting for her. 'Walk with me,' he requested.

They strolled along the field margin where the herd was grazing. Most of the cows had calves with them.

'Do they all have babies?' she asked.

He laughed. 'Most of them. There's one or two still to calve, back in the barn.'

'Will you keep them all?'

'I may keep a few of the young heifers – that is, the female ones. The bulls will have to go for slaughter.'

'For slaughter? Why?'

'Well, I can't keep them. They don't produce milk, and that's how I earn my living. If I kept them all I'd be overrun with cattle.'

'Well, why do you let them have so many then?' she asked.

He looked at her as if she was a child – a rather stupid child. 'If the cows don't have calves they don't give milk. It's as simple as that.'

She shook her head. 'Poor little things!'

'I'm afraid that is how it has to be. You can't be too soft-hearted if you're a farmer.'

He stopped walking and faced her. 'I have been think-ing about what you told me. Indeed, I have thought of nothing else all week. It seems to me that all that was in the past, and none of it was your fault. Nothing you have said makes any difference to who you are now. Can't we put it behind us?'

She looked into his face. 'It's easier said than done. Even if you can forget what I was, I cannot. I told you. I can't bear the thought of . . . of letting a man . . . do those things to me.'

'Suppose I were to say that I would not ask you to. That we could live together like brother and sister?'

'It wouldn't be fair on you. And it wouldn't work. Sooner or later, you would want more than that.'

'Perhaps, in time, you might come to feel differently.'

'That's just it,' she said. 'You would keep hoping that things might change, and I should keep wishing that they could. It would be too hard for both of us. You need a proper wife, Greg, not a . . . a half-baked one like I would be.'

He sighed deeply. 'Well, let us leave it for now. All I ask is, don't give up on us altogether.'

She knew she ought to finish it there and then, but he looked so wounded that she did not have the heart. They walked in silence back towards the farmhouse.

Back in the kitchen Daisy had made a sponge cake. She had just set it on the table when Jerry ran in, look-ing scared.

'Pa, it's Marigold. She's in trouble.'

Gregory pushed his feet back into his boots. 'I'm coming.' He looked round at Patty. 'Perhaps you should come and watch this.'

'Who's Marigold?' she asked, as she followed him out of the kitchen.

'One of the cows,' he said over his shoulder.

Patty screwed up her face as they entered the barn. The smell was worse than ever and it made her feel sick. In one of the stalls Jerry was holding up a lantern and in its light she saw a cow, head hanging and flanks heaving. Gregory ran his hand along the animals back, murmuring reassuring words, then he bent and thrust his arm inside her. Patty stared, horrified. Gregory grunted with effort and then withdrew his arm, covered to the elbow in blood and mucus.

'The calf's the wrong way round. It needs to be turned but my hand is too big. I can't get in far enough.' He looked round. 'Here, Patty. You've got small hands, but you're strong. Come here and I'll explain what you need to do.'

Patty stood transfixed. 'I can't! I can't do that!'

'Yes, you can. Come on. I don't want this calf to die.'

Patty shook her head desperately. 'I can't! I'm sorry. I just can't.'

He gave vent to a half-smothered oath. 'Jerry, fetch your sister. She's done this before. She won't let me down.'

Patty stood back and Jerry brushed past her. Then she turned and ran out of the barn. At the kitchen door she almost bumped into Daisy, who called, 'Watch the little 'un.' But Patty, after checking that the baby was still asleep, waited only to grab her coat and bonnet from the hook by the door and then she ran as fast as she could back to Avalon.

Later that night she wrote a short note, which she gave to Iris to deliver next day.

Dear Greg,

You have seen now that I could never make a farmer's wife. You need someone who will be a help to you, not a coward like me. I am going away soon and I think it will be better if we do not see each other again.

I shall miss you and the children, but perhaps when I am out of the way you will find someone else who can be everything you need her to be.

Your friend,
Patty

Later that morning Patty was up to her elbows in flour, preparing the pastry for a steak and kidney pie, when the front doorbell rang. A few minutes later Vera came into the kitchen.

'Lady Helena wants you in the library.'

'What now? Ask her if she can wait a few moments. I'm covered in flour.'

'I think you had better go straight away,' Vera said. 'She's got a gentleman with her.'

'A gentleman? What sort of gentleman?' Patty felt a flurry of anxiety. It was obviously not one of the local people, or Vera would have recognised him, but what could a stranger want with her?

'Smartly dressed. A professional gentleman of some sort. You'd better get up there.'

Patty rinsed her hands and pulled off her apron, which was doused in flour. Hastily tucking her hair under her cap she ran up the stairs and tapped on the library door. Bidden to enter, she found Lady Helena in the company of a small man wearing pince-nez on his rather sharp nose.

'Ah, here you are, Patty,' she said. 'Come in. This is Mr Weaver. He is a solicitor and he wants to speak to you.'

Patty's stomach lurched. A solicitor? That meant a lawyer. What could a lawyer want with her? Had one of her erstwhile clients laid a complaint against her, after all this time?

'Please do not be alarmed, Miss Jenkins,' Weaver said. 'There is nothing to worry about.' He looked at her employer. 'Do you think Miss Jenkins might be allowed to sit down?'

'Of course,' Lady Helena responded. 'Take a seat, Patty.'

Patty lowered herself onto the edge of a chair, glad that her long skirts hid the shaking of her knees.

Mr Weaver opened a briefcase and took out a manila folder. 'Am I right in thinking that you spent some months last year in the Brownlow Hill workhouse?'

'Yes,' Patty responded faintly.

'Do you remember a Miss Eleanor Pargeter?'

Patty shook her head. 'Was she one of the wardens?'

'No, she was an inmate like yourself. A rather eccentric lady, I believe.'

Something clicked in Patty's memory. 'You don't mean Mad Nelly, sir?'

'Is that what you called her? Why?'

'She was always going on about her father. He was a rich man and one day he was going to come and fetch her home. Well, we knew she couldn't have a father living. She was an old woman – and what was she doing in the workhouse if she had wealthy relatives?'

'I understand your doubts,' Weaver said, 'and of course you were correct that she could not have a living father. But in other respects her story was the truth. She did come from a wealthy family.'

'No? Really?'

'Let me explain. It is a sad story, I would say a tragic one, except that it does have a happy ending. Miss Pargeter's father, Sir John, was a rich man, as I said. He had interests in coal mining and in the railways. Her mother died when she was a young girl and after a few years her father married again. His new wife was a widow, with a son of her own. I fear it was not a happy arrangement for Miss Eleanor, though I have no evidence to back that up. All I know is that from that time onwards Eleanor suffered from recurrent bouts of illness, which were diagnosed as hysteria. The marriage was not of long duration, because the new Lady Pargeter died of typhus in the last great epidemic. When Sir John also died he left his estate equally between his daughter and his stepson, Marcus. Now, we come to the saddest part of the story. Marcus was a shiftless fellow. He gambled most of his share away and frequently borrowed money from his stepsister. Then he heard about the discovery of diamonds in South Africa and conceived the notion that he could redeem his debts and become rich by joining the rush to exploit it. He persuaded Eleanor to invest in a joint enterprise and promised her a good return on her capital. She believed him and signed the necessary documents and he took himself off the South Africa. She never heard from him again.'

'Oh, the scoundrel!' This interjection came from Lady Helena.

'Quite!' Weaver agreed. 'As a result, Eleanor was unable to pay her bills. The bailiffs were called in and she found herself out on the street. She had always been, shall we say fragile? This turn of events completely unhinged her and when she was taken in to the workhouse it was assumed that her tales of a wealthy father were pure fantasy.'

'Poor old thing,' Patty murmured. 'If only we'd known ... We used to laugh at her.'

'But you alone showed her kindness. You used to bake cakes and you gave some to her.'

Patty blinked. 'How do you know that?'

'All in good time,' the little man said. 'As it happened, Marcus's gamble paid off. He bought a mining concession and it turned out to be very profitable. He became a rich man, but he did not enjoy his riches for long. A year ago, he succumbed to malaria and died, intestate and without issue. You will appreciate that that left the authorities in somewhat of a dilemma. Who should inherit? When they examined his papers they found the original agreement under which Eleanor had loaned him the capital to finance his enterprise. Clearly, the fruits of that enterprise now belonged to her. The lawyers dealing with the matter in South Africa contacted me and asked me to trace her whereabouts. It took me a week or two, but I eventually located her in the workhouse.'

'Oh, that's wonderful!' Lady Helena exclaimed. 'So you were able to reinstate her in her own home?'

'Not precisely,' the lawyer said with a sigh. 'She was by then in a very fragile state of health. I found a home run by the Sisters of Mercy and had her transferred there and she lived out the last months of her life in comfort and with the best of care.'

'She is dead, then?' Patty said. 'But I am glad that it was proved she was telling the truth all the time. I wish we had understood.' She hesitated. It seemed odd that he had come all this way just to pass on this information, but she could not see what it had to do with her. She got up. 'It was kind of you to come and tell me. Thank you.'

'Wait,' Weaver said. 'You haven't understood the real purpose of my visit. You recall that I mentioned your kindness in sharing your cakes with her?'

'Oh, yes. I had forgotten. How do you know about that?'

'Eleanor never forgot. And before she died she made a will. Most of her money goes to the Sisters of Mercy. There is a bequest to the infirmary at the workhouse. There is also a legacy, a substantial one, to you.'

'Me? Do you mean she left me some money?'

'Quite a lot of money.'

Patty sat down again abruptly. 'How much?'

'One thousand pounds.'

Lady Helena gave a small gasp. Patty gazed at him, struggling to find words to respond.

'Do you mean, for me to do whatever I like with?'

'Certainly. But I hope you will take good advice about how to invest such a sum. Do you have a bank account?'

'Me? A bank account? No.'

Weaver produced a card case and held one out. 'If you would be so kind as to wait on me at my office, some-time in the next day or two, I will be happy to arrange that for you, and the money can then be transferred.'

Patty took the card. 'Oh, yes. Thank you.' The response came automatically.

Weaver put his documents back in his briefcase and rose to his feet. 'In that case, I think we have concluded the necessary formalities for today. I will take my leave.'

Helena rang a small bell on the table beside her and Vera appeared at the door with a promptitude that suggested she had been loitering in the hall. 'Show Mr Weaver out, please, Vera.'

Weaver made a small bow. 'Lady Helena.' Then, to Patty, 'Miss Jenkins. I look forward to renewing our acquaintance very soon.'

'Yes. Thank you.' Patty's thoughts were whirling.

As the door closed behind him Lady Helena got up and took hold of Patty's hand. 'Patty, this is wonderful news! You do realise, don't you, that if you invest this money in the three per cent bonds you will have an income for life? I am sure Sir Basil will be more than happy to advise you how to do that.'

Patty looked into her eyes. That's very kind of you, ma'am. But I know exactly what I am going to do with the money.'

Chapter 24

Three months later, on a day when the summer sun was hot on their backs, Patty and Vera stood outside a small shop, conveniently situated on the street leading to the place where the ferries from Liverpool docked, so that gentlemen returning after a day at the office or families heading for the pleasures of Birkenhead Park could not avoid passing it. Above the door was a sign that read PATTY'S PANTRY and inside it was possible to see tables spread with spotless white cloths and set with delicate china and fine silverware. In the window there was a display of Patty's finest baking. There were eclairs and cream buns, chocolate scones, fruit cake, slices of parkin and flapjacks, and in pride of place, sparkling in the light of a carefully placed oil lamp, was a Savoy cake.

From the waterfront came the sound of the gangplank being lowered from the ferry and the voices of passengers disembarking.

Vera touched Patty's arm. 'Come on, partner. Time to open up. Here come our first customers.'

They hurried inside and Patty turned the sign on the door from CLOSED to OPEN. In the kitchen Vera had turned up the heat under the big kettle that was already singing on the hob. Patty's stomach gave a lurch. Suppose no one came in? Suppose her display of cakes and pastries was not good enough to tempt them to pause on their way home to sample them? Suppose the whole project ended in failure?

The bell on the shop door tinkled. Patty wiped her sweating palms on the back of her apron and hurried out into the shop.

Gregory Armstrong stood in the doorway with his hat in his hand and sheepish smile on his handsome, sun-burned face. Daisy was at his side.

'We couldn't wait any longer for one of your cakes,' he said. 'We're not too early, are we? We wanted to be your first customers.

Patty caught a sharp breath. She wanted to burst out laughing, but already three elderly ladies were waiting for Greg to move out of the way so they could enter. Behind them, she could see a well-dressed gentleman with a small boy.

'No, you're not too early,' she said. 'I'm really glad you came. Please sit down. I'll be with you as soon as I've settled these ladies.

Moving from table to table, taking orders and serving her cakes, Patty's anxiety ebbed away. It was going to be all right! This was what she had always wanted. She had found her niche, the home she had never had, and the future looked bright.

AUTHOR'S NOTE

The background to the Brownlow Hill workhouse in Liverpool will be familiar to readers of my earlier books in this series. A new element in this story is the struggle for women to be allowed a proper education. In this a publication called *The English Woman's Review* played a leading part. It was edited from 1862 by Emily Davies. This brought her into contact with other women who were campaigning for the same rights, women such as Barbara Bodichon, Elizabeth Garret Anderson, (the first woman to qualify as a doctor) and her younger sister Millicent Fawcett. Also involved were Dorothea Beale, who became the first headmistress of Cheltenham Ladies College, and Frances Buss, who was the first principal of the North London Collegiate School for Ladies. Their activities prompted an anonymous writer to produce the following ditty:

Miss Buss and Miss Beale
Cupid's darts do not feel.
How different from us
Miss Beale and Miss Buss.

In this period universities refused to allow women to study as undergraduates. In 1869, Emily Davies, with the support of the women mentioned above, set up Girton College, Cambridge. Women were able to study the same subjects as men, but Cambridge refused to award them degrees until 1948!

The background to the Australian parts of the book was much less familiar, though I have visited the area more than once. For the historical data regarding the development of Rutherglen and its surroundings I am deeply indebted to Mr Kevin Mayhew of Chiltern who provided me with several documents, including an invaluable survey of the built environment and social structure of the area.

Make sure you've read the rest of the Workhouse series

All they have left is each other …

Life has always been tough for May and Gus Lavender. Their father went away to sea never to return, and then their mother falls victim to the typhus sweeping through Liverpool. Regarded as orphans by the authorities, May and Gus are sent to the Brownlow Hill Workhouse.

Like all workhouses, Brownlow is the last resort for the poor and destitute. May and Gus will have to rely on each other more than ever if they are to survive the hardships to come …

Keep reading for an exclusive preview …

Prologue

'They've got to go! I've told you. We've got five of our own. We can't cope with any more. They'll have to go.'

May could hear Mr Johnson shouting from downstairs. Then she heard the door bang as he went off to his work on the docks. She shifted her position in the narrow, crowded bed. Jenny's elbow was sticking into her ribs and Maisie's foot was right by her nose.

A sound reached her, a sniff followed by a half-stifled whine, like the cry of an animal in pain. Gus was crying, and trying not to be heard. She eased herself out of the bed and wrapped her shawl round her shoulders. The boys' bed was close by and by the smell of it one of them had wet himself – not Gus, her little brother never did that. She bent down and scooped him up in her arms and he buried his face in her shoulder, snuffling. She moved over to the one rickety chair and sat down with him on her lap.

'Don't cry, Gus. It'll be all right. You'll see. We'll be all right.'

She wanted to believe it, but it was hard. She had been three when their father disappeared, 'lost at sea', and Gus just a baby. That was nearly three years ago. They had never seen much of him, because he was a sailor and away from home most of the time. She had got used to being without him; but she had seen her mother grow thin and tired, taking in washing to keep them from starving.

Then, just a few days ago, she had come in from playing out in the cobbled yard, with its smell from the two privies shared between eight families, to find Mrs Johnson waiting for her. 'Your mam's poorly,' she had said. 'You're going to stay with us for a while.' She had watched people going in and out of the house where she had grown up, and one day four men had come out carrying a big box and Percy, Mrs Johnson's eldest, had said, 'Your ma's dead. That's a coffin. They're taking her to be buried.'

As soon as they had eaten their breakfast, thin porridge made for six but shared out between eight, Mrs Johnson put on her cap and shawl and told Percy to keep an eye on the others and see they didn't get up to mischief while she was out. When she got back she took Gus on her lap and pulled May close to her.

'Now, listen to me. You understand your mam is dead, don't you?'

'What's dead?' Gus asked.

'It means she's gone to heaven to live with Jesus.'

'When's she coming back?'

'She can't come back, love. When people die they can't come back. But she'll be watching out for you, looking down from heaven, wanting you to be good and brave. But now, there's no one to look after you and you can't stay here, because there's too many of us already. You can see that, can't you?'

May nodded.

'So a nice man is coming today and he's going to take you to live in a big house at the top of the hill with lots of other children. That'll be good, won't it? You'll have your own beds again, and plenty to eat and friends to play with, so you must go along with him like good children. Understand?'

Gus just sniffed miserably but May nodded. Anything had to be better than sharing a bed with the other girls and hearing Mr Johnson shout at his wife.

The man arrived not long afterwards, a tall, thin man in a hat that made him look even taller and a coat that looked as if he had spilled something down it and not wiped it off properly. He and Mrs Johnson talked for a few minutes and then he said, 'Right, you two. You come along with me.'

Mrs Johnson came to the entry from the court into the road to see them off. 'Now, you be good children, and May, you look after your brother.'

'I will,' May promised.

They set off, almost running to keep up with the man's long strides. Gus began to grizzle and May took hold of his hand to help him along. She tried to ask the man about the place they were going to, but he did not seem to want to talk, so she kept quiet and let her imagination wander.

When her mother was alive and not too tired to talk, she used to tell them stories. They were always stories about poor little girls who somehow met a mysterious stranger who turned out to be a prince and took them to live in his beautiful palace. When May had asked what a palace was, her mother said it meant a big house full of lots of fine things. Perhaps, she thought, that was what Mrs Johnson had meant by the big house where they were going to live.

3

Perhaps this man was really a prince in disguise, or perhaps he was the prince's servant who had been sent to fetch them.

It seemed a long way, but at last they found themselves walking along the side of a high brick wall.

'Not far now,' the man said.

May thought the wall did not look much like the outside of a palace, but then perhaps it was just a wall round the palace gardens and the palace itself was inside. They came to a big gate and the man knocked. May held her breath, waiting to see what was on the other side. There was no palace, just a cobbled yard surrounded by more high brick walls. It was cold and the ground was damp, as if the walls stopped the sun from ever reaching it. Two men in shabby clothes were sweeping away dead leaves. As they crossed the space May heard a woman's voice, high pitched and cracked, yelling something unintelligible. The man led them down a narrow alley and up a flight of steps to a door, on which he knocked.

A gruff voice called, 'Come in.'

The man opened the door and he put one hand on May's shoulder and the other on Gus's to propel them inside. 'The two new orphans, Governor.'

A man with a bushy beard and side whiskers was sitting behind a desk. 'Very well. Ask Mrs Court and Mr Taylor to come here.'

The man left and the one he had called 'governor' opened a big book and picked up a pen.

'Name?'

May's legs were beginning to shake. 'May Lavender, sir.'

'Age?'

'Five and a half, sir. I'll be six in May.'

4

'And the boy?'

'He's Gus – Augustus, sir.'

'Age?'

'He was three last August.'

The governor peered at her as if he thought she might be telling fibs. 'You are May, and your birthday is in May. And he is Augustus, and his birthday is in August?'

'Yes, please, sir. It was our father's idea, I think. That's what my mam told me.'

The governor peered at his book and muttered as if he was talking to himself rather than her. 'Father lost at sea, mother deceased. No other relations.' There was a knock at the door. 'Come in.'

Two people entered: a woman in a black dress with a white cap and apron, and a man in a grey suit. The governor looked up.

'Ah, here you are. Two new inmates. May Lavender and her brother Augustus. I'll leave them in your charge.'

The woman held out her hand. 'Come along, May. You come with me.'

'And you come with me, boy,' the man said.

Gus looked at him and shrank back, grabbing May's hand.

'Please, sir,' May said, 'let him come with me. I always take care of him.'

'You may have done so,' the man said, 'but now he is in my care and he will come with me.'

'But why can't we go together?' May begged. 'He's my brother!'

'That's as may be. But boys and girls don't live together here. Gus will sleep in the boys' dormitory and be taught in the boys' classes, and you will sleep and be taught with the girls. That is how things are here.'

'But ...' May began.

'Enough!' It was the governor's voice. 'You will learn not to argue, or you will regret it. Now, get along with you.'

Gus was still clinging to May's hand. She bent down to him. 'You must be a brave boy, Gus. Go along with the gentleman, like he asks.'

'No! No! I don't want to,' he wept, but the man stooped down and picked him up.

'You will have to learn to do as you are told, boy,' the man said. 'Now, shut your noise.'

He headed for the door and as he carried Gus down the stairs May could hear him crying, 'Let me go, let me go! I want May! May! May!'

The woman grabbed May's hand. 'Come along. There's nothing you can do. He'll get over it.'

As she was led down the stairs, May looked around her through eyes blurred with tears. 'Please, ma'am, where is this? It's not a palace, is it?'

'A palace?' The woman looked down at her and for a moment it seemed she was going to laugh. 'Whatever put that idea into your head? Don't you know what this place is?'

'No, ma'am. Mrs Johnson said a big house.'

'And you thought she meant a palace?' The woman's voice had softened. 'You poor mite. This is the workhouse.'

Will she ever be reunited with her real father?

Angelina was abandoned on the doorsteps of
Brownlow Workhouse when she was just a baby – her
only possession the rag doll she held in her arms.

Nicknamed 'Angel' for her golden curls, she is
adopted by Mr and Mrs McBride. At first Angel is so
happy to have found a caring family to save her from
the drudgery of the workhouse. But her new parents
are not the benevolent guardians they first appear.

Angel has lost all hope when she discovers that a
man has visited the workhouse, looking for the baby
girl he was forced to give up. A girl who isn't an
orphan after all …

Keep reading for an exclusive preview …

Prologue

Mist lies thick over the Mersey and, beyond the crowded buildings, the first faint lightening of the sky shows the dawn to be near. It is very cold. The streets are empty, save for one heavily cloaked figure, who walks with an uneven stride to the doors of the great building that squats menacingly at the top of Brownlow Hill. He carries in his arms a shawl-wrapped bundle, holding it close to his chest within the folds of his cloak. The doors of the workhouse are closed and no light burns in the window of the porter's lodge. The man hesitates, looking down at the burden he carries and then back over his shoulder towards the river. From out of the mist a ship's whistle sounds a warning.

'It will be light soon. Then someone is bound to open the gates. You won't be left alone long.'

His voice is choked with tears. He stoops and lays the bundle tenderly on the flagstones in front of the gate.

'I'm sorry! I'm sorry! I don't know what else to do. I have to go. You will be cared for – and I shall come back to find you when I can.'

He kisses the small face, looks up for a moment at the grim outline of the building, then turns and hobbles away as fast as he can towards the river.

It is cold and she is hungry. She begins to cry. For a long time nobody comes. She wants her mother, wants to be picked up and held and comforted. She cries louder. There is movement and light falls on her; then unfamiliar hands pick her up. She is carried, passed into other hands; strange faces peer down at her.

'Left outside like a parcel. Might have been there all night for all I know! Who could do such a thing?'

'Plenty have done worse. Let's have a look at her.'

She is unwrapped by brisk, ungentle hands.

'Well, it's a girl. Pretty little thing. How old would you say?'

'Not a newborn, that's for sure. A year, maybe a bit more.'

'Anything left with her, to show who left her here? No note or anything?'

'Nothing at all, except this rag doll.'

Raggy! She reaches out, feeing for the familiar shape. It is not there. She begins to cry again.

'Oh, shut your noise! I can't be doing with it.' The voice, like the hands, is harsh.

'Here, give her this. Maybe that will quiet her.'

The rag doll is thrust into her grasp. She holds it tight. It smells of home, and Mother.

Time passes. She is dumped in a chair and a spoon is pushed into her mouth. The food tastes strange and she spits it out. The spoon is pushed in again, more forcefully. She screams in anger and distress.

'Do without then, see if I care!'

She continues to scream. She is picked up and shaken roughly. Then, suddenly, other arms go round her, holding her gently, rocking her and a soft voice begins to sing:

'Lavender's blue, dilly dilly, lavender's green.

When I am king, dilly dilly, you shall be queen …'

She goes quiet. The arms that hold her are thin, the shoulder against which she lays her head is bony; not like her mother's, but she feels safe here. She looks up into a narrow, pale face and a lock of hair falls across her cheek. Her mother's hair was golden. This is more like the colour of polished wood. Voices go on over her head.

'I shall call her Angel. Don't you think she looks like a little angel?'

That is not her name. Her name is Amy. She tries to tell them, but it comes out as 'May-me'.

'She's trying to say my name! It's May. Say May.'

'May-me! May-me!'

'There's a clever girl!'

Days pass. Sometimes the girl called May is there, sometimes she is not. She is always gentle. She helps her to eat, changes her, plays with her. But when she is not there the woman with the hard hands takes over. She does not like that. She screams in protest. The nights are worst. Alone in the dark, listening to the cries of other children nearby, she clutches her rag doll and cannot help crying; and then she is picked up and shaken and dumped down again.

One night is different. May takes her with her, up some stairs, into a room where other faces peer down at her. There is a lot of chatter. 'What have you got there, May? Who is she? Do they know in the nursery you've got her?

3

Why have you brought her up here?' Then she is laid in a bed and May lies beside her and cuddles her close. She shuts her eyes and sleeps.

She wakes to shouts of alarm and a strange, frightening smell. Someone shouts 'Fire!' She is grabbed out of the bed and thrust into unfamiliar arms. There is noise and confusion. She cries for May, but May does not come. Then she is back in the nursery.

More days pass, but still May does not come. One day, a new face peers down at her. This one is framed in dark hair. The eyes are bright, but not gentle like May's.

'This one! I want this one.'

'Are you sure, ma'am? She's over a year old. I thought you were looking for a baby.'

'I don't care about her age. Just look at that golden hair and those blue eyes. She will be a beauty when she grows up. What is her name?'

'Angela, ma'am. She was baptised Angela.'

'Angela? That's rather a common name. Perhaps Angelina would be more suitable. Yes, Angelina will do very well. I'll take her.'

Can this orphan ever fulfil her nursing dreams?

After her mother's death, Dora is sent to live with her father and his other family. But the fact that Dora is mixed race and illegitimate sees her treated as little more than a servant by her step-mother and half siblings. This doesn't stop the son of the house abusing his position and Dora finds herself on the streets and pregnant ...

Sent to the local workhouse, Dora's future looks bleak but she still dreams of a better life where she can help others as her late mother did with her herbal remedies. But can a girl from a workhouse ever achieve anything, let alone become one of Florence Nightingale's nurses?

And don't miss Holly's new series, Frontline Nurses

Can she follow her heart while doing her duty?

After training with the First Aid Nursing Yeomanry, Leonora Malham Brown sets off to Europe with her new friend, Victoria, determined to do her bit for the war effort.

The battlefield is a difficult place for a woman so Leonora cuts her hair short and swaps her skirts for trousers in order to better cope with the demanding duties of a frontline nurse. But concealing her true identity becomes more complicated when she meets dashing Colonel Malkovic.

Torn between keeping her secret and their blossoming friendship, Leonora must choose between her duty and her heart …

Can she find the courage to do her duty?

When war breaks out in 1914, Leonora and her best friend, Victoria, head to Calais to volunteer with the First Aid Nursing Yeomanry. Determined to see her sweetheart, Colonel Malkovic, again Leonora soon decides to return to the front.

But once there, Leonora gets caught up in the danger and chaos of the battlefields and she loses hope of ever finding Sasha. Alone and in danger, Leonora must put into practice the very best of her nursing training if she is to return safely home.

*When war comes, friendship will see them through
the tough times*

In the midst of the First World War, Leonora is now a
volunteer with the Red Cross, while her best friend,
Victoria, is a nurse at the Front in Calais. Despite the
hardships of war, Leonora is delighted to be reunited
with her sweetheart, Colonel Sasha Malkovic.

Before long, Leonora falls pregnant but she daren't
tell Sasha for fear he would send her home. But
when she finally plucks up the courage to tell him,
tragedy strikes and he is reported missing in action.
Heartbroken and now a new mother all alone, Leonora
must turn to her friends back in England to help her …